"I didn't come to Darwin Island for this." Jack flicked a hand in Lina's general direction.

"For muffins?" She sat on the edge of the table and elegantly crossed one leg over the other. The high slit in her skirt allowed it to part and fall away, revealing her legs from toe to hip.

Logical thought eluded Jack for as long as he stared at the way her smooth legs gleamed in the moonlight. He tore his gaze away to stare at the interlocked canopies of the tall Nikau palms. "I didn't come here to get involved."

"Why *did* you come here?" She plucked a ripe kiwifruit from the platter. She brought the soft little oval to her mouth. With excruciating delicacy, she used her front teeth to break its furry bronze skin and her lips and tongue to peel it back, exposing the gold flesh. Her left check dimpled in a tiny grin as she caught a drop of sweet juice on the tip of her tongue.

Jack's body responded fiercely to her actions. "This isn't something I do. I don't allow myself to be seduced by strange women in strange places."

A tiny smile curled one corner of her mouth. "Am I seducing you?"

"Don't insult my intelligence, Lina."

"Certainly not. Although I'm afraid I may prick your ego a bit. I'm not trying to seduce you, Mr. DeVoy."

"Jack . . ."

She held his gaze and dared to slide her hands along his shirt front as she stood to face him. "I seduced you last night. I'm here now because it's your turn to seduce me."

BLAME IT ON PARADISE

CRYSTAL HUBBARD

Genesis Press, Inc.

INDIGO LOVE SPECTRUM

An imprint of Genesis Press, Inc.
Publishing Company

Genesis Press, Inc.
P.O. Box 101
Columbus, MS 39703

ISBN: 13 DIGIT : 978-1-58571-273-1
ISBN: 10 DIGIT : 1-58571-273-6
Manufactured in the United States of America

First Edition

Visit us at www.genesis-press.com
or call at 1-888-Indigo-1-4-0

DEDICATION

To Mary Croom Hicks, who made me scream in Michigan City, Indiana.

ACKNOWLEDGMENTS

My first Love Spectrum title, *Crush,* was borne of my lifelong affection for the United Kingdom and many of my experiences in Wales and England. The idea for *Blame It on Paradise* exploded in my head the day I saw an exceptionally attractive woman at Logan International Airport. Men were transfixed by that dark-skinned goddess from the other side of the world. Her waist-length black hair was akin to that of a Native American, her mouth, cheekbones and dark brown complexion were distinctly African, and her thin nose and gray eyes seemed typically Caucasian. I had never seen a person, male or female, so strikingly and oddly beautiful. She was kind enough to answer when I asked her where she was from, and she named an island near New Zealand.

To establish one of the settings for this book, I adopted one of the uninhabited Chatham Islands. With no bounds to my boldness in the telling of a story of my own invention, I took the liberty of moving the island closer to the International Date Line.

Nahant Island, the counterpart to my fictional Darwin, is real. Not only is it one of the prettiest pieces of land in New England, it is home to Bobbi Lerman, one of the best storytellers and most thorough researchers I've ever read.

My bibliography for this book topped out at three single spaced pages but I'd like to specifically thank the following individuals, groups and organizations for their assistance, generosity and patience in helping me bring Darwin Island to life:

Treehouse designer James Powell, the Treehouse Workshop, Cessna Aircraft Company, Dassault Aviation, the Chatham Islands Department of Conservation, the New Zealand Department of Conservation, Greg Horler of the Awarakau Farmstays, the Te Matarae Farmstays, Chatham Island Fish and Dive Charters, Attorney Robert Enyard and Pacific maritime historian Rhys Richards.

And finally I'd like to thank Sandy, Marjorie, Grant, Ellis and Yael, friends and stalwart travelers who went to the other side of the world before me and brought back stories that spurred me to follow in their footsteps.

PROLOGUE

Her long, lithe form perched atop the highest point of Tuanui Bay. About her face and bare shoulders, a mild breeze set tendrils of her almost waist-length hair dancing, as though it moved to the music of the ocean crashing against the volcanic rock upon which she stood. Unblinking, she watched the subtle artistry of the sunrise painting the sky in muted shades of pink that slowly replaced the pale grey of the between-time connecting night to dawn. She breathed deeply of the cool air, already smelling the heat to come once the sun assumed its throne high above the clouds.

She was completely alone, yet anyone who stumbled upon her might have looked up from the shore and spent a moment wondering if she were some ebony goddess of the sea silhouetted against the dawn, reasserting her ownership of the new day.

As the pastel pink bloomed into blinding yellow, she closed her eyes and tipped her face to receive dawn's kiss. An unexpected tickle of excitement moved over her skin, and she smiled. She tried to begin each day with the sunrise, right here atop her favorite spot on the island, yet never had she enjoyed such a strong feeling of anticipation. A thrilling current of expectation sizzled low in her belly and tingled in her fingertips.

Something was in the air, figuratively, if not literally. She was certain of it. Whether good or bad, she couldn't tell. But her gut instincts had never deceived her, and she trusted that something was about to happen. Accepting that what would come would inevitably do so, and that she would face it accordingly, she moved closer to the very edge of the precipice. Then without hesitation, without fear, she threw out her arms and dived off, hanging weightless for a joyous, infinitesimal moment before slicing into the inky black waters of the sea.

CHAPTER 1

"Hold onto your chairs, soldiers, and don't let your eyes deceive you." Reginald Wexler, co-founder and CEO of Coyle-Wexler Pharmaceuticals, punctuated his admonition with a sly smile. A slight bob of his rectangular head spurred his personal assistant into motion at the far end of the cavernous executive board room. The fidgety young man jerked open a pair of double-wide mahogany doors and stepped aside.

The executives of Coyle-Wexler operations—save the dearly departed Gardner Coyle—and a fleet of attorneys turned to watch an elegant, shapely woman make a cheerful and gracious entrance.

"Gentlemen," Reginald started, "and ladies," he added, acknowledging his trio of female executives: the Puerto Rican vice president of marketing, the African-American vice president of communications and the Korean vice president of customer service. "I'd like you to meet the new Mrs. Reginald Wexler."

Jackson DeVoy sat back in his plush leather chair, slowly swiveling to follow the new Mrs. Wexler's long and stately walk from the doorway to her husband's side at the head of the gigantic conference table. Jackson's heavy eyebrows met in the incisive scowl he normally reserved for opposing attorneys as he thoughtfully took his chin between his thumb and forefinger. He studied the woman. The new Mrs. Wexler looked like Ann-Margret, circa *Grumpy Old Men*. A red knit dress flattered her curvaceous figure, hugging it in all the right places, making her look like a belated Christmas present. Her auburn hair was swept into a simple twist that accentuated her cheekbones, and her makeup had been applied with a light and careful hand. Her coffee eyes were her most striking feature, and they seemed to laugh while her mouth merely smiled.

The *new* Mrs. Wexler? Jack cocked a suspicious eyebrow.

She responded to his expression with a surreptitious wink.

"Mr. Wexler, I'd like to be the first to congratulate you on your surprise nuptials. I don't know about anyone else here, but I wasn't aware that your excursion to the South Pacific six months ago was a honeymoon trip." Edison Burke bumped Jack's chair, hard, as he vaulted out of his seat to approach Reginald and his wife. His skinny arms and legs encased in an ill-fitting striped suit, he scurried to the head of the room and clamped Mrs. Wexler's hand between both of his, shaking it so hard that his frameless glasses bounced on the bridge of his nose. "I believe I speak for everyone in this room when I say that we had no idea that you were contemplating divorce, never mind remarriage."

Edison brought Mrs. Wexler's hand to his face and pressed his lips to the back of it. She absently wiped her hand on the skirt of her dress when Edison turned his silvery blue eyes on Reginald. "May I also say that your new wife is a vision of sheer loveliness, truly an upgrade, compared to the former Mrs. Wexler." He guffawed, shoving an elbow into Reginald's ribs.

In a gesture of infinite patience, Reginald passed a claw-like, liver-spotted hand through the white floss covering his head. "Burke. Sit."

"Yes sir." The words left Burke in a humble whisper as he backed toward his seat.

"I suppose you're all wondering why I've called you here this morning." Reginald addressed the forty-five people seated at the conference table, but he kept his gaze on his wife. "It was to meet my wife, yes, but—"

"Not your new wife," Jack said.

Mrs. Wexler's face broke into a smile, and then she chuckled. "Jack, how did you know?"

He stood, straightening his exquisitely tailored jacket as he did so. His presence alone commanded the attention of every man in the room, and his dark, golden good looks captivated Wexler's trio of female veeps.

"Your eyes." Jack neared Mrs. Wexler, still not quite believing what he was seeing. "You can change the body, but the eyes . . . they can't hide." He allowed Wexler's wife to give his hands a brief squeeze, and then he set a chaste kiss on her cheek. "You look wonderful, Millicent."

Reginald gave Jack a proud pat on the back. "Very good, Jackson, my boy. Once again, you've shown why you're my number one."

Millicent Wexler—the first and *only* Mrs. Wexler— beamed. She clapped her hands to Jack's face and gave

3

him a grandmotherly smooch full on the lips. "Jack, you're such a smart cookie!"

"Okay, Millie, enough's enough." Reginald impatiently ushered her into an empty chair. He picked up a remote control and used it to simultaneously dim the lights overhead and lower a projection screen at the front of the room. With the click of another button, an image appeared on the screen. Jack took his seat.

"This is Millicent Wexler, one year ago." Reginald paused to give his audience the chance to absorb the sight of Millicent Wexler's pale, doughy flesh overspilling the confines of a floral bathing suit. "Millicent topped the scales at an all-time personal high of two—"

"Must you, Reginald!" Mrs. Wexler's voice drowned out the rest of the number.

He rolled his eyes skyward and took a deep breath before continuing. "Honestly, Millie, everyone in this room knows you used to be—"

Jack felt the heat of the fiery stare Mrs. Wexler pinned on her husband.

Reginald snorted impatiently. "This is a scientific presentation," he stated gruffly. "Full disclosure is key here, and that includes your weight."

Mrs. Wexler stubbornly crossed her arms.

"Would *you* like to handle this presentation, Millie?"

"Actually, I would," she said, standing. "Thank you, Reginald." She plucked the remote from his palm before taking his shoulders and guiding him into her unoccupied chair.

"Ladies and gentlemen, that indeed is a photo of me from last year." Millicent began a leisurely stroll around the conference table. "That's me in the pool at our house on Cape Cod on our thirty-fifth anniversary. I weighed in the neighborhood of two hundred pounds. As many of you know, I've tried every weight loss aide offered by Coyle-Wexler and every other pharmaceutical company in the Western Hemisphere as well as all the diets on the bestseller lists, every homeopathic remedy, hypnosis, acupuncture and even a few things that aren't legal within the United States.

"Nothing worked for me. I tried low-carb, low-fat, all-vegetable, all-liquid, citrus, cabbage, soy, fasting, water binging . . ." She stopped to catch her breath. "I'm an older woman, but I'm not an old woman, no matter what you young hotshots might think. I wanted to improve my health as well as my looks, but nothing helped me manage my weight. Just when I began considering drastic surgical options, I discovered something better."

She clicked the remote. A leafy green plant appeared on screen.

"What's that?" Edison snickered. "The parsley diet?"

"It's mint," Millicent said. "It grows half a world away, in the mountains of Darwin Island. I spent six weeks on Darwin with Reginald, my sister and her husband. While we were there, we were served a delicious mint tea that's brewed from freshly picked young leaves. By the end of our third week, my sister and I had each lost nearly twelve pounds, and we weren't dieting. On the

5

contrary, we gorged ourselves on every delicacy the islanders set before us.

"By the end of the six weeks, I'd lost twenty pounds and my sister had lost sixteen. I brought some of the tea back with me, and once it was released from quarantine, I resumed drinking it. Within five months, I'd lost another sixty pounds, and I'd never felt better. I *ran* the Susan G. Komen Race for the Cure a few months ago, I took the 55-and-over doubles title in my indoor tennis league, and I've reached my goal weight. I'd fit right in on Darwin now. The women there are exceptionally fit and healthy, and we were told it was because of this mint tea. The women drink it the way we here in the United States drink soda."

Millicent switched photos, now showing a beach shot featuring a sampling of the island's female residents. Every man in the room sat up straighter, some shifting from side to side to get a better, unobstructed view of the screen.

"The women on Darwin are beautiful as well," Millicent said, "which probably has more to do with the various ethnicities of its residents rather than the tea."

Other than a slightly quirked eyebrow, Jack showed no outward reaction to the smiling, nubile figures on screen. Dressed in skimpy bathing suits, simple cotton dresses or topless, the women of Darwin ranged in complexion from strawberries and cream to ebony. Jack's eyebrows drew together in curiosity as he picked out a very fair-skinned woman with very full lips and a broad, flat nose, and then a dark-skinned woman with straight, honey-blonde hair. Jack knew that Aborigines could be born with blonde hair, but he'd never seen such a thing, even in photos.

Edison openly leered at the attractive women in the photo. "It's like that scene in *Mutiny on the Bounty*, the one where the native women choose their mates from among the English sailors."

Reginald grimaced. "Keep it in your pants, Burke. Millie, may I take it from here?"

She handed over the remote. Reginald raised the lights, drowning the image of the island beauties in fashionable track lighting. "According to Darwin's Ministry of Health, the average woman on the island is five-foot-seven and weighs 135 pounds. Her measurements are 35-24-36, and she lives to be 84 years old. On Darwin, obesity is unheard of for the natives."

The stout vice president of new developments raised a pudgy pink hand. "Does this Darwin mint have the same effect on men as it does on women?"

"Yes." Reginald nodded his appreciation for the question. "In fact, the tea's effect seems to work even faster."

"Figures," muttered the female vice president of marketing.

"People, my wife has given you a firsthand testimonial as to the effectiveness of Darwin mint, but as you know, our stockholders and the Food and Drug Administration require far more than that." Reginald clasped his hands behind his back.

Edison's snort resounded through the room. "You intend to market that weed under the Coyle-Wexler trademark?"

"That's exactly what I plan to do." Thirty years of sharpening his claws on pipsqueaks like Edison Burke put a gleeful shine in Reginald's eyes as he braced his hands wide on the glossy tabletop. "Do you have any objections, counselor?"

"N-No, sir." Edison's hands trembled slightly as he straightened his already straight tie.

Jack bowed his head to hide a grin.

Reginald directed their attention to the folders set before them on the table. "Over the past few months, I've had our research department working to chemically synthesize this tea. So far, we've had no success in reproducing it. In fact, our trials have been dismal failures. One of the women in our initial test study gained twenty pounds in eight days. Another version of the tea had side effects of, and I quote, 'temporary blindness, irritable bowel syndrome, acute sleeplessness and episodes of speaking gibberish.' Either the sample we're working with is too small, or there's something in this tea that cannot, and clearly should not, be duplicated in a lab."

"Why can't we just buy the rights to Darwin mint from the growers on the island?" Jack asked.

Reginald, grinning smugly, narrowed his eyes and pointed a finger at Jack. "That's where you come in, my boy." He greedily rubbed his hands together. "The mint grows exclusively in the Paradise Valley region of the Raina Mountains on Darwin Island, which is privately owned by J.T. Marchand, who has ignored all of our inquiries regarding Darwin mint tea and its outright purchase. Now, gentlemen—and ladies—clinical trials on the tea are ongoing, even as we speak. But once we get clearance from the FDA to market the tea, Coyle-Wexler Pharmaceuticals fully intends to be the sole producer and distributor."

Reginald strolled to the expanse of one-way glass forming the east wall of the boardroom. He gazed at an unparalleled view of Boston from sixty stories up as he said, "Darwin mint tea is what the world has been waiting for. It's a weight loss aid that has no discernible side effects. It's impossible to overuse it, as it seems to paradoxically act as an appetite stimulant if consumed in massive quantities. This tea will change the face, and the figures, of the world. J.T. Marchand is idling on the gold mine of the millennium, and I want in on it."

Reginald turned away from the wall of glass. "I'm sending my best man to work out a deal with J.T. Marchand. Burke . . ."

Surprised, Edison sat taller and offered the room a gloating smirk.

"I want you on standby, in case I need a second down there," Reginald finished.

His smirk morphing into a petulant pout, Edison sat back heavily in his chair.

Reginald issued his closing command. "Jack, pack your bags. You leave for Darwin today."

By the time he had departed Boston's Logan International Airport and arrived in Sydney, Australia, where he'd boarded a chartered flight bound for Christchurch, New Zealand, Jack felt comfortable in his knowledge of Darwin Island. He'd read the comprehensive report Coyle-Wexler's research department had prepared and now considered himself a walking encyclopedia of trivial information about Darwin.

J.T. Marchand was another subject entirely. In an Internet-driven information age, Marchand had a canny knack for staying out of newspapers, magazines and web sites. The hasty Internet search Jack had conducted on his own in the air above the Rocky Mountains had yielded only the most basic information.

Marchand, a descendant of the French, English and Aboriginal settlers who colonized the island in the late 1700s, inherited the whole of Darwin at an early age. Like the Vatican and the tiny country of Malta, Darwin Island was a sovereign entity under international law, which made Marchand the closest thing to a genuine potentate Jack ever hoped to meet. What most intimidated Jack was the fact that Marchand was a summa cum laude graduate of Stanford Law School and a corporate attorney with an undefeated record.

A perfect winning record was one thing Marchand and Jack had in common, and he mused on that as he stepped off of the charter from New Zealand to set foot on Darwin for the first time.

"Welcome to Darwin, the pearl of the South Pacific," greeted a woman with a bright smile, flawless terra cotta skin and a clipboard bearing the passenger manifesto. A warm, fragrant breeze made her long, black hair dance and shimmer about her shoulders and upper arms. It played in the wispy grasses of her low-slung skirt, which revealed a considerable expanse of her taut, honey-dark abdomen and rounded hips. The five male passengers disembarking after Jack trained their eyes on their hostess's exposed flesh and the straining contents of her floral bandeau top while she stamped Jack's passport and visa.

Jack had eyes only for the nearest taxi. "I need to get to the Warutara Hotel." He took off his double-breasted Burberry trench coat, which was no longer necessary now that he'd left the brutal New England January on the opposite side of the Earth. He pushed back the cuff of his left sleeve to set his watch to Darwin time, which was nineteen hours ahead of Boston.

"The Warutara, Mr. DeVoy?" The hostess returned his passport and visa before gently taking his arm, much to the envy of the other male travelers who had been on Jack's flight. She guided him toward the compact terminal attached to the small airstrip. "Are you sure that's where you—"

Speaking over her, Jack tactfully extracted himself from her grasp. "I'm in something of a hurry and I'm quite sure of my itinerary. If you could just point me in the direction of the rental car center, I'd really appreciate it."

The pretty native's mouth tightened before relaxing into its former welcoming smile. "Well, then, Mr. DeVoy, if you have any items to declare, you may do so at the customer service center inside the terminal. You'll find transportation waiting at the front of the terminal,

Mr. DeVoy. I'm afraid if you need assistance with your luggage, you'll find that—"

"I have everything I need right here." He impatiently indicated the leather garment bag slung over his shoulder and the valise and briefcase gripped in his hand. "This won't be a long stay."

Jack's helpful hostess seemed relieved. "Even so, welcome to Darwin Island, and I trust you'll have a memorable visit."

Jack grunted his thanks and hurried into the terminal, shouldering his way through a colorful mix of tourists and locals as he searched for the customer service center. There had been a mere ten passengers on his flight from Christchurch, New Zealand, to Darwin, and Jack spared little more than a glance as the arms and smiles of chattering family and friends swallowed his fellow passengers.

With his travel-rumpled business suit and his decidedly pale Boston pallor, Jack stood out as he paced in front of the terminal, wondering which vehicle and driver could possibly be his. He was accustomed to seeing stone-faced drivers bearing placards with DeVoy printed on them, but here and now, forced to choose among an open-topped Jeep with bald tires and no passenger seat, a wooden cart drawn by two extremely bored yet diabolical-looking long-haired goats, a rusting Stingray with a flat rear tire and a minivan already filled to capacity with cheerful, laughing locals, Jack decided to retreat into the bustling terminal to find customer service.

At the far end of the terminal, between a humming vending machine and the men's lavatory, Jack spied a high counter manned by a portly fellow wearing a splashy shirt printed with exotic birds. Jack's long, hurried strides carried him there quickly, and he marched directly to the front of the long line. "Excuse me. My name is Jackson DeVoy and I have an important business meeting in the city in less than an hour and I need to get to my hotel. I just flew in—"

"Your arms must be tired!" the desk clerk cut in. His golden-brown cheeks puffed with laughter at his own goofy humor as he slapped the desktop.

"—and I was told that transportation would be waiting for me." Jack clenched his jaw. "Where might I find my car and driver?"

"Do you have a reservation for a car and driver?"

The clerk's accent was odd, something between Australian English and something Jack couldn't quite place. Whatever it was, "reservation" came out as "riversation."

"Of course." Jack withdrew an envelope from his inner breast pocket. He opened it and yanked out his itinerary, which included the confirmation numbers for his flight, transportation and lodging. He set the paper before the counter clerk, who studied it as though he were auditing an income tax return.

The clerk smiled and cheerfully handed the paper back to Jack. "This reservation is no good. Next!"

The short woman who'd been first in line stepped forward, making a point to give Jack a small shove, and set a live chicken on the countertop. The bird escaped the

13

woman's grasp and frantically scrambled across the counter before leaping at Jack, who jerked himself clear of the bird's awkward flight path. The frenzied fowl hit the tile floor and began zigzagging through the terminal, much to the counter clerk's amusement and Jack's annoyance.

After shunting aside the next person in line, Jack again stood directly in front of the clerk. "Look. I need transportation. Why is my 'riversation' no good?"

The counter clerk watched the chicken's mistress chase her charge. "You booked Nathan's Limousine Service. Nathan himself drives the one car, but Nate will be on his back for the next few weeks. He slipped a disc yesterday, trying to land a striped marlin out on his boat. She was a beauty, about seventy kilograms, but she got the best of our Nate."

Jack drummed his fingers on the desktop. "What's the fastest way I can get to the city?"

"What city?"

"Wautangua, the capital."

"Wautangua's more of a town than a city, kiddo," volunteered a petite, dark-skinned woman in a Kansas City Royals T-shirt. She was standing at the nearby postal desk. "Christchurch is a city. Wellington is a city. Boston is a city, and I'm guessin' that's from where you're about, given your accent and your attitude. But Wautangua . . . that's a town."

Jack turned to the woman. "You're American." He approached her, daring to hope for a quick resolution to his transportation problem. "Finally, someone who speaks regular English."

The woman slipped on a pair of thick glasses that had been hanging from her neck by a fine braided leather cord. "Levora Wilkins Solomon." She offered her hand. Jack took it and she gave his hand two hard pumps that shook his garment bag from his shoulder to the crook of his elbow. "I came to Darwin twenty-five years ago to study the Moriori. I went and fell in love with one of them, and I've been here ever since." She crossed her arms over her nonexistent bosom. "So tell me, son. What brings you to Darwin and how can I help you get to it?"

"I'm here on business."

She stared at him, clearly waiting for him to elaborate.

"It's confidential."

She stood frozen a moment longer, but then tossed her hands up. "Good enough. Come on." She started for the exit, waving Jack along behind her. "My business here is finished, so I can ride you into Wautangua."

Jack offered a silent prayer of thanks as he fell into step beside Levora. They exited the terminal to see that the chicken was still kicking up a ruckus. Several laughing young boys darted after it in half-hearted pursuit, but the chicken always skipped out of reach, stopping just short of crossing the wide dirt road. Then it turned and ran erratically, skidding to a stop beneath the goat-drawn cart. The devilish-looking goats spooked and took off in a cloud of dust, clattering wheels and terrified bleating.

Mindless of the scene before him, Jack scanned the area for the practical four-wheeled vehicle he imagined Levora would drive. "Where's your car?"

"That was it." She pointed to the goat-powered speck disappearing into the horizon. "BeBe and CeCe don't like chickens. Never have, never will." Levora began walking in the direction her goats had taken.

Jack's shoulders fell. He stared at the sky, seething as he contemplated the nature of God, man and just how much pleasure he would take in sucking J.T. Marchand dry.

"Hey, you." Levora, her hands on the hips of her loose-fitting blue jeans, had doubled back for him. "Are you comin' or not?"

He glanced back at the airstrip, but he resisted the temptation to return to the plane and fly right back to Boston. Taking a firmer grip on the handle of his bag, he quickly caught up to Levora. "How far is Wautangua?"

"Mmm, 'bout ten miles." She kicked at a few broken oyster shells with the toe of her worn hiking boot. "Shouldn't take more than a couple hours to walk it. 'Course, we should catch up to BeBe and CeCe long before then. Unless they decide to go all the way home this time."

"Why do you drive a goat cart?"

"You got something against goats?"

"No. I just think it's unusual in this day and age to travel by goat-driven cart."

"A lot of things on Darwin are unusual. It's the nature of the place. Not too many folks drive cars here. We've got ambulances and fire trucks and all, but there was a law passed twenty-some years ago banning most other vehicles. It's never been enforced, really, considering who made the declaration, but most everybody abides by it. The only folks who drive are the ones who absolutely need to."

Jack fished out his cell phone. "I have to call my hotel and let them know that I'll be checking in late."

"Where're you staying?"

"The Hotel Warutara."

Levora slowed her step to closely examine a stand of tiger lilies growing on the side of the dirt road. "That's too bad."

Dread settled in Jack's belly. "Why's that?"

Levora snapped off one of the pale lemonade-colored blossoms. She handed the lovely bloom to Jack, who scarcely looked at it. "It really wasn't that great of a hotel. Of course, that's neither here nor there, since the Warutara collapsed in a typhoon three months ago."

The tiger lily fell from Jack's hand as he scowled and readjusted his bags. Grumbling under his breath, he again fell into step behind Levora, inadvertently crushing the delicate flower under his heel.

Wautangua was more of a village than a town, with no automobile traffic on the roads, which alternated between hard-packed dirt and gravel. Jack allowed Levora to lead him past well-kept, sprawling, single-story stucco homes and smaller, cozy stone bungalows set far from the main road to the center of Wautangua. Foot traffic picked up as they entered Wautangua, and Jack was only mildly surprised to see that Levora seemed to know every person she encountered by name. An even mix of tourists and natives ambled in and out of one-story storefronts with colorful plate glass windows, rough plank market stalls and a single gas station that doubled as a visitors' center. A three-story brick building, the one oasis of urban "civility" on the island, rose on the edge of town.

"This was the factory." Levora sat on the topmost of three stone stairs leading to the long walkway to the building's entrance. She took off one of her hiking boots. Gripping it by its heel, she hung it upside down, pouring sand and pebbles from it. "Back when the North and South were at war in America, they used to make commercial fishing nets here at the Marchand factory. It's been the governor's house, a hospital and a warehouse in the past, but now the place is used for offices. The Marchand family's owned the whole island since Methuselah came off the mountain. Are you here for the tea, Jack?"

Levora had single-handedly kept the conversation flowing during their long trek into town. She had told him all about her childhood in Kansas City, Kansas, her scholarship to Berkeley and the decision to study anthropology, her marriage to Moriori tribesman Errol Solomon, her daughter Louise and son Ben, who were currently enrolled at MIT and Penn respectively, and the small oyster farm her husband currently ran. She hadn't inquired further about Jack's business on the island, so he was more inclined to answer her question. In part.

"I won't say no. But I can't say yes."

"How old would you say I am, Jack? Even if you didn't know that both my babies are in college, how old would you think I was?"

"That's a loaded question, Levora, and you know it."

"Go on and answer. I promise, I won't kill you."

"Well, you've been on Darwin for twenty-five years, and you came while you were working on a graduate research project. Given those facts, I'd guess that you were fifty years old, even though you don't look a minute over forty."

Levora's eyes sparkled, their color rivaling a rich, dark, home-brewed coffee. "I worked for ten years before I started graduate school, Jack. I was thirty-four years old when I came to Darwin. I'll be sixty next week."

Jack studied Levora a little closer. She had maintained a good pace, never once stopping to rest or to catch her breath, even though she had been speaking incessantly. Tiny lines fanned from the outer corners of her black eyes, but only when she laughed or smiled, which had been often. Her teeth were bright, almost too white against her ebony skin. Jack noted a few strands of silver hair at her temples and in her stubby ponytail, but they complemented the twinkle in her eyes. Levora was slender, and she carried herself with such a lively step that it was hard for Jack to believe that she was closer to sixty than forty.

"A lot of people have come here to get their hands on the tea, Jack."

"Is it the fountain of youth? Is that why you stayed on Darwin?"

Levora laughed and tied her bootlaces. "It's just tea, kid." She stood and patted the front of his jacket, raising a puff of road dust. "And I stayed because of my hot island lover. Goodbye, Jack. And good luck with J.T."

As he traveled the lengthy stone path to the front of the building, Jack brushed off his clothes and stamped his feet to remove as much dust from himself as he could before he swung open the lobby doors. He was instantly comfortable in the elegant, if not luxurious, surroundings. Traces of the island were still evident, despite the corporate setting: with her silk blouse and headset phone, the receptionist wore a skirt made of brightly colored, papery Masi cloth.

Jack dropped his valise and briefcase at his feet and leaned over the tall counter wrapping around the receptionist's desk. "I'm from Coyle-Wexler Pharmaceuticals and I'm here to see J.T. Marchand. I had an appointment this afternoon, but I was unavoidably detained at the airport."

Without looking up at him, the receptionist removed a glossy magazine from atop a large appointment book. "Well, let's see here, Mr. . . ." Her eyes followed the path of her long red fingernail as it moved down the left side of the appointment book before coming to an abrupt stop. "You must be 'Coyle-Wexler rep.' " She peered at the large clock affixed high on one wall. "You're very late."

Jack scowled, but he managed to suppress the Bostonian instinct to snap, "No kidding, Einstein."

"J.T. is no longer on the premises." The receptionist shifted her gaze from the appointment book to the fashion magazine beside it. "You'll have to reschedule for tomorrow."

The muscles of Jack's neck tensed. "I'm in town for twenty-four hours. I need to see J.T. Marchand *today*. Can you give me a number to call, or a home address?"

The receptionist finally glanced up at him. Her eyes widened for an instant, becoming two deep pools of jet within the terra cotta of her face before her lids dropped, suggestively hooding her eyes. She took the left corner of her lower lip between her pearly teeth and gave Jack a long, leisurely appraisal. "I can give you *my* number. I guarantee that you'll have more fun with me than with J.T. Marchand."

Jack squinted in annoyance and shook his head. He took several long strides back toward the plate glass lobby front. He turned and knocked his head against the surrounding brick as he formed a mental picture of exactly how he would financially keelhaul J.T. Marchand.

The receptionist's voice dragged him from his vengeful reverie. "J.T. has an opening tomorrow morning at 7:30."

"I'll take it." He finally raised his head from the brick.

"Is there anything else I can do for you, Mr. . . . ?"

"Yes," Jack snapped pointedly. "I need a place to spend the night."

A feline grin slowly spread across the receptionist's face. Wearily, Jack sighed and rolled his eyes heavenward.

CHAPTER 2

For all of her forwardness, the receptionist proved useful in arranging a homestay for Jack. The one-bedroom cottage with its hand-woven thatched roof was owned by none other than J.T. Marchand, which—despite its rustic exterior—likely explained its tourist-friendly amenities. The first thing Jack did upon arriving was search the house for a phone directory, an address book, a list of emergency numbers—anything that would enable him to contact Marchand—but the cottage yielded nothing.

Jack succumbed to the allure of the large bathroom, which featured a whirlpool bath and an oversized shower stall. He stripped, leaving his clothes on the floor, mourning the custom-tailored suit ruined with sweat and road dust.

Billowy clouds of steam lazily floated through the room as Jack stepped into the shower stall. The gentle blasts of hot water washed away layers of grime and fatigue, leaving more room for Jack's growing frustration. He was sorely tempted to dress and search the island. There had to be a car for rent somewhere, and there were only so many places a person could hide on an island of less than two hundred square miles. But then Darwin was an alien landscape of dizzying cliffs, savage seas, treacherous coastlines, volcanic peaks, waterfalls, peat bogs, lagoons and endless beaches. Marchand could be hiding out in the thick patches of tropical forests Jack had viewed from above during the descent to Darwin.

The island's benefactor could be anywhere, and given the helpfulness of the locals so far, Jack decided he'd be better off getting a good night's sleep.

He took his time shaving after his shower, thinking up an alternate plan of attack for his early morning face-to-face. His original strategy had been to soft sell Marchand, to simply illustrate how partnering with Coyle-Wexler would make him almost as rich as God while benefiting a world gone crazy with fad diets and gastric surgeries.

Jack was in no mood for the soft sell, not after a 21-hour flight, a chicken chase, a 10-mile hike, a missed meeting and being forced to spend an extra day on the island. He switched into offensive mode. Between now and six A.M., he would outline a plan that would leave Marchand with little more than the volcano that had upchucked Darwin an eon ago.

He carefully ran the silky-sharp edge of his German-crafted razor along the lathered plane of his jaw. "The ol' snake probably never intended to see me today at all. Nice move, J.T. Way to throw your adversary off his game." He ran water over his blade to clean it of its dark stubble before splashing handfuls of water over his face to rinse away the last specks of shaving cream. He ran his wet hands through his shower damp hair as he stared at his reflection.

He tried to see himself as Marchand would. Of course, he'd be wearing a suit and not a towel swathed around his hips when he finally met Marchand, but there was no denying what the mirror showed him. It had been eleven years since he'd last tossed a game-winning touchdown pass, but he still had the durable and well-built physique that had led the Boston University Terriers to a bowl game. He had an imposing physical presence, when he wanted to.

A former girlfriend had dragged him to a yoga class, and to Jack's eternal shame, he had enjoyed it. Yoga had increased his strength, flexibility, concentration and confidence, not that he'd lacked those qualities before. Yoga had also given him the ability to control his physical presence, to appear less intimidating when he needed to—or more so, as the occasion warranted.

Jack intended to overwhelm J.T. Marchand in every possible way.

He gave his arms and back a good stretch as he exited the bathroom. "Thanks for the delay, J.T. The worst thing that could happen to you is me getting a good night's sleep."

Only trouble was, Jack wasn't sleepy. Even though it was a warm, moonlit night, his body was still on Eastern time. It was 10 P.M. on Darwin, so his body recognized its bedtime, but his mind was hungry for its 4 A.M. cup of Dunkin Donuts coffee.

Jack pulled the towel from his hips and deposited it on top of his ruined suit before he climbed into bed. "At least it's a king-size," he groaned, pulling a light flannel blanket up to his waist. He pillowed his head on one forearm and draped the other forearm over his middle. Closing his eyes, he tried to force himself to sleep.

He might have succeeded, if not for the scent of mango. His stomach growled as he sat up and noticed that the sliding doors leading to the back patio had been opened. He leaped out of bed and tugged on a pair of black sports briefs. Screen doors kept out animals and insects, but a two-legged creature had opened the glass doors while he showered.

He cautiously approached the screen doors, listening . . . nothing, other than the arrhythmic chirps and clicks of insects and the gentle movement of water. He quietly slid the door open farther and poked his head out for a more thorough look, but he saw nothing other than the mint-blue underlighting in a private lagoon and vast canopies of tall, palm-like trees hooding it from the moonlight.

"Wow," he exhaled. Jack still wasn't sleepy, but he suddenly felt more relaxed as he stared at the picturesque scene before him. The view left him speechless, so he had nothing to say when he noticed the netting-covered platter on the rattan table on the patio. His stomach grumbled with more enthusiasm when he went to the table and drew back the netting.

His last real meal had been on his first-class flight from Los Angeles to Sydney. He'd had packets of snack crackers on the chartered flights from Sydney to Christchurch and Christchurch to Darwin, so once he sat down at the table, he realized that he was starving. He began gorging himself on slices of fresh mango, green and gold kiwi, cantaloupe, honeydew melon and spiced ham, and practically swallowed whole a salad of marinated grape tomatoes, goat cheese and fresh basil. He particularly enjoyed a spicy roasted bird that tasted like chicken, only with a more robust, mildly gamey flavor.

He tore open a large crusty roll and chomped into the satin fluff of the interior. After a few cursory bites, he took a swig of the pale amber beverage in the goblet beside the platter. The drink was cool and refreshing, and Jack made special note of its subtle mint flavor.

"So this is it." He swirled the drink, watching the way it caught the moonlight. "The green gold of Darwin Island."

He set down the goblet and shoveled in another chunk of roasted poultry. The tea was good, but a cold Sam Adams would have been better. Jack enjoyed a bittersweet chuckle thinking about the last time he'd had a Sam Adams. It had been around the same time he'd last played football. Over the years, his tastes had evolved to appreciate the complexities of Czech pilsners and rare milk sugar vodkas. No matter how pretentious his palate became, it would never forget its humble origins belonging to the son of a dockworker who had bought him a Sam Adams on his twenty-first birthday.

Jack might have eaten himself sick if the ring of his cell phone hadn't drawn him away from the food and back into his room. Only one person had his cell phone number, so without looking at the text box, he knew who was calling.

Rather than waste words on a greeting, Jack got right to the point. "I had a transportation problem at the airport and missed my appointment. Marchand had left the office by the time I arrived. I've rescheduled for 7:30 tomorrow morning."

"Have you seen any other predators down there?" Reginald's voice crackled over the thousands of miles between them.

Jack knew exactly what Reginald meant by 'predators.' "Not a one. C-W's secret is still a secret."

"Are you sure?"

"Positive." Jack fought back a yawn. "For now, at least. This place is crawling with tourists, but none of them look like competition." He stood at the patio doors and stared at the water lapping at the man-made part of the lagoon. A sudden shift of shadow in his peripheral vision aroused the hairs at the back of his neck. Fully alert, he again stepped outside and peered into the darkness of the wild foliage surrounding the cottage and lagoon.

"Jack?"

"What?" he responded a bit too sharply.

"It's only a matter of time before word of the tea gets out, now that I've announced my plans to the company," grumbled Reginald.

"I know. C-W's secrets have been sprouting wings lately." Sensing a presence he could not see, Jack spoke in hushed tones.

"You'll get this done, won't you, Jack? Burke is champing at the bit for a shot at this acquisition, and I'm tempted to give it to him."

Jack returned his full attention to Reginald. This was the first time he'd heard even a hint of doubt regarding his negotiating skill, and Reginald had never before threatened him with Edison Burke. Burke's style was far different from Jack's. While Jack preferred to negotiate person to person, laying all the facts and incentives right out on the table, Burke's success had been built by stating half-truths and making side deals.

"Marchand's mine, Reginald," Jack stated. "I know this game and I always win it. I'll get J.T. Marchand. First thing tomorrow."

He disconnected the call and tossed the phone back into the bedroom. When he turned back toward the patio, he saw her.

More stunned than surprised, a pained groan seeped from deep in his chest. True to the advance billing given by Reginald's photos of Darwin's female population, every woman Jack had encountered since his arrival, Levora included, had been nothing less than beautiful.

The woman slowly crossing his patio had to be their queen, which was odd considering that, at first glance, she wasn't particularly attractive. At least not in any conventional sense.

Individually, Jack found her features peculiar. Her nose was rather thin and elongated, her odd-colored eyes set too wide and her lower lip much fuller than the upper one. But puzzled together, they comprised an amazingly alluring face. Stars of moonlight gleamed in her blue-black hair and made her dark brown skin glow. Tendrils of her long hair whispered against her exposed shoulders and collarbones, and the movement guided Jack's gaze lower, to her bare torso. Her breasts were magnificent. Round, high and tipped with tiny mahogany buds, they stoked a very specific hunger within the black knit of Jack's shorts. Her lightly muscled abdomen drew his eyes to the sensuous swell of her hips, around which she wore a sarong made of what seemed to be a black silk handkerchief.

She walked with the grace and body awareness of a prima ballerina. Hypnotized by the sylph-like movement of her thighs and calves, Jack could look away from her body only after she was standing directly in front him and had captured his gaze within the crystalline grey of her own.

When her lips parted as if to speak, Jack had to clench his hands to stop himself from touching his fingertip to the plumpness of her lower lip.

He took a healthy step back before he embarrassed both of them by poking her in her stomach—with a body part far more insistent than his hands. "I like your outfit," he blurted. He'd wanted to express admiration for the supple sheen of her skin, but then decided to keep his opening remarks more tame.

She'd never been self-conscious about her body. This was the first time she'd ever felt naked when she was half nude. Snared in the heat of the handsome American's serious hazel gaze, she prickled with glorious exhilaration. This was it. *He* was it, the unknown something she had been expecting. All day, her sense of expectation had been a low simmer in her belly. Now, standing before him, that pleasant sensation began to roil. Following her instincts had earned great rewards or big trouble time and time again, with no in between. Unsure which path the trend would take, she circled the out-of-place American, her island's most interesting new visitor.

"Is that a Moriori costume?"

She narrowed her eyes a bit. So he had done his homework. Many tourists came to Darwin with knowledge of the Maori, the indigenous tribesmen of neighboring New Zealand, but few took the time or interest to visit Darwin to learn of its indigenous people, the Moriori.

"Do you speak English?"

She reached past him and ran her fingertip along the rim of his tea goblet. Jack swallowed back a hard lump that traveled through his body and settled below his waist.

"*¿Usted habla español?*" he persisted.

She answered with an amused half smile.

Jack scrubbed a hand through his damp hair, leaving it more rakish. English, French and Maori were Darwin's official languages, and Jack wanted to kick himself for not even trying to learn basic Maori phrases during his long flight. He gave it one last try. "*Je parle français, et vous?*"

She smiled, and its radiance made him sweat between his toes. His thigh muscles weakened under the force of her clean, unadorned beauty. All at once, he was relieved to know that she couldn't understand him because it gave him the freedom to say whatever he wanted. He moved closer to her, so close that his words softly buffeted the top of her head as she sorted through the grapes on his tray.

"My work takes me all over the world," he told her. "I've seen the sun set beyond the Greek isles and doves fly over the Taj Mahal. I've heard angels sing in the Sistine Chapel, and watched children play in Buckingham fountain. I've seen some of the most beautiful sights in the world . . ." A lump caught in his throat, and he was unable to continue until he forced it back. "But . . . my God . . . I have never seen anything as beautiful as you. I thought this was the most godforsaken rock on the planet, but now I suddenly find myself thinking I'm in paradise."

She looked up at him, her eyes wide. Jack opened his mouth to apologize but then realized that she had not understood a word. He might have apologized anyway, had she not abruptly turned on her heel and started for the lagoon.

It never occurred to Jack to remain behind. He followed her to the water's edge and found it surprisingly warm as he climbed down the natural steps and into a tile-lined section of the lagoon. His guide dived into the water with the sleek, splashless ease of a dolphin, and she swam out beyond the tile and into the cooler ocean water. She was as agile as an otter, spinning onto her back to see that he still followed before she ducked under the water only to emerge several yards ahead of him moments later.

He had no trouble finding her in the bright moonlight when she exited the water on the other side of the lagoon. With her sheer sarong molded to her perfect buttocks, she appeared totally nude as she scrambled atop an outcropping of volcanic rock.

She sat on the edge of the rock and watched him climb up after her, enjoying the sight of his arm and leg muscles working under his pale peach skin. He was nimble for such a large man, and it didn't take him long to join her. She laughed when he shook like a St. Bernard, throwing salty water from his hair and body.

"Even your laugh is beautiful," he remarked as he sat beside her.

She gathered her hair in her hands and squeezed it. Jack watched a rivulet of water run down her shoulder and over her breast. He forced his eyes to her face, which was even lovelier with her hair slicked away from it, and they spent a long time mutely contemplating each other and the beauty of the starry ocean night.

Five minutes or five hours passed, Jack couldn't be sure which, before he decided to interrupt the perfect peace between them. "This is really nice, sitting here with you like this. 'Bathed in moonlight,' " he chuckled. "I read that in a poem in school once. The image stuck with me, but I didn't quite get it until now."

Even though she couldn't understand him, her eyes seemed to smile despite her intense expression.

The words began to pour from Jack. With bitter honesty, he told her of his beginnings in South Boston. "My father came to the United States from Ireland thirty-seven years ago. He got work at a shipyard in Quincy—that's south of Boston. He bought a two-bedroom clapboard shoebox of a house in Southie, and he married a tavern owner's daughter. Three years later, I came along. Jackson Heathcliff DeVoy. My dad's name is Sonny, and he thought it would be amusing to give all of his kids a name with the word 'son' in it. I have to thank one of the Brontës for my middle name. *Wuthering Heights* is one of my mother's favorite books. Ever read it?" Jack held her gaze for a long moment. "You have no idea what I'm saying, do you?"

She bowed her head, and Jack took that as a sign to continue, to hope that she could understand the emotion behind his words even if she couldn't translate their meaning.

"Harrison Rhett was born two years later, and Anderson Darcy finished off the set. Harry's a pocket edition of my dad and Andy's the goofy baby of the family. I love my brothers, don't get me wrong, but . . . I'm glad my parents had to stop at three. A dockworker's salary doesn't go far. There was always food on the table, but by the time I was eight years old, I never wanted to see another boiled potato or bowl of oatmeal again in my life."

Before he could censor himself, Jack was telling her about the embarrassments of going to school in third-hand clothes his mother purchased at church-run thrift shops, and the humiliation of being the only kid who had to use an old bread sleeve for a lunch bag.

"Being poor never seemed to bother my brother Harry." Jack grabbed a handful of tiny black stones. As he spoke, he methodically tossed them over the edge of the rock. "Harry was always running with the jocks and the rich kids. He got picked first for all the teams, he always got the prettiest girl. I was so glad when I got to high school because I had two years without him to look forward to. I'd started mowing lawns and doing odd jobs when I was eleven, so by the time I was a sophomore, I had the money to buy some nicer clothes. I bought my first car, a real jalopy, when I was sixteen, so things were looking pretty good. By the time I was eighteen, I was captain of the football team, in the top two percent of my class, and I had the prettiest girl in school, Beth O'Leary, lined up for the Harvest Homecoming Dance."

Jack kept to himself the rest of the Beth O'Leary story. Alone on the edge of the world with the attentive beauty who had taken him there, the Beth O'Leary tale suddenly lost its teeth. The golden, blue-eyed beauty of the Beth O'Leary in his memory seemed faded and two-dimensional compared to the dark goddess sitting before him.

He glossed over his stellar college football career at Boston University but savored the telling of his decision to pursue law and his acceptance to Harvard Law School. He avoided talking about his work and more specifically, his reason for coming to Darwin. The last thing he wanted was to taint this exquisite moment beneath the stars with talk of business.

"This is the kind of thing that happens in movies," he said with a chuckle. "You're nothing like the women I usually meet. I come across so many women hunting for a good match—financially, socially and physically, in that order. I've dodged a couple of bullets in the past several years."

Jack turned slightly, to fully face her. "It's not that they weren't nice, accomplished women. Clio was a divorce attorney who liked swing dancing, Cinnabon and NASCAR. Eighteen months after we started dating, she draws up a pre-nup and wants to get married. I couldn't do it. It was too soon, it didn't feel right, I was just starting my career . . . I had a lot of excuses that seemed great at the time, but now . . ." He shook his head, and in doing so, ridded himself of the memory. "So she left. Then there was Erica. She was a fashion designer. We lasted almost three years, probably because she wasn't in law. I know she wanted to get married, and she would have been a great wife and mother, but . . . I wasn't ready. There was just so much I wanted to accomplish with my career before I settled down."

Jack stared at his sea nymph, and in her silence, he realized what he'd never before admitted. "I didn't love them. I don't think I've ever been in love with any woman. I can't afford to fall in love, not until my future is secure." A slurry of unexpected emotions clogged his throat. "I must be jet-lagged. Nothing else explains why I'm suddenly wishing that I could spend the rest of my life right here on this rock, with you."

She sat back on her heels. Her hair had dried and hung in lanks about her face and shoulders, and her skin shimmered with crystals of salt and sand. She reached a small hand forth and cupped his face.

"If I didn't know better, I'd think you understood me." He covered her hand with his and pressed it to his cheek. The whispery softness of her innocent touch set his nerve endings ablaze. She stood on her knees and inched closer to him, finally resting between his thighs. Afraid to touch her for fear of not being able to stop, Jack kept still. She set her free hand on his shoulder, leaning deeper into the cradle of his legs and torso. Her breath at his ear and temple left him breathing hard, and he closed his eyes, committing every second of her warmth and sea scent to memory.

When she withdrew, Jack opened his eyes to see her sitting back from him, framed by the purple-grey light of dawn. Because of its location, Darwin received the first light of every new day before any other place on Earth. Longing flooded through him as he gazed at his anonymous companion in the newest light of day. He had never seen such beauty, and he knew he likely never would again. This moment was a masterpiece, and the most fitting final stroke would be a kiss.

"I wish I spoke your language." Jack lightly cupped her neck and touched his forehead to hers. "I want to kiss you, but I don't know how to ask you."

Her hands closed around his wrists as she lifted her face and tilted her head, aligning her lips with his. His breathing seemed to stop and he couldn't move, not until she had brought her mouth delicately to his.

His hands moved into her hair, cradling her head. He took command of the kiss, feeding his hunger for the sweet warmth of her mouth. Her breath quickened when he tipped her head back to suckle her earlobes and kiss her neck, the fingers of one hand tracing her spine before coming to rest at the small of her back. She leaned back, allowing him to support her, and eagerly offered the plum-dark buds he found himself craving.

He had no will to resist, not after she cupped the back of his head and guided his mouth to her left breast. With a fierce tenderness he never knew he possessed, he sent her into a writhing frenzy that left her lying on the rock, panting, her body rigid and arched into his. His final restraints fell away when she slipped her hand into his shorts and between his legs, and she moaned her approval of what she found there.

Her touch left him shuddering atop her, fighting to regain control of himself. His knit shorts and her sarong were all that stood between his desire to fill her and feel her heat closing around him. But a needle of reason injected Jack with some of his own inescapable common sense.

"We can't," he breathed heavily. He took her wrist, but he couldn't bring himself to remove her skilled hand from his hard flesh. "I won't." He groaned and collapsed onto his back, her hand never leaving him. He squinted against the brightening sunrise until she hunkered over him, blocking out the pink-tinged light. She kissed him, her hair teasing his shoulders and chest while her right hand continued its devilry in his shorts.

The silky heat of her mouth, the brush of her hair and breasts over the skin of his chest, and the expert pump of her hand sent a rocket of sensation exploding through Jack, and she smothered his loud response in a kiss.

Jack closed his eyes and thought he might actually lose consciousness. He lay there on his back, panting, overwrought and as weak as a newborn. "I wish I knew your name." His voice sounded distant to his own ears. She stroked his hair, and it had the effect of a lullaby. "I wish I could stay right here with you forever," he mumbled before resting his head on her soft thighs. With her fingers gently moving through his hair, he succumbed to the sleep that had eluded him hours earlier.

CHAPTER 3

"You're late."

Jack had tortured himself with those two words ever since he woke up on a black rock under a broiling morning sun. His night companion had disappeared so thoroughly, he would have thought the encounter a dream if the satisfied phantom memories of his body had not convinced him otherwise. He was no wilderness scout capable of telling the time by the position of the sun, but he'd known that it was well past seven when he dived back into the ocean and swam back to his cottage.

He'd spent two minutes showering, dressed in his remaining suit and gathered his cell phone and briefcase before fleeing the cottage. He'd trotted the two miles to Marchand's offices, leaping over mud puddles and skirting past bicyclists, pedestrians and rickety carts the way he'd once avoided grunting linesmen on the gridiron. Along the way, he'd cursed his own stupidity, Marchand and Darwin mint tea, and underneath it all had been the admonition, *You're late*.

Hearing the receptionist's deadpan delivery of the words made Jack's annoyance burn that much hotter. "I know I'm late. Last night, I was . . . Look, could you please just let J.T. Marchand know that I'm here?"

The receptionist dragged a red fingernail along her collarbone, which was exposed by her low-cut floral blouse. "J.T. waited for you, Mr. Coyle-Wexler Rep," she said, addressing him by the title written in her appointment book. "J.T. had another engagement this morning and had to leave at nine. You really are quite late."

Jack ground the heel of his hand into his eye in frustration. "Where can I find him?"

"Him who?"

Jack gnashed his teeth. "J.T. Marchand."

She giggled. "Do you know anything at all about J.T.? I suggest you not refer to J.T. as—"

"Although I appreciate your advice, I've been doing what I do for quite a long time without the help of a phone jockey," Jack trumpeted over her. "I know everything I need to know about your boss." He dropped all pretenses toward politeness. "Now if you don't mind, tell me where Marchand is, or do I have to search the building myself and—"

A stampede of jabbering business suits burst into the lobby, drowning out Jack's threat. The receptionist stood, her eyes wide in fear, amazement or annoyance. She held up her hands to ward off the army armed with cell phones, digital assistants and briefcases.

Jack refused to be moved from his prime position at the front of the receptionist's counter until a familiar voice on the fringe of the corporate wave stole his attention.

"Carol Crowley," he growled under his breath. He shoved his way to the edge of the fracas and circled around to the rival who was always a half step behind him in his business dealings. "You're a long way from Boston, Carol." He forced a pleasant grin. "What brings you to this side of the world?"

"Same thing that brought you, stud." Carol, her petite fame impeccably attired in navy blue Anne Klein, flipped shut her cell phone and gave her blonde locks a flirty flip. "I hear you can get a good cup of tea on this island, Jack."

"You know, I'm not really surprised to see you here. PharmaChemix seems to have a knack for sniffing out Coyle-Wexler's new product leads. But I have to wonder how the rest of those lemmings got in on it." He tipped his head toward the well-dressed corporate reps gathered around the receptionist like a flock of starving geese around a cob of fresh corn. The receptionist was invisible in the crowd, but Jack clearly heard her voice above the anxious murmurings of her audience.

"J.T. Marchand is available by appointment *only*." She stood on her chair, pointed her finger like a pistol and aimed it at Jack. "You. Before J.T. left, I took the liberty of rescheduling you for eleven tomorrow morning."

Jack gave her a hearty thumbs-up and mouthed, "Thank you." A chorus of voices requested appointments, but the receptionist's aggravatingly even voice silenced them. "I can't make appointments without the master schedule and the master schedule is with J.T., who is gone for the day."

An angry male voice rose above the others. "We just spent an hour jam-packed in a minivan with no floor, for heaven's sake, all for you to tell us that we have to *wait*

God-knows-how-long to make an appointment to see J.T. Marchand?"

The receptionist picked up a magazine and a pair of sunglasses. She set an OUT TO LUNCH sign on her counter. "Wonderful. We understand each other. Good day."

While the newly arrived pharmaceutical reps loitered like lost goslings in the lobby, Jack embarked on a manhunt. Rather, a woman hunt. With Carol Crowley doing a poor job of tailing him, he walked briskly through the bustling town center. His fair hair and skin, his height, his European-designed business suit and his hurry made him stand out among the tourists and easy-going, casually dressed locals and vendors in the busy marketplace.

He passed an elderly man calling out the prices of a water-speckled, rainbow assortment of fruits and vegetables packed in stacked crates around him. He shouldered his way through the crowd of patrons jockeying for position at a fish stand, where the day's freshest catches were prominently displayed. In deference to the morning heat, Jack loosened his tie and unbuttoned his collar as he turned sideways to avoid a collision with a group of laughing college-aged tourists.

Jack stopped at a news kiosk attended by a dark-skinned young man in dungaree cutoffs and an ancient Kool & the Gang T-shirt. He bought a *New York Times* and a *Boston Globe*, and he had to remind himself that he was on Darwin, not Mars. No matter how backward the place and populace seemed, it had something going for it if the *Times* and the *Globe* could be had.

He tucked the papers under his arm and resumed his search, not going far before he saw the very person he'd been looking for. "Levora!" He broke into a trot when he saw her untying BeBe and CeCe in front of an outdoor café. "Mrs. Solomon!"

She planted her hands on her hips and smiled at him once he was standing in front of her. "You had it right the first time. It's Levora. Mrs. Solomon is my mother-in-law, may she choke on a chicken bone." She scrunched up her nose as she studied him from head to foot. "Never properly dressed for the occasion, are you?"

He ignored her inquiry. "I need your help." He glanced back the way he'd come. Carol's overcoiffed blonde head was stalled in a heavy glut of spectators watching a trio of muscular Moriori street performers. "Is there someplace we can go to talk privately?"

Levora indicated her cart. "Hop in."

He swung his briefcase into the back of the empty cart and offered Levora a hand as she planted a foot on the driver's step.

She gave him a dazzling smile. "You're one refined city boy, Jack DeVoy." She tightly clasped his hand and allowed him to help her onto the backless bench. After climbing up himself, he looked back once more to see Carol's stylish but impractical navy pumps closing the distance between them.

With a click of her tongue, a flick of her flywhisk and a tug on the leather reins, Levora started her goats. Their long, shaggy hair blowing in the wind, BeBe and CeCe lurched along with the speed of snails on sand.

There's never an escaped chicken to give a pair of goats a turbo boost when you need one, Jack thought sullenly.

Levora skillfully steered her cart through the congestion of bicyclists, pedestrians and carts pulled by donkeys. She waited until they were on the outskirts of the town center, surrounded by nikau, the tall palms native to the island, before she asked, "How can I help you, Jack?"

He played his lowest card. "I need to find someone."

"J.T. Marchand?" she grinned.

"What gave me away?"

"The forty-five Brooks Brothers clones who flew in this morning. Suits tend to follow suits, and you're the suit that got here first. All that bunch talked about was grabbing up some Darwin mint tea and catching the next flight out. Ricky Nikuradse carted half of them into town in his minibus and the ingrates tipped him only ten bucks American. Cheapskates."

"Levora . . ." Jack prompted her to stay on track with him.

"My guess is that our big secret's out," she laughed. "America's got a bad case of Venus envy, and you came here to get first crack at J.T., to get that tea."

"I never said anything about the tea, Lev—Venus envy?"

She laughed lightly. "Women are very good at recognizing beauty, except when they look at themselves. They hear about the tea and they come here, looking for a magic fix-it-all to make them beautiful. What they don't know is that they're already beautiful. Each one of them. There's beauty in the stretch marks a woman earns during pregnancy, and in the fingernails she breaks washing dishes and scouring bathtubs. The tea has its own merits, I admit that, but it's only a part of the quest for true beauty and good health." She winked at him. "It's a good thing you aren't here for the tea. You'd be wasting your time."

He took a long hard look at Levora. Working on her husband's oyster farm had blunted her fingernails. He studied the lines at her eyes and mouth, the ones that came alive when she smiled and laughed. Flour and some sort of berry juice muddied her dungarees, and she seemed to always smell like vanilla. She was older than his mother, yet Levora was easily one of the most beautiful women he'd ever seen. "Venus envy," he muttered. "Women are strange."

"Yes, Jack," she happily agreed. "And that, too, makes us beautiful."

His own beliefs about the tea pushed aside, he focused on his assignment. "Can you take me to J.T. Marchand?"

She snorted. "If you hotshots did your homework properly, you'd know that privacy is very important to J.T. And J.T. is very important to Darwin Island."

"Does that mean you won't help me?"

"It means I *can't* help you. Your guess is as good as mine as far as J.T. Marchand's whereabouts are concerned. Some people just know how to disappear when they don't want to be bothered. J.T. does it better than anybody."

Tension crept into Jack's neck and lower back as he took his cell phone from his inner breast pocket. He dreaded the call he had to make: to tell Wexler that the secret of the tea was out, that the island was now overrun with rival companies stricken with Venus envy, and that he still had not met Marchand, let alone secured the rights to Darwin mint.

He breathed a short sigh of relief when he couldn't get a calling signal on his phone, so he put it away, took off his jacket, and then turned to stow it in the back of the cart as Levora brought BeBe and CeCe to a halt on the right side of the dirt road. "Look who we have here," she crooned.

Jack turned and looked. "You!" He added a stern finger point to the word he shouted at the raven-haired woman sitting in front of the lone thatch-and-stone cottage on the right side of the road.

"You two have met?" A surprised Levora held the reins in lax hands as BeBe and CeCe guided the cart's wheels into the deep ruts in the dirt drive beside the cottage.

"Oh, we've met, all right." Jack leaped from the cart before it fully stopped, and he started for the woman. It was a struggle to control his temper as he studied her in the clear, clean light of day. "You deliberately distracted me to make me miss my meeting, didn't you?"

Unimpressed by Jack's show of Yankee temper, his midnight paramour merely watched his lips move.

Jack whirled on Levora as he rolled up his shirtsleeves. "Lawrence Taylor used to send escorts to the hotel rooms of his rivals the night before big NFL games," he told her. "Someone sent *her* to me." He again jabbed a finger toward the woman in front of the cottage. "This is a sick little game you're playing, lady!"

Jack, angrier with himself than at Marchand or his unnamed sea nymph, failed to see the bewildered look exchanged by the two women.

"You're confusing me," Levora said. "You know Lina?"

"Lina?" he repeated, tossing up his hands. He stood straighter, thrusting his chest slightly forward, but she held her ground when he moved to stand directly in front of her. "Your name is Lina?"

Her fine eyebrows wrinkled. "Yes."

Jack's eyes bulged. Not only could she speak, even more frustrating, the sultry purr of her voice sent his blood rushing south. "You can speak?" he finally worked out for lack of anything better to say. "English?"

"Of course she speaks English." Levora approached them and gave Jack a playful shove. "Lina also speaks French, Spanish, Japanese, Maori, and when she really wants to impress, some mighty fine Italian."

"Mum, we just received an order for five-dozen cane-and-lime muffins and six-dozen ginger-raspberry muffins for the luncheon at the medical center next Friday," Lina said. "Do you think we'll be able to fill it on such short notice?"

"Anything for you, kid." She gave Lina's shoulders an affectionate squeeze before bidding Jack good morning, opening the front door of the cottage and disappearing inside.

A deep furrow split Jack's forehead as he eyeballed Lina. On the outside, he knew he appeared ferocious and cold, but on the inside . . . He cringed, admitting to himself that on the inside, he was a shuddering glob of need. Lina wore a formless, sleeveless dress of pale, airy cotton, and it was hard to stay angry when he couldn't stop thinking of what was under the dress. The strands of neon blue glinting in her hair further distracted him. Once she pinned him with her silvery eyes, Jack's anger swirled away.

"You never said you spoke English," he accused.

"I never said anything."

He tried to place her accent. She sounded mostly Australian, but she could have been English or perhaps even South African. "Where are you from?"

"I was born here on Darwin, but I went to university overseas. My dialect is something of a hodgepodge."

"How old are you?" By day, she looked even younger than she had at night. Given how the citizenry of Darwin aged, she could be anywhere from sixteen—God forbid—to thirty.

The tip of her tongue peeked from the corner of her lips. "I'm old enough to go skinny-dipping with a man at midnight."

The sweat rings wetting the armpits of Jack's starched white shirt rapidly began to expand. "We weren't skinny-dipping. We weren't naked." *Not completely*, he grumbled to himself.

Lina picked up a covered wicker basket of muffins that Jack had failed to notice before, and brushed past him. "I meant tonight." After hanging her basket over one arm, she stepped onto the side of the road and headed in the direction of the town center. Jack stood in the road, watching the shift and sway of her rear until she disappeared.

Lina waited until she had rounded the bend and was well out of sight before she sank heavily onto the black volcanic boulder that doubled as a road sign. A muffin bounced out of her basket when she set it heavily at her feet. She rested her elbows on her knees and buried her face in her hands and whispered, "Just once. It was only supposed to be one time."

She'd seen Jack, in Levora's company, walking into the town center as she herself had been leaving yesterday. Had Levora been alone, she would have drawn attention to herself, but the sight of Jack had paralyzed her for a moment. There was no shortage of tall, handsome, interesting men on Darwin. The bulk of the island's visitors were ordinary tourists, but a small percentage were more dangerous. They were adventurers drawn by Darwin's unusual landscape, treasure hunters looking to pick at the submerged wrecks of ships that had come off the worse against Darwin's deep, ragged harbors, or romantics looking for creative inspiration in one of Earth's lesser known corners. No matter their reason for coming, that sort typically left Darwin, but not before leaving a part of himself—usually a child—behind.

Unable to determine which sort Jack was, Lina had stood in the shadow of the news kiosk, tracking his progress alongside Levora. At first glance, he seemed the most destructive visitor of all to her island—the kind who came to take advantage of any and all native women foolish enough to succumb to his physical charms.

People from all over the world had settled in Darwin, producing a gene pool so wide and varied that most natives never knew what their children would look like upon birth. Lina herself had the nose of a French ancestor, the eyes of an English one and the dark complexion of her grandmother, an Australian-born Aborigine. Darwin tea brought women to the island all year round, but Darwin's women drew the men.

Even before she'd asked around about him, Lina had known that Jack was American. Levora loved Darwin, but she'd never surrendered her American citizenship, and she always befriended the Americans she encountered on the island. Jack had been stingy with information regarding his reason for coming to Darwin, but Lina wasn't especially interested in it. For what she had in mind, the less she knew about him, the better. Past experience had taught her and every other Darwin resident that stiffs in suits meant nothing but trouble. So she'd followed Levora and Jack, eyeing him with suspicion from a distance.

His impatient gaze had roamed right over her when he was looking around while Levora emptied her boot of road grit. Unreasonably insulted—he was the first man she had ever encountered who'd failed to at least notice her once she'd turned her eyes on him—she'd continued to watch him as he spoke to Levora. She couldn't hear what he was saying. She hadn't cared to, not when simply looking at him was so enjoyable. His honey-gold hair, easy to spot amid the shorter, darker heads around him, was on the long side of business professional. It was the hair of a busy man who cared about his appearance for professional reasons, rather than vanity. He had the strong, straight and square features of a movie star, but his shrewd, jewel-colored eyes radiated intelligence and cool cunning.

Unlike most visitors to Darwin, he hadn't looked awed or intimidated by what must have been a totally alien environment. His confidence was apparent in the way he moved, and Lina had found that brand of self-assurance mouth-watering.

She'd gone about the rest of her day after he disappeared into the old factory building. Later, a few careful inquiries had directed her to his homestay, where she had been able to study him discreetly through the thick foliage surrounding his temporary residence. When he'd popped into the shower, she'd arranged to have dinner brought to him, and she'd waited just beyond his terrace, hoping to steal another look at him.

She'd gotten a look all right, and it had been a pair of knit sports briefs short of a Full Monty. She had stared at him, stunned at how a man could be so beautiful in both form and movement. He possessed an elegant strength she wouldn't have expected from a man of his size and build, and her desire for a look had evolved into the need to touch.

Like most American men she'd met, he'd started talking and kept on talking once she'd approached him. The only difference with Jack was that he'd actually had something to say, interesting, intimate things that aroused her mind as thoroughly as his presence and touch had aroused her body.

Her simple desire to see him up close had taken an impulsive and unexpected turn. She'd attempted a feeble escape, by swimming across the lagoon. But he'd followed her, and in so doing he'd erased any reservations she might have had. The most stunning man she'd ever laid eyes on had followed her to her favorite spot on Darwin, and the combination had worked a spell that forced surrender to her hungriest carnal instinct.

In the end, as she'd watched him sleep, she'd been glad that he'd shown a bit of crucial restraint. God knew that she hadn't been able to.

One of the island's treasured black robins glided to an easy landing beside the lost muffin. "Two nights, then," Lina said, directing the words at the bird as though seeking its counsel. The robin eagerly pecked at the muffin as Lina carefully scooped up her basket and started down the road.

CHAPTER 4

Jack paced the bedroom, his loafers making no sound on the polished, bamboo flooring as he clicked off the floor and desk lamps and the ceiling fixture. Then he opened the drapes and sheers as far as they would go, flooding the room with moonlight. He had already opened the glass doors so he could easily hear outside noises.

So he could hear Lina.

He peeked at his watch even as he told himself that he wouldn't check the time again: 11:37.

He wrung his hands together. It was a myth that toilets swirled backwards in this part of the world, but time sure seemed to. This had been the longest day of Jack's life, despite how busy he'd been.

Once Lina had left, he'd had muffins and coffee at Levora's, at her insistence, and he'd listened as Levora told him about her baking business, which specialized in softball-sized muffins that shipped daily as far as Sydney and Canberra. The coconut-lime muffins Levora had served were unbelievably good, but Jack was more interested in learning more about J.T. Marchand than muffins. But every question he had asked about Marchand had been answered with some inane observation about Lina, who appeared to be Levora's favorite topic.

As if he needed her help in keeping Lina on his mind. He had another reason for being so determined to find Marchand. The faster he clinched the deal for the tea, the sooner he'd be free to devote a little time to Lina.

He'd once secured the rights to an herbal antihistamine produced by a tiny company in Seattle. Pharmaceutical reps from hundreds of companies had descended upon Seattle, each vying to get the drug. After three days of bargaining, negotiating and competing, Jack had gotten the deal done despite heavy competition from Carol Crowley. Jack had put millions in Coyle-Wexler's coffers and earned himself a hefty six-figure bonus. His winning record had withstood its fiercest challenge, and the victory had given Jack a feeling of self-assurance and joy that he'd never known.

Until last night.

Until he'd spent a night on a hunk of black glass with a woman who had appealed to his every sense.

Until Lina, Jack had never known the thrill of complete surrender, and instantly he'd become addicted. He'd moved through the minutes of the day, thankful that each tick of the clock brought him closer to midnight, yet snappish over the slowness with which each minute arrived. He'd almost wished that he could have just gone to bed and slept until midnight.

The idea of climbing into bed only made his thoughts circle more tightly around Lina, so Jack forced himself to review his day instead.

Hoping to learn more of what his newly arrived competitors knew, he had accepted Carol's invitation to join her and a group of lawyers for a late lunch at The Crab and Nickel, one of the island's two restaurants, and to Jack's surprise, a three-star Michelin rated establishment.

Jack had sat down to his second meal on Darwin, and it was exquisite. Yet it couldn't compare to his first with its dessert of Lina's kisses. It wasn't like him to lust so after a woman. He'd never had problems satisfying his physical needs, but this time the urge was specific. He wanted Lina, plain and simple.

Plain and simple. The two words described her perfectly, though she was anything but plain, and clearly not simple. Despite her skill with languages, she was an island girl untempered by MTV, McDonald's, Botox and *Sports Illustrated* swimsuit issues. She was natural, beautiful, the most precious treasure he had ever discovered. To be more accurate, he conceded that she had discovered him.

He had been able to push Lina out of his head just far enough to function with his fellow attorneys and pharmaceutical reps, and he'd learned far more than he'd anticipated. Most of them had heard of a tea with miraculous weight loss properties and they'd come for samples to take back for testing and research. With boxes of dried Darwin mint already purchased, most of them had planned to fly out of Darwin the next day.

Carol, as usual, was ahead of the game. She already knew that the boxed product had dismally failed Coyle-Wexler's laboratory testing and, like Jack, she wanted to buy the rights to the actual plant in its native habitat. And like the savvy attorney she was, she was digging her heels in for the full ride. She'd rented a cottage near the center of town and had paid for two weeks in advance.

Jack hoped it wouldn't take that long to find and deal with Marchand . . . but as he wore circles in the carpet, he decided that he might not mind two weeks in Darwin, not if they were spent with Lina.

"You're not dressed for skinny dipping," Jack said, Lina's emergence from the shadows stealing all but the obvious from his lips. He absently licked them as she neared him. With each step she took, her bare toes peeked from beneath her long, silky skirt. Rather than concealing the lines and hollows of her hips and legs, the sheer, floral-printed fabric of the low-slung skirt emphasized them. A glittering thread of gold loosely circled her bare midriff, the dangling end unerringly drawing Jack's gaze to her lower abdomen and the soft angles of her exposed hip bones. Her hair hung loose and floated on the breeze generated by her movements. She was standing toe-to-toe with Jack before he realized that she wore nothing other than the skirt, the gold chain and her luxurious wealth of hair. Her hair cloaked her bare breasts, but Jack caught teasing peeks of plum as she raised her face to his.

"Neither are you," Lina responded. She sidestepped him at the edge of the lagoon and went to the rattan table. A basket of Levora's banana-kiwi, honey-raisin, cinnamon-oat and coconut-lime muffins made a fragrant centerpiece surrounded by a grand assortment of fresh fruit, a carafe of mint tea and a chilled bottle of Peterson's Botrytis Semillon, a sweet white wine Jack had heard of but never tasted.

Lina ran her fingertip through the condensation beading on the chilled carafe. The film of moisture tempered the burst of heat she'd felt upon seeing Jack. He'd gotten some sun in the course of his day's travels, and his crisp white shirt highlighted his new tan. Pleated khaki trousers, a dark braided leather belt and Cordovan loafers completed his apparel. His clothing was average to the point of bland, yet Lina was captivated by the simplicity of his attractiveness.

"I didn't come to Darwin Island for this." Jack flicked a hand in her general direction.

"For muffins?" She sat on the edge of the table and elegantly crossed one leg over the other. The high slit in her skirt allowed it to part and fall away, revealing her legs from toe to hip.

Logical thought eluded Jack for as long as he stared at the way her smooth legs gleamed in the moonlight. He tore his gaze away to stare at the interlocked canopies of the tall nikau palms. "I didn't come here to get involved."

"Why *did* you come here?" She plucked a ripe kiwifruit from the platter. She brought the soft little oval to her mouth. With excruciating delicacy, she used her front teeth to break its furry bronze skin and her lips and tongue to peel it back, exposing the gold flesh. Her left cheek dimpled in a tiny grin as she caught a drop of sweet juice on the tip of her tongue.

Jack's body responded fiercely to her actions. "This isn't something I do. I don't allow myself to be seduced by strange women in strange places."

A tiny smile curled one corner of her mouth. "Am I seducing you?"

"Don't insult my intelligence, Lina."

"Certainly not. Although I'm afraid I may prick your ego a bit. I'm not trying to seduce you, Mr. DeVoy."

"Then why did you come here tonight?" he almost yelled, but only because he wanted so much to feel her lips against his once more.

"Why did you wait for me?" she calmly countered.

He marched toward her. She uncrossed her legs and sat up straighter, expectant. He didn't stop coming at her until he stood at the table, one of his legs wedged between hers. "You have the annoying habit of answering a question with a question. You should have been a lawyer."

"Mr. DeVoy—"

"Jack."

"Jack . . ." She held his gaze and dared to slide her hands along his shirt front as she stood to face him. "I seduced you last night. I'm here now because it's your turn to seduce me."

Jack gritted his teeth, breathing a little heavier through his nose. His hands went to her hips and found handfuls of her filmy skirt. Her soft, citrusy scent whittled away what little willpower he still possessed.

"This isn't something I make a habit of, Jack." She swallowed hard, and Jack was pleased to see that she was as intensely affected by their proximity as he. "I saw you in town yesterday and I wanted you."

He groaned low in his throat. His fingers splayed over her backside and he gave her a short, easy tug that brought her pelvis into contact with his.

"If I see something I want, I go out and get it," she said quietly. "I'm rather self-centered in that regard."

"No more than I am." His words caressed her lips, sending tremors of anticipation through her. She passed her hands over Jack's unyielding chest and shoulders on her way to threading her fingers through the hair at his nape.

"Welcome to my island, Jack." Her eyes closed as she caught his lower lip in a kiss. He took a deep breath, inhaling her, reveling in the tropical taste and softness of her mouth. He pushed one hand into her hair and wrapped an arm around her middle, drawing her still closer. She tilted her hips, angling the center of her desire directly against the hard knot behind his fly.

His hungry kisses swept over her face and throat, grazed down to her collarbones and her chest. A distant part of him felt shame—not over the course he'd chosen to pursue with her, but over how desperately he wanted to feel her beneath him and around him. He ached to bury himself in her.

Between the kisses he swept along her jaw line, he mumbled his desires, almost pleading with her.

She unhooked the single fastener at her hip. Her skirt fell away and she draped it across one end of the table, forming a silk tablecloth upon which she became the most tempting treat. Jack eased her onto her back, nibbling his way from her chin to her breastbone, her navel and the neat strip of midnight curls between her legs. He dropped to one knee to kiss her inner right thigh as he guided that leg over his shoulder.

Lina smiled into the night and spread her arms over the table, contentedly offering herself to Jack. She gazed dreamily into the night sky, thrilling in the quickening of her breathing and the rush of her blood.

"I'm going to look at you, Lina." He spoke to her in a low, almost business-like voice that managed to be incredibly seductive. "And then I'm going to kiss you, first with my breath . . . and then my lips . . . and then my tongue."

Her thighs quivered, her skin goosepimpling as his breath brushed the sensitive flesh between her thighs.

"I'm going to taste you," he murmured. "And then I'm going to have my fill of you."

A man of his word, Jack did exactly as pledged. She hadn't known what to expect, but he surpassed her expectations. He was artful. Unhurried. Thorough . . .

Loving? His hands trembled as he caressed her hips and thighs, as if he were both afraid to touch her or to let her go.

A low moan of satisfaction oozed from Lina's throat as her spine arced. Her hands clenched and unclenched, her toes curled and her lower body shivered in response to Jack's intimate work. His fingers dug into her backside when she convulsed against him, her gasping cries joining the symphony of the hidden wildlife around them.

He spread himself over her nude body, fully aware of the effect his clothed form had on her as he moved over her. He lightly closed his hands around her wrists, his gentle grip whispering along her arms as he brought his head even with her chest. With his nose, he nudged aside the strands of jet lying across her left breast, and his breath alone turned her nipple into a tight bud. But when he closed his lips around it, she arched into him, feeding him as much of her breast as he would take.

He nursed her into a writhing, cooing frenzy before his kisses followed her midline to her navel, and on down to the glistening darkness between her legs. Sumptuous, darting movements of his tongue delightfully tormented its target before it homed in on the bullseye. With a loud, breathy gasp, Lina closed her eyes. Her head and shoulders involuntarily pushed against the tabletop while her hips rose to meet each thrust of Jack's mouth.

"Jack . . . Jack, please . . ."

His name became her plea and she clutched at his shoulders, urging him to rise and continue his invasion more intimately. She half sat up and pulled him to her for a deep kiss that allowed her to tug open his shirt, popping three of its buttons into the shadows.

She locked her ankles at the small of his back and hunched over to grab at his belt. Jack was sure that she would have stripped him and mounted him right there under the stars if he hadn't scooped her up and carried her to the sliding doors. She clung to him, kissing him, her nude body making Jack clumsy and stupid with desire. He supported Lina with one hand and used the other to tug at the stubborn screen door.

Lina giggled against his lips when the thing wouldn't budge despite Jack's blind pulling and tugging. He broke free of Lina's kiss to give the door handle a hard wrench that yanked it half off its track.

"I'm sure the owner will understand, once you properly explain the circumstances," Lina teased between the kisses she dotted along the rim of his ear.

Jack's knees went soft while the rest of him became painfully hard when the tip of her tongue sweetly dipped into his ear.

The cottage was much smaller than any of the hotel suites he had stayed in, but his invisible hosts kept the place exceptionally clean, cozy and inviting, right down to the midnight muffin and fruit platter. The temporary residence was more like a friend's guest home than a hotel—except for the contents of the hospitality basket in the bathroom.

After positioning Lina on his bed, Jack popped into the bathroom to retrieve the strand of condoms his thorough hosts had included among the miniature shampoos, lotions, mouthwash and disposable razors.

He stood at the side of the bed and forced himself to take his time as he undressed. His leisured, almost indifferent striptease was meant to give himself time to gain a much-needed measure of self-control. As he revealed his chiseled, well proportioned physique, he robbed Lina of her self restraint.

She sat up on her knees and took him by the shoulders. Kissing him, she guided him onto the bed. She took one of the condoms and used her teeth to open the packet. Her silky hair tickled over Jack's torso when she lowered her head, using her mouth to slide the condom onto Jack's steely flesh before boldly straddling him. With his hands at her hips, she completed their union with one hard thrust that made her jaw clamp shut.

"I'm sorry." His touch light, Jack laid a hand along her jawline. "I didn't mean to hurt you." He swallowed back a gasp. The apology was the one coherent thought he could express through the mindless pleasure of being locked inside her snug heat.

"You didn't." The muscles of her abdomen and hips contracted and relaxed in concert with her deep, raspy breathing. "It's just . . . it's been a while for me."

She allowed herself to acclimate to his size, to the vastness of him within her. When she began to move her hips, to undulate upon him in a steadily increasing rhythm, Jack welcomed the possibility that he could literally die from pleasure.

It had been a while for him, too, so long that his flesh couldn't remember ever having been treated so well. Lina cloaked him with her body and Jack wrapped his arms around her. Her weight upon him and her heat around him carried him to an unfamiliar place of keen physical awareness. Her hair formed a black tent beneath which she kissed him. Bodies locked from lips to hips, limbs intertwined and hearts throbbing in syncopation, they existed in a paradise of two.

No longer able to hold back the eruption building within him, Jack clasped Lina to him and rolled her beneath him. He supported the small of her back with one hand, raising her hips just enough to give him complete control. She responded with a whimper of gratification, digging her fingertips into the hard meat of his hip and buttocks. Jack squeezed his eyes shut tight and buried his face in the sweat-glossed warmth of her neck.

Yoga had honed Jack's control to the point where he could prolong this exquisite torture for both of them. He braced his weight on his left elbow and gazed at the way passion shaped her features, and the vision fueled him. He shifted his hips a little and moved his right knee a bit higher. The subtle change in position created delicious friction that sent Lina into a breathless delirium.

Her body clamped around him, inside and out, and tore his release from him. He stiffened, his abdominal muscles bunching against her flat belly. He cried out and breathed hard in her ear, his fists clenched at the sides of her head as spasm after spasm seized him.

"Lina," he exhaled loudly, pressing his lips to the tiny beads of perspiration glossing her shoulder before catching her gaze. "Dear God, that was . . . what did you do to me?"

She took his chin and steered his mouth to hers. She let her kisses speak for her, telling him how he had done just as well by her.

Soft kisses and tender caresses eased them back into their separate selves, and neither of them spoke to disrupt the tranquility. Snuggling into Jack's embrace upon the tangled bed sheet, Lina laughed lightly as she rested her head upon his shoulder.

"Do I even want to know what's so funny?" he asked.

"I was just thinking." With the tip of her finger, she circled the tawny disk of flesh capping Jack's right pectoral muscle.

"About what?"

"About you."

"Do tell."

"I thought you would be an utter stiff when I saw you in town." She ran her hand along his thigh. "A sexy stiff, but a stiff just the same. Turns out I was right. And wrong."

Jack grasped her buttock to press her hips to his as he rolled onto his side to face her. "Thank you. I think."

He lifted a thin lock of her hair from her forehead and delicately draped it over her shoulder, giving himself an unobstructed view of her face. With her straight hair, light eyes and dark skin, she was truly an original, like no other woman he had ever seen. He inwardly celebrated the spin of the genetic dial that had produced such a visually stunning final product.

"You're staring," Lina said softly.

"You're a curiosity."

"Am I?"

"Your hair and your eyes . . . they're so unusual for someone with such dark skin."

"My hair comes from one of my grandmothers," she told him. "My skin color comes from the other. She was an Aborigine. She lived with her mum in Australia until she was relocated. She was sent to live with a white Australian family in the Northern Territory when she was eleven. She was fourteen when the family moved to Darwin."

Jack kinked an eyebrow. "Relocated?"

"My grandmum's father was white. English. Her mother was Aborigine. At the time, the Australian government was concerned about an unwanted third race being created through the intermarriage of Aborigines and Caucasians. Light-skinned or half-caste Aboriginal children were forcibly removed from their parents and sent to live in camps. They were schooled, adopted by white families, and later married to Caucasians. The belief at the time was that by the third generation of intermarriage with whites, the Aboriginal blood would no longer manifest itself."

"If you can't kill them, breed them out," Jack murmured. "It's an ancient form of genocide."

"As you're seeing now," Lina smiled, "nature has a way of reasserting herself."

Jack stroked her cheek, his thumb moving lightly over her lower lip. "Her work is quite exquisite."

"Indeed," she agreed, studying Jack's face as intently as he studied hers. She stroked his hair from his forehead and admired the way sleepiness softened the serious set of his features. Lina wondered if the honest, open emotion she saw in his clear gaze was his or a reflection of her own. Jack DeVoy had gotten under her skin in more ways than she'd anticipated. The longer she basked in the light of his eyes, the less secure she felt lying in his arms. "I should go now." She started to shrug her way out of his embrace.

"You can't."

She stilled. The lock of her hair slowly slid from her shoulder, and the movement reminded Jack of the dying note of a lovely song.

"What I mean is . . ." He cleared his throat to camouflage his sudden anxiousness. "I'd rather you didn't."

"Why?"

He shifted his head closer to hers on the pillow they shared and spent a long moment pondering his answer. He couldn't tell her that she was like a narcotic, an exotic, addictive drug that he'd go itchy without.

"Jack? Why can't I leave?"

He rose on his elbow and splayed his hand over her heart. "Because I'm not finished seducing you."

CHAPTER 5

Lina woke up to the pale grey of early dawn and the fragrance of flowers on the humid breeze. She rose slightly on her left elbow to peer at Jack, who slept with his back to the patio doors. His shoulder blocked the sleek, Sharper Image mini alarm clock on the nightstand, but judging from the brightening sky, it was about five A.M.

Time to go, she thought, although her body made no effort to obey the directive.

She spent a moment watching Jack sleep. She had always considered her lovely little island to be nothing less than paradise, but she had never expected to discover a god walking among the mortals. She lightly stroked her fingers over Jack's shoulder and arm, along his torso and his waist. The terrain of his sculpted physique was irresistible. He was that rare male creature who had a fantastic body along with the stamina and imagination to make the most pleasing use of it.

Goosebumps rose on his skin and his muscles twitched when her fingers glided over his abdomen and along the sensitive arrangement of flesh resting on his right thigh. It sprang to rigid life and saluted the new day under Lina's careful touch. She thought of a dozen creative acts she could have performed to rouse the rest of Jack DeVoy, but her sense of responsibility—and the condom wrappers on the nightstand, the floor, the bathroom sink and the edge of the lagoon—forced reason to prevail.

She had to get to work early, and starting anew with Jack would knock her entire day off schedule.

After setting a chaste kiss on his forehead, she slipped out of bed. She eased open the patio doors, stepped over the remains of the screen door, and looked back over her shoulder to see Jack shifting onto his stomach. Affection surged through her as her eyes devoured the sight of his bare shoulders, back, buttocks and legs. Even his feet were sexy enough to make her take a tiny step back toward the bedroom.

Jack's right arm went under his pillow while his left slowly swept the fresh vacancy beside him. His head was rising from the pillow when Lina scurried away on tiptoe, pausing only to snatch her discarded skirt from the patio table.

His vision bleary with sleep, Jack turned his head in time to see a multicolored flutter of silk disappearing from his line of sight. With a heavy sigh, he nestled his head deeper into the pillow. He inhaled and breathed deeply of Lina's scent, but then had to roll slightly onto his left hip to accommodate the lengthening ridge of flesh between his legs.

Dear God, he thought. *If her scent can do this to me, what's going to happen the next time I see her? And touch her . . .*

He groaned into the pillow bunched at his face. "There must be something in the water that's making me act this way. Or maybe it's in the tea," he chuckled dryly. Nothing else could explain his wholehearted attraction and interest in a simple island girl he'd only just met.

Once his body calmed, he pulled himself out of bed, spent a few minutes giving himself a good long stretch, and then collected the condom wrappers as he made his way to the bathroom. Even after his exertions with Lina and after only a few hours of sleep, he stepped into the hot shower feeling fully rested and relaxed. Among the many things Lina had given him was a renewed sense of confidence as he turned his mind from his night with her to his morning with J.T. Marchand.

"I know why you're here, fella, and I'm telling you right now that you're gonna leave empty-handed." Levora punctuated her words with sharp pokes of her finger to Jack's chest.

He stole an anxious peek at his watch. He had ten minutes to get to the Marchand Building, which meant that he had no time at all for whatever had Levora's finger locked and loaded. "Could we talk about this in an hour or so? I really can't miss my appointment this morning." He would have hurried on down the street if Levora hadn't practically bodytackled him into a bright white mailbox. Curious passersby paused on the congested sidewalk to watch the spectacle the pair made.

"I know what your appointment is about, you low-down dirty schemer!" Levora, her small frame swallowed by an oversized red T-shirt, jutted her chin at Jack. "This isn't the first time that a slick salamander has come from the States to steal what I'm not willing to sell. I should have known what you were here for the minute I saw you. I must be getting dumb in my old age!"

"Listen." Jack forced himself to remain patient. "I have no idea what you're talking about. Can it wait? Please?"

"Who sent you, Jack? Is that even your real name?"

He threw a glance down the road. The Marchand Building was less than a hundred yards away, and Jack's patience evaporated. "What the hell are you accusing me of, Levora?"

She blinked, stunned by his fierce tone and the way his upper body seemed to swell. She took a small step back, but stubbornly clenched her hands into fists as she said, "You came to Darwin to get my muffins!"

Jack's face screwed itself into an expression of confusion and indignation that would have been comical, had he not been so exasperated.

"I just assumed that you were here for the Darwin mint tea, like the rest of those suited knuckleheads, but I haven't seen you with a single box of the stuff. That got me thinking. Most of the knuckleheads are gone, but you're still here. Why?" She answered herself. "You're after the recipes for my muffins, that's why! You've had my muffins every day since you got here, and you seemed awfully fidgety when you were at my place yesterday. You would have stolen them right out of my kitchen, wouldn't you, if I had turned my back long—"

"For God's sake, Levora, this is only my third day here, and they're good muffins," Jack interjected. He'd devoured three of Levora's muffins—the coconut-lime, lemon-ginger and kiwi-banana—between rounds on the floor and in the lagoon with Lina. "I didn't know that I should have asked your permission before I ate them. They come to my cottage every day. I thought they were part of the owner's hospitality."

Levora stared into his eyes. "You're a lawyer, aren't you?"

"Yes. My name—my *real* name—is Jackson DeVoy. I work out of Boston." He looked at his watch again and swore under his breath.

Levora's forehead wrinkled in suspicion. "Are you with Iggy's Bread of the World?"

"Whose bread of the what?"

"Iggy's. My daughter's up in school in Massachusetts. Iggy's is the only baking company in Boston I can think of that would be interested in my recipes. Or even good enough to duplicate them."

Jack started walking toward the Marchand Building. "I'm not here for your recipes, although I can truly understand why someone would try to steal them. I'm not in the food industry."

Levora grabbed his briefcase, stopping him once more. "My business partner would never sell my recipes without my consent, Jack. Remember that when you're in your important meeting at the Marchand factory. I don't appreciate some big-headed American lawyer trying to wrangle a deal behind my back."

Jack tried to tug his briefcase from her grip. "I'm not here to steal your muffins, Levora. I promise."

"You wouldn't lie to me about this, would you?"

"No," issued from between his gritted teeth.

"But you're a lawyer," she argued, tightening her hold.

"I'm really good at what I do, Levora. I don't have to lie to get what I want."

"Well, then . . . okay." She still sounded unsure. But to Jack's relief, she released his briefcase.

He gave her a quick smile and fell into a brisk stride. A moment later, Levora caught the tail of his jacket, pulling him up short. "If I ever wanted to sell my recipes, and I'm not saying I do, mind you, could you represent me?"

"Levora, I promise I'll do anything you want if you'll just let me go. Deal?"

The instant she freed him, he raced off.

Levora formed a megaphone with her hands and hollered after him. "I'm holding you to your promise, Jack!"

Lina shook beads of water from a bouquet of fresh Dickson roses before placing the heavy mauve blossoms in the straw basket slung over her left arm. She thanked the florist before leaving his stall and merging into the flow of foot traffic passing through the marketplace. Stalls and kiosks filled with fresh produce, baked goods, handmade crafts, clothing and souvenirs lined the center of Main Street in the town center. A slow-moving river of pedestrians ambled in opposite directions on either side of the outdoor market, which competed for tourist dollars with the shops, cafes and restaurants in the permanent structures lining Main Street.

Lina was ready to leave the town center to stop by Levora's when, through the swarm of tourists, she spied her newest favorite face at an outdoor café. Jack sat alone at a small wrought-iron table, a notebook computer opened before him. He sat back in his chair and looked off to one side as he spoke into a cell phone the size of a credit card. His tie had been loosened, his top button undone and he looked like he was wilting within his gray wool suit. But for the staccato movements of his lips as he spoke into the phone, his face was rigid.

He's in the middle of something, Lina thought, taking a hesitant step in his direction. She was still deciding whether to approach him when he shifted his gaze and spotted her.

His face instantly transformed. His brow smoothed out, his eyes widened and sparked to life and his mouth softened as he spoke a few more words before clapping the phone shut. He leaned forward, closed his laptop and he smiled. It was a tiny smile, like the glimmer of the sun behind a cloud emptied of rain, but it sent a luscious current of warmth through Lina.

She started for his table, sidestepping a bicyclist and hopping out of the path of a noisy group of Japanese tourists. She used her basket to push through the line of patrons waiting to be seated at the café. When she reached him, Jack stood and pulled out a white wrought-iron chair for her.

"Special occasion?" he asked when she sat her basket of roses on the black and silver streaked schist tile at their feet.

She crossed her slender arms on the table and leaned on them. "Levora uses the petals to infuse the milk for her rose and champagne muffins. They're for some actor's wedding in Sydney tomorrow."

"Levora and her muffins," Jack grumbled with a shake of his head.

Lina gave him a questioning look.

"I ran into her this morning. And I ended up missing something very important."

"I'm sure it's not the end of the world, Jack."

She smiled, and he couldn't help responding with one of his own. She was a fast-acting antidote to the frustration-induced headache throbbing behind his left eye. His day had gone from bad to nightmarish after he'd sprinted away from Levora. He'd arrived at the Marchand factory in time for the most unhelpful receptionist in the world to tell him that J.T., a stickler for punctuality, had left the building three minutes prior to Jack's arrival. Not only that, Marchand would be out of the office with no plans to return until Monday morning.

And it was only Thursday.

He had booked his fourth—and hopefully final—appointment for Monday, and then he'd walked back to the marketplace. He'd parked himself at a table at the

Taiko Café, raided the emergency aspirin supply he kept in his briefcase, and he'd begun the painful process of updating Reginald.

The conversation had not gone well. To complete the failure of Jack's day, Reginald had gone so far as to utter the "B" word—again threatening to send Burke down to assist him.

Determined to connect with J.T. Marchand or die in the attempt, Jack had settled into combat mode and begun mapping out his strategy to Reginald.

And then he'd seen her. A fleeting glimpse of her face through a drift of idly moving bodies had drained the fight right out of him. He'd ended his call to Reginald in mid-sentence and focused on Lina.

The stark whiteness of her halter top glowed against the luscious darkness of her skin, and the frayed threads of her faded denim cut-offs caressed her thighs. Electric highlights crackled in her sleek ponytail. The spongy soles of her black flip-flops had slapped out an announcement of her arrival at Jack's table before she'd taken the chair he offered. Once she'd smiled her thanks, Jack completely forgot all about Reginald Wexler and J.T. Marchand.

"You've been here for three days." Lina's slim fingers pinched off a piece of Havarti cheese sticking from the interior of the braided roll set before Jack. "How much of my island have you actually seen?"

"Main Street, mostly." He took a long swallow of the tea he'd ordered over an hour ago. It was warm and watered down with melted ice cubes, yet it invigorated him almost as much as Lina's company. "And a sunrise over Tuanui Bay."

"You learned the name of my favorite place. Very good." She drummed her elegant fingers on her forearm. "Jack . . ."

"Yes?" he chuckled after she spent a long, silent moment staring at him with one eyebrow raised.

She spent another quiet moment chewing the bit of his sandwich. "Let me show you paradise."

Her sultry words, shaped by her lovely lips, achieved the impossible. For the first time since his first day at Coyle-Wexler, Jack DeVoy turned off his cell phone.

After a quick shopping excursion that had left Jack with a new, island-chic wardrobe, Lina had embarked on her mission with a vengeance, showing him Darwin's past and present. A long walk in the Rekohu Reserve had taken him back in time to an adolescent Darwin dominated by giant palms, tree ferns and birdlife that existed nowhere else in the world. An hour or two spent in the tidal pool at the base of an inactive volcano, a crowded tourist spot, had given him the chance to watch Lina frolic in her native habitat. Seeing her dive in and out of the sunlit waterfalls in an iridescent blue-green bathing suit was like watching the ballet of a mermaid. Jack had swum with her behind the wall of water, where she shared the secret of a cathedral-like cave, and he had so wanted to ease her onto the damp clay floor and love her as he had the night before.

Lina saved the best activity for last, and Jack was thrilled when they chartered a sleek, 32-foot fiberglass power boat and took to the ocean, but once they lost sight of the shore, Jack found himself falling in love anew with the motion of the boat and the freedom of being on the open sea.

"You're a natural sailor, Jack." Lina reclined on a chaise behind the captain's wheel. She had changed into a black bikini made of little more than string and sinful wishes, and Jack had a little trouble minding his coordinates.

"I've always liked the water." He spoke into the wind, breathing deeply of the salty air. "I grew up in South Boston, so I was always close to the harbor. I never got to sail boats like these back then, but I got out every chance I could with my overprivileged college pals."

"That was then." Lina propped herself up on her elbows and watched Jack's back. "What about now?"

His shoulders sank a little. "I'm thirty-three years old and I have a corner office at a multibillion-dollar corporation. I'm on track to retire at forty-five and the first thing I intend to do is buy a small fleet of boats and start my own sailing school. Or maybe I'll just buy a yacht and sail the world. Just me, the sea, and some good wood under my feet."

The wistful longing in his voice did not fool Lina. "It sounds like a lonely life."

"There hasn't been much room for relationships in my line of work. The company comes first. Always."

"No."

Jack looked over his shoulder. "No what?"

Lina swung her long legs over the edge of the chaise and sat upright. "No, *you* should come first. Never place a company before yourself or the people you care about. A company can't make you happy."

He turned back to the water before him. "No, but it's making me rich. Trust me, that'll make me happy."

"That's all you people have ever cared about," she muttered, her disdain obvious. "Even in this day and age, you people come to Darwin not to enjoy its beauty, but to try to claim resources you imagine can make you wealthy."

A flush of guilty color traveled across Jack's cheeks.

"This is precisely why no one likes white people, and why you're so worried that the rest of us are going to do to you what you've done to us for centuries."

"What are you talking about?" Jack squawked.

"You go where you're not wanted and muck everything up," Lina declared. "How many island people have gone to *your* lands throughout history and stolen *your* natural resources and enslaved the population?"

"I've never enslaved anyone!" Jack cried in alarm, completely caught off guard by her argument.

"You know what I mean," Lina charged calmly. "*Your* people—"

"*Your* people," he interrupted, "should have fought against intruders."

"That's always the answer, isn't it? Fighting to establish not what's right but who's got the greater might."

"You can't fault European explorers for wanting to know more about the world," Jack argued.

"They weren't seeking knowledge," Lina pointed out. "They wanted fortunes. White men risked life and limb traveling to the islands not with open hands to explore but to grab whatever they could to take back with them."

"All those exploited islanders you're referring to could have left to do the same thing," Jack argued.

"They didn't want to. They were happy right where they were. Perhaps if *your* people had come to the islands searching for happiness instead of wealth, the world wouldn't be in such sorry straits now!"

"Stop with the 'your people' stuff, will you?" Jack said. "They're *your* people, too, or haven't you looked in a mirror lately? Your eyes . . ." All the fight drained from him as he contemplated the turbulent beauty of her sparkling eyes.

"Are you implying that I have white eyes?" she accused.

"You have beautiful eyes," Jack sighed. "Not white. Not black. Just yours." His gaze wandered over the rest of her. "And your skin . . . I love how it looks against mine, and the way it feels." His tone softened, his words melting into the breeze. "I'm guilty, Lina. I came here to conquer this island, to find a fortune, just like you said. Instead . . ." he faltered, unsure if he wanted to confess anything further.

The gleaming blond hardwood of the deck kept its quiet as Lina moved to stand behind him. She slipped her arms around him and secretly delighted in the way he relaxed into her embrace. "My island has conquered you," she finished for him.

"Something like that," Jack admitted.

"This fortune you seek, Jack," Lina started, "will it greet you with kisses every morning when you wake up on your 'round-the-world yacht? Will it caress you as you watch the sun sink into tropic seas? Will your riches give you a son with your golden hair, or a daughter with your lovely hazel eyes? No matter how much of it you acquire, your money won't buy a thing that matters, Jack."

He took his hand off the throttle to cover both of hers, which were clasped at his abdomen, atop the waistband of his new black surfer shorts. She was right. He admitted it, if only to himself. He wanted all of the things she'd mentioned, right down to the children. Only he wanted it all with someone truly special. Someone like . . . "Lina?"

She leaned around him, to face him. "Hmm?"

"How is it that some smart man hasn't put a ring on your finger?"

She shrugged one shoulder. "Just lucky, I guess."

"Are you against marriage?"

"Only to the men who've proposed to me."

He tried not to imagine the number of hopeful paramours who would have wanted to bind her to them forever.

"I've seen too many lives ruined when men like you come to my island and marry women like me."

"I think I should be offended."

"Don't be. It's an inescapable fact that you and I are different."

"You're black and I'm white. So what? Underneath it all, we're all the same."

She scoffed. "You and I couldn't be more different, Jack," she said stubbornly. "Our differences run deeper than skin."

"Lina, you don't know me well enough to make judgments about who or what I am."

"Do you love me, Jack?"

His heart skipped a long, hard beat in response to the unexpected question. His experience as a lawyer made it very easy for him to evade a wholly honest answer. "I don't know you, Lina," he offered.

"Do you respect me?"

"Of course."

"Well, that's all we need, isn't it? Respect for one another. That alone will stop us falling into the same trap that so many other tourist-native partnerships tumble into."

Confused by his need to argue on the side of love, Jack fine-tuned his argument. "What about Levora and her husband? She came here to research a thesis but fell in love, and she stayed."

Her arms still around him, Lina positioned herself between Jack and the dashboard. "Errol and Levora are different. They're the exception, not the rule. Levora had to come to the other side of the world to find the person she was meant to spend the rest of her life with. She hadn't planned on it or even wished for it. It just happened. It was that easy. Most of us aren't that lucky. Most of us waste far too much time hoping to find someone merely good enough. I won't ever settle for just good enough. I want perfect. I want true love."

A hot blush warmed her cheeks. Fearing that she'd said too much, she ducked beneath Jack's left arm and went to the opening in the brass railing surrounding the deck. She stood on one of the swim steps for a moment, a hand braced on either side of the rail, before she dove cleanly into the water. Long, graceful strokes carried her away from the yacht, and she rolled and turned in the water as a creature truly borne to it.

Jack watched her tumble, float and twirl, and then climb back on board. Envy clogged his chest as he watched the sea trickle over her skin, tracing every curve and hollow. The breeze subtly altered the landscape of her body, raising goose pimples and hardening soft peaks. She reclined on her chaise, her arms over her head, and the sun licked droplets of seawater from her. Nature made love to her the way Jack wanted to, and helped him see how plainly she had no need of a husband, or any other man. Especially one who would go back to his own side of the world, leaving her with no more than his respect.

He inhaled a deep, pensive breath through his nose and stepped closer to the dashboard. Lina's questions had affected him strangely; he felt as if his skull had suddenly turned transparent and she'd picked through his brain to find his innermost desires.

The oddly affecting moment on the boat didn't stall their afternoon, but it certainly changed its tone and timbre. Lina maintained a quiet, perhaps even cautious distance. At sunset, as she walked him back to his home-stay with mango-flavored shaved ices in hand, she seemed lost in her own thoughts.

"Would you have dinner with me?" Jack asked once they were standing on the road in front of his cottage. "I could take you to The Crab and Nickel." He took a step closer to her. "Or we could stay in. I have no idea what my hosts have on the menu, but everything served so far has been excellent."

She absently hooked her fingers over the waistband of his trunks, but then quickly snatched them away. "I'm sorry," she said through a raging blush, "I shouldn't have done that."

Jack laughed softly. There's something more dangerous about sunlight than moonlight, he reasoned. At night, there had been no secrets, no inhibitions between them. Never had he questioned his motives, intents or desires. Everything actually made sense. Daylight made the rest of the world more apparent, made it too easy to recognize how different their lives were, and even easier to see that eventually . . . soon . . . he would leave. Daylight provided clarity, with each brush of skin and each glance eliciting a pinprick of uncertainty. Jack suspected that the unobscured view forced Lina to question exactly what they were doing.

That thought saddened him in a way he had never experienced.

"I can't join you for dinner tonight, Jack. I have plans. It's a birthday party. I have to be there since the whole thing was my—"

"You don't have to explain," he said, cutting short the sudden awkwardness between them. He took a few steps back, toward the door of the cottage.

Lina flipped a heavy lock of her damp hair from her face. She felt the need to explain anyway. "It's for a good friend. I can't miss it."

"I understand. Have a good time."

She peered at him, mildly concerned by his diffident tone. A peculiar feeling rose within her. Confusion? Alarm? Regret? Spending the day with Jack had been too comfortable. Too pleasant. It had illustrated just how hard it would be to do the inevitable—to say goodbye to him for good. If the difficulty of this parting was any indication of how painful it would be to say goodbye to him when he left Darwin, perhaps it was best to end things, for good and for all, right now.

"Will I see you later?" Jack hoped that he didn't sound as eager as he felt.

She hedged her answer. "The party might run late. It's a beach thing, and they get out of hand sometimes. I should go now." *Even though I don't want to.* "To get ready," she added, buying herself another two seconds of his company.

Jack stared at his sandals. "Goodnight, Lina."

She hesitated, then quietly said, "Goodbye, Jack."

He winced at the finality of her words.

She turned and started down the palm-lined road, and Jack stood on his front pathway watching her, hoping that she would at least look back.

CHAPTER 6

Lina hurried away from Jack's homestay, chanting under her breath, the hem of her sheer black cover-up tickling her knees as she went. "Don't look back, don't you *dare* look back," she whispered. She picked up her speed and practically raced around a turn, and only then did she halt and spin around. Her view of Jack's place was hidden by dense foliage and a cluster of giant rocks, one of which she slumped against.

She pressed her fingers to her lips as if she could re-seal her goodbye to Jack behind them. It had been such a simple thing, and in the moment, so easy. But now, only seconds later, her soul smarted at the thought of never seeing him again. How could she enjoy a party when all she wanted to do was sprint back to Jack's homestay, throw open the door and fling herself into his arms?

Dropping the half-melted slush of her shaved ice, she spun to hammer both fists against the unyielding boulder. "How could I have been so stupid?" she asked between gritted teeth. She'd always prided herself on being too smart, too sensible, to fall for visitors to the island. Tall, handsome foreigners were good for one thing only, and to be fair, Jack was better at that than any of the other men she'd dallied with. Not that she had a large basis for comparison, but Jack truly was a rare sort.

Spending the day with him had been as stimulating and enjoyable as their nights had been, and that more than anything else had scared her into bidding him goodbye.

Even if he were on Darwin for more than a few days, there was no way their relationship could survive. Jack was an outsider, one born and bred to the hurry and noise of an American city. He was no more capable of transplanting his life to Darwin than a shark could adjust to life in a tree. The rational part of her brain understood that what she and Jack had been enjoying was the taste of the unknown, and with it the freedom to indulge physical desires made more delicious by the knowledge that it was all temporary. That there would be a clean break at the end with no penalties to pay, no genuine emotion to bog down the experience.

But when she closed her eyes and pictured Jack, Lina knew that it was already too late. In trying so hard to give him nothing meaningful, she'd already given him too much. "Just like a silly island girl," she admonished herself, topping it with a kick to the rock that would surely raise a bruise on her big toe. But in all fairness, not all the native-foreigner couplings had resulted in heartache. All she had to do was look around the crowded town center to see the results of the intermarriages between the Japanese, Africans, South Americans and Europeans who had settled on Darwin throughout its history.

But Jack hadn't come to find love, and Lina doubted that he'd stay, even if he'd stumbled upon it by accident. He'd come to Darwin to find fortune. He hadn't explained how, and Lina had an aversion to mixing business and pleasure, so she hadn't inquired further. But she hadn't missed Jack's message that money meant more to him than anything else. That fact alone was enough to forge a gap between them that Lina wouldn't be willing to bridge.

She shook her head, as if she could so easily clear Jack from it, and started back down the road. "I've got a party to prepare for," she told herself. "That'll be just the thing to get my head right again." She picked up her ice cup to dispose of it properly. "If I can get through tonight without Jack, I'm sure I'll be able to let him go." *Without letting him take the biggest part of my heart with him.*

"A beach thing," Jack indignantly huffed as he loosely tucked in the white linen shirt Lina had helped him pick out earlier on Main Street. "The whole damn island is beach."

He slipped his wallet into the rear pocket of the formless cotton trousers he'd acquired along with the shirt. He also wore his new hiking sandals, another one of Lina's selections, when he left the cottage, presumably for an evening stroll.

An evening stroll along the beach, of course.

Following his clumsy parting with Lina, he'd tried to dull his loneliness by throwing himself back into work, his reason for being on Darwin in the first place and always a reliable point of retreat. There were always e-mails to answer, voice mail to retrieve—surely from Reginald Wexler—and most important, a battle plan to strategize before his Monday meeting with J.T. Marchand. The endless river of job-related obligations had gotten him through his breakups with Clio and Erica, but this time, as he'd sat on the patio staring at the uncovered dinner platter his hosts had delivered to him, his work had seemed as bland and unappealing as watching saw grass grow. He hadn't even mustered enough interest to turn his cell phone back on.

He'd left both his appetite and his cell phone on the patio and gone inside to take a long hot shower. Memories of what he'd done with Lina the last time he'd been in the shower led to a longer, colder dousing that convinced him that he needed to get out of the cottage.

He'd quickly dressed, musing on the prank-playing nature of Fate. He'd left a particularly nasty New England snowstorm with no clue that he'd fly into the arms of an island goddess who'd seduce him in both body and mind. Boston was mean, chaotic, gray and cold beside the tranquil blues, greens and warmth of Darwin.

The thought of going back to Boston made Jack's neck stiffen, so he shoved it away as he exited his homestay and started along the dirt road in the direction that Lina had taken earlier.

His hands in his pockets, Jack strolled in no special hurry with no idea where the torch-lit road would take him or if Lina would be at the end of it. Instead of enjoying the wind-hewn beauty of the bracken surrounding him, he used his observation skills on the foot traffic around him. The people walking on the right side of the road, toward the town center, moved at a leisured pace, the same one Jack had developed in the course of his day with Lina.

An older couple walking in the opposite direction raised their hands in greeting as they approached Jack. His response was delayed, but he eventually nodded back. The blue-black spirals and dots of the older gentleman's striking Maori facial tattoos, the *ta moko* Jack had read of briefly, had initially caught him off guard.

Five young men sharing the left side of the road with Jack hurried past him, laughing and joking. But for their thick Aussie accents, they reminded Jack of himself and his football teammates on spring break twelve years ago, when all they had to worry about was finding the next party. "S'cuse us, mate," one of them said cheerfully when a corner of a red cooler carried by two of them grazed Jack's leg. "Sorry, sir," said the other one.

"No problem," Jack said offhandedly, the younger man's use of the word "sir" making him feel like an old man. Jack wasn't so old that he couldn't read certain clues. Whether it was Cape Cod, Daytona Beach or Darwin Island, Jack recognized the key piece of equipment needed for a beach party. He picked up his pace and followed the red cooler. It wasn't until he heard distant laughter and music that he broke into an easy run and sped past his unwitting guides.

"Mr. Coyle-Wexler Representative," said a voice behind Jack's right shoulder. "It's good to see you getting out and enjoying the island instead of chasing down J.T. Marchand."

Jack had been watching the festivities from a reasonable distance, within the cover of a stand of nikau palms. He stepped into the open at the greeting from Marchand's receptionist. "Good evening, Miss . . . ?" He felt the slightest twitch of shame that he'd never gotten her name despite his interactions with her.

"Kiri," she said with a coquettish tilt of her head. It was a practiced move that allowed her long black hair, which she wore loose, to fall from one shoulder, revealing a narrow floral bandeau top that barely contained the ampleness of her bosom. "And do you have a name other than Coyle-Wexler Representative?"

"You can call me Jack."

"Now that we're finally on a first name basis, Jack, let's enjoy the party." She looped her arm through his and pulled him toward the buffet tables. Jack's appetite roared to life at the sight of the strange and colorful foods before him. He had sampled exotic cuisine before; it was one of the perks of work-related travel. But he recognized none of the foods displayed before him. He was grateful for Kiri's patience in introducing him to the new fruits and vegetables.

She plucked a few black-purple orbs from their arrangement upon a sheet of paperbark. "These are Illawarra plums." She offered to feed one to him, but he took it from her and fed himself. The sweet flesh was firm, and a rich berry flavor exploded in his mouth. Kiri pointed to each fruit as she described it. "The pale lemon ones are aspen fruit, and these yellow-green fruits are Kakadu plums."

Jack glanced at an arrangement of halved kiwifruits. He was very familiar with the green ones; his mouth began to water in memory of his introduction to the gold variety. He grabbed a couple of bunya bunya nuts, examined them closely, and then popped one into his mouth. After chewing it for a moment, he said, "They look like a cross between hazelnuts and macadamias, but they taste like chestnuts." He took a few more with him as Kiri led him farther down the long table.

He sampled the native raspberries, which were smaller, fuzzier and juicier than the variety he knew from home, and the velvet succulence of the sweet flesh reminded him that he'd gone in search of Lina. He bided his time with Kiri, hoping for an opening to bring her up.

The fruits gave way to a raw bar complete with oyster shuckers. One of the nut-brown young men shook back a head full of long, wavy black hair before addressing Jack. "You're the bloke at the Te Taniki homestay," he said in an accent that made Jack think of the Australian sitting behind him on his flight from Sydney to Christchurch.

Since he was slurping down one of Darwin's famous sweet rock oysters, Jack could only nod.

"Well, that's al'right!" the shucker said merrily.

Jack discarded his empty shell in the bin provided. "This is some hootenanny," he remarked, taking up another oyster and scanning the crowd for Lina. "Looks like the whole island turned out."

" 'Hootenanny?' " The oyster shucker nudged his co-worker with an elbow. "Did ya hear that, mate? 'Hootenanny!' " He turned back to Jack. "You Yanks sure got an odd turn or two of phrase." He laughed as he wiped his hands on the front of his apron before he untied it and balled it up. "Good to see you Kiri, doll. It's off to the shed with a get in behind to the dog. The girls need milking, so it's into my gummies and I'll catch you later." With a final nod and smile at Jack, the young man leaped over the table and trotted away.

"Could you translate that?" Jack asked Kiri under his breath.

"He said goodbye."

"You Darwinians sure have an odd turn of phrase or two," Jack muttered.

"I'm Fijian," Kiri told him. "And oyster boy Derek was born in Tasmania. Darwin seduces, Jack. It becomes home, no matter where you were born." She began heaping a plate with lobster, scallops, eel, crayfish and *paua*—abalone, in Jack's part of the world. "The local seafood, our *kaimoana*, is unrivaled," she assured him. She offered her plate to him, and lifted a tiny red crustacean to his mouth.

"You eat baby lobsters here?" Jack wondered, politely refusing the dainty creature. "That's illegal where I come from."

"This is a yabby. A freshwater crayfish. It has a beautiful, toasty flavor."

Deciding to stick with what looked most familiar, Jack opted to sample an Australian scallop served on its pearly purple half shell.

"Who's the host of this party?" he asked.

Kiri's full lips drew into a smirk. "J.T. Marchand."

Jack's eyebrows rose. "Who's it for?"

"Sally Huatare. She's head housekeeper at Marchand Manor."

Jack scanned the crowd with as much feigned disinterest as he could muster with Kiri tugging at him and speaking nonstop at his elbow. There were plenty of men around, but none who fit the image Jack had formed of the Stanford-educated attorney and demagogue of a small island kingdom. Most of the men on the beach were too young, buff and undressed, or too old, relaxed and tattooed to be J.T. Marchand. Jack's brow wrinkled in frustration as he tried to reconcile the reclusive man of power he'd researched with the generous employer who would throw an extravagant beach party for a servant. Jack decided to bide his time and wait for a suitable opening in which he could ask Kiri to point out Marchand.

She led him farther along the buffet. Barbequed meats and vegetables flavored with cinnamon, cumin, ginger, saffron and even vanilla assailed his senses before he encountered the sweet brilliance of the dessert table.

"This is passion fruit tart," Kiri told Jack as she tried to slip a thin wedge between his lips. He took it from her, all the while eyeing the other desserts arranged among fragrant and colorful blossoms set upon beds of ice. "Levora Solomon's rose petal ice cream," Kiri said, pointing to a pale pink confection before introducing the rest of the desserts. "Pineapple sorbet, cinnamon ice cream with poached pears and raspberry vacherin." Kiri selected the last dessert for herself. "The vacherin is my favorite. It's a meringue shell filled with fruit salad and topped with raspberry sorbet." She spooned a luscious dollop of whipped cream onto the plate beside the meringue shell. "It's paradise on a plate, Jack."

Male and female servers, some topless and in native dress and others in traditional Western beachwear, chatted amiably with the party guests. The line between worker and guest blurred with the servers leaping over tables to join the group dancing in the sand apart from the buffet.

"There are so many people here," Jack mentioned casually. "Sally must be pretty popular."

"Sally is friend or kin to just about everyone here." Kiri leaned closer to Jack and used her spoon to point out a short, dark-haired woman who appeared to be about Levora's age. "I grew up with her oldest daughter. She's in America now, living in California. She went to school there. J.T. paid her way through college."

Jack leaped, inwardly thanking Kiri for the perfect opening. "Is J.T. Marchand still here? You don't have to introduce me. If you could just point—"

"I was wondering when you'd get around to that." Kiri bumped him with her hip, careful not to spill her dessert, and tipped her chin toward the mob of dancers. "J.T. loves to dance."

Jack followed Kiri's line of sight, trying to pick out the right man, but he was distracted by a woman. Once his eyes fixed themselves on her, he couldn't tear them away. Lina, dressed in white, moved to the beat of an island song played by a live band. She wore a clingy T-shirt that exposed most of her torso and abdomen. One sleeve was short while the other was little more than a loop of fabric capping her shoulder. The asymmetrical hemline of her flounced miniskirt barely concealed the inviting rounds of her bottom. In some ways, she seemed more nude than if she'd actually been naked.

He forgot all about J.T. Marchand as he watched Lina. He forgot about Kiri and the food sliding from the plate gripped in his suddenly lax hand. He watched Lina move to the ancient rhythms of instruments that duplicated the sounds of rain, bird songs, bass vibrations and human voices. As he watched, he realized that it wasn't completely accurate to call what she was doing dancing. Her upraised arms undulated like underwater plants. With her bare feet planted in the sand, her hips wrote slow and sinuous figure eights in an invitation addressed to Jack. He accepted, without hesitation, and went to her.

He wasn't much of a dancer, but he knew how to shape his movements to music. Lina lowered her hands to his waist and welcomed him into her space. With a tiny smile she staggered her legs with his and let him lead. Hips to hips and belly to belly, their bodies fused as much as their clothing permitted. Jack closed his eyes, breathed the spicy scent of her hair, and he reveled in the softness of her body against his, nourishing himself on her warmth and the light touch of her hands at his back and hips.

Her loose chignon hadn't withstood the rigors of her dancing, and Jack smoothed stray tendrils from her face as she gazed up at him. "I'm not usually a party crasher," he murmured.

"I'm glad you decided to become one tonight. I was missing you."

He tried to cough up the hard lump suddenly blocking his throat. No woman had ever looked at him the way Lina looked at him now. It would have been easy to blame it on the moonlight, the spell cast by the sensual, primitive music, or even the ambience created by the hot, fit bodies dancing around them. She gazed at him openly, her clear, bright eyes gleaming with a combination of desire and affection that sent heat searing through Jack's veins. It wasn't the moon, the music or the company that put such magical light in Lina's eyes. He was seeing his own feelings mirrored in them.

The sight should have sent him running back to his homestay.

Lina had the same instinct, to flee the heat in Jack's eyes before it consumed her. "I'd like to get something to drink, Jack. Will you come with me?"

She drew away and Jack followed, loosely holding her hand. She led him to the bar set up opposite the buffet, and she ordered a pink gin-and-lemon granita, which she sipped at as she guided Jack farther away from the main thrust of the party.

"Where are we going?" he asked, even as he spotted the bone-white cabin of the closed lifeguard tower well outside the circle of torchlight from the party.

"Someplace quiet."

She skipped ahead of him and her skirt flipped up, giving him a tantalizing peek of her bottom and the tiny triangle of fabric forming the back of her thong underpants.

Jack caught up to her once she had climbed the two steep flights of creaky, weather-beaten stairs and had rested her beverage atop the sun-bleached wood railing edging the tower deck. She stood with her back to the tumbling sea, her elbows resting on the top beam, one of her feet propped on the lowest one.

Jack opened his mouth to comment on the vast carpet of velvet that was the night sky, to marvel at the pungent salt scent of the ocean. Instead, he took Lina's face in his hands and lowered his lips to hers, capturing her mouth in a kiss that took both of them by surprise with its urgency and depth. Her lips were cool and had the sweet, tart taste of her slushy drink. He was an addict, she was his drug, and he didn't even try to curb the intensity of his lust for her.

With a soft whimper of surrender, Lina melted around him. Her hands found their way beneath his shirt and into the waist of his loose-fitting trousers; she raised her right knee to run it along his outer thigh and hip. To bring her even closer, he gripped her buttocks and ground the cradle of her pelvis into his.

Their gasps and groans mingled with the crashes and sighs of the waves below. Jack's lips never left Lina's skin, even as she turned to face the ocean. He filled his hands with her breasts, his thumbs teasing their hard peaks through the whispery fabric of her top. She stroked him with her backside, her skirt rising with each downward motion. She blindly reached back and found one end of Jack's drawstring, gave it a light tug, and the small bow unlooped, loosening his trousers enough to free him.

She arched her back and set one foot on the lowest beam, her thighs quivering as Jack hooked a finger around the white silk of her thong and slipped it aside. Lina took the meat of her lower lip between her teeth when Jack's strong hands gripped her hips, and she gasped aloud when he steered himself into her. She fastened her hands on the top beam, her fingernails etching tiny crescents into the weathered wood, and she tossed her head back, giving Jack's lips free access to her neck as she reached back and wrapped one arm around his head.

His fingers plucked and kneaded her breasts, which he had exposed to the sea breeze. Lina controlled the rhythm of their mating, almost matching it to the music they heard faintly in the distance. Jack squinted in torturous pleasure with each movement of her buttocks against his pelvis. Sure that such pleasure would kill him if endured for much longer, he slid a hand along her sweat-sheened abdomen. It traveled lower, and lower still, until his longest finger found the jewel set atop the place where they were joined. He stroked it with his finger, laving it with the nectar generated by their union. Not long after, her body shook, inside and out. Her darkness locked around him, imprisoning him, a short bark of rapture exploding from her. Her hand fastened in his hair and she turned her face to his, her mouth opening against his in a voracious kiss. She tried to choke out his name, but it was hard enough remembering her own with such keen pulses of satisfaction cycling through her.

Jack tore his mouth from hers, grunting his frustration at having to hold back his own eruption. "Lina," he managed breathlessly, "let me go."

She answered with a low growl and the resolute pumping of her backside against him.

Heavy droplets of cold sweat formed on Jack's forehead. They ran into his eyes, stinging them. His arm and leg muscles ached from the effort it took to suppress his release. "Lina, I can't . . ."

He started to move his hand from the dampness between her legs, but she clamped her hand around his wrist, holding his magical fingers in place.

"Sweetheart, I'm sorry." He tore his hand and the rest of himself from her. He clumsily turned away, his shoulders hunching as he spent himself into a dense clump of bracken and gorse in the shadows beyond the tower.

Something with weight skittered deep in the darkness.

"Bullseye?" Lina laughed. She wrapped her arms around his waist and hugged his back to her chest.

Jack tidied himself before turning to properly take her into his arms. "You make me crazy, you know that?"

"That's a compliment, I hope."

Her chignon had come undone and her hair now hung loose about her shoulders in the way that Jack now decided was his favorite style. He cupped her face and aimed it at his with a slight shake of his head.

"What?" she smiled.

He stared at her in wonder. Wonder at why the age-less, guileless, island goddess in his arms had blessed him with her attention and generosity. He'd never been so carried away that he'd thrown caution to the wind and made love to a woman without the proper protection. He'd never been so out of his head that, for a fleeting moment, he hadn't feared the possibility of making a baby with her. A permanent, unbreakable bond with her.

He mentally shook himself out of his preposterous reverie.

Lina stroked a fingertip along his cheek. "You seemed so far away for a minute there."

"Yeah," Jack sighed, staring beyond her and out at the water beating against the black rocks. *And one day soon I really will be far away,* he thought dismally as his arms went around her to press her close.

"Jack?" She shifted in his embrace.

"I'm sorry." He focused his full attention on her. "I'm just . . ." *Falling in love?* "Losing my mind," he finished with a sigh.

"Good. I thought it was just me."

She blessed him with a smile that made him want her again so fiercely, he felt it from the ends of his hair to his toenails. He answered her smile with a kiss that left her panting for breath. Still kissing her, he walked her backward until she was pressed against the slatted side of the lifeguard cabin. As he slowly lowered himself to one knee, he eased her top up, again exposing her breasts to the night.

"I never imagined God made women like you, Lina." He lowered his gaze, unable to look at her face with his heart so naked in his eyes.

A grin played at her lips as she lightly stroked his hair and silently enjoyed his particular beauty. Moonlight charged the sun-gold in his hair and softened his almost too masculine features. The cords and veins of his forearms stood out beneath a golden haze of hair as his hands palmed the twin weights of her breasts. She would not have guessed that such strong hands were capable of such tenderness, such mastery of her flesh as his fingers searched out her most sensitive places.

When he replaced his thumbs with his mouth, her knees would have buckled if not for the support of his hands at her hips.

"Good heavens," she breathed, her head pressed into the wall of the cabin, her eyes drowsing shut in renewed pleasure.

His lips moved over the lower curve of her breast, along her ribcage and down to her navel. The tip of his tongue dipped into her belly button, sending an arrow of sensation directly to the moistness between her thighs. Jack used one hand to delve into it and she parted her legs, letting him prop one of them over his shoulder. He kissed the trembling flesh of her upper inner thigh, taunting her with his proximity to her most secret place.

She uttered a purr of satisfaction when his tongue breached the curls hiding the center of her pleasure. A sharp cry tore from her when he drew on it, gently scraping his teeth against it.

"Jack," she gasped, his name both plea and promise. She gripped the meatiest part of his shoulders and moved her hips to meet each thrust of his tongue. "Jack," trembled from her lips as he intensified his efforts. "Jack!"

She shoved away from him with the last cry of his name. He stood, alarmed.

"Lina, what—" He didn't get to finish that either.

His head whipped around to follow her, and he saw her climb onto the lowest beam of the railing and reach for the frayed rope attached to the big bell mounted on a pole at the corner of the railing. She gave it three hard tugs before she bolted down the stairs and ran, full speed, toward the surf.

Jack raced after her, but stopped short of trailing her into the choppy waves battering the shore. "Lina!" He doubted that she heard him over the crash of the water as it struck the rocky shore.

The warning bell summoned a pair of medical vans, their yellow roof lights flashing, speeding along the shoreline to the vicinity of the tower. With relief Jack watched teams of lifeguards spill from the vans, and he ran with them as they splashed into the water.

"Stay back, mate," one of them directed with a hand to Jack's chest. "No one's allowed in the water. The undertow's a killer tonight."

"I'm a strong swimmer," Jack insisted. "I can handle myself. A woman went in there a minute ago and she hasn't surfaced." Saying the words aloud sent spikes of panic through his chest. "I should have stopped her. I didn't realize . . . the undertow . . ." Fear trapped his breath in his lungs.

"We haven't lost one yet, mate, and we won't start tonight." The lifeguard left Jack with that reassurance before zooming off after his companions.

The medical vans had outraced the crowd pursuing them, but those people now gathered around them as their spotlights scoured the water. They pointed at the water, craned their necks to see what was going on, their voices blending into a hushed murmur of concern.

Jack spotted it first, the spot of white bobbing on a wave that broke angrily against the rocks. "God no," snagged in his throat as a swell of frothing water swallowed up the spot of white he knew was Lina.

Jack mindlessly ran along the shoreline, circling around the rocks, his eyes never leaving the dark sea as two questions swirled in his head. *Where are you, Lina? Why the hell did you run into the water?*

The answer to both questions surfaced on the dark side of the rocks. Lina, one-arming a limp figure to her body, crested a wave that carried her and her companion to shore. The ocean bubbled at her ankles as she struggled to drag the still form from the waterline.

Jack rushed to her, his blood chilling at the sight of the blue figure whose weight carried Lina to the sand. "He's not breathing," she gasped before coughing violently. She scrambled to her hands and knees and hacked out salt water. "Jack, help him . . . he's so heavy . . ."

Jack easily lifted the unconscious boy. The kid couldn't have been more than twelve or thirteen, and his water-logged T-shirt and shorts dampened Jack's clothing. A frightening purple pallor tinted his brown skin, and unless the boy got medical attention fast, Jack feared that Lina's valiant effort would be for nothing.

"Help!" Jack shouted as he ran the boy to one of the medical vans. "I don't think he's breathing!"

The van's driver spotted Jack and began flashing the spotlight, calling in the lifeguards from the water. Two more medics pulled a gurney from the back of the van in time for Jack to place the boy upon it. In the light from the van's interior, Jack noticed the blood streaking the side of the boy's face.

"He must've hit the rocks pretty darn hard," one of the Aussie medics said as he probed the boy's neck with his fingertips. "I've got a weak pulse and I'm starting CPR," he told his partner. "Radio ahead to the medical center and tell 'em we're en route as soon as we get this boy stabilized."

Jack slowly stepped back into the crowd, watching the swift and effective actions of the paramedic team. The boy was soon breathing on his own and hooked up to an IV line. "He's stable," one of the medics said. "I've cleaned the blood from his head but there's no wound. Kid got lucky. I don't know why they never heed the warnings to stay out of the water."

"Maybe the rock's what bled when the kid hit it," the other medic joked dryly as he helped his partner load the gurney into the van.

Fresh panic bloomed in Jack's chest. "Lina."

He raced back the way he'd come. The wind off the ocean whipped at his hair and damp clothing as he fought against it to reach Lina, who lay motionless in the sand. Jack fell to his knees beside her. The sand around her told the story of her collapse as Jack pulled her onto his lap. She'd taken a few steps from the place where she had dragged the boy, and the sand was dark with blood where she had fallen.

Jack gripped her chin and brusquely turned her face to his. "Sweetheart, wake up for me!" Getting no response, he curled over her, clapping his ear to the wet fabric molded to her chest. Her heartbeat was loud and strong, but Jack couldn't rouse her. He sat back up to find the palm of his hand covered in blood. "Help me!" he yelled toward the remaining medical van. "I've got an injured woman here!"

He scooped Lina's boneless form into his arms and frantically hurried toward the remaining medical van, which met him more than halfway. "She went into the water after that kid," Jack breathlessly explained to the paramedic tending to Lina. "They hit the rocks before she pulled him out. It was her blood on him, not his."

"Thanks, mate," the paramedic said distractedly as he peered into Lina's eyes with a penlight. "Her pupils are responsive but sluggish." His fingers moved through the salty hanks of her hair. "I've got a laceration at midline, approximately three inches long, and profuse bleeding. We gotta get her in."

The medical team wasted no time prepping Lina's wound and boarding her into the medical van. As dozens of people looked on, the medics moved with the cautious haste Jack would have expected an injured head of state to receive. He would have been impressed, had he not been so worried.

He moved to the back of the van and had one foot on the rear bumper ledge, ready to boost himself into the cabin when the medic stopped him. "No passengers allowed, mate, sorry. We're taking her to Waurutangua Medical Center. They'll take good care of her and you can catch up with her there."

"Will she be okay?" Jack asked, stepping out of the way to allow the medic into the van.

"Don't know, mate," he said. "You never can tell with head wounds."

CHAPTER 7

"I've been standing here for twenty minutes and no one's been able to tell me a thing." Jack spoke between gritted teeth. He forced himself to remain polite when all he wanted to do was pitch a few potted palms through the plate glass windows of the medical center's lobby. "A woman was brought here a little while ago, and she was injured quite badly. I need to see her. Would you please tell me where she is?"

"I'm sorry, sir," said the fourth smiling desk nurse Jack had encountered since his arrival in the overly pastel reception area. "What's your name again?"

"Jackson DeVoy!" Jack hollered. "Everyone in this damned hospital knows my name because I've given it to you people a hundred times! Give me the name of your superior. You can't possibly have final say as to who sees who and when." He gave the front of the counter a sudden, sharp kick. "I want to see Lina, and I demand to see her now. I'm an attorney, and I won't leave here until I get some answers! Do you understand me?"

The nurse scowled in a moment of deep thought before her face suddenly broke into a smile. "I get it," she laughed airily, clearly unimpressed with Jack's occupation and show of temper. "*Terms of Endearment*. You scare me into helping you. You're almost as good as Shirley

MacLaine, Mr. DeVoy. Now, who are you here to see again?"

Jack closed his eyes and counted backwards from 100. He reached 89 before he calmly said, "Her name is Lina. I don't know her last name."

The nurse's eyes roamed over his tousled hair and rumpled, blood-smeared clothing. "No? She must not be a very close friend."

Jack slammed his palms down on the counter separating him from the nurse. "She's my—" He stopped short. She was his what? His lover? His fling? His . . . what exactly? "Please," he started as benevolently as he possibly could. "Please tell me how she is. She . . ." He paused to clear the sudden tightness in his throat. "There was a lot of blood, and I couldn't wake her. I need to know if she's going to be okay."

The nurse's black eyes softened before she lowered them to her clipboard. Her finger moved across a piece of paper with print too small for Jack to read upside down. "We've had three emergency drops tonight, a sixty-year-old man, a thirteen-year-old boy and a twenty-nine-year-old woman, but no one by the name of Lina."

"Lina could be a nickname," Jack suggested. "That woman who was brought in tonight, she had a head injury, didn't she? It was a three-inch laceration along the midline. How could I know that if I wasn't with her when it happened?" He bunched the front of his shirt up in his hands and showed it to the nurse. "This is her blood." His voice softened. "I held her in my arms after it happened. The paramedic said he couldn't tell how seriously she was hurt, but I need to know how she is. If she'll be all right."

"I understand your concern, but I can't disclose patient information to you, Mr. DeVoy, unless you're family," the nurse said gently. "I'm sorry."

He sighed heavily. "I know. I apologize. I'm just . . . she's . . . I'm worried about her, is all."

"Perhaps you should have a seat," the nurse suggested. "We've placed a call to her next of kin. I'm sure they'll be along soon, and perhaps they could help you."

"Thank you." Wearied by worry and frustration, Jack retreated to one of the light blue molded plastic chairs lining the front window. He slumped heavily into it, knocking his head against the plate glass. He started to bring his hands to his face, but then he noticed the blood caked in the creases of his palms and around the beds of his fingernails. He stared at it, half hoping that Lina's blood could imbue him with the same uncommon strength and determination that had driven her into the treacherous waters of an angry ocean to save someone he had neither heard nor seen.

She had given no thought to her own safety or survival. She had dropped everything and acted only in the best interest of someone else, had risked her own life for that of a stranger.

Jack leaned back in the chair and closed his eyes, ashamed of the certainty that he was incapable of that level of selflessness.

Jack's nostrils twitched. A second later, his right hand batted blindly at an annoying tickle near his right ear. He bolted upright in his uncomfortable plastic chair when the tickle moved to his left ear.

"What the hell . . . ?" he started.

A little girl dressed in nothing but a grass skirt squatted on the chair to his right. A bit too slowly, she hid a long piece of grass from her skirt behind her back. Her round brown belly jiggled as she giggled at Jack's expression of surprise and irritation.

It could be worse, Jack thought grudgingly. *It's definitely better than being awakened by a bum pissing on your leg on the Red Line.* He squinted against the bright sunlight framing the little girl as he rose and went to the reception desk.

"Good morning, Mr. DeVoy," greeted a fresh desk nurse, who leaned around the young woman she was helping. "I have a message for you, from last night's duty nurse."

He excused himself as he reached past the young woman, who had the same brown skin and sweet smile as Jack's tickling alarm clock. He took the note and retreated to read it.

> *Mr. DeVoy:*
> *Your friend was released against medical advice at three this morning. She's gone home.*

Jack crumpled the note in his hand, pressed his fist to his eyes.

Lina was at home.

"So where the hell is that?" he asked himself in a loud whisper.

He turned back toward the reception desk. But sure that the nurse wouldn't give him any personal information on Lina, he instead started for the glass double doors of the exit. He began walking down the main road, toward the center of town. The hospital couldn't reveal Lina's address, but he knew Levora could. The question was, would she . . .

Worry, fatigue and impatience had clouded Jack's thoughts as he'd spoken with Levora. She'd seemed surprised that he didn't know Lina's address, almost as surprised as he'd been when she directed him to Marchand Manor. For a fleeting instant, he'd felt betrayed, positive that Lina had indeed been a distraction sent by the mysterious J.T. Marchand to keep him too busy to chase down the exclusive rights to Darwin mint tea. But then Levora had told him that Lina lived in a small house behind the estate, and Jack's suspicions had faded.

Levora's directions were good, and as he rounded the sprawling, two-story brick mansion, Jack paid little attention to its whitewashed columns and the smooth, blacktop driveway curving through the emerald lawn to the front door. No one stopped him as he traveled through the estate, although gardeners and other employees cheerfully waved at him.

He paused when he came to a stand of nikau well out of sight of the estate. Three of the enormous palms supported a treehouse built approximately thirty feet from the ground. The circular floor and roof were connected by 10-foot panels made of polarized one-way glass. The walls were so well made that they appeared to be a single seamless cylinder of glass. A wide porch with a retractable roof and a bamboo railing ringed the treehouse, completing the whimsical domicile. A gated stairway winding around one of the outer palms granted access to the treehouse.

Jack carefully looked around. This was the only house behind the estate. The gate was open, so he invited himself up.

At the top of the stairs, he saw her. Her slender form was curled up in the middle of a giant hammock that swung in a gentle arc between two fat branches of nikau. A rattan rocking chair was at the railing surrounding the treehouse, and beside it sat a wicker basket full of yarn and a pair of knitting needles, which led Jack to think that Levora had been acting as nursemaid.

Jack grabbed the chair by its wide armrests and quietly carried it to Lina's side. The sturdy bamboo planking beneath his feet kept silent as he sat down and examined her in the clear light. A long white bandage covered the place above and behind her right ear where she had split open her head, but her sleeveless white slip dress did little to hide the bruises and abrasions she had sustained against the rocks.

Blotchy patches of purple-black and blue-green decorated her upper arms, and Jack winced at an especially nasty-looking scrape peeking from under the hem of her sheer dress, which had ridden up to the middle of her thighs. He ached deep inside at the sight of the ugly injuries marring her gorgeous skin. But the ache lessened, and the tension in Jack's face vanished when his eyes landed on Lina's feet. She wore a pair of white anklet socks. The image was so sweet, Jack's stomach turned as he thought of how easily her beautiful body could have been broken against the rocks.

His elbows propped on his knees, he dropped his face into his hands and began taking deep, quiet breaths, instinctively practicing the yoga techniques he relied on in moments of stress and anxiety. Once his head and chest cleared, he raised his head to see Lina's sleepy eyes fixed on him.

"You look tired."

Her soft voice soothed away the last bits of worry clinging to his heart, and he leaned over her. "I didn't sleep well last night," he explained.

"There's blood on your shirt." She was looking at his shirtfront, which was covered in splotchy reddish-brown stains.

"It's not mine." He reached for her, to cup her face, but at the last second he closed his hand and ran his knuckles along her jawline.

"Levora told me that you slept at the hospital." Lina turned onto her back, grimacing slightly in pain. "She saw you in the lobby when she and Errol came to pick me up this morning. I'm afraid I didn't notice much of anything when he carried me out. In fact, I barely remember him carrying me out."

"I was worried about you." *And Levora could have awakened me,* he thought to himself.

"I'm fine," Lina yawned. "But thank you." She took in his rumpled clothing, the golden stubble covering the lower half of his face and the weary wrinkles under his eyes. "You should get some rest."

"Yeah," he agreed on a gruff sigh. He was working up the energy and will to leave when her hand lighted on his. Whether she meant it as such or not, Jack took her gesture as an invitation to join her in the hammock. Jostling her as little as possible, he eased onto the hammock, careful not to overbalance it and send them both spinning onto the floor.

"You're shivering," he said as she nestled into his embrace. "Are you cold?"

"It's a side effect of the painkillers," she explained.

He impulsively kissed her forehead and her temple. "You amaze me. You didn't hesitate. You ran right into that water and got that kid out." He held her closer and pressed kisses to the top of her head.

"You amaze me, too." Her words warmed a spot on his neck. "Just by being here."

"I'm an idiot. I didn't even ask how the kid was doing when I was at the hospital."

"He's stable. They're keeping him another day for observation. He took in a lot of water."

"Is he related to you?" Jack asked.

"No. Why?"

"The hospital wouldn't give me any information about your condition because I wasn't family," Jack explained. "I was just wondering how you know so much about the boy's condition."

"I made it my business, Jack. I try to take care of everyone on my island."

"Well, that kid was lucky that you do. How did you see him out there?"

"I didn't. I heard him," she said. "I don't know how. I was incredibly distracted at the time."

"I don't know if I should be embarrassed at how easily you overcame my ability to distract."

She rested a hand on his chest. Her fingers lightly danced at the base of his throat as she said, "Jack, if you were any better at what you were doing, that boy would have died." She shifted her head to meet his eyes. "I might have, too."

He clasped her fingers, maybe a bit too hard, and brought them to his lips. He kissed them before tenderly cupping her chin and kissing her lips with a reverence that surprised her as much as him. He watched the light play in her eyes until their lids drifted shut. Jack gently repositioned her to rest her head on his chest. In slumber, her arms went around him, and Jack's heart surged so strongly, he feared the force of it would awaken her.

Jack jogged up the walkway of his homestay and burst through the front door, his sandals leaving part of the dirt road on the floor as he made his way into the bedroom. He'd left Lina asleep in the hammock, and he wanted to shower, change and return before she woke up and missed him. Telling himself that he was probably being presumptuous to assume that she would miss him, he had stripped off his shirt and started the water in the shower before he noticed the well-dressed figure squatting at the edge of the lagoon.

Jack threw open the sliding screen doors and stepped onto the patio. "Can I help you?" he asked the trespasser.

"Nice place you have here." Edison Burke smiled, his chemically whitened teeth blazing beneath his long nose as he stood to face Jack. "It's not the Ritz-Carlton, but I suppose it'll do in a pinch." His gaze wandered over Jack, scrutinizing him as though he were an item up for auction. "I see it didn't take you long to go native. Interesting."

Jack glowered at Edison, unsure as to whom he was angrier with—Burke, just for being Burke—or himself. From the moment he'd seen Lina dancing at the beach party, he hadn't thought of Coyle-Wexler, Reginald or the tea. And now, here stood Edison Burke, the most bitter reminder of why he'd come to Darwin in the first place.

"Aren't you going to ask me why I'm here?" Burke said brightly.

"No."

Burke recoiled at Jack's short snap of an answer, but he continued to enjoy the moment. "When Rex couldn't reach you by phone or e-mail in the past two days, he sent me down on the corporate jet. I'd never been in the Gulfstream before," Burke giggled. "Ever had a personal masseuse work the kinks out of your sacroiliac at six thousand feet, DeVoy?"

Jack seethed. "After the hundredth time, it's pretty much the same as getting a rub on the ground."

"Well then, your return trip won't be all that much fun, will it?" Still smiling, Burke pushed past Jack and into the bedroom. He picked up the briefcase Jack hadn't noticed before, opened it, and drew out a thin sheaf of papers. He dropped them on the foot of the bed as Jack came back inside. "This is your travel manifesto. The Gulfstream is waiting for you in Christchurch. Rex wants to see you, ASAP."

Jack's jaw locked so tightly, his rear molars cracked. He studied the travel documents but only because it was something to do other than crumple them in his fist and drive them through Burke's grin. His charter from Darwin to Christchurch would leave in one hour, so he scarcely had time to pack and find transportation to the airport, never mind shower in the water that was surely running cold by now.

He scrubbed his hand over his eyes as he realized he wouldn't have time to return to Lina.

Feeling slightly sick to his stomach, he went to the nightstand and snatched up his cell phone to see that eleven messages awaited him. His back to Burke, who sidled closer, he punched in his retrieval code and listened to them. Each was from Reginald and they became more and more stringent. The deadly calm of the last message left no uncertainty in Jack's mind as to what he had to do next.

"Unless you've been eaten by sharks, Jack, I expect to see you in my office within the hour of your arrival in Boston," Reginald said in the bloodless fashion he typically reserved for Burke. "Do not disappoint me, Jackson. Your future at Coyle-Wexler depends on it."

Jack pitched the phone onto the nightstand, where it struck the wooden top and skidded onto the floor.

"You might want to give me your file on Marchand," Burke whispered over his shoulder. "I'll need to get up to speed before my meeting on Tuesday. I assume you've met him? Opened a dialogue? I'm sure I can close whatever deal you've started. You have started negotiations, haven't you, Jack? Or have you been otherwise occupied?"

Jack whipped around and stared at Burke through narrowed eyes. He refused to satisfy him by answering his questions, delight him with the lack of progress he'd made, or even ask how he knew that Jack had definitely been otherwise occupied. Jack went to the closet and dragged out his valise and garment bag. He set his bags on the bed and began stuffing his clothes into them, hesitating only when he came to one of the new linen shirts Lina had chosen for him.

I'll leave a note for her with Levora on the way to the airport, he told himself as he put on a clean shirt. *I have to let her know that I left because I* had *to, not because I wanted—*

Burke's continued babbling penetrated Jack's reverie. "It came as quite a shock to me when Rex sent me down here, especially on such short notice. One minute I'm putting for par on the eleventh green at Brookline, and the next I'm on my way here." Burke stepped out onto the patio but soon returned, grunting under the weight of two suitcases, a valise, an over-the-shoulder garment bag and what looked suspiciously like a purse. "And here I plan to stay," he repeated breathlessly, "to succeed where you've failed, Jacky boy."

Jack angrily zipped his valise shut, dragged it off the bed and started for the door.

"Don't look so down, Jack." Burke's smile transformed into a sour grimace. "You're Rex's golden boy. You're bulletproof. And there's no shame in failure."

Jack turned in the doorway. "That means a lot, coming from you. You've dealt with failure more than any other attorney I know."

Settled in a vanilla leather seat in the Coyle-Wexler jet miles above the Pacific Ocean, Jack rapped his knuckles on the mahogany-inlaid armrest. An overly attentive flight attendant set a meal before him, wild mushroom encrusted filet mignon with white truffle risotto, while her partner poured a sample of a rare white Beaujolais. The trip home would be long with nothing other than Reginald's dissatisfaction to look forward to at the end of it, but that wasn't the reason Jack had no appetite for the sumptuous, steaming meal before him.

All but physically, he was firmly rooted in a hammock suspended from nikau palms on one of the tiniest islands in the world. He closed his eyes and found that he could pretend that the quiet hum of the plane was actually Lina's soft snore in his ear, but try as he might, he couldn't imagine her reaction when she woke up and found him gone. Not just gone from the treehouse, but gone from the island, without even so much as a goodbye.

Jack bristled at the fresh memory of Burke chasing him down the road with his own cell phone, telling him that Reginald was on the line. One look at the text box of his cell told him that Burke had placed the call to Reginald, who had ranted at him for so long that Jack had lost the precious few minutes he'd needed to stop at Levora's to leave a note for Lina. He'd had to hustle to the airport after hitching a ride in the jalopy of a minivan that served as the town taxi.

He cringed when he pictured Lina waking up and wondering where he was. News traveled at the speed of thought on the island, and Lina surely already knew that he had gone. He prayed that she heard it from Levora. It killed him to think of her going to the homestay to look for him only to be greeted by Edison Burke and his glow-in-the-dark teeth.

The thought of Burke leering at Lina stiffened the hairs at the back of Jack's neck, and he had half a mind to storm the cockpit and demand that he be returned to Darwin immediately.

But Jack remained in his butter-soft seat, his eyes fixed dully on the billowy clouds beneath the plane. He was nauseous and achy, and he chalked it up to lack of sleep, concern for Lina's health and the renewed stress of failing to secure the Darwin mint tea for Coyle-Wexler. Closing his eyes, he turned away from the window and snapped down the shade. No matter how much he wanted to, he couldn't ignore the truth: he was leaving Darwin, and it was literally making him sick.

He'd known that he'd leave, but he hadn't readied himself for it. In half a day, he would be back in Boston, where grim-faced strangers packed the wet, wintry streets, and then he would return to his house, where he had everything except a lover, friends or even a pet to share it.

Jack's belly knotted tightly at the most bleak thought of all, that leaving Lina was the best thing, the only thing, he could do for her. He had nothing to offer, certainly nothing that could compete with the friends and freedom she enjoyed on Darwin.

He shoved aside the gold-edged table supporting his cold dinner and downed the watery dregs of the second gin and tonic he'd been served after takeoff, all the while thinking that perhaps, hopefully, it was best that he had disappeared from her life as suddenly as she had appeared in his.

CHAPTER 8

Jack sat at Reginald Wexler's right hand in the board-room, hiding a smile of wicked satisfaction behind his curled fingers as he stared at Burke, who perched at the opposite end of the long conference table. For the past three weeks, beginning with his return to Boston, Jack had been under virtual house arrest, with Reginald acting as warden. After briefing Reginald immediately upon his return, Jack had been assigned to a team working on the acquisition of a hemorrhoidal ointment formulated by a medical school in Canada. The assignment was meant to be a punishment, but Jack had handled it in stride, taking care of the contracts in half a day. That alone was enough to get back in Reginald's good graces, but things had gotten even better when Burke returned from Darwin.

Jack stared at him, snickering under his breath. Jack had certainly failed to secure the rights to the tea, but unlike Burke, he hadn't been deported after twenty-eight hours on the island. Accused of "lewd and lascivious acts performed in the vicinity of minor children, the elderly and domesticated animals," Burke had been booted back to the other side of the world under the threat of "harshest prosecution" if he ever dared return to Darwin. According to the documents filed on the American side of the equation, J.T. Marchand had initiated Burke's deportation proceedings personally. As bad as Jack's own post-Darwin sit-down with Reginald had been, unlike Burke, he hadn't left his meeting looking like he'd been fed his own pancreas.

J.T. Marchand had put Jack through the wringer, but after his treatment of Burke, Jack resolved to shake the man's hand for that alone if ever they met.

And it looked like they would, given the reason for this emergency meeting of Coyle-Wexler's legal and research teams and board of directors.

"I called you all here today because of J.T. Marchand," Reginald said, getting right down to business. "Inspired by Burke's . . . *performance* . . . on Darwin," Reginald scowled, "Marchand's people initiated contact with me. Marchand has decided to come to Boston, rather than allow another C-W representative to set foot on the island. We'll be dealing with a shark, people, an attorney who has a one-hundred percent win record when it comes to protecting personal interests and those of Darwin Island. Marchand successfully fought the efforts of the New Zealand government to incorporate the island, and when the general himself leads the Darwinian army of attorneys and advisors through those doors, I want every one of them overwhelmed by the sight of Coyle-Wexler's front line."

Jack lowered his eyes, ashamed to admit that Burke wasn't the only Coyle-Wexler rep who'd offended the island. At least once a day since his return, he'd wanted to kick himself for leaving the way he had, and with each day that passed without trying to contact Lina, he felt even worse. Guilt was a big part of his bad feeling, but there was something bigger beneath it, something that he knew he could work out if he just talked to her once more and explained the reason for his vanishing act.

The rest of the room fell away as Jack began to strategize. *I'll call the island and get Levora's phone number,* he thought. *If she doesn't have a phone, which wouldn't surprise me, I'll try the receptionist at the Marchand Building. She seems to know everyone on the island. Better yet, I'll just take the weekend and go back there to explain in person. Lina deserves that much. And I absolutely have to see her again.*

Reginald's battle talk was a vague prattling in his ear as the lawyer part of Jack's brain played devil's advocate. *What if she's already found another grateful partner to share her bed?* The thought made him sick with jealousy, and he squirmed in his chair.

No, that isn't possible, he reasoned. The very notion felt wrong and grossly unfair to Lina. She had never treated him as though he were interchangeable. Or even replaceable.

Guilt soured his stomach as he realized how wrong he'd been. He shouldn't have left her the way he did, and the more he thought of it, the more he began to believe that perhaps he shouldn't have left her at all. J.T. Marchand's impending arrival was the most vivid reminder of why he'd gone to Darwin, and now it had become the most glaring symbol of all he'd left behind.

Jack was on the verge of standing up and running to the airport when an announcement came through the intercom built into the table. "Mr. Wexler? The lobby just gave us the heads-up. J.T. Marchand is on the way in the express elevator."

"Thank you," Reginald said. He stood and leaned on his hands on the table, his eagerness apparent to everyone in the room. Still and wary, Jack watched a wave of excited expectation travel from person to person around the table. The sudden tension in the grand room seemed to heighten Jack's senses, making every breath, every heartbeat audible. One by one, every head except Jack's turned to watch the doors, eager to see the mysterious and elusive magnate who had handed ace attorney Jackson DeVoy his sole defeat.

The express elevator wasn't as fast as Jack thought it was, because it seemed to take hours for Marchand to reach the top floor. His heartbeat grew louder with each passing second, and Jack suddenly wanted to grab Reginald by his two-hundred dollar tie and demand to know why he had sprung Marchand on them like a jack-in-the-box. Just when Jack thought he couldn't keep his calm façade up a moment longer, the double doors swung open to break the silence in the room.

"Mr. Wexler," announced Reginald's gray-haired private secretary, "may I present J.T. Marchand."

The vice presidents of marketing, communications and customer service gasped in unison, and Jack turned to see what held everyone else spellbound.

A woman swept into the room, her determined stride elegant, regal and sure. Her black suit appeared to be made of a light, tightly-woven wool that moved with the whispery ease of silk. The loose-fitting pants had a blade-sharp crease and the double-breasted jacket was fully buttoned, yet the plunging opening revealed that the woman wore nothing but lovely dark skin underneath it. She wore no makeup but for a bit of sheer gloss that made her lips glisten. With her hair loose and finger-combed from her face, she looked more suited to a high fashion runway than a boardroom, but the serious set of her unusual features made it perfectly clear that the lady meant business.

It took a while for Reginald's eyes to return to their normal size, and he still hadn't spoken by the time she reached him at the head of the table. His tongue making a tangle of his words, Reginald babbled indecipherable syllables as he offered his hand to her. "This is quite a big, uh, shock—er, *surprise*. Yes, quite a surprise, M-Mist—er, Miss—uh, Mrs. Marchand, is it?"

"Ms.," she said, taking his hand in both of hers. She gave it a squeeze that made the old man wince. "Mr. Wexler, I'm Jaslyn Thérèse Marchand. I see you've been expecting me, although you seem somewhat . . . perplexed."

Jack's ears rang and hot blood rushed into them. His mouth fell open with an audible pop that would have been embarrassing had anyone been paying any attention at all to him. But all eyes, Jack's especially, were on J.T. Marchand as she surveyed the people assembled around the table. She narrowed her eyes slightly when she spied Burke, who tried to hide behind a red leather binder embossed with a shiny gold "C-W."

Jack kept staring at her until her gaze finally lit on him.

Surprise creased her brow and confusion flickered in her light eyes, but she quickly regained her coolly indifferent expression.

Jack stood, buttoning his jacket as he did so just to give his hands something to do other than smooth back the gleaming black tress dangling near her temple.

"Mr. Marchand is a *Ms.*," Reginald said, stepping between them to announce the obvious. "It seems our research wasn't as thorough as we'd believed. You're not exactly what we imagined, Ms. Marchand."

"You were expecting a man?" she said briskly, sparing a quick glance at the female vice presidents.

"W-Well, yes," Reginald stammered uncomfortably. "Given your career track record and your position on Darwin, I just assumed that you'd be . . ." He stared at the ceiling, avoiding her eyes.

"Yes?" she prompted impatiently.

"Male," Reginald finished with a lame laugh. "And older. And . . ."

Jack watched the female vice presidents lean forward, and he wondered if they, like him, expected Reginald to disclose his full list of assumptions about J.T. Marchand.

"Not quite so alone," Reginald finally remarked. "Shall we wait a moment for the rest of your team to arrive?"

"There's no team, sir," she said. "I feel more than capable of handling this business on my own."

Eyebrows raised, eyes widened and spines stiffened all around the conference table. Never had Reginald assembled them to face a lone warrior. The three female vice presidents were the only ones who seemed to be enjoying themselves.

Reginald rapped his big knuckles on the table. "I admire your confidence, young lady. It's well earned, from what little we were able to rustle up about you. You certainly manage to keep quite a low profile, Ms. Marchand."

"I like to keep my private life private," she said. "I've found that a non-gender specific name allows for more open dialogue between myself and the men with whom I wish to conduct business." With a quick sweep of her hand, she stroked her hair completely away from her face. Her sharp-eyed gaze swept over Jack. "Mr. DeVoy," she said woodenly. "Or would you prefer Mr. Coyle-Wexler representative? I'm afraid we failed to make a genuine connection on Darwin."

Reginald made no effort to conceal his surprise and delight. "You've met?" His head pivoted as he looked from Jaslyn—*Lina*—to Jack. "I was under the impression that you two hadn't met at all. You undersold your visit, Jack." Reginald laughed heartily even as he set a hand at the small of Lina's back and ushered her toward the chair at his left. "I take back everything I said when you got back from Darwin, boy," Reginald whispered merrily as he pulled out a chair for himself. "Your master plan made no sense to me, but it worked. This is the first time a big tuna has ever flopped right into our board room!"

"Don't underestimate this woman, Reginald," Jack murmured as he took his seat. "I have a feeling that she has an agenda of her own."

Lina stood behind the chair Reginald had offered her. "We have much to discuss, Mr. Wexler," she said briskly. "Please, sit down."

Reginald did so, and Jack wondered if he realized that he'd just relinquished control of the meeting to Lina. She slipped her hands into her pants pockets as she made her way to the glass wall. Her stride was bold yet relaxed, and completely unlike her unhurried island gait. The laid-back, passionate island girl Jack had abandoned was now the picture of elite urban sophistication and style as she faced Coyle-Wexler's commander and fifty of his top corporate officers by herself. Even as his guilt turned to anger, Jack found himself responding to this version of Lina as ardently as he had the first.

Which only made him angrier.

"You want Darwin mint and I don't want to give it to you, so naturally we're at an impasse before we even begin." Lina folded her arms over her chest and sauntered to the conference table. She stopped directly behind the vice president of international sales. The heavyset man promptly burst into a sweat and seemed to be holding his breath as Lina gripped the back of his leather chair and leaned on it. "That mint is one of Darwin's few natural resources, and it's a dear commodity to the residents of the island. It's also a principle draw for tourists, as I'm sure Mrs. Wexler would attest."

When Lina moved on, a loud breath exploded from the vice president of international sales. She next leaned between two researchers and spent a long moment reading the paperwork displayed before them. One of the researchers, a tall, angular man with thick glasses, appeared to be sniffing Lina's hair as it dangled before him.

Jack gritted his teeth in envy, remembering the way that fresh-scented curtain of jet felt trailing over the bare skin of his torso.

"Uh uh." Lina tapped the document. "You can't synthesize the tea. The chemical structure is too varied, and you could never acquire the one ingredient that makes the tea so distinct."

"What ingredient would that be?" Jack asked, his voice filling the distance between them.

"Water," Lina said.

"We have water in Boston."

"Is your water filtered through an isolated geothermal artesian aquifer entombed in rock and clay two thousand meters beneath the mountains of Darwin?"

The stout researcher in gold-rimmed glasses partly raised his hand to beg the floor, as though he were a shy kindergartner on his first day of school. "Er, Mr. DeVoy, the volcanic rock would impart dozens, perhaps hundreds, of different mineral compounds to the water. It would take a long time to identify which ones and determine proper concentrations."

"How long?" Reginald asked through a chilly smile.

"If I were to guess . . ." The researcher stared at the subdued overhead lighting for a moment. "Years."

Lina resumed her travels around the table. Jack's shoulders stiffened when she absently brushed a speck of lint from one lawyer's shoulder and handed another one a fresh ballpoint pen from her own inner breast pocket when he started shaking the one he'd been using.

She was commanding without being arrogant, and she remained fully aware of everything going on around her. She was amazing, so much so that Jack unconsciously held his breath when she paused behind his chair.

"I won't have my island or its resources bastardized for the financial gain of Coyle-Wexler Pharmaceuticals." The purity of Lina's voice and her peculiar accent softened the firmness of her words. "As owner of the land upon which the mint grows, I'm well within my rights to refuse you access to the property, and subsequently, the mint. It's been lovely visiting your offices and meeting you lovely people, but if you'll excuse me, my flight home leaves in a few <u>hours.</u> Good day, gentlemen." She tipped her head toward Reginald, encompassing Jack with a frozen glare. "And ladies." She bowed to the trio of female vice presidents, the only people of color in the room aside from herself. With a sharp turn and whirl of her hair, she exited the room.

Reginald stared dumbly at Jack. "What just happened here?"

"She said no," Jack snapped.

Reginald took to his heels and hurried after Lina, catching her at the elevators where she was lightly stroking a fingertip over the giant waxy leaf of a tall potted plant adorning the elevator lobby. "Hold on, now, Ms. Marchand," he chuckled nervously. "You came halfway around the world and now you're ready to leave without even hearing our offer?"

"Yes," Lina responded. "I also wish to make it clear that representatives from this firm are most," her glaze flickered toward Jack, "unwelcome on Darwin."

"You proved rather elusive for our agents." Reginald snapped his fingers toward the door of the conference room where Jack, Burke and several other attorneys and vice presidents stood watching the activity at the elevator. Burke scurried forward at Reginald's bidding. Never one to respond to a snap, Jack hung back.

"Not you!" Reginald angrily waved off Burke. "Jack, I need *you*."

Lina studied Reginald's face. Sweat beaded above his upper lip, and his smile was a bit too glassy. "Please, Ms. Marchand," he said. "At least just listen to our offer. Jackson DeVoy is prepared to present our proposal, aren't you, Jack?"

Lina shifted her gaze from Reginald to Jack. He could control his body language and facial expression, but he couldn't stop his eyes from speaking to her. Unless she was imagining things, he was suffering the same chaotic emotions she was.

"I'd love the chance to argue our case before *Ms. Marchand*," Jack answered.

Reginald gave him a quizzical look. "Yes, well," he started impatiently. "Hear us out then, Ms. Marchand. We just may change your mind about doing business with Coyle-Wexler."

Jack couldn't read her silence, which seemed to last forever, or at least until the express elevator doors finally opened, and she stepped into the car. As the doors slid shut she said, "The penthouse, Harborfront Regency. One hour."

"Not you."

Lina blocked Burke's path when he and Jack attempted to enter her suite of rooms atop the Harborfront Regency.

"I'm an integral part of this deal, too," Burke stubbornly protested.

"Mr. Burke, during your brief visit to Darwin you verbally assaulted my receptionist, you attempted to break into my office, you refused to pay for your homestay because—and I quote—'The bed sheets were scratchy.' " Her fists stuck to her hips, Lina stood toe to toe with Burke. She was a head shorter, but Burke retreated a step. "Do I even have to remind you of what you and your companion were caught doing in the restroom of The Crab and Nickel, or how much you were required to pay to have the walls steam cleaned?"

Burke blinked. "I think I'll just wait in the lobby, Jack," he mumbled in a rush.

Lina turned and started toward the east side of the penthouse, which housed a full office and a spacious sitting room. Jack followed her. She still wore her sexy suit, but her feet were bare as she padded soundlessly across the thick, burgundy carpeting. She went to the desk, a long, wide, dark-stained affair that gave the room a distinctly masculine feel and dwarfed Lina's petite figure.

When she sat in the matching leather wing chair behind the desk, she took pleasure in neglecting to offer Jack a seat.

"We live in an age where a name is power," Jack said. "If you know a person's name, time, effort and the Internet are the only things you need to discover everything about that person."

"Indeed," Lina agreed. "Tell me, is cloaking your identity the secret to your success, Mr. DeVoy?"

"I suppose you think you're entitled to a monopoly on anonymity?" Jack responded with a lift of an eyebrow. "Why did you tell me that your name is Lina?"

"I didn't tell you my name at all," she reminded him. "Levora told you. Lina is a nickname I've had since childhood. It comes from my first name, 'Jas-LEEN.' My parents always called me Lina." She leaned back in the chair and put her feet on the desk, crossing them at the ankle.

Lina almost smiled at the look of horror on Jack's face. The Harborfront Regency was probably Boston's finest hotel and was renowned for the somber Chippendale and Hepplewhite antiques furnishing its penthouse. Lina could easily picture the fussy hotel manager, who had personally handled her check-in, having a conniption at the sight of her bare feet resting upon the priceless desk.

His hands on his hips and his feet wide apart, Jack remained impassive. "Is there something you'd like to tell me?"

"Is there something you'd like to say to *me*?" she countered.

He seemed offended. "What's that supposed to mean?"

"You used me, Jack."

He was unsure what bothered him most, her accusation or her breezy delivery. He fired back with, "You *deceived* me."

Everything he'd planned to say and everything he'd felt in the boardroom seemed to wilt in the heat of his rising anger at both himself and Lina. In the ten blocks between the Coyle-Wexler building and the Harborfront Regency, he'd reviewed his stay on Darwin in fast-forward. He'd been so enthralled by Lina that he hadn't seen the forest for the trees, and he'd come to hate Kiri and Levora just a tiny bit for allowing him to continually make a fool of himself. So many of Kiri's pointed comments and Levora's peculiar remarks and observations made sense now that he'd finally met J.T. Marchand.

Lina.

He'd gone silly in the head because of her. Never before had he let a woman scramble his brains so much that he was blinded to what was right in front of him. Even as his ire grew, he grudgingly admired her ability to have a full, uninhibited life outside the responsibilities of being Jaslyn Thérèse Marchand.

Lina put her feet back on the floor and swiveled in her chair. Boston Harbor filled her view, but she was too angry to appreciate its quaint beauty. The fact that she knew she had no right to be angry only made her angrier. She had pursued Jackson DeVoy, the strapping tourist whose attractiveness went beyond skin. She had volunteered to be in the mess she was in by starting something that had no way of finishing well.

She'd done the very thing she consistently advised Kiri and the other island girls against—she'd fallen in love with a visitor. She squinted her eyes tight and fisted her hands, pressing them to her eyes. She hated admitting it, but only one thing was causing this much toxic anger to flood her system: she was in love with Jack DeVoy.

Seeing him so unexpectedly in the Coyle-Wexler boardroom had only proven what she'd suspected over the past weeks. Her first response to seeing him again hadn't been rage or hurt but a surge of love so strong that it had made her dizzy. She had been so happy to see him, his awful vanishing act had suddenly lost its lingering sting.

She couldn't pinpoint exactly when it had happened, the moment she'd fallen for him. It might have been as early as the first sight of him in town, or when he'd spoken to her so openly atop their rock in Tuanui Bay. She knew for sure that her feelings for him had gone from casual to certifiable the afternoon she'd approached him at the café. He'd looked up at her and in that first fleeting moment, she'd felt that snap.

That emotion had grown during their time on the yacht, and had become even more powerful during their dance at the beach party. And when she'd opened her eyes to see him gazing down at her in the hammock after her night in the hospital, she'd known for sure that she was lost. She loved him. Which was a shame, because she hated him, too.

"If anyone has the right to be angry here, it's me," Jack said.

Gripping the arms of her chair, she swiveled to face him again. "I stopped being angry right after that grinning idiot Edison Burke left Darwin. And let me make one thing perfectly clear before your ego completely misinterprets this situation. I don't care that you left. What pissed me off, Jack, is that you didn't have the decency to say goodbye." She clamped her jaw until she was sure that she could control the waver in her voice. "I could have settled for goodbye, I'd prepared for it. You left me wondering and wishing and . . . and wanting you, damn it. I went to the homestay and found that Burke creature." She grimaced and shuddered. "I've never liked surprises, and I like them even less now."

"You should have told me your name," Jack muttered coldly.

"You should have told me yours!"

"You deliberately ran around that island half-naked, like a savage, and all along you were the very person I went there to find!"

She leaped to her feet. "I *told* you Darwin was my island!"

"Yeah, and it was like a star laying claim to the night," Jack yelled. "I thought you were being poetic."

Her eyes widened, her jaw dropped. "A savage poet. Is that what I am to you?"

"I don't know what you are." Jack brusquely rubbed his hand through his hair. "I certainly don't know *who* you are."

"Of course you know me, Jack. I held nothing back on Darwin. I wanted to, and I wish now that I had. But I couldn't. You'd know that if you hadn't disappeared without so much as a backward glance."

"That's unfair." Jack took a few steps toward her, his finger raised in accusation. "I haven't stopped thinking about you since—"

She cut him off, unwilling to let go of her anger long enough to hear his explanation. "I'm waiting for your proposal."

"My what?"

"Your offer," she said tersely. "Coyle-Wexler's package. Let's hear it and make quick work of getting out of each other's lives once and for all."

His heart pounded hard enough to hurt at the cool indifference of her words. He knew that he deserved her anger, so he accepted it. But the thought of being cut out of her life altogether was so much harder to take.

To buy himself time to think of something to say that would change her mind, Jack set his briefcase on her desk, opened it, and withdrew the package he had structured with Reginald's approval. Without looking at him, she took the blood-red folder and opened it, pacing the thick carpeting as she read the terms outlined on the thick sheets of ivory letterhead.

No matter what she thought of Jack, Lina had to admit that Coyle-Wexler's offer was incredible. As owner of Darwin Island and all of its properties and naturally occurring resources, J.T. Marchand would receive a fifty-percent share of all profits, in all markets

both domestic and international, from the sale of
Darwin mint tea. That was just the start. She would also
receive a fifty-fifty partnership in licensing with an
equal voice in marketing, advertising and distribution,
both domestic and international. She would have use of
one of Coyle-Wexler's private jets, and Reginald Wexler
was willing to provide a permanent office for her personal use at Coyle-Wexler's home base in Boston, as
well as an apartment. She would also have full access to
the company's chalet in Zurich and its villa on the
Italian Riviera. She harrumphed softly. Switzerland and
Italy were nice, but Darwin was paradise, and even
better than that, it was home.

Jack studied her face as her eyes scoured the proposal.
He knew that she wasn't impressed even before she
snapped the folder shut and said, "Not good enough."

He rolled his eyes and sighed in frustration. "What
more could you possibly want?"

For the briefest instant, her forehead relaxed and Jack
saw the open, honest face of the woman he had loved on
Darwin. In her clear, lambent eyes he saw the answer to
his question. He raised his hand to touch her and his lips
parted to speak, but then her longing expression disappeared and the brittle, passionless glare of the lady lawyer
returned.

"Nothing," she said. "I'm sorry to have wasted your
time." *Both domestic and international,* she was tempted
to add.

"The financial arrangement alone will make you millions," Jack said.

Lina went back to the desk, sat down, and opened her sleek, silver laptop. She slipped on a pair of glasses with heavy black frames and began typing on her keyboard.

"I didn't know you wore glasses," he remarked.

She typed a few more words before peering at him over the top of her Clark Kent glasses. "You're still here?" she snapped impatiently.

Jack choked back his pride. "Can't we talk about what happened instead of sniping at each other?"

"You left. That's what happened." She turned back to her computer. "End of conversation."

"I didn't want to leave," he angrily confessed. "I went back to my homestay—excuse me, *your* homestay—to find Edison Burke and a one-way ticket to Boston waiting for me. I had less than an hour to pack and get to the airport. I had to come back here, Lina. I had no choice."

She took off her glasses and set them on the desk blotter before crossing her forearms on the desk and leaning toward him. "You had a choice. In every situation, everyone always has choices. They might not be very good ones, or even the ones you want, but you always have them. You chose wrong. If it's any consolation, you're not the only one at fault here. I made the wrong choice, too, when I picked *you*."

"Now you're just being cruel."

She guiltily dropped her eyes.

He braced his hands far apart on the desk and leaned down toward her. "Was it a mistake, everything that happened between us? You can honestly say that?"

She cast her face down and turned her head to avoid his gaze, and she busied her hands by tucking locks of her hair behind her ears. Jack's stomach growled hungrily as his gaze traced the lyrical line of her jaw, throat and exposed collarbone.

He rounded to her side of the desk, and she stood as if to challenge him. "I made assumptions about you on Darwin," Jack began apologetically. He was so near her, he could smell the citrusy spice of her hair. "That's the worst thing a lawyer can do."

"That's one of the differences between us, Jack. I saw you as a man, not an occupation. It never occurred to me that you came to Darwin for the same reason as Carol Crowley and Edison Burke and the rest of those parasites." She laughed sadly. "And to think Levora feared you were there to steal her muffin recipes."

A slight smile softened Jack's expression. "They're worth stealing. I've been craving the coconut-lime ever since I got back."

She passed a hand through her hair, lacing the air with its delicious aroma. Jack's hackles went tense under the power of the scent he had reveled in during the days and nights he'd spent on Darwin. Levora's muffins weren't the only thing he'd been craving, and the scent of Lina's hair seemed to seep into his skin, starting all kinds of telltale responses.

"Jack—"

"I know," he said over her. "Enough chit-chat about Levora's muffins. Enough talk about everything." He wanted to use his mouth in more effective ways to let her know how much he had missed her. How much he still wanted her.

He realized that she must have seen the naked hunger in his eyes when she said, "I want you to leave." She lightly rested her hand on his lapel. "If you don't, I'll just be right back where I was three weeks ago."

He brushed her left temple with the backs of his fingers. "Would that be so bad?"

"I don't think it would be bad at all. That's the problem."

Her eyes went to his lips as her fingers plucked at the sides of his jacket. He cupped her face, lowered his mouth to hers, and felt her breath on his lips just as loud pounding issued from the next room.

CHAPTER 9

"Jackson!" Reginald shouted the name over the sound of his fist banging on the double doors of the penthouse. "Are you still in there?"

Jack and Lina abruptly pulled apart. She used both hands to smooth her clothing fully back into place as she started for the foyer. Following her, Jack took choppy breaths and adjusted the front of his slacks and his jacket to conceal the effect Lina's almost-kiss had on him. At the doors, he grabbed the brass handles, stopping her from opening the doors. Her flushed skin burned with heat and he was tempted to grab her and kiss her in spite of the muffled voices on the other side of the heavy doors.

"Let's get this over with, Jack," she said quietly.

His hands tightened on the twin handles. It would be so easy to just keep the door shut, to turn all the locks, latch the bolts and keep the world outside where it belonged: outside.

Lina peeled his hands from the fancy door handles. She held his hands for a lingering moment before she freed them and tossed open the doors. She shared a peeved look with Jack when Reginald led Burke into the suite.

"When you said an hour I didn't know if you meant an hour for us to present the proposal, or that you wanted to see us in an hour," Reginald said. "Forgive us for intruding, but quite frankly, I couldn't wait to find out if my MVP hit it out of the park," Reginald added with a stern nod.

"Or got his second strike," Burke muttered hopefully.

"At least I'm in the game," Jack shot from the corner of his mouth. He turned to Reginald. "We were in the middle of heated negotiations when you arrived."

"Actually, I've made my decision." Lina went to the bar, and Reginald happily trailed after her. She took her time collecting a bottle of Waiwera Infinity water and a crystal tumbler. She deliberately neglected to take drink orders for anyone else before she took a seat on a brown velvet chaise.

Burke scurried to her side. "Can I get that for you, Ms. Marchand?" he asked, indicating the water-pouring duties.

"Touch me or my beverage and I'll crack your windpipe with my elbow," Lina said. Her tone was so pleasant, Burke seemed to think she was kidding.

"You island people are so . . . *expressive*," he laughed with a snort, reaching for the clear glass bottle.

Lina scarcely glanced at him as she brought the tumbler down, pinning Burke's knuckles to the table. "Your offer is incredibly generous," she started over Burke's girlish whimper of pain. "You've made it nearly impossible to refuse."

Reginald gave Jack a hearty clap on the shoulder. "It's a slightly revised package from the one Jack would have presented on Darwin, given the chance," he said cheerfully. "We decided to add in the office space, the apartment and use of the corporate jet as additional incentives. As you've seen, the offer is more than generous. It's downright embarrassing, actually, which is why we included the writ of confidentiality. If word of your platinum agreement got out, we'd never be able to acquire another product without giving away the shirts off our backs. You see, Ms. Marchand, the world of corporate acquisitions, especially in pharmaceuticals, is a highly competitive, cut-throat—"

"Mr. Wexler," Lina began with the patience one would show a large, slow-witted child, "I'm not exactly a rookie, as you might say here in Boston. I handle not only Darwin's legal affairs but those of several international conglomerates, including the European arm of Caduceus Pharmaceuticals."

Reginald gulped loudly. To Jack it sounded as though he were finally swallowing his patronizing attitude. "Caduceus, you say?"

"The fourth largest pharmaceutical company in the world," Lina clarified.

"Ms. Marchand, if Caduceus has made you an offer on the tea, I assure you, Coyle-Wexler can meet or beat it."

"The tea is not available to Caduceus, Coyle-Wexler, or any other company that wishes to invade my island and turn it into a factory. Which is why I pass on your offer," she finished, freeing Burke's hand. "I'm not interested in climbing into bed with Coyle-Wexler Pharmaceuticals."

With Lina perched on the chaise like an Egyptian queen, it took a moment for the men to focus more on her actual words and less on the image they conjured. Once her rejection registered, Burke stopped rubbing his offended hand, Reginald's smile faded away and Jack clenched his jaw to keep from smiling.

Reginald stepped closer to her, his hands outstretched. "I don't understand, Ms. Marchand. Coyle-Wexler has made you an offer you can't possibly refuse."

"But I just did." She poured a glass of water and took a dainty sip of it.

"I urge you to reconsider. Perhaps I could explain some of the finer details to you, points that you might not have quite understood. Ms. Marchand, I honestly think you owe us the courtesy of spending some time really thinking about this offer before you—"

"I understand everything perfectly, Mr. Wexler. This situation is far from complicated. I can't bear the thought of my tea being hyped as a miracle weight loss product by some lacquered and fluffed actress or model whose figure actually resulted from the careful sculpting of a surgeon's knife, eating disorders or drugs. Darwin mint tea is an integral part of my island's tourist trade, which is a major keystone of its economy. You take the tea, you crimp our livelihood. You can't have it, you won't get it, so stop asking for it. Your offer is refused."

Reginald's mouth pulled into a fussy sneer. Jack enjoyed a moment of vindication, glad that Reginald finally had a personal taste of how difficult J.T. Marchand could be.

Burke scurried to the foyer and back again, this time carrying his briefcase. "May I interject here?"

"Now would be the perfect time for your contribution to these proceedings." Reginald lowered his eyes and stepped aside to give Burke the floor. Jack didn't like Reginald's guilty expression any more than he did the gleeful one suddenly brightening Burke's pinched features.

Burke opened his briefcase and pulled out a fresh, blood-red Coyle-Wexler folder, which he presented to Lina. She hesitated, and then snatched it from him, startling him into hopping back a step. He tried to cover the cowardly move with a nervous laugh as Lina opened the folder and pulled out a stack of eight-by-ten photographs. Her face hardened, her lovely features becoming mask-like as she intently examined the documents.

"According to our research, Darwin's mint tea is a major factor in the island's booming tourism," Burke began, his voice slicker than ever as he broke the extended silence. "We can't do anything about the allure of the tea, but we can certainly use other methods to put a significant dent in tourism to Darwin."

Lina curled the papers and photos in her fist as she stood, glaring at Burke and Reginald. "You and you," she spat, pointing at them in turn. "See yourselves out." She aimed a steely look at Jack. "You stay."

Rubbing his bruised knuckles, Burke didn't wait around for a second invitation to leave. He grabbed his briefcase and disappeared while Reginald made a slower retreat. "I'm sorry it's come to this, Ms. Marchand. I'd hoped that we could conduct our business more civilly. In the end, I'm sure you'll find that a partnership between Darwin and Coyle-Wexler is best for everyone concerned, and given time, you'll—"

"Leave!" Lina ordered sharply.

Her fury had an unexpected effect on Jack. Without knowing what Burke's folder contained, he instinctively took her side. Whatever had enraged and hurt her so had originated with Coyle-Wexler, and Jack was eager to find out what it was.

"I'm going, I'm going," Reginald said amiably. "Ms. Marchand," he said, nodding goodbye. "Jack." He gave Jack a conspiratorial wink that wasn't lost on Lina.

She waited until the front door had closed behind Reginald before she flung the folder's contents at Jack. She let loose a stream of invective in a mish-mosh of languages that left him thinking that she was possessed. When he kneeled to gather the photos from the carpet, he froze in place, staring at them, and he understood the reason for her outburst.

Burke had acquired photographs of Darwin's worst. Only trouble was, the photos had been taken out of context. In Burke's first photo, the friendly Maori street performers that had entertained outside The Crab and Nickel looked like thugs menacing a frightened, purse-clutching Carol Crowley.

Jack remembered Darwin's busy, rural airport as chaotic, but in a harmless, sunny, *Gilligan's Island* kind of way. Burke's photographer had used lighting tricks and digital alterations to depict a dark, overcrowded space congested with people who looked like refugees from a Third World war zone.

The worst photo, the one that likely had truly triggered Lina's rage, also initiated a slurry of emotion in Jack. He stared at a moment frozen in time, a moment he'd experienced firsthand. One of Darwin's Ocean Rescue medical vans, the blinding lights atop it burning into the night, idled on the sand with its back doors wide open. A dark, long-limbed figure in a soggy white T-shirt and miniskirt lay upon a gurney being thrust into the van. A black smear covered one side of the patient's head, and Jack knew from experience that blood looked black in moonlight. He tried to swallow over the dry lump lodged in his throat as he remembered how pangs of fear and worry had coursed through him. He'd been so scared that night, of losing Lina so soon after finding her.

He hadn't realized it until now. He hadn't stopped thinking about Lina or dreaming about her since his return to Boston, and he'd shown extreme patience in waiting for his longing for her to fade. But then she'd come to Coyle-Wexler, in effect to him, and he knew for a fact that no amount of time would change the one thing he'd been unable to admit: that he was in love with her.

His jaw locked in anger. Burke must have started working on his smear campaign the minute he'd been deported, and he'd obviously had Carol Crowley's assistance. He decided to further investigate Burke's relationship with Carol. If it were as intimate as Jack suspected, it would certainly explain how Carol and the other parasites had gotten wind of Coyle-Wexler's interest in Darwin mint.

"I wouldn't have thought it possible for you to insult me more than you already have."

Jack looked up from the photos and saw Lina's bare toes peeking from her pants cuffs. He stood up and tore the photos in half. "I had no part in this, and I certainly don't condone it."

"You're a part of it as long as you're a part of Coyle-Wexler." Her chin and lower lip quivered.

"This is just a scare tactic. Reginald thinks he can bully you into doing what he wants."

"A name gives you power, Jack, remember? It took my research staff less than two hours to uncover Edison Burke's style of conducting business, specifically the less savory methods he uses on behalf of Coyle-Wexler. You were smart, Jack, not to give Kiri your name. She would have ferreted out as much information as she could prior to our meeting, and I would have used every bit of it to disarm you. It was easy to derail Burke. Once he landed on Darwin, all we had to do was watch and wait for him to give us a reason to deport him."

"Burke's an idiot," Jack exhaled. "He's a fool, and Reginald knows it."

"Then why does Reginald Wexler keep him around?" Lina demanded. "Perhaps it's because Burke is good at the things Mr. Wexler has no stomach for. It's slimy, slithery, sycophantic reptiles like Burke Edison that sully the reputations of all lawyers."

Jack slapped a hand to his forehead. *How could I be so naïve?* he asked himself. Burke was best at lying, scheming, sidling and gossiping—the four horsemen of apocalyptic law. And Jack would not put it past Reginald to resort to such weapons when it came to his determination to acquire the products he wanted for Coyle-Wexler. It also finally explained Reginald's reasons for keeping Burke in his employ.

"I won't let Coyle-Wexler destroy Darwin's reputation or its number one economic resource," Lina said.

"How do you plan to stop them? Bad word of mouth travels faster than good word of mouth, and people are more willing to believe negative things than positive ones."

Lina turned away and went back to the windows. Jack had seemed genuinely surprised by Burke's plan, but she wouldn't dare trust him with any confidence related to business. She'd trust Jackson DeVoy with her life. Mr. Coyle-Wexler representative, on the other hand, was another matter entirely.

"This is a very unpleasant place," she said quietly as she stared at the waterfront and the narrow, winding streets so far below her. "So cold and damp. Too many cars and too many people crowding the streets, and no one looks happy. The sky seems so much higher here than on Darwin. So far away, so out of reach."

A dry laugh escaped Jack. "You can't touch the sky on Darwin, either."

"Every morning at sunrise, the sky touches *me*. It touched us once, or have you forgotten?"

He closed his eyes and saw the memory, and it felt as real as the moment he'd lived it.

"Hotels are one of the reasons I hate leaving Darwin," she said. "I don't care for them, and I can't bear to think of spending the next few months here."

Jack looked around the penthouse, which he knew for a fact went for five-thousand dollars a week. Lina had every conceivable amenity at her disposal, and a professional private staff of seven, including a personal chef, stood at the ready to cater to her every request. "Are you sure you can't manage?" he asked sarcastically. Then her words really hit him. "You're staying for a few *months*? Well, if you're staying that long, you really can't do better than the Regency."

"A hotel is a hotel, even if the bathroom fixtures are made of 24-karat gold and the headboard reads 'John Quincy Adams Slept Here.' " She backed away from the windows and took a seat at the desk. After slipping her glasses back on, she logged onto the Internet on her laptop. "Every night I spend here is another night in hell, and I can't go home until I settle Coyle-Wexler once and for all."

"Lina, how are you going to stop Burke's campaign? He's a yutz, but he could really cause some damage. You have to know that tourism is one of the few industries where bad publicity is not better than no publicity."

"I'm going to give Reginald Wexler what he wants."

He faced her, his eyes narrowed in suspicion. "You're going to give him the tea? Just like that?"

"I'm going to give him *some* tea." She bowed her head to the wash of blue-white light from her monitor. "I'll give him enough of the fresh product for his researchers to process, and twelve weeks to do it. Even if they can't reproduce the tea synthetically, there's every possibility that Coyle-Wexler might identify and reproduce the key substance responsible for the weight loss effect he believes the tea to have."

"Do you think those are legitimate possibilities?"

She avoided his eyes, but Jack caught a glimpse of her smile, which suddenly looked rather devilish. "Anything's possible, Jack."

"You're sending them on a snipe hunt, aren't you?"

"I'm making them work for what they want, if that's what you mean. I've been through this before, when a French biotech firm wanted to market Darwin mint. It took them twelve weeks to run their tests and trials. I'll give Coyle-Wexler the tea, twelve weeks, and nothing more."

Her fingers flew over the keyboard, and Jack itched to know what she was really up to. Not to spy for Coyle-Wexler, but to share in her amusement. He had a hard time hiding his own excitement at the thought of her spending three months in New England. "Lina, if you're sure that you'll be miserable here, I know a place where you might be more comfortable."

Still typing, she absently mumbled, "Another hotel?"

"No. A homestay."

One step on the thick, triple-padded heather-grey carpet of the foyer invited Lina to unzip her damp boots and pull her feet free of the tight black leather. She left her boots slumping against the wall near the front door before moving through a short entry hall that opened into a large, airy living room with a thirty-foot ceiling.

Her luggage had already been delivered by courier, and recently, judging by the droplets of melted snow dotting the sleek black dressage leather of her twin-wheeled garment bags. The tight huddle of T. Anthony bags sat unobtrusively at one end of the sofa, which Lina passed on her way to the wall of floor-to-ceiling glass doors.

In some ways, this homestay was as impersonal as the luxury hotel she'd abandoned in Boston. The furniture, a custom-designed collection by the look of its austere chrome lines and understated black leather, was tasteful, sparse and artistically arranged in the vast space. Fixtures strategically embedded in the ceiling mimicked natural light, which the overcast, wintry day kept hidden.

The view from the glass doors more than compensated for what the décor lacked in personality.

As she stared at a bare expanse of blue-gray Atlantic, Lina drew in a long breath. Like a sudden rush of wind through an old attic, Lina's exhalation carried away all of the anxiety and tension that had settled in her chest. So occupied by the urgent e-mails she'd had to send from her laptop within the confines of the car Coyle-Wexler had arranged for her, she had noticed little of the scenery in the course of her forty-minute ride north of Boston. Upon exiting the car at a sprawling, gray-shingled building of contemporary design, she noticed a vaguely familiar sea-bite in the air, but she hadn't been able to taste salt or hear the murmur of waves against the shore.

With the high ceilings above her and her toes burrowing into the soft warmth of the thick carpeting, she watched foam-edged waves rush against the shore in a futile attempt to batter an outcropping of pale rock. She slid open one of the doors. Leaning into a blast of frigid sea air, she inhaled, searing her lungs with the clean freshness of the water.

She stepped onto the wide planking of the rear deck and went to the wood railing, well out of the safety of the overhanging roof. The New England winter penetrated her thin wool suit and she crossed her arms over her chest, shivering, the toes of her right foot crossed over her left.

She felt as though she were standing on the very edge of the opposite side of the world. This shore wasn't a thing like the coast in Darwin, where warmth, softness and green dominated. Cold air bit her nose and ears, and the butterscotch sand that stretched left and right as far as she could see was the only thing that broke the monotonous canvas of gray-blue sky and water. *Not a thing like Darwin,* she told herself, *but still beautiful in its own way.*

Grudgingly admitting that her new surroundings were much better than the hotel, she stepped back into the warmth of the living room to explore her new accommodations.

She liked the tall, wide, glassed-in fireplace, which shared a wall with the formal dining room. The all-white kitchen was well stocked, and she took a bottled water with her when she left it to continue her tour.

The décor could use the warmth of a woman's touch, but it was better than the false sense of home offered by the hotel. The furniture had clearly been chosen with care to match the oceanfront view and not with an eye toward an impressive display of wealth, although she knew that the sleek, museum-quality pieces had to be obscenely expensive.

Lina climbed the open staircase gracefully spiraling from the entry hall to the upper floor. She was pleased to discover that three bedrooms had full, spectacular views of the ocean, with the huge master bedroom having the best view of all with its wall of one-way glass.

She flopped backwards onto the king-sized bed, splashing a little of her water over the light grey duvet cover.

"Excellent recommendation, Jack," she smiled to herself as she counted the blades of the motionless ceiling fan suspended high over her head. "I'll have to think of a very special way to thank you."

She rolled onto her stomach and watched the ocean pound the shore, and the forceful image gave her a few provocative ideas about exactly how to thank him. Like the ocean, her thoughts built in intensity, and they flooded her lower belly with phantom memories of the waves Jack had created within her on Darwin.

She'd missed him, plain and simple. She'd spent each day since his abrupt departure trying so hard not to think of him that she gave herself tension headaches that abated only when she let her memories of him wash over her. Despite her best efforts, she had failed in making herself hate him enough to forget him. And then seeing his shock and—annoyance?—in Wexler's boardroom, when she'd revealed herself to be the very J.T. Marchand he'd sought on Darwin, well . . . that look had almost won her forgiveness.

But not quite.

She hopped off the bed and set her water on the gleaming onyx surface of a black dresser spanning half the length of one wall. The dresser shared a wall with a work-station complete with a computer, two printers, two telephones, a scanner, a fax machine and a paper shredder.

Facing the foot of the grand bed was a massive armoire that matched the dresser. An almost impercep-tible seam marked the place where the doors opened, but for all her pressing, pulling and banging, Lina couldn't open it. Glancing around, she spotted a streamlined black remote on one of the nightstands flanking the bed.

Scrambling across the bed on her hands and knees, she settled into the nest of pillows nearest the windowed wall before grabbing the remote control and pressing the POWER button. The doors of the armoire whispered apart, disappearing to reveal a full entertainment chamber with a giant, flat-screen television at its center. The television blipped on, tuned to CNN.

After experimenting with a few more buttons, she discovered the radio feature and managed to exchange the mind-numbing chatter of the television for the amusing noise of a local radio station. With Boy George and Culture Club crooning in the background, she resumed her investigation of the master bedroom.

The walk-in closet set between the dresser and workstation was straightforward, and she grasped a pair of black knobs to part the doors. They, too, were automated, and the mere touch sent the doors sliding into their hidden pockets. The overhead lights came on as well, fully illuminating the deep, wide space.

She stumbled back a step, surprised to see clothes already filling the closet. Business suits dominated, dangling from their shaped cedar hangers and organized into groups of black, navy and gray. Lina drew a suit from the nearest rack. It was tailored so well that the jacket maintained its shape even on the hanger.

Several items wrapped in dry cleaner's plastic caught Lina's eye from the farthest end of the rack and seeded a thick lump in her chest. She rifled through the bagged items, recognizing each one. They were items she'd helped pick out on Darwin.

CHAPTER 10

Jack's index finger spent one second hovering over the doorbell before he lowered it. *What the hell am I doing*, he asked himself before stepping up to the security console affixed to the doorframe. *This is my house. I don't need permission to enter it. And it's not as if she showed me the courtesy of knocking that first night she came to me on Darwin.*

Despite his assertive reaffirmation of home ownership, Jack didn't want to scare Lina with his sudden presence, so he hesitated once more before punching in the digits of his security code. He made a mental note to give Lina the code as well, so that she could come and go freely.

If she was still there, of course.

He'd had his secretary arrange for a car to bring her to Nahant, the pretty little rocky island he called home. It was close to Boston, the skyline of the chaotic city plainly visible from his rear deck even on cloudy days. But in all the ways that mattered most to him, Nahant was worlds away from Boston. He was certain that some of those ways mattered to Lina, and convinced that she'd be more comfortable on Nahant, he'd made sure that she ended up there.

Question was, had she remained . . .

There was only one way to find out, and he tapped the ENTER key. A quiet beep signaled the release of the front door locks, and Jack went into his house. Painful arrows of relief shot through his gut when he saw a sexy pair of women's boots lazily resting against the wall. He forgot to unbutton his black cashmere overcoat in his haste to take it off, and an embarrassed blush warmed his cold-kissed cheeks as he tried to dial down his eagerness to see Lina. After hanging his coat in the foyer closet, he carried his briefcase into the kitchen, half hoping to find her there enjoying the dinner he'd had delivered to her.

The kitchen was empty. He set his briefcase on the deserted oval of the table in the breakfast nook and quickly crossed the living room to peek into the dining room. The stylized chandelier burned brightly, but the long glass table and twelve chrome chairs beneath it were empty. Cloaking his disappointment in logic, he told himself that it was late, that she'd probably already eaten and gone to bed, and he started for the stairs.

But then a flicker of light from the deck caught his eye, and his steps slowed as he changed direction and headed for the sliding glass doors.

Lina sat on the deck, bundled in a blanket from the waist down. One of Jack's sweaters, a thick, hand-knitted charcoal-grey fisherman's sweater she'd found in his closet, kept all the rest of her toasty.

Dinner, much to her surprise and delight, had been brought to her a little over an hour ago. Friendly and efficient deliverymen wearing white chef's smocks under their parkas had delivered her dinner and laid the meal on the deck, at her request, although given the cold temperatures, they'd recommended she dine in the kitchen or the dining room. After explaining that she'd been shut up inside long enough, the men acceded to her wish, even lighting a votive candle for her that they'd found in Jack's kitchen.

The men were Cape Verdean, and Lina had taken advantage of the chance to practice her Portuguese and the more difficult Caboverdiano.

"You are the most beautiful and most gracious woman to ever visit Mr. DeVoy," one of the men had said before leaving, his smile a toothy flash of white against his bronze skin.

"*Ela é a única mulher para visitar Sr. DeVoy*," his partner had added with a wink after accepting Lina's generous tip.

Hmm, Lina had thought with interest, translating his Portuguese in her head as she'd returned to the deck. *So they think that I'm the* only *woman to visit Jack's home . . .*

Her speculations regarding Jack's past female houseguests vanished the instant she'd lifted the small silver dome concealing her first course. The savory scent of a thick, creamy soup tickled her nose and started her stomach grumbling.

"So this is New England's famous clam chowder," she muttered before gently blowing on her first spoonful. She'd barely eaten all day and couldn't wait for the soup to properly cool before she shoved the first taste into her mouth. It was so good, she had moaned out loud as she'd tasted the plump, tender clams and the potatoes that melted on her tongue.

She'd made quick work of the chowder before uncovering her second course. The tantalizing aroma of crab-and-breadcrumb stuffed shrimp piqued her appetite anew, and she'd taken up her cutlery for a hearty first bite. Crispy on the outside, succulent and spicy on the inside, the sweetness of the shrimp and crab was heightened by the buttery goodness of the breadcrumbs, and almost had her writhing in her cushioned chair. She ditched her knife and fork to eat it with her hands, after which she'd toasted the brilliance of the unknown chef with the cold Sam Adams lager her traveling wait staff had opened for her.

She'd next sampled the Tuscan bread, its crispy crust leaving crumbs on the front of Jack's sweater. The bread was heavenly, almost as good as Levora's best sourdough. She'd noted its characteristics, the satiny, moist interior with its big air bubbles and the sweet tang of its sourdough flavor, to take back to Levora.

The beer had nicely complemented the meal, rounding out all the flavors, including those of her final course, a salad of fresh, ripe pear slices, crumbled gorgonzola and toasted spiced walnuts atop a nest of frisée and arugula. A light drizzle of raspberry vinaigrette had made the salad one of best she'd ever had.

In a haze of culinary satisfaction, she'd curled up in her chair with her beer and her blanket, one forearm lazily draped over her full belly. Even now, as she gazed upon the darkened sea, she again wondered how to go about thanking Jack, this time for the wonderful meal. A growing and insistent part of her regretted that he hadn't been there to share it with her.

She lifted the votive and watched the tiny flame fight for life against the swirl of the wind off the water. It wasn't her birthday, but she didn't think it out of order to make a wish as she blew out the candle. Focusing all of her concentration on the object of her wish, she pursed her lips and aimed a quick, hard breath at the guttering flame.

The glass door behind her slid open with a soft whoosh. With the smoky spirit of her dying wish still twisting into the air, she set the votive holder back down on the table and turned to see Jack. *Oh heavens, it works,* she thought in amazement.

Silent and unsmiling, he sidestepped her, remaining well out of reach. He stopped at the railing, propping both hands on it as he leaned into the night.

Lina wanted to say something to him, but she couldn't work a greeting past the emotion paralyzing her vocal chords. His presence reawakened the strong feelings of exhilaration and terror she'd first felt upon realizing that she was in his house. That she was now on *his* island.

She quietly cleared her throat. "This isn't a homestay. It's a home. Yours."

He meant to keep his eyes on the water. It was his habit to come home after his eighteen-hour days in Boston and allow the ocean to medicate him. Watching the hypnotic movement of the water, listening to its unique symphony . . . it was better than antidepressants, better than booze, better than anything. Except, he now realized, the sexy allure of Lina's throaty rasp.

"Dinner was quite delicious," she said.

He finally turned halfway, crossing his arms over his chest as he leaned against the corner of the railing.

"And this . . ." She lifted her Sam Adams and gently swirled the last inch of liquid in the bottle. "It's very nearly as good as Darwin's mint tea."

Lina wondered how long he'd been home before he'd ventured onto the deck. He was still wearing the suit she'd seen him in that morning at the Coyle-Wexler offices, but now his tie was gone and his hair was slightly spiky in front, as though he'd been scrubbing his hand through it.

"I like your outfit," she said.

Jack clamped his jaw to suppress a smile. She was throwing his first words to her back at him.

"Is it an Oxxford?" With no response from him, she answered herself. "It must be. No one else designs such an attractive silhouette. Personally, I've always believed that it's the man that makes the suit, and not the suit that makes the man."

The clouds had cleared to display a fat pearl moon. Jack looked away from Lina, hoping that the moon's light wouldn't reveal the blush creeping from his collar. His three-thousand dollar suit was indeed an Oxxford. Reginald Wexler had recommended the Chicago-based company years ago, on Jack's first day at Coyle-Wexler, when he'd shown up for his first meeting in the worsted wool suit he'd worn to his law school graduation, a suit his mother had purchased on sale at the venerable Filene's Basement "for a steal" at ninety-nine bucks.

"Do you speak English?" Lina asked, reclaiming Jack's attention in time for him to see her bring the rim of the beer bottle to her lower lip.

A sly smile fought its way through Jack's determination to remain impassive.

"*¿Usted habla español?*" she asked.

He watched the tip of her tongue taste the rim of the bottle, and a short, choppy exhalation slipped from his parted lips. She set the bottle on the table, tilted her head, and thrust the fingers of both hands into her hair, smoothing the glimmering fall of darkness from her face. His sweater seemed to have swallowed her whole, the sleeves bunching at her elbows and coming down over her hands. But as she moved her head, enough of her neck was exposed to make Jack forget about the frigid night air at his back and instead worry about the mounting heat situated behind the zipper of his over-priced trousers.

Guiding her hair over one shoulder, she gave him a smile that wrapped around his heart and gave it a fearsome squeeze. "*Je parle français.*" she uttered softly. "*Et vous?*"

Jack wanted to slap himself, hoping that it would help him resist the sorcery of hearing his owns words spoken by Lina. They had started the day as adversaries and had now come full circle back to where they'd been on Darwin. With the tension in his trousers rapidly becoming a yearning pain, Jack realized that whether they were on Darwin in the South Pacific, or on Nahant in the Atlantic, there was no place he'd rather be than with Lina.

Laughing lightly to himself, he bowed his head and rubbed his eyes with his thumb and forefinger.

"*Avete una risata bella,*" Lina said, complimenting his laugh in the language she saved for the most special occasions, and in so doing, she closed the coffin on Jack's free will. She pushed back her chair and drew aside the blanket, which Jack recognized as part of a set from one of the never-used spare rooms. She stood, and Jack hoped that she would come to him just as she had on Darwin, exactly as she had on Darwin.

His chest sank into his stomach when she stepped toward the deck doors, but it merrily bounced back in place once the table no longer obscured her lower half. His sweater was too big for her, and it exposed the supple lengths of her bare legs as she circled around the table. She opened the deck doors and climbed the single step leading into the living room, giving Jack a teasing glimpse of her bare bottom in the process.

A few steps into the living room, she turned. "I want to kiss you, but I don't know how to ask you."

Jack made a vague note to thank her for leaving the door open, which spared him crashing through the tempered, polarized glass to get to her. Breathing hard, he quickly closed the short distance between them, clasped his hands to the small of her back and the back of her head, and he brought his mouth hard upon hers. Like one of the tropical vines of Darwin, she wrapped herself around him and eagerly returned his kisses.

One easy motion robbed her of the sweater, leaving her fully exposed to the cold air rushing through the open deck door and the heat generated by Jack's touch. He kept silent, his eyes communicating with her in a common language older than speech as he tore off his jacket and allowed Lina to help him strip away the rest of his suit.

Right there on the cushiony carpet, he reacquainted himself with every inch of her as she learned anew the secret, intimate responses of his body. Through touch they expressed how much they had missed each other, how eager they were to relive the moments they had spent together on Darwin. Neither spoke, not even after they were joined at the hands, heart and hips and climbing beyond frustrated need, voracious want, even blind lust.

Consumed by her inside and out, Jack stifled a cry in her neck when he could no longer hold off the inevitable climax that would join them completely even as it ripped them apart. Lina rode the wave with him, a sharp, desperate cry climbing from her throat as her fingertips burrowed into the hard meat of his shoulders.

Jack caught her cries with hard kisses that softened as they floated back to the place where cold ocean air tickled their bare skin. Without completely leaving her, Jack dragged his suit coat over her to give her a measure of protection against the cold.

There was so much he wanted to say to her, things that only just now seemed to have occurred to him, but he couldn't find the words to articulate them. 'I love you' just wasn't big enough, not when he was so unsure about the depth of her feelings for him.

Lina lost herself in his eyes as he gazed upon her between kissing her nose and lips and tickling her with a lock of her own hair. He had taken her to paradise with a quiet urgency unlike their couplings on Darwin. Something had happened to him, or *was* happening to him, and all she could do was hope that it was the same thing that had happened to her . . . the complete and irretrievable loss of her heart.

Jack noticed the subtle change in her expression and chose that moment to ask, "Are you going to stay here? With me?"

"I'd like to, yes." She was certain that his question, and her answer, were fraught with more meaning than he realized.

"You'll have a car at your disposal, 24/7. The commute really isn't bad between Nahant and Boston, but then again, I usually leave for the office at six and don't get home until nine or so. You'll be very comfortable at C-W. I'll make sure that you get an office with a view of the harbor. The trials on the tea will be over before you know it, and in the meantime we can keep trying to hammer out a package agreeable to you and C-W, if the trials fail to yield the desired results. Now, what was the name of that biotech firm in France? I'm wondering if they'd be willing to share their science with Coyle-Wexler. There might be something use—"

She stopped his words by pressing him onto his back and climbing astride him. "Do you want me to stay here?"

"Absolutely." His body was already responding to her new position as he gazed up at her slender, nubile form and the tumble of black silk draping her chest and shoulders.

"Then no business." She rose over him, repositioning herself once more. "Not here," she gasped, her eyes locking with his as she welcomed him in one easy, fluid motion that made his abdomen quicken. "Not ever."

Jack grunted his agreement. It was the only way he could respond with her torturously slow movements stealing his ability to form rational thought.

With all business talk banned while they were in Nahant, Jack decided to pursue another topic later as they lay tangled, face to face, in the warmth of his enormous bed. "Do you actually own Darwin?"

"It's a small island, Jack, probably no bigger than Nahant. The land has been in my family for almost three centuries. When my parents were killed, the island became mine. It was held in trust for me until I turned twenty-five."

"I'm sorry." He cupped her face and stroked a thumb over her cheek.

"Trust me, twenty-five wasn't so bad, and it's rather young to come into the responsibility of an island, its infrastructure and its population."

"I don't mean that. I'm sorry about your parents."

"I am, too. I was five when they died. My father lost control of their car on a rain-slicked road, and that was that. Levora and Errol were my parents' best friends, and they took me in."

"Was it Levora's idea that you attend Stanford?"

"No. I knew that I wanted to go to school in America and that I wanted to be an attorney. Stanford was the first school that offered me a scholarship."

Jack blinked. "A scholarship? But you own an island."

"I'm not rich, Jack, at least not by American standards."

"I've seen Marchand Manor. It's not exactly a hovel."

"It's just a house."

"It's a mansion."

"A mansion is nothing more than a big house." She raised herself on one elbow. "I don't want a mansion, I never did. I've always wanted a home. Marchand Manor stopped being a home the night my parents died."

He deliberately missed her point. "Is that why you live in the trees behind the mansion?"

"I love that treehouse. My father designed it. It was meant to be an office, but he never got the chance to use it."

"I've known some lawyers who look like they should be swinging from trees, but you're the only one I've ever met who practices from one."

"It might seem unconventional, but it suits me and my clients. People on Darwin pay for my legal services with bushels of kiwi fruit, or by agreeing to provide meals to the guests in my homestays. My parents left me a bit of money that I've invested with good results, but I still have to work for a living, same as most other people, Jack. In fact, I'll be in handling some business in Toronto next week, and soon after that, I have a scheduled visit to Madrid."

"You wouldn't have to work another day in your life if you accepted Coyle-Wexler's offer for the tea."

"That's business," she reminded him. "Forbidden subject. And just so you know, I enjoy working, and the work I do. I get along quite well with legal consulting overseas."

"But you could be rich."

"Money won't make me rich, Jack," she said before planting a chaste kiss on the end of his nose.

A few days after her shocking appearance in the Coyle-Wexler conference room, Lina was comfortably settled in a corner office with Kiri, the receptionist from Hades, installed at the door in prime watchdog position.

Having informed Reginald of the French firm's past interest in the tea, Jack had been given a new assignment, that of acquiring the company's research. Whether for sport or business, Lina refused to divulge any more information about the French company, particularly the firm's name. The resultant arguments she and Jack had in her office led to chilly behavior between them in the halls at Coyle-Wexler, but the frost had a way of vaporizing once they were together at the end of the day in Nahant. By the end of her first week, their daily office rows had become an oddly amusing form of foreplay.

When Jack came into her office late Friday afternoon, one look at his face told Lina that he wasn't there to stage another fight about a French pharmaceutical company.

"I was wondering what you were doing this weekend," Jack asked, absently toying with the brass nameplate gleaming at the front of her desk.

Lina sat back in her leather chair and laced her fingers over her midsection. "I haven't been in town long, Jack. I'm afraid I haven't had time to fill my social calendar."

"Oh." Jack scrubbed his right hand over the back of his head as he backed toward the door. "Well, then . . . I guess I'll just, uh, leave you to finish up whatever you were doing."

"You're being quite strange, Jack." Lina pressed back a smile. "Is there something special you'd like to do this weekend?"

"No. Yes. Well, there's a work-related function I'm supposed to attend," he explained. "I don't want to go, but Reginald will expect to see me there."

"What sort of function is it?"

He dropped his eyes to his shoes. "It's nothing, really. Just—"

"A wedding."

He turned the brilliant dark blue of his eyes on her. "How'd you know?"

"Millicent Wexler stopped in earlier today." Lina stood, and she exchanged her comfortable leather chair for the hard, narrow windowsill.

As she looked down on the gleaming gold dome of the State House and the sparse greenery of the Commons and Public Gardens, Lina could have been a benevolent goddess surveying her mortal realm. Jack wanted to go to the wedding even less now because it meant one fewer evening alone with Lina.

"Mrs. Wexler wanted to meet 'the woman who's keeping Reggie up nights,'" Lina continued. "That's me, according to her. We chatted, she tried to get chummy about the tea, and then she went and invited me to her cousin's wedding."

"Nephew," Jack corrected.

Lina shrugged. "Whichever. I got the impression that it's going to be quite the to-do."

"Yeah," Jack sighed. "The Wexlers spare no expense when it comes to marrying off one of their own, especially when he's getting hitched to one of Boston's wealthiest Brahmin families. I'd rather have hot needles shoved under my eyelids than go to this thing. I probably attend more Wexler family functions than DeVoy family functions. But at least I can write my tuxes off as business expenses." He groaned. "The last thing I want to do is spend my Saturday night at a wedding."

Lina's mouth pulled into an enigmatic smile. "Are you against marriage?"

Jack recognized his own words, and he prefaced his answer with a telling smirk. "I love marriage. It's weddings I hate."

"Weddings are wonderful," Lina said. "I went to them all the time when I was an undergrad. My girlfriends and I would scan the society pages and pick the most promising looking ceremonies to attend."

"You were a wedding crasher?"

"There's a name for it?"

"There was a movie about it. It's one of my brother Anderson's favorites. He borrowed one of my tuxes and tried to crash some baseball player's wedding at the Park Plaza Castle last year. He got tossed out on his can."

"Interesting," Lina chuckled. "And all this time, I assumed that my friends and I were so clever and original. We never got tossed, though, so I guess we were lucky if nothing else."

Jack seated himself in one of the wing chairs facing Lina's desk. Reginald had gone top-of-the-line in outfitting Lina's office. The leather chair at her desk was the same model as his, so Jack knew that Reginald had shelled out a princely sum to assure Lina's comfort. The twin wing chairs were taller, wider and more luxurious than the pieces Jack had, which sent a twinge of jealousy flickering through him.

Shaking it off, he asked, "What made you crash weddings?"

"Originally, for a kick, because we were bored." Lina strolled over to a long, low cabinet along one wall.

She pressed a button on the Capresso coffee maker, and Jack immediately recognized the scent of the amber potion beginning to brew within it.

"We kept doing it for the food," she finished, taking two porcelain mugs from a lower section of the cabinet.

"Sure you did," Jack said.

"No, really," Lina insisted. "Dorm food was awful compared to what I'd grown up with on Darwin. At wedding receptions, we'd get the best food in exchange for witty conversation and a dance or two with doddering Uncle William or weird Cousin Wingfield."

Lina prepared their tea and Jack tried to picture her ten years younger, doing the Macarena at a stranger's wedding. It was easier to envision her now, dancing barefoot in the sand in celebration of her own nuptials.

"What . . ." Lina wrinkled her brow at Jack's intense study of her.

"Hmm?" he said, snapping out of his reverie.

"You looked so far away for a moment."

"I suppose I was. So are you going to the wedding tomorrow?"

"Absolutely. It'll be the first American wedding that I've actually been invited to. It was sort of fun searching through the couple's seven bridal registries to find a gift."

Jack accepted the steaming cup of tea Lina brought to him. "My secretary handles that sort of thing for me. I have no idea what I'm giving them."

"Shame on you, Jack." Lina leaned against her desk, facing him. "The least you could do is shop for them yourself. I did. I went online and got them the sinfully overpriced Riedel Vinum martini glasses they wanted."

"I'm sure that my gift will be just as nice." Jack lightly blew on his tea. "My secretary's got great taste. She sent my parents to Cape Cod for a week for their wedding anniversary last year."

"How generous of her," Lina said facetiously. "I can only imagine what *you* gave them. They're *your* parents, after all."

"My money paid for the Cape trip, so that means it was from me. Janet just booked it for me."

Lina stared at him and she couldn't help wondering how he could be so relentlessly detached. "You're unbelievable."

"Thank you," Jack grinned.

"That wasn't a compliment." She set her tea cup on her desk with a sharp tap. "You couldn't be bothered to shop for your own parents? Was it even your idea to send them on a trip?"

"Janet suggested it, but—"

"It isn't the same, Jack." Lina displayed her own stubborn streak by tightly crossing her arms over her chest. "Anyone can open a wallet and shell out cash. It means much more when you open your heart and spend the currency you hoard there."

Jack set his cup beside hers, grumbling under his breath. Her argument was airtight. He conceded defeat with, "I hate you."

Lina rounded the desk. "No, you don't," she snickered, settling back in her leather chair.

"You're right again. I don't. Would you like to go to the wedding with me?"

"What I would like and what I should do are two different things."

"I was invited. You were invited. We were going anyway, we might as well go together," Jack reasoned.

She gently swirled her tea before she raised her eyes to him and said, "Are you sure that's wise?"

Jack's eyebrows lifted. "I don't see why it wouldn't be. I'm the primary attorney in the midst of an acquisition deal with a highly desirable vendor. It's just good business to escort you to a wedding that Millicent Wexler expects both of us to attend."

"People aren't as oblivious as we might believe them to be," she said. "I don't want to compromise your standing here." As she held his gaze, Lina knew that she didn't have to say anything more, that Jack understood her meaning perfectly.

"No one's going to have a problem with you and me being together at the wedding," he assured her.

"What if they knew we were together all the time and not just for the sake of a business appearance?"

Jack stared past her and lost himself in the cloudless sky. He had no idea how his co-workers, or Reginald, would react if they knew he and Lina were much more than business associates. Office romances were frowned upon, but they existed. An interracial office romance would have lit up Coyle-Wexler's gossip grapevine like the Esplanade on the Fourth of July, and the last thing Jack wanted was to have his private life discussed around the water cooler. Or worse, discussed by Reginald Wexler.

"I want to take you to the wedding," Jack said earnestly. "As long as we keep it professional, there shouldn't be a problem."

"Then that's what we'll do," Lina said with a sweet smile. "We'll just keep it professional."

CHAPTER 11

Jack realized that he shouldn't have worried about Lina and the Macarena.

He was far more concerned with what she was doing with Shakira's "Hips Don't Lie" as she danced with three bridesmaids and the new Mrs. Dalton "Trip" Wexler III. The bride and groom were both twenty-four years old; far too young, in Jack's opinion, to be getting married.

Or to have gotten married, Jack reminded himself as he polished off the rum and Coke he'd been nursing. Both the wedding and the reception were held at the bride's parents' "winter" house, a sickeningly lovely display of real estate excess in Weston that gave them a place to escape the hustle and noise of their primary residence, a brownstone on Commonwealth Avenue in Boston.

The 30-room Weston mansion was off-limits, but the 12-room carriage house comfortably accommodated guests spilling over from the heated tents containing most of the two hundred invitees.

The two white tents, designed to look like actual buildings complete with floor-to-ceiling sectioned windows, ran together, with the bar and banquet area leading to the ballroom. A string ensemble from the Boston Symphony orchestra had played early on, during the "drink and drop" part of the reception, the time during which guests got loaded at the open bar and dropped twenty different kinds of hot and cold hors d'oeurves all over the white outdoor carpet while the bridal party posed for photos.

Dinner was a lavish buffet featuring six food stations—Thai, Italian, Mexican, sushi, Chinese and French. The food, exquisitely prepared by the much-in-demand Currier & Chives, was as good as the food Jack had enjoyed at the beach party on Darwin, and served to remind him of how much more he'd enjoyed that beach party than any wedding he'd been to.

Even though Lina was the only person of color in attendance who wasn't there as a server or bus person, she seemed to be having a great time. The bride, Garrett "Corky" Burlingame-Wexler, had made a point to take Lina from Jack and introduce her to people she would likely never see again. To Lina's credit, she remembered every name and chatted amiably about nothing with them so well she might have known them for years rather than minutes.

Just as easily as she'd discussed an article in a recent *American Society of International Law* journal with one of the founding partner's of Trip's firm, she'd next turned and conversed in Spanish with the man preparing and serving taquitos at the Mexican table. Lina congratulated him upon the birth of his new son with the same interest and enthusiasm she'd shown the lawyer who'd tried to get the best of her in an argument about the Japanese Supreme Court's ruling on the commercial activity exception to sovereign immunity.

Jack noticed how none of the other guests, himself included, actually spoke to the servers, other than to order drinks or food. Few even bothered with thank yous, as though common courtesy was already included in the catering charges, like a pre-paid gratuity.

When Lina wanted to dance, Jack held himself back. He hadn't expected her to remain glued to his side, but he certainly hadn't counted on her complete self-assurance and ease. She was as comfortable with hundreds of blue-blooded strangers as she had been at the beach party on Darwin. Jack wished that he had a little of her confidence. He'd gone to the same law school as Trip Wexler, and he'd worked with many of the other people at the wedding, yet, as always at occasions like this, Jack still felt totally out of place. He had the same education, wardrobe, corporate ties and net worth, but he still viewed himself as less than an equal. And he figured that they had arrived at the same assessment, that he'd never be more than a son of Southie masquerading as a member of the social elite.

After setting his empty tumbler on a tray carried by a passing waiter, Jack shoved his hands in his pockets and meandered closer to the dance floor, to get a better view of Lina. The bridesmaids, most of whom were younger and prettier than the bride, had been charmed by Lina's accent and origin, and were instantly drawn to her. They formed a circle around her, drunkenly dancing around her as though worshipping the greatest among them.

The DJ, a college friend of Corky's younger brother, was quite skilled and kept the party moving by mixing jaunty old standards preferred by the older guests with clean versions of contemporary pop and hip-hop songs that the younger people wildly enjoyed. Dressed in a fiery shade of red that would look good on no other woman, Lina stood out even more as she danced. The obvious strength and grace of her body complemented her ability to interpret a song. Her subtle glances at Jack tempted him to join her, but he couldn't. Or wouldn't. He couldn't make himself let go in front of his colleagues and co-workers, and he'd die before he let Reginald see him shaking his groove thing with Lina. Along with several other tuxedoed men too concerned with the opinions of others to let go of their inhibitions and have fun, Jack stood to one side and observed.

"This is my third wedding in four months," said a stocky redhead whose bulldog shoulders severely challenged the handiwork of the tailor who'd constructed his tux. "I guess I'm at that age when all my pals itch to get hitched." He reached into his jacket and withdrew a monogrammed silver flask. He took a swig and then offered it around. Jack held up a hand in polite refusal. "I give it two years, tops," the redhead said. "Trip's not the marrying kind. And lucky for him, Corky didn't ask him to sign a prenup. Even if the marriage cracks up, he's all set."

"Spoken like a true divorce attorney," said a man Jack recognized as one of Trip's groomsmen.

"Spoken like a true best man," the redhead said. "I know Trip. When it comes to women, he likes, shall I say, a little more variety than marriage typically allows."

"There's some variety right there," another groomsman said, subtly pointing toward the dance floor where Lina was putting an island spin on the Cupid Shuffle. "I have it from a reliable source that she's conducting some sort of supersecret business with Coyle-Wexler. Now would be a good time to invest in C-W, from what I hear. She's a part of some new weight loss aid that—"

"Hell, I'll buy a ton of it if it builds babes like her," said the redhead. He stepped closer to the other groomsmen. "You should have come to Trip's bachelor party." He lowered his voice. "I hired three girls, a Korean, a Puerto Rican and this black girl with an ass like . . ." Unable to find the proper words, the redhead bit his lower lip, clenched his fists and grunted in delight. "Man, it was a seven-seater! It was big and round and soft . . . it was like being squeezed by a pair of giant marshmallows."

Every man but Jack laughed along with the redhead, who continued his tale. "She was wild, too. Took on each of us and begged me for seconds. You hear a lot of things about black girls, but take it from me, if you ever get the chance, go for it. Now if you gentlemen will excuse me . . ." He cracked his knuckles and gave his neck an exaggerated stretch. "It's time for me to make the acquaintance of Coyle-Wexler's hired help. Jeez, I feel like I'm gonna explode, just looking at that sweet thing. Talk about brown sugar." He slapped a high five with one of his pals. "You won't even recognize her if you see her tomorrow. She'll be walking like she's got rickets."

Jack didn't realize how tightly he'd been clenching his jaw until he released it to address the redhead. "May I have a word with you, son?" he said, draping an arm over the shorter man's shoulders. Before he could answer, Jack started walking him toward the back of the carriage house.

"You're Jackson DeVoy, aren't you?" the redhead asked, failing to recognize the warning inherent in Jack's use of the word 'son.' "I've heard a lot about you. You're kind of a legend among Boston barristers."

"Is that so?" Jack patiently waited for a few well-heeled partygoers to exit the house before he guided the redhead into the rear foyer. "What have you heard?"

"You're at C-W, so you have to know who that black chick is," the redhead drooled. "She's been giving me the eye, so I figure I'll go for it. Chicks like to hook up at weddings, and I want to get my hooks into that one before some other fella wises up and gets her." He shut up long enough to see that Jack was steering him into the spacious bathroom off the foyer. "What are we doing here?" he managed just before Jack clamped a hand to the back of his neck and forced his head into the toilet bowl.

Jack flushed the toilet with his free hand, literally drowning out the redhead's horrified screams. The clumsy redhead's flailing was no match for Jack's superior strength and indignation, so he remained in place until Jack pulled him out. "You're frickin' crazy!" the bedraggled redhead sputtered, backing away from Jack, who used a hand towel to dab water from the front of his tux. "Is this some kind of damn joke? I'll have you arrested for assault!"

"Do that," Jack said calmly as the redhead fished his cell phone from an inner breast pocket. "And I'll place a call to Shariq Hillen and give him the same play-by-play of Trip Wexler's bachelor party that you gave me."

The redhead's thumb pressed a button, disconnecting his phone call. "Mr. Hillen's a partner at my firm. Y-You know him?"

Jack gave a very lawyerly response. "We played high school football together."

"Mr. DeVoy, I didn't mean anything by what I said about that black chick," the redhead smiled weakly. "I think maybe I had too much to drink tonight or something. I just ran off at the mouth a little back there. I'd appreciate it, truly, if we could just keep this thing between us."

Jack took his time washing his hands and tidying his hair. He grabbed another towel from the neatly folded stack on a chrome warming table, and he draped it over the redhead's saturated shoulder as he made his way to the door. "Dry off, kid," he said. "And call it an evening."

Jack returned to the ballroom tent, but instead of lurking on the fringes of the portable parquet dance floor, he went directly to Lina. A slow, sweet, evocative Corinne Bailey Rae tune was playing, and Lina was having her toes crushed by the vice president of new developments. Jack tapped him on the shoulder and cut in without securing permission.

"I'll find you later," Lina assured the displaced vice president. "I've got plenty of dances left in me."

The rotund vice president reluctantly backed away, but he soon found comfort in the trays of miniature chocolate desserts making the rounds.

Jack danced close to Lina. "This isn't exactly professional," she told him. He held her even closer, tucking her hand to his heart as he gazed into her eyes. Lina's smile wavered. All evening, Jack had been standoffish if not cool. Rather than feeling abandoned, Lina had thrilled in secretly teasing him. He was unquestionably the handsomest man in attendance, and every move she made had been designed to lure him to her. Now that he was where she wanted him to be, she was concerned rather than thrilled. She'd never seen him like this, his face tense and angry, his touch possessive to the point of defiance. "You look a bit off," she said.

"I'm fine." He forced a smile that had no real warmth behind it until Lina crossed her eyes to make him laugh.

Another Coyle-Wexler employee, a man from technical services, tapped Jack's shoulder, hoping to cut in. A dark look from Jack sent him scurrying away to chose a partner from the pool of inebriated bridesmaids.

Lina whispered in Jack's ear, "I'd be flattered if I actually believed you sent that man away because you wanted to keep me all to yourself."

"Then you should be flattered," Jack murmured. "Let's say we get out of here. I'll pick up a DVD and we can watch it in bed."

"Jack, surely you know there are better things to do in bed than watch a film."

"Really?" He feigned shock. "Do you think you could show me some of them?"

Lina laughed, and the sound was as arousing to Jack as her touch.

"I've put my time in here and I'm ready to spend the rest of my night with you," he said. "I see enough of these yahoos at work. The last thing I want to do is spend a Saturday night watching the vice president of new product development bump bellies with his wife."

Lina glanced around the dance floor until she spotted her former partner with his wife. The two looked like Mr. and Mrs. Pac-Man. "He came to me at C-W two days ago, asking about the tea," Lina said. "He wants it for his wife."

"Well, she needs something," Jack said. "So does he. They're both at risk for heart disease, diabetes, high blood pressure, apnea and joint problems if they don't reduce their weight."

Lina draped her arms over his shoulders. "I think that's the sexiest thing you've ever said to me, Mr. DeVoy."

"The risks of obesity? Oh yeah, that's a real turn on."

She again brought her mouth close to his ear. "Because your concern centers around health, not appearances. That, Mr. DeVoy, is terribly sexy. I think it's time we said our goodbyes and go pretend to watch a movie."

The next week, when Lina flew off to Toronto, was one of the longest in Jack's life, and only partly because

Lina left Kiri at Coyle-Wexler to "protect Darwin's interests." Kiri admirably performed the task. When a gaggle of young Coyle-Wexler administrative assistants descended upon her to see if she could sell them Darwin mint tea "under the table," Kiri soundly berated each in turn for being slaves to the "homogeneous, unreasonable and ridiculous standard of beauty propagated by the American media." After Kiri loudly pointed out their rhinoplasties, hair extensions, permanent waves, blonde dye jobs, perilously high heels and heavily applied cosmetics, they managed to escape, and had threatened to quit if they ever found themselves on the receiving end of another tirade.

Jack typically spent his weekends at work, but on the Saturday Lina was expected to return from Toronto, he cut his day at the office short. His concentration was shot anyway, since his mind was fixed on counting the minutes that would bring Lina closer to Nahant. He was at home, contemplating what to do to welcome her back when the phone rang. He would have let the machine get it if he hadn't been expecting Lina to call from Logan Airport.

He got it by the third ring. "Hello?"

"Jackie, you're home!"

He grimaced at the ceiling. "What's up, Mom?"

"I don't mean to bother you, Jackie," Connie DeVoy began hesitantly, "but I wanted to invite you to the house next Sunday. It's, well, you know, Harry's birthday, and your dad and I would really like to have you come down."

"Mom, I have plans. I've got to, um—" He cut himself off before a lie could reach his lips. "We'll see, Mom. Okay?"

"But Jackie . . . it's been so long. You didn't come home for Thanksgiving or Christmas, you didn't even call for New Year's. That boss of yours tells you to go halfway across the world on a moment's notice, and you're off like a whistle. Why do you—"

He spoke over her, effectively ending her tirade. "I have a lot of work to do, Ma. You know this is a crucial time for me."

"You always have a lot of work, and I understand that. But just this once, couldn't you—"

"I'll try. That's the best I can do, okay?"

"Your brothers would really like to see you. So would me and Dad."

The chime of the doorbell echoed through the living room and Jack was equally thankful and annoyed—thankful for the excuse to end the call with his mother, annoyed that someone else was now interrupting his afternoon. "Mom, I have to go. There's someone at the door."

"Next Sunday at one, don't forget, Jackie," his mother managed before he turned off the cordless phone, set it down, and then trotted to the door. He opened it to find Lina standing on the doorstep while a driver withdrew her garment bag from the trunk of a shiny black Lincoln.

"Hey," Jack greeted warmly. "I wasn't expecting you for another few hours. You were supposed to call me when you arrived. I would have picked you up."

Lina moved into his embrace, leaning heavily against him. "I took an earlier flight. I didn't want to trouble you, so I hired a car to bring me home."

Home . . . the word echoed in Jack's head and his heart swelled as he kissed the top of her head. "Did the trip go well?"

She nodded against his chest.

"Are you going to tell me why you had to go there?"

Her face still buried in his sweater, she shook her head.

"Are you okay?"

She drew back a little, to face him. "I'm a bit peaky, I think. I ordered a kidney pie from room service my first night in Toronto, and the sight of it threw me off everything but digestive biscuits and weak tea for the rest of the week."

Jack grinned as he cupped her face and studied it. "I'm not trying to be funny, but you look a little pale."

She smiled wanly. "I'm sure it's nothing a good meal and a good rest can't fix."

A short ways behind her, the Lincoln driver cleared his throat. Lina pulled away to pay him, but Jack intervened after reading the name of the service on the nametag clipped to the driver's lapel. "I believe I have an account with your service." He rattled off an account number, which the driver typed into his handheld computer log.

"There it is, Jackson DeVoy," the driver said. "Your receipt will arrive in the mail within three business days." He touched the brim of his smart black cap and bowed in farewell. "Enjoy the rest of your weekend. Sir, madam."

Jack grabbed Lina's luggage and carried it up to the bedroom. After kicking off her shoes, Lina went to the sofa, grabbed the blanket she had taken to storing there, and proceeded onto the deck. She bypassed the teak chairs, opting for the matching sun lounger instead. Jack joined her, slipping under the blanket and shifting her so that she lay in his embrace.

"It's thirty-nine degrees out here," he told her. In his boots, jeans and thick crew neck sweater, he scarcely felt the cold, but he felt the urge to parent Lina, who'd come out in a silk blouse, wool slacks and a light jacket.

"I'm hoping the cold air will refresh me." She hoped it would do a lot more than refresh her; she wanted it to clear away the nausea she'd suffered most of her trip.

Jack's fingers lightly played in her hair. "How was your flight?"

"Not bad. I slept through most of it, despite the best efforts of a loud-mouthed stockbroker who kept screaming into his cell phone about some dazzling new Japanese computer software company that just went public."

"Did he mention the name of the company?" Jack perked up. "I'll bet it was Kobeyashi Technologies. They're ten years ahead of everyone else when it comes to new interfacing technology. I'd love to add some shares of that to my portfolio. Or could it have been Siyuri Robotics?"

"I don't know, I don't care, and I wouldn't tell you anyway," she yawned. "Is money all that matters to you, Jack?"

"Money is the only thing that keeps the wolves from the door. You grew up in a place where food falls from the trees, and where you can sleep outside all year and walk everywhere. It was different where I grew up."

Lina pulled her arm from under the blanket and pointed south, over the water. "That's South Boston over there, isn't it? You didn't grow up too far from here."

Jack glanced at the shadowy skyline. "The distance between Southie and Nahant isn't measured in miles. My dad worked two jobs to keep up with the mortgage on a clapboard house that should have been condemned during Prohibition. My mother was the queen of day-old bread. She knew to the minute how late she could mail in the electric bill payment before our service was cut off. My family was poor, Lina. I don't ever want to be poor again."

"You had two parents who loved you enough to make sure you had what you needed. It may not have been the best, or what you wanted, but everything they did got you to where you are now. You'll have to work harder to convince me that you were poor."

He hugged her closer, squinting at Boston as though he could peer directly into his father's shabby little house. His mother was probably in the miniscule kitchen preparing the traditional Saturday night supper of baked beans and hotdogs, which her husband and at least two of her three sons would consume in the living room while they hooted and hollered at whoever the Bruins were playing on the plasma television he'd given his parents for Christmas.

His mother would sit in the kitchen at the old chrome-edged table with last week's *Boston Globe Magazine* crossword opened before her on the dull laminate surface. She'd pore over the puzzle clues, oblivious to the ruckus of her husband and sons in the adjoining room.

In his memory, those hockey Saturday nights were the only moments he'd ever seen his mother spend on herself, the only time when she put aside laundry, dusting, mopping, scouring, sweeping, washing dishes, vacuuming, cooking, mending, breaking up fights and all the other things she'd done for her family without complaint and without compensation, and most times, without even a simple thanks.

"My mother called a little while ago," Jack began hesitantly. "She wants me to come by next Sunday. It's my brother's birthday."

"Which brother?"

"Harrison. Harry. He's turning thirty, and he's already been married for ten years. He and his wife Beth were high school sweethearts. We actually dated a couple of times."

"You and Harry?" Lina teased.

"Me and Beth, wiseguy. When I was a senior in high school, Beth was a sophomore, but she was the hottest girl in school. I took her to the Christmas dance that year. Over Christmas break, she came to the house, presumably to watch videos. She saw Harry, and the rest kind of wrote itself. They've been together ever since."

"Cuckolded, just like King Arthur," Lina laughed.

"It was all for the best in the end. I only wanted Beth because every other guy wanted her. But Harry genuinely liked her. They got married two years after they graduated from high school. It was funny because they weren't even legally old enough to drink at their own wedding. They lived in a tiny little basement apartment in Southie while Harry saved up to put a down payment on a house. He found a three-story brick rowhouse close to both sets of in-laws. It still needs a lot of work, but I gotta hand it to him. It has amazing potential. The neighborhood is experiencing an economic revival, so it'll have excellent resale value. Real estate is an incredible investment. I've tried to tell Harry to finish fixing the place up, sell it and—"

"He probably doesn't want to hear you go on about a financial investment when he thinks of it as an investment in his family," Lina said over him.

"They don't have any children."

She clucked her tongue. "Jack, you're impossible."

"Will you be here on Sunday, or are you flying off again?"

"I'm needed in Madrid early next week. I was planning to leave on Sunday."

"Oh. I was wondering if perhaps you'd like to go to the party with me. But since you have to be in Spain, I guess—"

"Jack," she cut in, "Spain can wait. Family shouldn't have to."

CHAPTER 12

Early Sunday morning, Lina woke up alone in Jack's bed. During the week, he typically rose and left the house before dawn, long before she lifted her head from the pillow. Sundays he would sleep in at least until seven, so his absence gave her a bit of a start. She threw off the warm covers and swung her legs to the floor. Her tiny white camisole and matching bikini panties offered no warmth against the morning chill, and her skin instantly broke out in goose pimples as she made her way out of the bedroom and down the stairs.

The soft sound of measured breathing caught her ear and drew her to the living room. She found Jack facing the ocean, standing on a long, narrow gray rubber mat. Lina stopped midway down the stairs, watching his pre-cise movements from behind as well as their reflection in the sliding glass doors in front of him. He moved with the same mesmerizing power and grace as the giant nikaus at home when they bent and swayed in storm-strengthened breezes. Lina barely noticed Jack's rumpled white T-shirt and plain gray gym shorts. The perfect musculature of his legs and arms held her enraptured, sending a tingle through her at the memory of how his legs felt between hers, with their crispy-soft golden hair brushing the smoothness of her own naturally hairless limbs.

He took to the floor, arms straight, palms flat on the mat, his back and head arching toward the ceiling with his hips and legs flat. This new pose gave Lina a peek of Jack's abdominal muscles. She bit her lower lip, hungry for the feel of those hard abs working against her belly as he filled her and cloaked her with his weight.

Jack broke his pose and stood with an easy grace she didn't typically see in such large men. She never would have expected a man like Jackson DeVoy to embrace a discipline like yoga, something that seemed so foreign for a Southie dockworker's son. But then Jack had embraced her, too, and she was sure that she was one of the most foreign elements he had ever invited into his life. *There's hope for you yet, Mr. DeVoy,* she smiled to herself.

She was certain that this was a part of his life that was sacred to him and that she probably shouldn't intrude. But she couldn't stop herself from descending the stairs and quietly moving across the carpet. Jack, lost in concentration, seemed not to notice her until she was standing behind him, aligning her arms and legs with his, shadowing his poses.

Jack noticed her, and his heart surged at her sudden proximity. He didn't break his routine, but he slowed it, allowing her to keep up with him. When he pressed his palms together and stretched his prayerful hands upward, Lina faced him, copying the pose. His hands separated, slowly lowering to shoulder height as he bent his knee to slide his right foot toward Lina, bringing his inner right thigh along her outer left thigh. A perfect mimic, Lina followed him into an effective warrior pose of her own.

The pose suited her, Jack realized as his gaze connected with hers. Fierce yet gentle, fearless but cautious, savage and civilized, Lina was the ultimate modern warrior. Without breaking form from the neck down, Jack leaned his head forward until his lips met hers. One by one, his body parts slipped out of the warrior stance to form around Lina, who continued to follow his lead.

Jack's solitary Sunday morning yoga session became a lengthy, unhurried wrestling match that left him and Lina knotted together atop their discarded clothing on the yoga mat. She arched into him, purring into his mouth with each languorous movement of his hips, and Jack felt that he couldn't possibly get close enough to her, to feel her intensely enough. He glimpsed their reflection in the sliding doors, and the sight sent Jack's passions soaring even higher. His peach-hued form wrapped in the dark of Lina's was the most erotic and beautiful image he'd ever seen. If only he could, he would have photographed it, to preserve the moment forever. But his enjoyment of living it overcame all other thoughts, and his body erupted.

Lina responded powerfully, every part of her stiffening for a moment before hard pulses carried her to the height of carnal exultation, bringing Jack along for the ride. Their moment in paradise seemed infinite and too short at the same time, and they remained locked together even after they returned to the soft rubber mat on Jack's living room floor. Through soft kisses and feather-light touches, they offered their Sunday good mornings before climbing once more to the summit of paradise.

Wedged in like sticks of gum on the sunken plaid sofa, Sonny, Connie, Harrison and Anderson DeVoy sat facing Lina, who had been given the seat of honor: Sonny's dark brown Barcalounger with the removable beverage and remote control holders.

Lina enjoyed her vantage point because it gave her an unobstructed view of Jack's immediate family, minus his sister-in-law Beth. Each of them tried so hard not to stare at her that they spent a great deal of time with their heads spinning all around the small living room.

During the drive to his old neighborhood, Jack had given Lina his family's most basic statistics. His mother, Connie, was the stereotypical housewife. Jack reminded Lina that his father had worked at the same shipyard in Quincy for the past thirty-seven years, and that Harrison and Anderson had followed him there after their graduations from South Boston Vocational Tech High School. Like their father, Harrison and Anderson were tall and stacked with hard muscle. Upon first meeting the other DeVoy men, Lina noted an edginess to the way they moved, and she realized that Jack's self-assured and elegant body mechanics were learned rather than organic.

Of the three "boys," Jack looked most like his father. At fifty-five, Sonny DeVoy was still a ruggedly handsome man with strong, craggy features reminiscent of Clint Eastwood. With his graying blond hair and the mischievous twinkle in his hazel eyes, he called to Lina's mind the lonesome cowboys on the covers of the novels about the American Old West that Levora's husband enjoyed reading.

The DeVoy living room was small, and it seemed tinier still with all four DeVoy men assembled in it. Anderson, the blondest, broadest and tallest, occupied more space than anyone, and he sighed gratefully when Connie pried herself off the sofa, giving him a little more room.

"M-Miss Marchand," Connie started, smoothing her brown plaid skirt in a way that betrayed her nervousness, "Jackie, uh, Jackson didn't mention that he would be bringing a lady friend with him this afternoon."

"We didn't know Jackie had any ladies in his life, friend or otherwise," Anderson snickered, his pale blue eyes twinkling.

Lina's ear for languages and dialects perked as she listened to the DeVoys speak. Just as he'd re-trained his body mechanics, Jack had worked on his speech. He sounded as if he'd grown up in Kansas with Levora, unlike Connie and Anderson, who stitched their words together by turning *r*'s into *ah*'s and dropping *ing*'s.

Sonny gave Anderson an elbow to the ribs that would have sent a smaller man hurtling off the sofa and through the archway into the kitchen. "Don't mind him." Sonny's gruff voice boomed with an Irish brogue, the rough edges of which had been softened by almost four decades in New England. "Despite the best efforts of his ma 'n me, Andy's got the social grace of a drunken baboon."

"Isn't it about time that we cut a cake or something?" Jack interjected. His family had been too quiet for too long, although Lina was taking their unabashed eye-balling in stride. She seemed just as comfortable in the shabby old living room as she'd been in the Coyle-Wexler boardroom and her own treehouse on Darwin. If she noticed the threadbare spots on the ancient green carpet, or the cracked armrests of the Barcalounger, she gave no indication. She seemed especially indulgent of the way his family members stared at her, then hastily looked away when she caught one of them at it.

"You in some kind of a hurry to go, Jackie?" Harrison asked before his maple eyes raked over Lina. "Fair enough, 'cause I can see why. Nice catch, big brother. I guess your tastes in girls have changed a bit since high school."

"I'd say they've improved." A chill radiated from the right side of Lina's chair, where Jack half sat on the arm.

Lina glanced up at Jack's icy expression, then turned her gaze back to Harrison. If Anderson was the playful baby of the bunch and Jack the overachieving number one son, dark-haired Harrison was clearly the sullen middle child.

"Mrs. DeVoy?" Lina scooted out of the big chair. "Perhaps there's something I can help you with in the kitchen."

Jack swung his legs out of the way, almost tipping over a rickety bamboo stand bearing a scrawny spider plant, to allow Lina to pass by him. She caressed his cheek before disappearing into the kitchen with his mother.

"So, uh, happy birthday, Harry." Jack spoke over the sound of Lina's voice from the kitchen. Daring a glance at her, he saw that just as she had at Coyle-Wexler, she had instantly acclimated to her new surroundings and taken control in his mother's kitchen, urging her to sit while she made the coffee and set out cups.

Jack handed Harrison a big blue envelope. "It's nothing fancy, just a gift card. I figured you could get what you wanted."

Harrison tore open the envelope and looked at the card. His eyes moved over the greeting before he opened the gift card envelope inside the card. He grunted when he noted the $500 written in the balance box. "Who picked this out?" he asked, displaying the birthday card.

"What difference does it make?"

"I just want to know if the card is from you or from *her*." Harrison threw his head in the direction of the kitchen.

Anderson reached across his father and tapped Harrison's knee. "I wouldn't complain if Jack's Caribbean queen gave me a card." His eyes seemed to glaze over as he stared into the kitchen. "Or anything else, for that matter."

"She's not Caribbean," Jack said. "She's from the South Pacific. She's part Aborigine, part French, part English—"

Sonny harrumphed.

"And part African," Jack told his brother as though he hadn't been interrupted by his father's open disapproval of all things English. "And quit looking at her ass."

With a guilty start, Anderson jerked his gaze back to the living room. He picked up the remote control from the low coffee table, aimed it at the television, and tuned in his favorite sports channel. "Cool, the Celtics are playing. I say it'll be the C's by ten points. Want some of that, Harry?"

Still glaring at Jack, Harry stood and flipped the birthday and gift cards back at him. "Keep your gift and *her* card, Jack. I don't want either of 'em."

"Fine."

When Jack made no move to retrieve the items from the carpet, Anderson grabbed them up. "Five hundred dollars!" He shoved the card back at Harrison. "Man, you and Beth could use this right now."

Jack's eyebrows drew closer together. "What's going on?" He peered at Harrison. "Do you need money?"

"I don't need a damn thing, especially from you, Jackie," Harrison spat.

Jack bristled. "I wasn't offering."

"C'mon, Harry," Anderson implored. "It might take weeks for the yard and the union to work out a contract. You and Beth still gotta eat, you're gonna have to heat your house in the meantime. Jack's got coin up the ying-yang. He's in a position to help."

"Look, boys," came Sonny's low growl, which was suddenly heavy with the lilt of County Kerry. "This isn't the time to be discussin' your brother's finances. We can talk about it later."

"There's nothing to talk about." Harrison stood on the bare patch of faded linoleum between the front door and the base of the stairway. "I don't need no help from Moneybags Jack. I'll get something to tide me over until the yard opens again."

"You guys are on strike?" Jack said. "Since when?"

"Tomorrow will be day seventy-five," Anderson said.

Jack got to his feet. "You've all been out of work for two and a half months?"

"I guess you don't read the regular news, bro," Anderson said. "*The Wall Street Journal* must not have covered our little strike."

"I think of it as more of a working vacation," Sonny said with a bitter grin. "Your mum's been keeping me busy. I've retiled the bathroom and laid new vinyl tile in the basement. Tomorrow I start tearing out this old carpet. Your mum's picked out a nice new Berber she got for a steal at Building 19 1/2 ."

"Building 19 1/2?" Jack echoed with a mouth of disgust.

"What's that?" Lina called from the archway.

Jack turned to explain. "Building 19 1/2 is the only place where you can buy irregular Wrangler jeans, wooden Spaulding tennis racquets from1973 and factory close-out carpeting all under the same roof." He shifted to address his mother, who was deeper in the kitchen. "If you wanted new flooring, Ma, why didn't you just tell me? Get Dad to take you to Boston Design, someplace nice. I'll pay for it."

Harrison made a snorting noise that drew Lina back into the living room.

"I can help with money, Pop," Jack went on. "What do you need?" But before Sonny could answer, Jack said, "Have Mom call my secretary tomorrow with a figure, and I'll see that the funds are wired directly into your checking account."

"You're a real piece of work, Jack," Harrison burst out with a grimace. "Why don't you take your flashy car and your imported supermodel and go on back to Nahant? Leave us poor union stiffs to solve our own problems!"

Connie bustled through the archway, wringing her hands. "Boys, please, we have a guest. And Harry, it's your birthday. Can't you and Jack just try to get along, at least for today?"

"Look, Ma, this was a bad idea." Harrison grabbed a well-worn, flannel-lined denim jacket from a peg affixed to the wall near the front door. "I'm leaving. I got some stuff to do around the house anyway."

"But we haven't even cut the cake," Connie persisted.

To Jack's eye, his mother suddenly looked twenty years older. She'd married Sonny DeVoy young, at twenty-one and fresh out of secretarial school. Jack's birth and Sonny's pride had ended her hopes for a career, and she'd become a housewife. With her silver-streaked blonde bob and hand-knitted sweater, she now looked every bit like the grandmother she hoped to soon become. "Please don't stomp off angry, Harry. I hardly ever get to see my boys all together anymore."

"It's *my* birthday, Ma." Harry shoved his arms into his coat. "And I don't want to spend it with *him*." He jutted his square chin toward Jack.

"No problem." Jack stood as Lina stepped into view beside Connie. "Lina, let's go."

"Oh, no you don't," Harrison sang darkly, shaking his longish brown hair from his eyes. "You don't get to make the dramatic exit while the rest of us sit here and listen to

Ma cry about missing you. You stay, Jack. You're the one she wants here anyway!"

"Harry!" Connie wailed, her tears starting as Harrison angrily wrenched the doorknob.

Anderson stood and swallowed his mother in a one-armed embrace. "Don't cry, Ma," he consoled.

"Look what you've done now, you ungrateful yits!" Sonny roared to his feet, which sent Anderson back down to the sofa. "Can't you boys be in the same room for five minutes without goin' at each other?"

"It's not my fault that he can't accept a simple gift!" Jack yelled.

"You can't resist a chance to shove your money under our noses, can you, Jack?" Harry accused in an angry spray of spittle.

"I earn a good living! Is that a crime?" Jack fired back.

"Stop it, *stop it*, STOP IT!"

Lina's voice took on a shrill quality that seemed to suck the air from the room. Connie and the DeVoy men froze silently in place, staring at the harpy in blue jeans positioned in the living room.

Harrison broke the silence. "I'm goin' home."

Lina stormed over to the door and shut it. "No, you're not. You're going to hang that coat back up, you're going to sit down in that kitchen and you're going to enjoy a big slice of the wonderful chocolate cake your mother took the time to prepare for you.

"And you," she turned on Jack. "Has it never occurred to you to show your love without using your checkbook?"

Connie continued to sniffle into her sleeve. Lina approached her and laid a gentle hand on her shoulder. "I'd like to apologize to you, Mrs. DeVoy. I'm sorry that your children place their petty disagreements above your feelings. I can't imagine that this is the first time it's ever happened. I sincerely hope that Jack and Harrison plan to beg your forgiveness for starting such a row in front of a stranger."

"Begging your pardon, Miss Marchand, but Jack and Harry have got a long history of sort of hating each other," Anderson said.

Connie whimpered as if she'd been struck. Sonny gathered her in his arms, tenderly pressing his lips to her hair.

"Begging *your* pardon, but you're wrong, Anderson," Lina said. "Jealousy isn't the same as hate."

Harry shot a derisive sneer at Lina. "Jackson Heathcliff DeVoy ain't got a thing I want, doll."

"Back at you," Jack snarled.

"Do you hear yourselves when you're tearing into each other? You're fakes, the pair of you," Lina scoffed. "Jack, you told me all about Harry's pretty wife and the house he's been restoring himself. And from what I've seen of you, Harry, your brother's financial security drives you mad. I've never had siblings, but from where I'm standing the both of you would do well to smother your egos, iron out your differences and learn to help each other."

She whirled on Jack, angrily wielding a finger worthy of the most irritated schoolmarm. "Jackson DeVoy, you are a man entirely bereft of emotional attachments, other than to your infernal job. You rely exclusively on the kindness of strangers. You have them delivering your food, tidying your house, cleaning your clothes—"

"Buying birthday cards for your brother," Harrison piped in.

"When was the last time *you* purchased a birthday card, Mr. DeVoy?" Lina shot toward Harrison's corner. "I'd wager that pretty Beth is the card buyer in your family, and likely forges your name to the inside as well."

Color blazed in Harrison's ruddy cheeks.

"She shoots, she scores!" Anderson laughed. "Caribbean queen 1, the home team zip!"

Sonny made a hissing noise that sounded remarkably like "Shut the hell up."

"I have a life, Lina," Jack snapped at her. "If I didn't, I'd have time to schlep down here for tea parties and gossip with my brothers."

"When was the last time you went to dinner with a friend, Jack?" she demanded.

"I dine with Reginald and Millicent Wexler a few times a year," he said.

"You're not Reginald Wexler's friend." Lina's eyes went cold. "You're his pet."

Harrison laughed but the sound had no merriment. "She's got you there, bro."

Jack's face stiffened. "I didn't bring you here to insult me or—"

"I didn't come here to listen to you and your brother tear each other's hearts out!" Lina's eyes blazed with unshed tears. "If you actually hated each other as adamantly as you pretend, your cruelty toward one another wouldn't be so effective. Since you've forgotten, let me remind you: you're brothers. You love each other the way everyone in this room seems to love both of you."

Muttering under her breath about overdramatic Americans, Lina went back into the kitchen, where the rattle of coffee mugs drowned out her words.

Sonny loudly cleared his throat. "A woman shouldn't talk to a roomful of men like that, and certainly not under their own roof!" He lowered his voice and directed his next words at Jack. "When's she goin' back to that island of hers?"

"When are you going back to *yours*?" Lina retorted smartly, stepping into the room with the coffee pot, cups and a cracked porcelain cream pot upon a tin tray, which she set on the low coffee table.

"She's got you there, Dad," Anderson snickered as Lina moved past him.

Lina narrowed her eyes at Anderson. "As for you," she said in a low voice of warning, "quit staring at my ass."

A bright flush of guilt rose in Anderson's cheeks and he busied himself with adding cream to one of the cups of coffee.

Lina went to the pegboard near the front door and retrieved her wool cloak. "Mrs. DeVoy, I'd like to catch some air. May I ask you to accompany me for walk? Perhaps there's a pub or café nearby. We could sit and get to know each other a little better while your menfolk settle things here."

Connie wiped her eyes, and she worked out a smile. "I think I'd like that, Ms. Marchand."

"Connie, where'dya think you're goin'?" Sonny asked. Lowering his voice, he said, "You can't take her just anywhere around here."

Lina guessed correctly that the brown wool coat hanging from a peg was Connie's, and Jack's mother allowed her to help her into it. "I think I'll take her to the Green Shamrock," Connie said as she resolutely buttoned and belted her coat. "I haven't been there in ten years."

"You can't take her there," Sonny insisted.

"Why not?" Connie said with a touch of defiance.

"Because she's . . . they won't . . . there'll be *questions*," he finally finished.

Connie straightened her spine and grabbed her boxy black purse, which had been hanging beneath her coat on the peg. "I'm fairly confident that Ms. Marchand is capable of handling anything anyone might ask her. So am I." She looked at Jack and Harrison. "We'll leave you to it, then."

And with that, Lina shunted Harrison aside to open the front door, and she and Connie vanished into the sunny afternoon.

His head down and one hand shoved deep in his coat pocket, Harrison closed the door behind them and lightly kicked at the base of it with the scuffed toe of his work boot. He kept his other hand on the doorknob, but he made no further move to leave.

For one fleeting second, Jack saw his brother not as a thirty-year-old laborer who matched him pound for pound and inch for inch, but as the stubborn ten-year-old who used to kick the door when denied the chance to tag along with Jack and his twelve-year-old cohorts.

Jack had never excluded Harrison from his street hockey or stickball games because he was the goofy younger brother. On the contrary, it had been because Harrison was always better. Harrison had the faster reflexes, the stronger arm, the better swing. Jack had hated being shown up by his little brother.

He still hated it.

Jack had gone to college and law school, and he'd succeeded beyond even his own expectations. But Harrison . . . he'd gone to work at the shipyards with Sonny, he'd married a pretty girl and bought a house close by that he'd soon fill with children. Harrison was still outdoing him, and Jack couldn't stand it.

Lina was right. He envied the way Harrison had found happiness in building the same life their father had, while he had done everything he could to make his own life as different as possible.

"Harry, I was wondering if you'd take a ride in the BMW," Jack said uneasily. "There's a funny knocking sound when I accelerate. The mechanics at the dealership haven't been able to pinpoint the problem, but I figured you could."

One, two, three, four more kicks sounded against the door before Harrison gave it a rest. "I have my coat on, so I might as well," he mumbled. "Maybe I'll take you by the gym. Beth hated that she couldn't come see you this afternoon."

"Beth went to work out this afternoon instead of coming to your birthday party?" Jack wondered.

"She's working, not working out." Harrison uncomfortably avoided Jack's gaze. "She took a gig babysitting in the daycare at BS&A. It pays all right, and the hours fit around her shift at NECCO."

Jack pursed his lips in a silent whisper. Beth worked long hours at "NECCO," the New England Candy Company, through the week, and now she was spending her weekends taking care of the overprivileged children belonging to the members of the ultra elite Boston Sports & Athletic club? Jack decided that he'd have to find a way to slip Harrison enough money to keep Beth home on the weekends.

"Coyle-Wexler's got a corporate membership at BS&A, doesn't it?"

Jack nodded, not bothering to mention that he'd taken yoga classes there.

"Yeah, one of Beth's Saturday morning regulars is a little boy named Joseph. His ma is an attorney for Coyle-Wexler. Say, you might know her. Adrian something?"

"Adrian Allen. We're, uh, old friends. Co-workers."

Harrison eyed Jack for a moment too long. "That's what your pal Adrian said to Beth when Beth told her that you were her brother-in-law. Small world, ain't it, bro?"

"Too small at times." Jack reached into his pocket, withdrew his key ring and tossed it to Harrison, who caught it cleanly. "In the mood for a diagnostic spin?"

Harrison stroked his thumb over the BMW emblem on the tiny leather key ring. "Andy says you've got an M5 now. Is that right?"

Jack nodded. "It's sweet. You'll like it."

"I'll bet," Harrison said through a tiny smile. He chucked the key ring into the air and snatched it back, cleanly. "Let's go for a spin, Jackie. It'll make it easier for me to work out that knock."

Jack hung his Burberry jacket on the pegboard, then popped into the kitchen. He found Lina sitting at the table in one of the hard plastic chairs, her head hung over a steaming cup of fresh coffee, a stack of photo albums at her right hand. He kneeled at her side, and she turned in her seat to face him.

"Did you make up with your brother?" she asked.

"We reached an agreement on mutual disarmament." He glanced at the photo albums. "I suppose Ma gave you my complete pictorial history from birth through last Christmas?"

Lina chuckled lightly. "She's upstairs now, looking for some award you won in the sixth grade."

"My state spelling bee ribbon?"

"The baton-twirling."

"Like hell." Jack's eyes bugged in shock. "I was never a baton twirler."

"Anderson was pulling my leg, then." She laughed, but it turned into a yawn.

"I'm sorry about this afternoon." He took her hands and kissed them. "I didn't bring you here to get stuck in the middle of a whole family drama." A wan smile came to her face, which looked strangely dull in color. He cupped her neck in both hands. "Are you okay?"

She nodded, perhaps a bit too vigorously. "I'm just a little tired. I had a glass of sherry at the pub with your mother. Perhaps I should have eaten something first."

"We can grab something on the way home," he told her, taking her hand. "Come on. Let's say goodbye to my parents and get out of here."

She rose from her chair. He tried to catch her mouth in a kiss, but she drew her head back. "Perhaps your father's kitchen isn't the best place for this. He doesn't approve of me."

"I don't need my father's approval to kiss you," Jack said quietly. "Whatever his issues are, they're his issues. Not ours."

"I can't imagine that I'm the kind of woman they expected you to bring home to them."

"I've never brought any woman home to meet them, so they had no idea what to expect."

"You know what I mean, Jack."

"My parents aren't racists, Lina. My father . . . he's like most people. He fears the unknown. Besides, he likes you. He admires anyone with the guts to stand up to him."

"Good," she chuckled wryly. "I'd hate to see what he would've been like had he hated me."

"He agreed with what you said about me and Harry. Then he and Anderson left for the hardware store, talking about what a great ass you have."

"I'm not sorry for attacking you and your brother like that. You made me so angry. I'd give anything to have brothers or sisters to fight with, and to be able to bring my boyfriend home to meet my parents. You take each other so much for granted. I couldn't watch it for one second longer without saying something."

"You did in five minutes what Harrison and I haven't been able to do in ten years." Jack stroked his hands through the wave of hair trailing down her back. "You really are an amazing woman. You're one surprise right after the other."

"That's me," she said, dropping her eyes. "Miss Bundle-of-Surprises." She pressed her body to his and draped her arms around his neck. "Let's order in tonight, from that place with the wonderful chowder and stuffed shrimp," she whispered, her breath a silky caress against the shell of his ear. "The sooner we get back home, the sooner we can ravage one another on my last night before Spain."

"Jackie, you're back," Connie said merrily, popping into the kitchen with two more photo albums and a fat blue ribbon clutched to her chest. Jack and Lina sprang apart. "Where's Harry?"

"He's at home with Beth. She's looking really good these days."

"Is everything okay between you two?"

"We're good, Ma." When the concern failed to leave his mother's eyes, he added, "Honestly. We had a really good talk about a lot of stuff."

Connie seemed to spend a moment weighing Jack's words, then smiled. "I'm so glad." She set the albums on the table. "Lina and I had a wonderful time at the Sham. The house was empty when we came back, so I thought I'd show her a few of your baby pictures. You were such an adorable baby, Jackie. You had the cutest little bum. You looked so beautiful naked."

"Still do," Lina said under her breath.

"Mom," Jack said loudly, "Lina and I are going to head out now. She's got an early flight to Madrid tomorrow morning and we—*she*—uh, Lina, I meant to say, needs to get to bed early."

Connie's smile melted a little. "Oh, well, if you have to go . . ."

"It's just that Lina's not feeling that great, Ma."

"Are you coming down with something?" Connie moved around the table to lay one hand across Lina's forehead and the other at the base of her neck. "You don't feel warm. You actually feel a little cool. Have you eaten anything today?"

"Not since breakfast," Lina recalled.

"Jack, shame on you." Connie guided Lina back into her chair. "No wonder she's out of sorts. I've got a lovely boiled dinner that I planned to serve before the cake. You two make yourselves comfortable, and—"

"Ma, honestly, we have to go."

Lina grasped Jack's forearm. "No, we don't. Not yet. Please?"

Jack looked down at her, confused. "You want to stay here for dinner?"

Lina spent a moment watching Jack's mother pull a heavy Dutch oven from the refrigerator and set it on the gas stove. She collected plates from a cabinet and set them on the table, and she gave Lina's cheek a loving pat as she squeezed past her and Jack to collect cutlery. "I'd really like to stay, Jack," she said softly.

He sat in the chair beside her and stared at the moisture suddenly glazing her eyes. "Why?" he mouthed.

"Because I miss being mothered," she whispered.

CHAPTER 13

"Jack?"

"Hmm?"

"Where are all the black people?"

Harrison had discovered the source of the slight knock, but the BMW might have had worse problems if Jack had kept staring at Lina in stunned silence as he drove west on Berkeley. "What?" he coughed, focusing on the road before he jumped a curb and wrapped them around a fire hydrant.

"I haven't seen any black people on Nahant since I arrived, and I've only seen a few working at Coyle-Wexler," Lina said. "Where are the black people in Boston?"

Jack gripped the steering wheel a little tighter with his left hand and downshifted with his right. "They're everywhere, Lina." He scoured the sidewalks, feeling like an idiot as he looked for proof. "See?" He pointed to an attractive, older couple bundled in fur and leather on the opposite side of the intersection of Berkeley and Tremont Street.

Lina watched as the older gentleman approached a driver, who'd double parked a sleek, shiny sedan in front of a high-rise condominium complex on Tremont. The older man briefly touched hands with the driver, surely slipping him a tip, before opening the car door for a woman Lina took to be his wife after catching a glimpse of the big diamond on her left hand. The couple had matching silvery-gray hair, but the man's complexion was several shades darker than that of his cocoa-brown wife. In keeping with the flow of traffic, Jack whizzed past them before Lina could see much more, but the sight of them did little more than beg more questions.

"That couple looked quite wealthy," Lina observed. "I haven't seen any regular black people."

He slowed and brought the car to a stop at Columbus Ave. "Okay," he mumbled around a noncommittal grunt.

Lina turned in her seat. "So you'll take me to them?"

It took a moment for the heat of her stare to force a response from Jack. "You mean now?"

"We're out, so why not?"

"It'll be dark soon."

"Your point being?"

"Some of those neighborhoods aren't safe."

"Oh honestly, Jack, you're being ridiculous," Lina chastised. "I'd really like to see people who look like me for a change. If you don't want to take me, fine. I'll have the Coyle-Wexler car drive me when I get back from Spain."

Jack spent a full two seconds deliberating the choice he was about to make, all the time allowed him before the light turned green. He put on his left turn signal, then outraced an oncoming car to make the turn onto Columbus. Traveling south, he instantly regretted acceding to Lina's wish.

"This is the more cosmopolitan part of Columbus," Jack told her as they passed ritzy boutiques, chic gyms, gourmet restaurants and neat brownstones.

"I suppose it is," Lina said, eyeing a young man in a furry pink parka walking a snow-white Chihuahua with a diamond-studded collar.

They drove several more blocks in silence before crossing Massachusetts Avenue. Lina sat up straighter, noticing how the brownstones had grown more depressed, with boarded windows and graffiti spray painted on front stoops. For the first time since landing in Boston, she saw a heterogeneous mix of people—black, white, Hispanic and Asian. Their skin colors varied, but they all wore the same dismal, flat expressions as they moved about their depressed neighborhood. The sight of them made Lina miss Darwin even more.

They passed an athletic center that, Jack explained, had been named for a Boston Celtics player who'd died young. Jack also pointed out Roxbury Community College. Lina wanted to stop and tour the campus, but she accepted Jack's explanation that since it was Sunday, the buildings would be closed for the weekend.

Lina was amazed at how the neighborhoods here and in Southie were different yet painfully the same. The brick, multilevel rowhouses were similar, the automobiles were pretty much the same, too. Even the corner stores were alike, only as they traveled farther southwest, storefronts and sandwich boards changed from O'Grady's Market and Paddy's Subs & Salads to Almeida's Groceria and Peoples Soul Food.

But when they approached a playground near the Jackson Square T station, where Jack was considering an illegal U-turn, Lina wouldn't take no for an answer when he refused to pull over.

"But you like basketball, you said so yourself," Lina argued, her face toward a group of lanky black men shooting hoops on the playground courts. "I'd really like to watch, just for a little while."

Jack laughed in disbelief. A red light forced him to wait to make his turn, and Lina took that opportunity to exit the car.

"Lina!" Jack called after her.

She slammed the door, cutting off Jack's yelling, and picked her way through the traffic idling at the red light.

Jack was boxed in by a divider on his left and another car on his right. He tracked Lina with his eyes, growing more annoyed by the minute as she walked to the basketball courts as though she'd been paid to officiate. He watched her so intently, the cars behind him had to use their horns to spur him into motion when the light turned green. Earning more angry honks from other drivers, Jack bullied his way to the right side of the road and wedged the BMW into the first available parking spot.

He exited the car so quickly, he almost got his door taken off by a low-riding Honda quivering from the reverb of a bass-heavy rap song. Spitting colorful curses, Jack jogged to the basketball courts. He found Lina sitting on the first row of the five-tiered concrete bleachers. Her hands on her knees, she leaned forward, intently watching the game with a smile.

"They're really good, Jack," she said, raising a gloved hand to point at a tall, muscular man wearing a strappy T-shirt and dark blue track pants. "Especially him. I haven't seen a live basketball game since I left Stanford, so this is a treat. You should have seen the three-pointer he landed from the top of the key while you were parking the car."

"While I was—!" Glancing at the men on the court, Jack forced himself to stay calm and to speak in low tones. "The only reason I had to park was because for some insane reason, you jumped out of my car! You've seen what you came here to see, so can we go now?"

Lina peeled her gaze from the three-on-three in front of her to look at Jack. "You're scared."

"The hell I'm scared," he said.

Lina peered at him a bit more closely. "You're scared to be in this neighborhood?"

"It's Roxbury, Lina." He kept his eyes on the distant sidewalk, where two young black men in baggy black jeans and hooded sweatshirts stood staring and pointing at his BMW. "Things happen here."

"It's not dark yet," she said, "so we'll be fine for a while longer." She looked back at the courts and the tall, broad-shouldered men playing basketball. She felt a chill through her fashionable pea coat and Burberry scarf, so she was amazed that the basketball players could function stripped down to their T-shirts with their breath curling into the air.

"This isn't the best place for either of us to be, Lina," Jack said pointedly.

"I'm afraid I really don't understand," she said. "You'll sleep with me but you won't watch these men play basketball?"

Flames of embarrassment licked at Jack's ears when the two players closest to the bleachers turned at Lina's words. "Let's just get back in the car and go home. Please."

"I'm watching the game. Okay?"

"We got us a pretty lady to entertain, let's go!" one of the players announced, clapping his hands.

Jack bristled at the overly appreciative grins Lina received from the players, one of whom glared Jack's way. Their open interest in Lina wasn't as unseemly as the best man's behavior at the wedding, but Jack had known how to handle that situation. He had no idea what to do about six black men, each about his size, ogling his girl on a Roxbury playground. Holding on to the hope that it would be easier to reason with Lina, he said, "Five more minutes, and then we're out of here. Understand?"

Her mouth firm and one delicate eyebrow arched in defiance, Lina pinned an accusatory eye on Jack. "Just because *you're* scared, don't try to bully me into—"

"I told you, I'm not scared of those guys," Jack insisted. Quietly.

"Then what's the problem? This is a public park. We have every right to watch them play."

Jack answered her so quietly, she barely heard him. "I'm more concerned about other guys, the ones we can't see right now. People get mugged and killed around here."

"People get mugged and killed everywhere," she said. "It's a sad fact of the world we live in. Brilliant!" she cried, applauding a deft hook shot from under the basket. "Heavens, did you see that, Jack?"

He was totally unwilling to acknowledge the shot, which would have made the highlight reel on any sports broadcast. "Anybody can dump a hook from that angle," he grumbled.

"Anybody in the NBA maybe," Lina said shrewdly.

"I could make that shot," Jack said.

She tipped her chin toward the game. "Prove it."

Jack stiffened. "You want me to play? Now? With those guys?"

"Pocket your fear and go for a shoot-around," Lina smiled.

"I can't just come down here and cut into someone else's game. This isn't my neighborhood. That's not how it's done."

"That's too bad. I think I'd have enjoyed watching you work up a sweat."

As much as Jack wanted to head north to his own neck of the woods, he was drawn to the action on the court. He'd left his coat in the car, and as the sun sank lower in the western sky, the air grew cooler. He warmed his hands by rubbing them along his jeans. The best way to warm them would be to step out onto the court and join the game. As much as he wanted to do just that, Jack sat on his hands instead. Football was his sport of choice, but he wasn't a slouch at basketball or any other game that involved a ball. The men on the court were talented, and Jack thought it would be fun to test himself against such skill. It wouldn't be a thing like playing in the pickup games at Coyle-Wexler's in-house gym. These guys were artisans, not overweight office hounds who illustrated the widely held belief that white men can't jump.

Jack and Lina watched the entire game, which ended with a showy dunk by the man who'd promised to entertain his audience. Lina started to applaud, but Jack took her elbow. The streetlights were beginning to glow against the cobalt sky and Jack wanted to get back to his car. Which seemed so much farther away now that a few of the basketball players were approaching them.

"We on for next week?" one of the men called to the group as he tugged on a sweatshirt with UMASS emblazoned across the front.

"Yeah," shrugged a man with a bald head that gleamed in the streetlight, "unless Mina drops the baby. Her due date is tomorrow. Doc says she won't let her go more than a week past her due date 'cause of her blood pressure."

"Page me at the office if I'm not at home and let me know what's up," UMASS offered.

"Still burning the midnight oil?" the bald man chuckled.

"Gotta meet the deadline for the Gillette campaign," UMASS said. "It's my biggest account."

"Excuse me," Lina interjected then, stopping them before they completely passed the bleachers. "That was quite a good game. You all were wonderful."

"You lit a fire, girl," UMASS grinned. "We always play better with spectators. The prettier, the better."

"We'd better be getting home now," Jack said. He smiled stiffly at the basketball player.

Lina took a tiny step forward, removing the possessive hand Jack had set at the small of her back. "Do you play here every week?" she asked UMASS.

"For the most part. There's always somebody on these courts."

Jack looked around UMASS to see another group of black men assembling to play on the court. The rest of the first group had finished dressing in sweatshirts and zippered jackets, collected their duffel bags, and were quickly closing the distance between the courts and the bleachers.

"It's time to go home," Jack said more stringently to Lina. He offered an awkward smile to UMASS. "We have a long drive ahead of us, so if you'll excu—"

"It's like that, huh?" one of the other players said, eyeing Lina with disgust. "You come slummin' to watch the brothers play, but you go back home with *that*?"

The intensity of the man's emotion made Lina flinch. "I'm sorry?" she managed, genuinely surprised at his sudden and unprovoked anger.

Clearly angry, the man dropped his duffel bag and made a move toward Lina. UMASS intercepted him, pushing him back a step. "Don't you have to be at the shop early tomorrow, R.J.?"

"I know my business, man," R.J. spat. "I don't need you tellin' me."

"Why you gotta be all up in somebody's face?" UMASS asked him, still blocking his path to Lina and Jack.

"Why she gotta bring her doughboy to our 'hood?" R.J. persisted, his arms wide as he maneuvered around UMASS as easily as he'd moved on the court.

"I'm sorry, but I'm not from any 'hood' around here," Lina said. "I saw you and your friends playing, and I—" She turned to Jack. "What's a 'doughboy'?"

"Ignore him, baby." UMASS flashed Lina a disarming smile that hardened the muscles in Jack's face. "I hope to see you around here more often, but right now I think it's time to drive my friend here home."

R.J. shrugged out of reach of UMASS's grip. "Let me carry my black ass to doughboy's 'hood and see how much peace I get. You stay here and try to cure that snow-blind sister. I'll walk home."

"She ain't even from around here," UMASS said. "Didn't you listen when she talked?"

Jack grew increasingly anxious as two of the new players on the court briefly turned toward the disagreement between UMASS and R.J. "Lina, let's go," Jack urged her.

"Where you from, baby?" UMASS asked Lina as R.J. stalked off. "I can't place your accent."

"I'm from Darwin Island," Lina said.

"Never heard of it," UMASS laughed. "Is it in the Bahamas?"

"South Pacific."

"You're awful far from home." UMASS set his gym bag at Lina's feet and shoved his hands into the pockets of his sweatpants. "What brings you to Boston?"

"Business," Lina told him.

UMASS cast a short glance at Jack. "I see."

"Lina!" Jack's voice carried, bringing the game on the court to a complete halt.

"Jack?" she responded evenly.

"I can't imagine what kind of business a beautiful woman like you could be in," UMASS said as though Jack had never interrupted.

"Well—" Lina started.

Jack quietly cut her off. "When you're ready to go home, I'll be waiting in the car. Unless you'd rather get a lift from your new friend here."

Lina watched him leave. His deliberate, measured steps betrayed the fact that he was fuming, and Lina thought it wise to extinguish the heat before it burst into full flame. "I really did enjoy meeting you," she said to UMASS. "Perhaps we'll see you play again."

"Doubt it," Lina caught as she hurried after Jack.

"What's the matter with you?" she snapped, catching his arm. "I was just talking to that man, nothing more!"

Jack opened the passenger door, practically shoved her in, got behind the wheel, and whirled on her. "I won't take a beating for you!"

Aghast, Lina's mouth hung open. Jack had started the car and dangerously pulled into traffic before Lina could work out words. "Have you gone insane?"

Jack struggled to remain calm. "You can't just go to some park in Roxbury at night and flirt with a gang of homeboys without expecting to get your ass handed to you. This isn't Darwin, Lina. We don't party on the beach singing 'We Are the World.' "

"By my recollection, there was no singing involved the last time we were on a beach together." She had to hold onto the door to keep from hitting the dashboard when Jack stopped too abruptly to accommodate the driver making a left turn in front of him. "Those basketball players were nice, and I wasn't flirting." Jack wildly changed lanes, bouncing Lina against the door. "If you wish to kill me, according to your own logic you should have just left me there in the park."

"This is all a big joke to you, isn't it?" Jack spat.

"I'm not finding any of this funny at the moment," Lina said, bracing herself by clutching her seatbelt with one hand and her elbow rest with the other. "I'd appreciate an explanation as to why you're so upset with me."

"Did you not see what just happened?" Jack finally turned to her. "R.J. was not happy about us being there together."

"That's his problem."

"Yes, well it could have become our problem if he'd decided to grab a few of his teammates and express his disapproval another way."

"But he didn't," Lina soothed.

"We got lucky."

They rode in silence, back the way they had come. The litter on the sidewalk gradually disappeared, the run-down brownstones became spiffy showcase-worthy homes. Liquor stores and corner convenience marts became gourmet sandwich shops and antique stores. High-rise condos gave way to high-rise office buildings, and as Jack steered the car onto the onramp for I-95

North, Lina broke the silence between them. "Are things really so bad here between black and white people that those men might have fought with you, because of me?"

Jack shifted into fifth and then set his hand on Lina's thigh. He gave it a warm squeeze. "Men fight with each other for all kinds of stupid reasons. Same as you probably got stupid looks from the people at the Shamrock, I got stupid looks at that playground."

"R.J. was angry with me, not you. I suppose he thinks I'm betraying my own race by being with you. Never mind that I have just as much French and English in me as African and Aborigine. It's so different on Darwin," she sighed, covering his hand with hers.

"Is it?"

"Most Darwin natives are mixed with something else. It's hard to hate another race when you've got some of it in your own blood. Our bigotry is generally imported. It comes with some of the people who've settled there from elsewhere."

"Boston has a long history of racial conflict, Lina. It's gotten a lot better, but there are a lot of old scars that haven't completely healed."

"Perhaps it's time people worked harder to learn from that history and build a more harmonious future," Lina suggested.

"Easier said than done. Bostonians are stubborn."

"You're changing your history, Jack. Just by being with me. You could have changed it even more if you'd played ball with those men."

"It's not my job to integrate a Roxbury basketball court."

"Perhaps it should be. Perhaps it would have made you, R.J. and UMASS see that you have much more in common than you realize."

"Like what?" Jack chuckled.

"The love of a game. And a definite attraction to at least one black woman."

Two days after a corned beef and cabbage dinner with Jack's mother, Lina got a phone call from her other mother. "Where are you, kiddo?" Levora asked from her side of the world. "You sound like you're in a cave."

"I'm in Madrid." Lina's right hand sweated around the cell phone clutched at her ear. "I'm in the bathroom of my hotel suite."

"Have you had your big ministry meeting yet?"

"No, I stayed in Massachusetts for an extra day, and . . . well . . . I haven't been feeling top of the line lately. I stopped at a pharmacy for a few things before I checked into the hotel, and then I spent an hour rescheduling my meetings for tomorrow."

"Are you getting enough sleep and eating well? You've taken on so much. You should probably think about taking a multivitamin."

Lina moved sideways along the lengthy bathroom counter, straightening the assembly of small, pastel cardboard boxes lined up along the edge. "Actually, I think I may have to start taking a more specialized kind of vitamin."

Levora's concern radiated across the miles and through the phone. "Do you need to see a doctor, sweetie?"

Lina moved back down the line, peering at the plastic sticks, bars, domes, paddles and cups she'd rested upon their respective boxes. She'd thought that her schedule had left her feeling lethargic and overwrought. But after a bout of violent nausea that had nothing to do with her smooth flight to Spain, Lina had forced herself to consider a specific truth. She'd gone to a pharmacy before she'd even checked into her hotel, and her purchases were now glaring evidence of what she had suspected for a couple of weeks. Plus signs, wiggly lines and pink ovals danced before her eyes as she absently responded to Levora's question. "Yes, I think will have to see a doctor . . ." Her voice trailed off when she raised the last stick and peered at the word slowly materializing in the miniscule text box: EMBARAZADA.

Pregnant, she translated in her head, swallowing hard.

"You sound funny, babe," Levora said. "Are you sure you're okay?"

"Levora?" she squeaked. "I have to call you back . . ."

Three weeks and thousands of miles after her surprise in Madrid, Lina returned to Massachusetts and Jack's embrace. She called him from Logan Airport and he insisted on picking her up, greeting her at the baggage claim with three dozen white roses, champagne and the sort of kisses one typically did not share in public.

Once they were back in Nahant, she made a fuss over the roses, traded the champagne for Orange-Mango Nantucket Nectar, and allowed the kisses to develop into a proper reception under the soft covers of Jack's big bed. Cutting him off when he began to fill her in on Kiri's goings-on at Coyle-Wexler, she listened with interest as he told her of his non-business related pursuits during her jaunt overseas.

"I gave my dad a few names and numbers of attorneys who've had good results mediating strike resolutions," Jack said. "They work pro bono, so it wouldn't cost the dockworkers' union a thing to consult with them. I don't know if he passed them on to his labor board, but he seemed to appreciate the gesture."

"Were you genuinely trying to help your brothers and father get back to work?"

He raised himself on one elbow and stared into her eyes. "Of course."

"Then what you did was more than a gesture. It was an act of love." She laced her fingers at his nape and gently urged him back on top of her.

His hands played in her hair as he studied her face. "Funny you should mention acts of love. We're going to have a baby."

Lina's heart flew into her throat.

"Beth is eight weeks along," he explained. "She finally told everyone last week. She was scared to say anything because Harry's still not working. I don't think I've ever seen Harry so happy. Andy's really excited too, about being an uncle, and my parents are 'over the moon' about it. Their words, not mine."

"How is Beth feeling?" Lina anxiously chewed a corner of her lip. "Perhaps you should introduce her to yoga. It's quite a good way for women to keep fit during pregnancy. Is she on a folic acid supplement?"

"Hell if I know," he chuckled. "You sure know a lot about prenatal health issues."

She carefully phrased her next question. "How do *you* feel about the pregnancy?"

He thought for a moment. "It made me think of you. I couldn't wait to tell you."

Three weeks was such a short time, but it had felt like months. Being at Coyle-Wexler from sunrise to well past sunset had not been enough to distract him from Lina's absence. The first two nights had been the worst, missing her so much he'd fallen asleep in a jumble of blankets on the deck in her favorite spot. The next several nights were almost as bad because he'd returned to his bed only to be tormented by the sweet, citrusy scent she'd left on his pillows. The next week he'd been steamrolled by the suggestive note she'd written on the menu of one of his favorite take-out places. Her handwriting, with its wide loops and elegant slants, was almost as provocative as her words, and Jack had spent a good part of the night standing in an icy shower.

The cold showers clarified a lot more than Jack wanted to see, specifically that her body wasn't all that he missed about her.

There was also the way she looked in his shirts and sweaters, and the tastiness of her pout when he lowered the god-awful pop music she liked to listen to while she soaked in the bathtub. She had also taken to joining him for his yoga routines at daybreak. He'd enjoyed the solitude of his exercise, but now he treasured Lina's company and loved teaching her how to position her body. She never failed to impress him with her flexibility and strength. And imagination. And her single-minded dedication to making him call in sick, to spend the day with her in bed.

Which they had. But only once.

As her return to Nahant had drawn closer, Jack also had begun to long for the moments they'd spent sitting on the deck, knotted together beneath a blanket watching the tides tumble onto shore. She was back, for now, and he already dreaded the moment when she would have to leave again.

Her gaze never wavering from his, Lina drank in the sight of him. Something had changed in her absence, something within him that she now saw in his eyes. He'd never shown any inhibitions when it came to sharing his body, but his eyes had been another matter entirely. Maybe her harsh words at his parents' house had done it, but the veil had lifted and Jack's emotions were before her as beautiful and bare as the rest of him. He had brought up the subject of babies, and now was as good a time as any to tell him her news.

But her voice had no strength in it when she said, "I'd like to bend your ear for a moment, Jack."

"Can it wait until after this?" He took her mouth in a kiss that made her eyelids drift shut and her heart flutter.

"Well . . ." she managed on a sigh.

"Let me just finish this . . ." He shifted on top of her, one of his hands moving between them. He caught her answering gasp in a kiss and continued to touch her until her back arched and she begged for something other than his ear.

Later, long after Lina had fallen asleep with her body nestled into his, Jack thought about his brother and the baby growing in Beth. He stroked a hand over Lina's abdomen and recalled how concave her belly had been when they'd first met. She was still firm and toned, but her abdomen had lost a bit of its flatness. Attributing it to the rich foods she'd consumed abroad over the past three weeks, Jack cradled her abdomen in one hand and closed his eyes. And in that twilight space between wakefulness and dreams, terror mingled with joy as Jack imagined himself in Harrison's shoes, with a child of his own tucked under the heart of the woman in his arms.

CHAPTER 14

Jack hummed softly to himself as he stood in the Coyle-Wexler Print Center—the vaingloriously named copier and office supply room—waiting for two hundred copies to finish running. Ordinarily, he'd have had his secretary handle the mundane task of copying a document, but since this letter wasn't Coyle-Wexler related, Jack thought it best to handle his non-company endeavor himself. His father and brothers wouldn't accept money from him, but Jack was surprised at how much more satisfaction he got out of spending his legal expertise on them. His family's gratitude and Lina's pride in his efforts had started to make him finally see why so many big-name Boston barristers did so much pro bono work.

Lost in his thoughts or hypnotized by the piercing light from the copier, Jack didn't notice that someone else had joined him in the room until she spoke.

"Adrian," he said abruptly in an attempt to cover his initial startled reaction. "I didn't see you there."

"Since when do you run your own copies?" she asked with a sly smile. "I was under the impression that your secretary lived to tend to your every need."

"This one's not specific to Coyle-Wexler," Jack confessed. "It's a letter to the members of my father's dock-workers' union. They're on strike and they've hit a

roadblock in negotiations and . . ." A flush of embarrassment warmed Jack's face. "I've been trying to help."

"A dockworkers' union has you on retainer?" Adrian
eyed him shrewdly. "How can they afford you?"

"Because I'm doing it as a favor."

A genuine smile lit up Adrian's face, giving her cocoa
complexion a warm, rosy glow. She wore a red wool suit
that was perfect for the office without hiding her great
figure. She ran a hand through her short black hair before
resting her fist on her hip. "This is an interesting new
side to you, Jack," she observed. "I have to say, I
approve."

He gave her a noncommittal shrug as he collected his
copies.

"I approve of Ms. Marchand, too," Adrian added.
"She's a fascinating woman. Gorgeous, too. She reminds
me of Naomi Campbell, without the assault charges."

Jack smirked. "Don't be fooled by that smile of hers.
She's plenty aggressive when she needs to be."

"You like that in a woman?" Adrian teased. "I didn't
know that."

Jack's finger went to his collar, which suddenly felt a
bit too tight. Early in his Coyle-Wexler career, he and
Adrian Allen had enjoyed a brief flirtation that might
have grown into something more serious if Jack had had
the guts to actually follow through on any of their tenta-
tively planned dates. Too concerned with what Reginald
Wexler and Gardner Coyle would have thought of an
office romance, particularly one with an African-
American woman, Jack had buried himself in work and

allowed the friendship to wither from neglect. "Hey, um, how's . . . uh . . ." He searched for the right name, and tried to picture a fancy wedding invitation he'd received years ago. "Daniel?" Jack finally blurted to mask his discomfort.

"It's Dennis," Adrian answered, lining her document up on the copier table. "He's fine. We celebrated our five-year anniversary last month."

"Five years already?" Jack whistled. "He's a podiatrist, isn't he?"

Adrian punched in the number of copies she wanted. "Pediatrician."

0-for-2 so far, Jackie boy, he chastised himself. "And how's your baby? You had a little girl, right? Janet?"

Adrian shook her head, her twinkling eyes revealing her amusement at Jack's struggle.

"Jessica?"

"Fourth strike," Adrian laughed. "Try again. You'll get it. There aren't that many names that start with 'J.' "

Jack thought a moment, then snapped his fingers. "Jennifer!"

"It's Joseph, and he's almost a year old now. But he liked the baby doll your secretary sent him under your name." Adrian chuckled as she lowered the copier cover and pushed START.

"Look, Adrian, I'm sorry," Jack conceded. "I should have read the birth announcement more carefully, and—"

"It's okay, Jack," she assured him. "Playing with dolls at this age will teach him to be compassionate and loving. When he has children of his own, he'll—"

"It's not just that," he tried to explain. "I'm sorry about all of it. You're one of the most amazing women I've ever met, yet that wasn't enough to make me get over my stupid notions about who I should get involved with back when we were . . . well . . ."

"Were what?" she asked softly.

"The new kids at Coyle-Wexler," he said with a weak smile. "Stuck in the trenches together."

She narrowed her eyes a bit. "The trenches?"

Jack dumbly scratched the side of his head, wondering how his average-sized mouth could accommodate so much of his foot. "I didn't mean it like that."

"The trenches are great, Jack," Adrian said. "You know, it's funny. We started here within two weeks of each other. We've both got Ivy League parchments and we both work hard, yet you're in a corner office with your own administrative assistant, and I'm still 'in the trenches.' "

"I don't know what to say, Adrian. Do you want me to apologize for my advancement?"

"Of course not, Jack, you worked hard for it. I just think you and the rest of the corner office folk might well remember that those of us 'in the trenches' are no less devoted to our careers or Coyle-Wexler than they are. I'll get my corner office one day, but I'm not in as big a hurry for it as you were, Jack. I met a wonderful man and fell in love. Then we had a baby, and I learned the true definition of love." Adrian spent a silent moment wistfully smiling. "My family is so important to me. I know it's blasphemy for me to say so here, but Dennis and Joseph mean more to me than my job. Even though my devotion to them might have slowed my advancement here, I wouldn't change a thing about my history here, Jack." She gave him a pointed look that Jack couldn't possibly misinterpret. "There's not one single thing I would want to do over differently."

A little stung, Jack said, "I wish I could say the same thing. I haven't felt as sure of myself as I usually do ever since I came back from the South Pacific."

"You've been a different man since Jaslyn Marchand came to town," Adrian grinned. "Don't think we haven't noticed."

"Who's 'we'?"

"Pretty much everyone from the parking garage attendants to Reginald Wexler. I think she's good for you, Jack."

"Define 'good,' " he said wryly.

"There are a lot of ladies around here who see green every time they see her. There's a broken heart in every other cubicle in the secretarial pool, now that you're off the market."

"Present company included?" his ego asked jokingly.

Adrian responded with a dry laugh. "Let's get one thing straight, DeVoy. Back in our day, I didn't expect us to fall head over ass in love and go flying up a rainbow. I've always respected you as a co-worker, and have always considered you something of a friend. At the very least, I knew that you were someone I could rely on when it came to business. You arrived at C-W determined to make a name and a career for yourself. I knew early on that nothing would get in the way of that. I don't mean to sound cruel, but I expected nothing from you, Jack."

"And that's exactly what I gave you, huh?"

"I didn't say that. I don't mean it that way. You're a good man. I've known that all along." She nodded toward the letters clutched in his hand. "I'm glad you're finally starting to realize it, too. For what it's worth, you're one of the few people around here I truly respect. That's as good as friendship, if you ask me."

"Then I'll take it, and gladly."

"I'm really happy with my life," Adrian said as she gathered the copies she'd made. "I hope you are, too."

"I am," he readily acknowledged. "More than I thought possible."

"Good." She patted his shoulder as they left the room. "Make sure you invite Mr. Wexler to the wedding. I think it would be good for him." With a playful wink, she turned down the corridor and disappeared around a corner.

Jack stood in front of the ridiculously massive desk Coyle-Wexler central supply had provided for Lina. With his feet wide apart and his hands on his hips, he looked as though he were digging in his heels for a take-no-prisoners face-off with the grizzled general of a rebel army.

Kiri was on guard outside Lina's office, so anyone passing by with the hope of peeping through the glass walls ended up being unceremoniously instructed to go about their business.

"I'm going to ask you one more time," Jack threatened inside the office. "Did you bring coconut-lime muffins back with you or not?"

Lina sat facing the door. Beyond Jack and the walls of her office, she spied Edison Burke, who carried an open folder as he slowly walked by. His eyes were on her office rather than the documents in his hand. Maintaining her serious expression, she glanced up at Jack, determined to put on a five-star performance for Burke. "Mr. DeVoy," she said briskly, "of the many duties I had to fulfill during my recent trek to Darwin, acquiring your favorite muffins remained at the bottom of my list of priorities. However, I did manage to procure one dozen muffins that I believe meet the specifications you designated during my two-hour phone call to you from Madrid."

"I can't help but wonder, Ms. Marchand, why you failed to mention said muffins yesterday, upon your return." He threw his hands up in mock frustration, purely for the benefit of the snoops passing the office. "Was it your intention to deliberately deprive me of the one souvenir I expressly requested?"

Lina slammed her palms on her desktop, shot to her feet, and with a fierce whip of her hair, she kept her voice low and seductive as she said, "Quite frankly, muffins were the last thing on my mind when I saw you in the airport yesterday." She looked past him, narrowing her eyes at Burke. His thin eyebrows rose in alarm, and he quickly scurried out of sight. Lina returned her silvery gaze to Jack. "If I'd known that you only loved me for my muffins, I might've just stayed in Darwin."

"The muffins don't have a damn thing to do with why I love—"

Shocked out of their little charade by his unwitting admission, Jack stumbled back a step. Lina's mouth worked but Jack's inadvertent confession left her too stunned to speak. Mercifully, before the sudden awkwardness between them became too uncomfortable, Kiri interrupted them via intercom.

"Mr. Coyle-Wexler Representative?" crackled Kiri's sarcastic voice. "Reginald Wexler wishes to see you in his office. Immediately."

"I'd better go." Jack backed toward the door. "It's . . . uh . . . I'm not sure what Mr. Wexler wants, but . . . we can talk more about what happened here . . . what I said . . . You know, never mind. Just forget—"

"Jack," Lina said quietly.

"That just slipped out," he hastily explained, his hand on the doorknob. "I don't . . . I didn't . . ." He exhaled sharply and slapped a hand over his face.

"Jack," she said a bit louder.

"Look." He tossed up a hand in supplication. "Let's just forget I said anything. This isn't the time and it's certainly not the place, so—"

"Jack!" Standing at her desk, Lina cut him off, her small fists propped at her waist, her eyes fixed on his. "I love you, too."

His fingers suddenly gone numb, Jack opened the door, walked through it, and closed it quietly behind him. *I almost made it,* he chuckled to himself as he started for Reginald's office.

Burke was already in Reginald's office. Jack assumed that he was fresh from his latest spy mission on Lina, and he discovered how right he was the moment he stepped up to Reginald's desk.

"This might seem very sordid, Jack, but you'll have to believe that I had a perfectly good reason for it." Leaning back in his chair, Reginald raised an arm and directed Jack's attention to an array of photographs displayed at the end of his desk.

Jack's mouth went dry and the tips of his ears burned as he stared at a series of glossy eight by ten photographs. The first depicted him and Lina on his deck, snuggling under a blanket, at sunset on Nahant. The second showed the two of them leaving his parents' house on Harrison's birthday and the third was a shot of them embracing at an arrival gate at Logan, crushing a huge bouquet of white roses between them.

"I have to say, the one with the roses is my favorite." A scowl deepened the creases in Reginald's forehead. "How long has this been going on?"

The muscles in Jack's jaw hardened. "Why don't you tell me, Reginald?"

The old man looked to Burke, who eagerly responded. "Well, as far as I can tell, your relationship with Ms. Marchand began quite soon after she first arrived in Boston. We were flagged once she checked out of the Harborfront Regency. It took about a week or so, but we tracked her to Nahant. Imagine our surprise,

Jackson, when we discovered that her forwarding address was *your* address."

Jack grabbed the shoulder of Burke's jacket and hauled him to his feet. "You sneaking, spying son-of-a—!"

"Jackson, calm down," Reginald said. "Burke was acting on my orders."

Jack's hands opened and Burke slithered back into his seat, scooting it well out of Jack's reach. "You had me under surveillance?" he fired at Reginald.

Reginald remained eerily calm. "I had Ms. Marchand under surveillance. I had no idea that would include you, so I think I deserve an explanation."

"Of course you do, sir," Burke tossed in with a snooty toss of his head. "Although I wonder if you can believe anything this man says, given his duplicity."

Jack screwed his face up in a look of utter disbelief. "Get the hell out of here, Burke, before I toss you out."

Burke almost tripped over the arm of his chair in his haste to get as far from Jack as possible. "You heard him, sir! He threatened me with bodily harm!"

Reginald impatiently rolled his eyes and reached for the Cuban-made humidor on his desk. "Get out, Burke, before I let Jackson toss you out."

His lower lip pursed in a petulant pout, Burke snapped shut his folder and skittered to the door. Jack half expected him to mutter "Well, I never!" before slamming the door behind him.

Reginald opened one of the sliding top drawers concealed in the cherry wood humidor and withdrew a cutting tool accented with 24K gold. He offered one of his precious Partagas Salomon cigars to Jack, who passed on it, before taking one himself. "I hate that kid, Jack, I really do," he said as he dragged the long cigar under his nose. "He's fussy, like a little girl."

"Perhaps you should let him go," Jack suggested with a sardonic lift of an eyebrow.

Reginald stuck the twisted end of the cigar into the cutter and guillotined it. "Burke is a necessary weasel. As much as I hate to admit it, his talents come in useful from time to time."

Jack crossed his arms over his chest and tipped his head toward the photographs. "That's not talent. That's desperation."

"I'm sorry about those, Jack. If I'd known that you were already on it, I never would have let Burke off his leash." He lit the cigar and took a series of long, deep draws on it. Plumes of smoke the same color as his hair formed a haze about his head. "You really should try one of these, Jack. They're Cuba's best."

Jack gritted his teeth and forced himself to be patient. If he'd heard Reginald's ode to the Cuban stogie once, he'd heard it a thousand times.

"A perfect draw, every time." Reginald stared lovingly at the cigar. "You know, I got this package for a steal." Passing a liver-spotted hand over the highly polished finish of the humidor, he said, "I got the box and two dozen cigars for four thousand dollars." He took another long draw on the cigar. "Sweet as vanilla, Jack."

Jack silently wondered how something that tasted like vanilla could smell like wet raccoon fur.

"You know, I had high hopes for you when you joined this firm." Reginald sat back in his leather chair and laced his fingers over his stomach. "I'm glad to see that you know how to find creative ways to solve difficult problems. You should have told me about your involvement with this woman."

"I won't apologize for my relationship with Lina, sir, because quite frankly, it's none of your business."

Reginald's white eyebrows met in confusion. "Who's Lina?"

"Ms. Marchand."

"Oh." He sat forward. "Well. Be that as it may, I have to confess that if I were thirty years younger, I'd have employed a similar strategy to get what I wanted." A lascivious snicker squeezed past Reginald's stogie. "Oh, yes. Millicent wants to go back to Darwin, and I think I might just go with her. She can get the tea and I'll get some T & A. Remember the photos of all those broads from the slide show Millie and I presented in January? I took those photos. Millie thought I was just doing research for the presentation."

Jack stared at his feet to hide a snarl of distaste. This was his first glimpse of the dirty old man wrapped in Reginald's five-thousand dollar suits.

"I'm looking forward to hearing the details," Reginald said. "Have your girl call mine and set up something, let's say lunch at the Union Oyster House."

"Details?" Jack looked up. "Of what?"

"About what you've gotten out of J.T. Marchand during your island interludes," Reginald laughed, greedily wringing his hands together. "Millie's convinced that no woman could ever resist your charms. And all this time, I thought your success was built on cold, efficient brain power, not beauty. Is Marchand any closer to signing over her precious tea?"

"We don't discuss business at home."

Reginald blinked in surprise. He tapped a finger against his desktop and grinned. " 'Home,' is it? You're going the extra mile to suck her in, aren't you? Women love that, Jack. You're good, boy."

"I'm not trying to put anything over on her," Jack said. "Either you'll get what you need through the tea trials or you won't. I'm not trying to trick her into signing with Coyle-Wexler."

Reginald's smile melted. "Am I to believe that you and that island woman are up in Nahant playing house for real? Jack, tell me you're joking."

Jack glanced at the Chippendale highboy housing Reginald's fifty-year old port and twelve-year old Scotch. His gaze wandered over the pair of John Singleton Copley originals hung on the walls before settling on the sprawling view of Boston Harbor behind Reginald. Jack looked everywhere but at the old man's eyes as he wondered why he'd ever wanted anything that Reginald had, why he'd wanted to someday be just like Reginald.

Elbows on his desk, Reginald leaned forward, still sucking on his cigar. "Give me a sneak preview of what she's like. I'll bet she's a wildcat between the sheets, isn't she?"

Jack stood up a bit straighter, pulled his shoulders back a little, and slightly lowered his chin. Whether

Reginald knew a fighting stance when he saw one didn't matter. It had the desired effect, and Reginald sat back in his chair. "I don't like this line of questioning, sir," Jack said.

"And I don't like your tone, son."

"My tone and I have work to do, so if there's nothing else . . ."

"You're a smart man, Jack. Surely you understand the ramifications of what you're doing with Ms. Marchand."

"What am I doing?" Jack picked up the photos and sorted through them one by one. "There's nothing incriminating here." He let the first photo flutter to the desktop. "I'm enjoying my view with a business associate." The second photo fell. "I took a business associate to my mother's for her Irish soda bread and a New England boiled dinner. And this," he sent the third photo flying toward Reginald on an air current, "this is an embrace, nothing more." He quickly turned from the old man before Reginald could see the lie etched on his face.

Reginald collected the photos and very neatly stacked them. "Now I know how your adversaries must feel once you start presenting your arguments, Jack." He spent a long moment thinking and smoking. "So in all the time the two of you have spent together, Ms. Marchand has given you no information we can use to advance our pursuit of Darwin's tea?"

"No," Jack snapped. "She hasn't."

Reginald studied the top photo, the one taken of Jack and Lina on the deck at dusk. "I didn't realize this was you, at first. You look so . . . human." He pulled his overpriced cigar from his mouth and ground out the burnt end in a heavy Baccarat crystal ashtray. "Let me ask you something, Jack. If Ms. Marchand *had* told you something we could use, would you tell me?"

"No," Jack decided right there on the spot. "I could never betray her."

Reginald's jaw slowly fell. "Are you—are you in love with this woman?"

Jack's eyes fell on the top photo. He and Lina had spent so many nights sitting on the deck, doing no more than talking as they watched the water. At first, he hadn't recognized himself any more than Reginald had. The man in that photo looked so relaxed and content. Jack's first thought upon seeing it was that Anderson, the happy, carefree DeVoy son, had somehow traded places with him.

Anderson had at least three girlfriends at any given time, but for Jack, there was only one woman. A barefoot island goddess whose silence had seduced him, whose wrath had built a shaky bridge between him and his family . . . and whose "I love you" made him happier than he'd ever thought possible.

"Yes," he finally answered, thinking back on Adrian's words. "I'm head over ass in love with her."

"Well," Reginald sighed heavily. "I guess that changes things. . . ."

CHAPTER 15

Lina stood before the full-length mirrors lining one wall of the master bathroom. Dressed all in white, she wore loose-fitting pants with a drawstring waist and a sheer mohair sweater over a cotton camisole. The furry sweater delineated her upper body against the stark white surroundings of the bathroom as she gathered her hair in one hand and twisted it into a loose knot at the back of her head.

It had taken an hour for her to achieve the look of casual comfort, but it still felt wrong. *White's too virginal,* she decided, peering at her reflection more studiously. *That's a bit incongruous with the subject I plan to address with Jack tonight.*

She had to tell him as soon as he returned from Coyle-Wexler. Her visit to her OB/GYN two weeks ago on Darwin had confirmed the result she'd gotten in Spain. She was at eight weeks now, and it was time that Jack knew. "I should have just blurted it out when he told me about Beth," she said aloud, moving into the bedroom. "Jack, dearest, you and Harry have much more in common than you realize. You're both going to become fathers and uncles at nearly the same time," she practiced.

Her knees weakened and she sat heavily on the foot of the bed. Cold, sticky sweat coated her palms while howler monkeys chased their tails in her belly. Very little frightened her, but the thought of telling Jack about the baby . . .

She forgot about changing clothes. She scampered over the bed to the nightstand and picked up the phone. It became a lifeline as she picked up the receiver and dialed the digits that would connect her to Levora, whose cheerful voice did much to calm her nerves.

"Hey, Mama," Levora greeted. "I was just sitting down to a cup of Kona. Did the muffins keep for Jack?"

"He'll have them tonight," Lina said, to herself adding, *if he still has an appetite after what I have to tell him.*

"How are you feeling, kiddo? Still fighting back the tummy trouble?"

"I'm scared. I'm really scared."

"That's natural with your first," Levora soothed. "You were so young the first time I was pregnant, so you probably don't really remember what a basket case I was. I was terrified at the thought of being responsible for such a tiny, helpless person."

Her knees drawn up to her chest, Lina huddled in a nest of pillows at the head of Jack's side of the bed. "That's not what scares me. That's actually the part I'm looking forward to. I was ten when Louise was born, and I can recall the first time you let me hold her. She was the littlest thing, and I remember how sweet her breath smelled, and the softness of the skin of her bum." She slid a hand over her abdomen. She had no tangible proof of the life tucked in there, but she felt its presence as strongly as she felt the beat of her own heart. "I want this baby more than I ever imagined I could. I'm not afraid of becoming a mother."

"So why're you calling me in the middle of my coffee break instead of putting a nice hot casserole on the table for Jack's dinner?" Levora teased.

"He's why I'm scared."

Levora sobered. "Handled the news badly, did he?"

"He doesn't know yet. I'm telling him tonight and I'm afraid of how he might react."

"Maybe you should wait a few more weeks before you say anything to anyone, kiddo. It's still really early yet, and you never know what could—"

"He loves me, Levora."

"Oh, sweetie . . ."

"It slipped out this afternoon. We were at Coyle-Wexler, performing our sworn enemy routine, and he said it. Mostly. I love him, too, and I told him. I have to tell him that we're having a baby."

A dull thud stole Lina's attention. Her head spun toward the doorway, and she saw Jack, the blood draining from his face, his hands lax at his sides, and his briefcase fallen dead at his feet.

Lina's voice rasped through the dryness of her throat. "Levora? I have to call you back . . ."

Once he was capable of movement, Jack threw up his hands and stepped over his briefcase. "Can this day get any worse?" He stared through the ceiling as if it were God's basement, still ranting. "That wasn't a challenge, because obviously, You've outdone Yourself so far."

Lina hung up the phone. "Who are you talking to?" she asked, pleased that she sounded completely normal for a woman who had just inadvertently changed a man's life, completely and forever. "Would you like some water? I think I need water."

She started for the bathroom, which had a tiny fridge built into the lower section of the linen closet. She grabbed a bottle of water, and the cold neck of the cobalt glass bottle gave her something to cling to as Jack dogged her steps.

"You're pregnant?" he nearly shouted.

"Yes. Almost nine weeks now."

"You're having a baby," he stated uncertainly.

"Well, unless 'pregnant' means something different here than in other English speaking parts of the world, then—"

"This is unbelievable!" Jack cried over her. He followed her back into the bedroom, and then began wearing out a patch of carpeting near the windowed wall.

Sitting on the foot of the bed, Lina elegantly crossed one leg over the other. Her heart pounded so hard and fast, the fine hairs of her sweater seemed to vibrate. "And why's that?"

"You aren't . . . you didn't . . ." He tore off his jacket and threw it over the back of the office chair. "You run around half naked on that damned rock of yours, just waiting to seduce some unsuspecting tourist, knowing full well that something like this could happen! Why didn't you do anything to prevent it?"

Lina's apprehension drained away and anger flooded into its place. It seemed to enter her bloodstream, loosening the muscles of her neck and shoulders and adding amplitude to her voice. "I didn't force you into anything, Jack. And if I'm not mistaken, contraceptive devices exist for men as well as for women, in Darwin *and* in Nahant! As I recall, we went through the complimentary condoms at your homestay as though they were snack mints, so it's not as if we'd completely lost our heads." She vaulted to her feet and gave him a good hard poke in the chest. "Before you, Jack, I hadn't been with anyone for more than two years, and I couldn't be with anyone else once you left. I wasn't taking or wearing anything to prevent pregnancy because I wasn't doing anything that could knock me up!

"This baby wasn't planned, but neither did I plan on falling headfirst in love with you." Her bottled water tipped over onto the bed when she got up and marched to the closet. Jack darted forward to grab the bottle, to stop its contents from saturating his custom-made mattress. "I wanted to tell you my own way, and I'm sorry you overheard it like that," she said, opening the closet. She dragged out her garment bag and unzipped the top of it. "I understand this is a shock to you, given the determination you've shown in keeping yourself alienated from everyone other than your financial advisor."

"What are you talking about?" he grumbled. "And what are you *doing?*" he demanded when she began snatching her blouses, pants and jackets from their hangers and shoving them haphazardly into the garment bag.

"This is a shock to me, too, Jack." Her voice cracked, and she abruptly turned to throw open a dresser drawer. "But I couldn't be happier!" Quiet tears dropped onto the armful of silky, lacy undergarments she scooped up and forced into the garment bag. She struck the tears away before she faced Jack again. "I'm not asking you for anything. My baby and I will have everything we need on Darwin." She moved to his nightstand and picked up the phone.

"Calm down so we can discuss this like two responsible adults." He grabbed handfuls of her underwear and put them back into their recently abandoned drawer. "Of course," he muttered under his breath, "if we'd been responsible in the first place, we wouldn't be in this mess."

"I heard that," she called over to him. "Yes," she said into the phone after the party she had dialed picked up. "This is Jaslyn Thérèse Marchand and I need my driver as soon as possible . . . Yes. Thank you." She hung up and went to her bag, shunting Jack aside with her shoulder so she could force the zipper closed. "I'm going back to the hotel. I think we need to spend some time apart." Clasping the retractable handle of her garment bag, she began dragging it to the staircase.

Jack hurried ahead of her, to carry the heavy bag down the stairs before she attempted to do it herself. "You can't go now."

"Is that so? Well, you didn't waste any time getting my bag down the stairs, did you?" She took it from him and parked it by the front door.

"You shouldn't be lugging luggage in your condition."

"I'm perfectly healthy and capable of doing whatever I like," she insisted stubbornly.

"Don't go, Lina," Jack said wearily.

"Why not?"

"Because you're pregnant." He vigorously unknotted his tie as he paced the living room.

"Is that the only reason I should stay?"

"Yes! We need to talk about this, consider our options."

Still pacing, he failed to notice the heartbreak reshaping Lina's features. She took her coat from the closet in the entry hall. "I have one option, and I'm taking it. I'll stay in Boston for what's left of the tea trials, and then I'm going back to Darwin. I can give my child a home there, a real home."

"Have you forgotten that I have a say in this, too?" Jack's frustration erupted. "I can't just pick up and go to the other side of the world. I've built a life here and I won't just leave it! It's not fair for you to expect me to."

"I don't," she said very precisely. "I know how much your life here means to you."

"You are the most self-righteous, supercilious person I've ever met!"

"We've more than *met*, Mr. DeVoy! Go twist your body in knots or check the totals in your stock portfolio or whatever it is you do when I'm not around. Let me leave in peace."

"He's my baby, too, Lina. I think I deserve more than 'I'm pregnant, I'm leaving.' "

She threw up her hands. "You're right. How unkind of me. Okay, Jack, I'm all ears. Tell me, how should we proceed? What do we do now?"

"Have you seen a doctor? Are you even sure you're pregnant?"

"I took eight over-the-counter tests in Spain and my physician confirmed those results two weeks ago. That's why I went back to Darwin after Madrid. I wanted to see my own physician."

Jack lightly pounded a fist into his palm. "Lina, we used condoms. We were careful."

"Obviously not careful enough. Particularly the night of the beach party."

"Bullseye," Jack recalled with a defeated chuckle. "I thought I got out in time."

"Funny you should phrase it like that." Lina cracked a weak smile. Biology, timing and carelessness aside, that night with Jack had been so powerful, so all consuming, as if their souls had mated along with their bodies. She shook herself out of her glassy-eyed recollection of that moment to see Jack looking at her with such tenderness, she knew that he had been thinking of it, too. "On Darwin, the night we met . . . did you mean any of the things you said to me?"

He heard the tremble in her voice, and he would have gone to her if his feet had not been rooted to the carpet. "Yes. Even more now than then."

"Baby or not, I was planning to return to Darwin soon, Jack. I'm tired and I want to go home."

"But Lina, this is . . ." He wanted to tell her that this was her home too, but in all honesty, he couldn't. She couldn't leave Darwin any more than the moon could leave night.

"I can't leave New England right now," he said, more to convince himself than her. "There are too many loose ends at Coyle-Wexler. Reginald called me into his office today because he wanted to show me photos of us. He had Burke hire someone to watch you, to try to get a leg up on securing the rights to the tea."

"No business," she said softly.

"Make an exception for this."

"You're his attorney, Jack. You're violating confidentiality by revealing any of his business tactics to me. Anyway, if Wexler's going to watch anyone, it should be Edison Burke. He and Carol Crowley were stitched at the hip on Darwin. She works for one of your competitors, doesn't she?"

"She and Burke are a couple?" Jack wrinkled his nose. "I didn't think Burke liked blondes. Blonde women, that is."

"She was deported along with him. She was the woman with him in the boys' loo at The Crab and Nickel. I, for one, will never eat there again. I might even have the place razed and the earth sown with salt."

Jack thoughtfully stroked his chin. "Interesting. I think that information will be extremely useful to Mr. Wexler."

"I'm sure Mr. Wexler would be even more pleased to know that at a time like this, his interests are the ones you have at heart."

"Don't be ridiculous."

"You know, I'd prefer it if I were competing against a string of beautiful women. It's rather humbling to know that I've lost you to a creepy old man."

They stood a few feet apart, looking at each other. Jack refused to drop his gaze. He deserved the disappointment shaping Lina's lovely face, and he wouldn't shy away from it.

No longer able to stomach the shock hardening Jack's face, Lina broke away first, thankful for the ringing of the doorbell. She slipped on her heavy black coat and turned up the high collar to face the cold, dark night, and then opened the door for the driver. She directed him to her bag.

Jack moved forward and took her arm, gently pulling her out of earshot of the driver. He stroked her arms, wishing he could feel her warmth through the tight weave of her wool coat. Her lithe body, which normally melted against him, stayed rigid, even when he bowed his head and touched his forehead to hers. "He knows I love you," Jack murmured.

"He who?"

"The creepy old man. Reginald asked me if I loved you today, after he saw those pictures. I told him yes."

Jack imagined that he felt her shiver. Her lips parted, her breathing became a bit heavier. He might have lowered his mouth to hers if she had not drawn away from him and backed toward the door. "There really is hope for you yet, counselor," she said somberly before turning and hurrying out to the waiting car.

Jack lay on the gray rubber yoga mat, in the aptly named Savasana, or corpse position. It was the position Jack began every yoga routine in, but this morning he couldn't force himself out of it. He'd spent his first night without Lina since her arrival in Boston, and it had been long. Time had taken on a gooey quality, the minutes sticking together rather than separating into orderly clicks marking the passage of the seconds separating him from Lina. After fidgeting on his sheets all night, he'd been glad to see the first glimmer of dawn, because it meant that he'd gotten through the night without her to face a new day, to start over with a fresh slate. He'd lumbered downstairs, rolled out his yoga mat, and struck the Savasana.

And he hadn't been able to move out of it. He lay on his back, his feet and knees slightly apart, his arms out and palms up. He tried to focus on centering his breathing and relaxing his body, but all he could think of was Lina and how she had looked at him when she'd said her goodbyes. There was nothing fresh or new to look forward to, now that the sun was rising. There was only the solid weight of loss and the refreshed memory of what had happened the night before.

He'd witnessed the death of whatever respect Lina had for him, followed by the birth of renewed disappointment.

Maybe that was why he couldn't relax enough to move past Savasana.

The sun's light was breaking into glittering shards upon the ocean when Jack managed to lift himself from the floor, roll his mat back up, and shuffle back upstairs.

He crawled into bed, his back to his million-dollar ocean view, and tugged the duvet up to his chin. *This shouldn't be so hard,* he told himself. *She's only in Boston.*

Boston was close, but Lina still too far away. More than miles separated them this time, and he felt farther from her than he had when he was the one who'd left. Jack flung off the covers and scooted out of bed, a surge of indignation spurring him into starting his day.

"It's not my fault she left," he resolutely stated to the empty room. "She shouldn't have sprung it on me . . ." But on the heels of that came a niggling truth: the news wouldn't have been sprung if he hadn't been trying to sneak up on her, to surprise her.

He sank heavily to the edge of his bed, catching his face in his hands. He missed her so much he ached with it, and the saddest part of it all was that she wasn't even gone, not really. What would he do once she, and their baby, actually returned to Darwin?

The thought gave Jack a stomachache that nearly sent him back under the covers. For only the second time in his career, Jack took a sick day, and once again it was because of Lina.

"I see you managed to find reasonable housing," Jack said, greeting Lina at the door to the penthouse suite of the Harborfront Regency.

"There was an actor here when I checked in last night, but apparently a guest on Coyle-Wexler's tab trumps an actor who received the suite compliments of the hotel." Lina stepped aside, allowing Jack to enter. Her eyes raked over him, noting his blue jeans and plain dark T-shirt.

"Do you know who the actor was?"

"I believe the hotel manager said it was Zander Baron. I'm told he's quite popular."

"I'll say," Jack agreed. "Anderson loves Zander Baron movies."

"I've never seen one," Lina said.

"He's got one playing now," Jack told her. "It's probably just a lot of car chases, gunplay and sex with one sexy broad after another, but I could take you to see it, if you're interested."

Lina threw an amused smile over her shoulder as she led Jack into the bedroom instead of the office. A colorful assortment of thick folders, foreign newspapers and magazines and travel documents littered half the bed. The covers were rumpled on the other half, and judging by her light white cotton pants and camisole, Jack suspected that she had only just rolled out of bed. The luggage under her eyes matched his, which led him to believe that she'd done little sleeping in the big bed.

"Have a seat, if you'd like," Lina offered with a tip of her head toward the sitting area of the room. She scurried around the bed, clearing away her papers but not before Jack caught a glimpse of the front pages of *La Repubblica*, which Jack knew to be an Italian newspaper, and *El Universo*, which Jack assumed came from a Spanish-speaking country that he couldn't guess. He wondered if she had plans to go away again soon, and the question was on his lips when Lina, slipping out of her camisole, rushed to him and planted her lips upon his.

"I knew you'd come," she murmured against them as she threaded her fingers in his hair. "I waited for you all night. I can't believe it took you so long!"

His arms flattening her chest against his, he sank onto the nearest surface with her, which turned out to be the compact loveseat. The hard cushions with their stiff damask covering had little give, and Jack's long body settled onto it uncomfortably as Lina wrapped herself around him, inviting him to fill his hands with her.

Her happiness at his arrival translated into eager desire. Refusing to break their kisses to watch what she was doing with her hands, she blindly worked at the button-fly of his jeans. She reminded herself to debate later which made her happier—that he had come to her, or that he had actually taken a day off work to do it.

He wants me, she told herself. She gritted her teeth, savoring Jack's touch upon her most sensitive places. *He wants* us.

Jack's entire body ached from the effort it took to stop himself from pitching her upon the bed and diving into her. Lina rewarded his restraint after freeing him and straddled him there on the loveseat, but even when she lay temporarily sated atop him afterward, Jack wanted more of her.

"I came over here to talk, and look at us," he chuckled.

"We talked." Lina nuzzled his neck with her nose. "We just didn't use words."

Jack stroked her hair, neatly arranging it over her bare back. "You have an alarming effect on me, Ms. Marchand."

"Good."

"I spent most of the night tossing and turning and thinking about everything."

Lina involuntarily stiffened. So far, Jack hadn't said anything stupid, but his tone set warning bells ringing between her ears.

"This whole thing between us is still so new, and it came about so suddenly," Jack went on.

She sat up, her shift in position giving him a lovely view of her. "What are you trying to say, Jack?"

The fear glittering in her pale eyes softened the hard delivery of her question, and shamed Jack into staring at her collarbones rather than her face when he spoke again.

"We both have complicated careers on top of everything else, and it's going to be hard enough to balance a relationship involving just the two of us," he continued, articulating his nascent thoughts about the pregnancy. "I meant what I said at the office yesterday. It wouldn't have slipped out if it weren't true. You and I need time to build on what we already have, and I'm not so sure about the wisdom of bringing a new life into it this soon. Maybe we should consider other options . . . *all* of our options . . . while we still have time."

He raised his gaze to Lina's face to see that she understood him perfectly. And her response to his suggestion was written just as clearly. Her mouth softened, her eyes glistened. A tiny muscle pulsed at the base of her jaw. She slightly bowed her head, and a lock of her hair fell to cloak half her face in shadow. She had the simple beauty of a somber Madonna, and Jack suddenly wished for a third leg with which to kick himself. Lina had told him that she loved him, and she hadn't done it for any reason other than because it was the truth.

He studied her face, and picked out the faint scar left over from her daring rescue on Darwin. Jack wanted to kick himself once more. Lina had jumped into a killing sea to save someone else's child. She would never, under any circumstance, dispose of her own. *Of* our *own,* Jack mentally corrected himself.

"I'm sorry." He sat up and held her tight, peppering her with kisses and wishing that he could take back what he'd said. "We can do this. We can manage it."

Lina gently pulled away from him. She retrieved her pants and camisole from the carpet and quickly slipped into them. After grabbing a brush from the massive dresser, Lina returned to the loveseat and handed the brush to Jack. She sat in the gap between his legs, using one of his thighs for an armrest. "You might as well make yourself useful while you try to talk me into considering *our* options," she said icily.

"Forget I said all that." Jack sat up a little straighter, using the armrest for back support. Never in his life had he brushed a woman's hair, but he set about the task because it gave him another excuse to touch Lina.

"Oh right," Lina muttered bitterly. "Instead of exercising our options, you've decided that we can 'manage' this baby. How do you propose we go about that?"

"I don't understand why you're being so hostile."

"You want to discuss this as though it's merely another legal matter for you to win at."

"I don't mean to." Jack paused to collect a lock of hair that had strayed to fall alongside her face. The light from the tall, wide windows caught in her hair, making it crackle with bluish highlights. "This has never happened to me before, so you'll have to forgive me for not knowing the precise way to react."

Lina refused to let him off the hook. "How do you propose we go about managing this baby?"

"Well, first of all, you'd have to move here."

"Here." The word fell from her mouth with a dull thud. "To Boston."

"Boston has some of the best doctors and medical facilities in the world."

"As opposed to the tribal witch doctors who patched me up on Darwin," she snapped.

"That's not what I meant."

"But it's what you think."

Exasperated, Jack began brushing a little harder. "Darwin is a great place, but—"

"Then why don't you move?"

"—it's—what?"

"Move to Darwin." She half turned. "Come home with me when the tea trials are complete." The movement of Jack's hand and the brush through her hair vanquished Lina's frustrated anger, but reluctant acceptance of where she stood with him moved in to replace it when it took him a long time to respond.

"I can't," he said at last.

Lina bit her lip, pained by the way he'd rejected her plea with no thought at all.

Jack set the brush on a cloisonné end table before reaching around Lina to take her hands. "Even after the tea trials are done we'll still have to evaluate how to proceed with the product. Reginald has two more acquisitions lined up for me, and—"

"You don't have to feed me excuses," she said over him. "You certainly don't have to hide behind them."

"They're not excuses, Lina, they're reasons."

"Little difference."

"They're still legitimate."

"Unlike our child."

"Oh, come on, Lina." He hugged her to his chest, fitting her head into the crook of his neck and shoulder. "That's not fair. It wouldn't do you, me or the baby any good to rush into marriage just because we accidentally made a baby."

"I haven't asked for a proposal. I've asked no more of you than you've asked of me. Why should I be the one to move here? Why can't you move, or is your work that much more important than your child?"

"My work is what will have to support him," Jack argued. "I won't have my son grow up the way I did, wearing brand new secondhand clothes and eating no-name canned goods."

With a grunt of annoyance, Lina threw off Jack's arms and got to her feet. "You were clothed! You were fed! You had two parents and you were loved. That's what's important, you fool. Those are the only things you truly needed!"

"My child will know that I love him!" Matching her for volume, Jack stood to face her.

"Measured purely by the amount of money you spend," Lina charged.

"Don't start with me about money, Lina."

"Don't use that tone with me, Jack."

He stopped short of wagging a finger in her face when he said, "Your self-righteous—"

"Not self-righteous," Lina blurted, propping her fists on her hips, "just *right*."

"Damn it, Lina!"

"Damn *you*, Jack, for being so blind!"

Jack stepped away from her, stopping only when he'd reached the windows on the far side of the room. He took a few deep, yoga breaths before continuing. "I didn't come her to fight with you."

Her arms crossed over her chest, Lina glowered at him. "Nor to fight for me, it appears."

"I fight for you every day!" Jack whirled on her. "When people whisper about us in the corridors at C-W, or when my perverted colleagues share their sick fantasies at parties and when homeboys talk smack about you being with me. I fight! You don't know what it's like here for a couple like us."

"If it's so bad, why would you want our child to be raised here?"

Jack inwardly chastised himself for forgetting that she was a lawyer, and she could call upon reason to trump passion even when the arguments were personal. Well, he was an attorney too, and reminded her of it by saying, "Can you honestly tell me that there's no bigotry on Darwin?"

She dropped her head and slowly walked to the windows. Darwin was paradise, but it wasn't perfect. Errol Solomon's family hadn't wanted him to marry Levora. Not because she was African American, but because she was American. And in reviewing her own behavior, Lina had to acknowledge that she, like many of the islanders, had eyed Jack with suspicion because he was a foreigner. Suspicion wasn't the same thing as bigotry, but the former had a way of leading to the latter.

Everything about his relationship with Lina had led Jack to do things he ordinarily didn't, and shouting was one of them. He maintained a normal tone when he said, "If the baby is born and raised here, we can give him the very best start in life."

"On Darwin, we can better insulate him from people who'll hate him just because of the color of his skin," she countered.

"Hate is everywhere, Lina."

"Not here." She placed a hand over her heart. "Or here." She took his hand and pressed it to her abdomen.

Jack drew her in for a long, hard embrace.

"I want to be with you," she said. "But I can't move here. I can't *live* here."

"Is it really that bad?" Jack spoke into her hair, deliberately ignoring the fact that after three days on Darwin he hadn't wanted to return to Boston. "You've been here for so long already. You couldn't get used to it somehow?"

"It's so loud and busy. People don't look at you when you pass them on the street unless it's to snarl at you to stop looking at them, or to tell you to get out of their way. It's cold—"

"It's winter. It'll warm up."

"It's too crowded."

"You could stay on Nahant. You don't have to go into Boston."

She cupped his face and held it, her eyes boring into his. "Nahant is your island. Not mine. It isn't home."

"It could be," he smiled weakly.

Returning his smile, she slowly shook her head.

Jack tightened his arms around her, unable to hold her close enough. "What are we going to do?"

"We're going to have a baby," she answered. "I'm going back to Darwin, and you're going to stay on Nahant."

"So we're back where we started."

"Yes," she whispered. "Right back at our finish."

CHAPTER 16

Harrison and Anderson DeVoy's heavy work boots left dark smudges on the mirror-finished surface of the white marble stairs as Jack led them up to the master bedroom. "Nice digs, bro," Harrison remarked as he openly stared around the place. "How long have you been out here? Four years?"

"Five," Anderson offered helpfully before he left his brothers to settle in the bedroom with the remote to Jack's television.

Jack ushered Harrison into the bathroom, and he winced when Harrison dropped his heavy toolbox on the marble floor. The pale champagne tiles had been imported from Italy, and the only reason Jack had wanted them was because the interior decorator had said they were cut from the most expensive marble in the world.

Pushing the ostentatious floor tiles from his mind, Jack said, "I'm sorry I never had you out before now."

Harrison shrugged a big shoulder. "It's okay. You get busy, time flies. It's like that with family." He kneeled to get a closer look at a big hole in the wall near the door. "What the hell did you do here, hit it with a hammer?"

Jack sat on the edge of the wide bathtub. He and his brother both wore old jeans and flannel shirts—Jack's from Ralph Lauren, Harrison's from Wal-Mart—and for the first time in a long time, they actually looked like brothers. "I'm glad you brought Anderson along. He hasn't been out here in ages."

"The kid keeps busy." Harrison unclipped the tape measure from his tool belt. "He came to my house to watch the Bruins cream Pittsburgh last night. Ma and Pop stopped over, too. Baby, baby, baby, that's all Ma and Beth can talk about these days."

Jack studied his thumbnail. He'd last seen his family on the night of Harrison's birthday, six weeks ago. Lina had occupied a few weeks of that time, but her abrupt departure had left him stuffing his days with work.

"You know, you guys could come out here for a change some Saturday night," Jack offered. "My satellite dish gets at least a hundred sports channels."

Harrison uttered a noncommittal grunt. "It wouldn't be the same."

"No, I guess not."

Harrison pulled a coil of repair mesh from his toolbox, along with a small tub of drywall compound. "You could come down to the city and join us, you know. If you're waitin' around for a hand-lettered invitation engraved in gold, that's the closest you're gonna get."

"Look, Harry, I owe you an apology," Jack started. "For a lot of things."

Harry smiled as he stirred water into the white powder in the little plastic tub. "Like missing me and Beth's wedding because that law professor invited you to his house on the Cape? And the time you blanked on Ma and Pop's thirty-fifth anniversary party because it was

the same night as Reginald Wexler's customer appreciation day?"

"C-W's clients spend millions on our products. If I
have to put on a penguin suit once a year and slap them
on the back for doing business with us, then I do it."

"And that's more important than Ma and Pop?"

"No. Of course not. But if I want to get ahead, sometimes I have to do things I'd rather not do."

Harrison shook his head regretfully. "Reggie Wexler
says jump, Jackie boy says, 'Is over the moon high
enough?' "

"I'm not proud of the way I've behaved. Especially
recently."

"If you want to confess your sins, Jackie, you
should've called a priest over to patch this wall, not me."

"I called you because I need to talk to you."

Harrison laughed. It was a full, throaty sound, just
like their father's, and Jack's pangs of guilt grew sharper.

"Remember the woman I brought to your birthday
party?"

"Is that a trick question?" Harrison grinned, dropping
to one knee to use a utility knife to tidy the ragged edge of
the hole. "She's not exactly the type you forget. Where is
she, anyway? Mom said you guys were out here 'rooming'
together. That's her nice way of sayin' shackin' up.'"

"Lina moved back to the Harborfront Regency a
while ago." *Nineteen days ago, to be exact,* Jack calculated
in his head.

Harrison sat back on his heels and faced Jack. "You
guys have a fight?"

Jack leaned over and rooted through Harrison's toolbox for a putty knife. "We're having a baby." He handed the tool over to Harrison. "That led to a fight."

"No, sir!" Harrison said, giving it his Southie best so that it contracted into "Nosuh," the ultimate expression of disbelief in Eastern Massachusetts.

"She's due about the same time as Beth, in late September."

Harrison worked steadily on patching the hole, but Jack knew that he was listening as well.

"There's still a quality of unreality to the whole thing, even though I've had a couple weeks to get used to the idea. I plan everything, Harry. When I get up in the morning, when I fall asleep at night, when I work out, what I eat . . . I leave nothing to chance. But this baby came out of nowhere."

"You sound like a frickin' kid." Harrison scraped the excess compound from the patch and tossed his putty knife into one of the twin marble basins. It landed with a worrying clink that Jack forced himself to overlook. " 'I didn't plan it,' " Harrison mimicked in a high-pitched whine. "You didn't have a single condom in your night-stand when you decided to play Who's Got the Sock Monkey with that girl?"

"If you really must know, I keep them in the medicine cabinet." Jack did a double take. " 'Who's Got the Sock Monkey?' Is that what you and Beth call it?"

Harrison coughed to cover a blush. "Never you mind about me and Beth. The point is, you had rubbers, you didn't use 'em, and now your Caribbean Queen's walkin' around with a Jackie Jr. cookin' behind her bellybutton."

"She's from the South Pacific, and she gets part of the blame, too."

"Do you think she did it on purpose?"

"No. God, no. I might not have found out about it if I hadn't walked in on her phone conversation. She was telling someone else." Jack was still stung by the fact that Lina would tell someone else before mentioning her pregnancy to him.

"So she told you because she had to, you flipped out—"

"Not because of her," Jack interrupted. "Well, not only because of her. I had a bad day at work."

"—and she left," Harrison finished.

A familiar spike of regret pierced Jack's heart, inflaming the wound caused by her departure.

"Have you talked to her?"

"We talk every day. She's in Montreal this week, and last night we were on the phone until about two this morning."

"Have you seen her?"

Jack stood and stretched while Harrison cleaned his tools in the basin. "All the time. She's still at Coyle-Wexler, and we had lunch a couple days ago. It almost got out of hand."

"They get a little whacko over the littlest things," Harrison said knowingly. "It's the hormones or something. How out of hand was it?"

Jack thought back on his ill-fated luncheon with Lina, which had taken place at the rooftop restaurant at the Harborfront Regency. Over New England crab cakes with roasted corn, what had started as innocent conversation about Coyle-Wexler's progress with the tea trials had become sizzling banter that led to the hasty decision to take advantage of the fresh queen-sized bed in Lina's penthouse. The moment the elevator doors had closed them in, Jack, unable to stop himself, had taken Lina in his arms and assaulted her with kisses. She had returned his ardor, driving him half out of his head with desire simply by tracing the rim of his ear with the tip of her tongue. He'd hoisted her onto the gold rail affixed to the back wall of the car and would have taken her right there had the elevator not stopped and opened to a fleet of wide-mouthed housekeepers staring at his bare rump. The heat of Jack's embarrassment had managed to cool his burners, and with an uncomfortable smile he'd hiked up his trousers and followed Lina into the penthouse. Where she'd promptly collapsed into a fit of laughter that left her crying and wheezing.

The mood broken, common sense prevailed, and Lina and Jack had spent the rest of the day talking, but not touching.

Jack almost smiled. "Is it my imagination, or does pregnancy make a woman even sexier?"

"Only if you love her." Dawning comprehension spread across Harrison's face and he froze in the middle of using an Egyptian cotton hand towel to dry off his putty knife. "If you're in love with her, Jackie, why don't you two just get hitched?"

"She won't ever leave Darwin Island. I can't leave Coyle-Wexler."

"You're a real idiot, Jackie," Anderson butted in, entering the room and joining the discussion in the middle. "Lina's the perfect girl for you."

"I thought you were watching television," Jack grumbled.

"Yeah, well what's goin' on in here is way more interesting." Anderson helped himself to a palmful of Jack's aftershave, a skin-conditioning astringent imported from Japan. "Besides, with a hundred and two sports channels to choose from, I couldn't decide what I wanted to watch."

"What makes you think that Lina is so perfect for me?" Jack asked his baby brother.

"The fact that she's not like any other chick you've ever been with." Anderson leaned against the wall, crossing one ankle over the other. "Most guys lift weights on their lunch hour or run to work out, but you twist around like a frickin' Auntie Anne's original during the ass-crack of dawn. Most guys pop open a Bud after work, but you uncork some fancy green beer from some country with a name I can't pronounce. You don't dig the regular, Jackie, you never have. Why should it be different when it comes to fallin' in love? Ordinary's never been good enough for you; you hardly even notice it. Lina ain't ordinary. Not by a long shot."

Jack stared at his baby brother, wondering when the kid had done so much growing up. He realized that there was work yet to be done when Anderson pushed away from the wall and said, "Say, you got any chips and salsa downstairs? I sure could go for some nachos right now."

Anderson left to raid the pantry while Harrison packed up his tools and snapped the lid back on the dry-wall compound. "I gotta agree with Andy, but you still got yourself a real pickle of a problem, Jack," Harrison said.

"You're thirty years old and you sound like an old man," Jack complained before he realized that he was hearing his father's words through his brother's mouth. "The tea trials at Coyle-Wexler will be over soon, and one way or the other Lina will be leaving. She's been hopping all over the globe since she got here, and it kills me to think that one of these days she'll leave and she won't hop back."

"Then you're just gonna have to let her go."

All the air seemed to rush out of Jack's lungs.

"Or," Harrison said, picking up his toolbox, "you're gonna have to do some hoppin' yourself."

"Have Mom and Dad said anything about Lina?"

Harrison grinned. "They both keep saying, 'Just imagine what their babies will look like.' Dad says it like he's expecting something from a Stephen King movie, and Mom says it like she's going to have a pack of little Halle Berrys running around the house. Mom really likes Lina. She's more worried about whether Lina can cook a good corned beef than anything else."

"I haven't told them about the baby, and I'd appreciate it if you wouldn't either," Jack said.

"It's your news to tell, Jackie. But you gotta let me be there when you do. I haven't seen Dad's head spin since the time Andy got drunk with his buddies and they shaved his head."

While Harrison made predictions regarding his father's reaction to Jack's baby news, Jack himself spent a long moment contemplating his own thoughts on a totally unrelated matter. When he finally spoke, he gave Harrison pause. "Remember that Thanksgiving Football Classic my senior year, when we played Mattapan?"

"I remember the brawl after the game better than I remember anything that happened on the field," Harrison said. "You got a shiner so bad you ended up with two stitches above your eye."

"What started that fight?"

Harrison shrugged a heavy shoulder. "Bunch of stupid kids acting stupid because we got beat by some black kids from Mattapan."

"I see Shariq Hillen from time to time."

"Mattapan's quarterback? No foolin'?"

"He's an attorney with Dunton, Howse, Thompson & Auffrey, in Boston. He's probably one of the best defense attorneys in the state."

"Wow." Harrison used the broken nail of his left thumb to scrape putty from the cuticle of his right thumb. "I guess Hillen's doing good for himself."

"Every time I see him, I think about that game we lost to his team, and the names I called him afterward. He's always very polite, very gracious toward me, but in the back of my mind, I know he still sees me as that ignorant Southie prick who called him just about the worst thing you can call a black person."

"We were all ignorant pricks back then, Jackie," Harrison tried to console him. "We were dumb kids."

"Yeah, with a bunch of ignorant parents in the background egging us on. Every time I see Shariq, I want to apologize, but then on the other hand I feel like I should just let well enough alone."

"Being with Lina's really made you reexamine your whole life, huh, bro?"

"She's not like anyone I've ever dated before. Not by a long shot."

Harrison caught a laugh at the back of his throat. "All your babes have been beauties, Jack. You never settled for less than the cover girls."

"I've never dated a black woman before. When I first started at Coyle-Wexler, I had a little bit of a flirtation going on with Adrian Allen, another attorney, but it never led to anything. We were both new and I was definitely more interested in building my career than building a relationship. She's married and she's got a kid. She seems so happy. I met her husband at one of the Coyle-Wexler holiday parties a few years ago. Seems like a good guy. Definitely a lucky guy. She's wicked smart and she's drop-dead gorgeous."

"Can I ask you a real doofus question, bro?"

Jack nodded. "Fire away."

"Is it . . ." Harrison uncomfortably cleared his throat. "Is it different being with Lina?"

"Different how?"

"You know. Is it different with her than it was with the white girls you've dated?"

A quiet laugh escaped Jack as he said, "Yes. I love Lina. That makes all the difference in the world."

Back downstairs, Jack and Harrison enjoyed a couple of Sam Adams out on the deck. Talk turned to Anderson and the two dates he'd scheduled for the same night—with twins, no less—and the progress the dockworkers' union was making with the help of one of the attorneys Jack had recommended. Nightfall quickly drove the temperatures down, and the two men went back inside.

"I better get going before Beth starts callin' around," Harrison said. He started for the front door with Jack trailing after him. "I never know if she's going to greet me with kisses, tears or a tartar sauce pizza when I come home these days."

"No, sir," Jack groaned, reverting back to his Southie roots.

"A small cheese from Prince Pizza with tartar sauce from The Lobster Claw slathered all over it," Harrison said. All three DeVoys shuddered. "It's her first major craving. She can't get enough of the stuff. She keeps me busy hustlin' my hump from Saugus to Reading and back to Southie twice a week."

Once Anderson trotted outside to sit behind the wheel of Harrison's car, an old Ford Bronco that Harrison kept one step ahead of the salvage yard, Jack pulled a square of paper from his back pocket. He pressed it into Harrison's hand. "I got a few estimates for that patch job, and that's the average there."

Without looking at the folded check, Harrison shoved it back. "I don't want your money, Jackie. I've been working at MacNeil's Auto Repair. Our noses are still above water."

"You should get paid for your work. Besides, I'd rather pay you than some stranger. I know where to find you if it turns out that you did a shoddy job."

Harrison hesitated a moment longer before sticking the check in his back pocket. "You could have done just as good. Pop taught you how to scrape and spackle same as he did me and Andy. Do a better job with the hammer next time. Make it really convincing."

Jack tried too hard to look innocent.

"You left the hammer on your bed, dude," Harrison said, his short, snappy Southie 'dude' wholly unlike the California surfer version. "If you ever want to talk . . ." He took a deep breath and rolled his eyes. "You don't have to abuse an innocent house to get me out here."

"Thanks, Harry."

He patted his pocket. "Back at you, bro. But don't expect me to pay *you* if I ever need legal advice."

Jack gave his brother a light punch in the arm. "Dude, you couldn't afford me."

Jack wasn't far behind his brothers when they left Nahant for Boston. Traffic was light for a late Sunday afternoon, so Jack was able to see Harrison's battered old Bronco exit I-93. Jack took the same exit, only he continued straight to Berkeley Street rather than driving left to go into Southie with his brothers.

He traveled west on Berkeley, then turned left, traveling south on Tremont Street. He half-heartedly fiddled with his CD player as he passed the Reggie Lewis Track & Athletic Center and Roxbury Community College. He gave up on music altogether and turned off the CD player when the playground near the Jackson Square T station came into view. Jack had felt fine when he left the house, but now that he was driving in reverse to parallel park in a spot near the basketball courts, his heart began to throb in his ears.

Once parked, he sat in the car, watching a group of men play. One of the men looked at Jack and then did a double take. Jack recognized him, as well as R.J. and perhaps one other man who he'd seen play the day he'd come to the park with Lina. There was no invitation in UMASS's expression, but there was no menace or intimidation either. UMASS nodded, and it was so subtle, Jack might have imagined it.

UMASS spoke a few words to one of his teammates, who then peered at Jack. They started toward him, and Jack's first instinct was to grab the keys in the ignition and start the car. His heart still battering his sternum, Jack started the engine, but only so he could lower the passenger window as UMASS approached.

Working the basketball gracefully from hand to hand, UMASS bent over to speak to Jack through the window. "Slummin' again?"

"Nope." Jack tipped his head toward his backseat. "I happen to know for a fact that this a good place to catch a good ball game."

UMASS peered into the backseat, where Jack's gym bag was slumped. The two men looked at each other. Just when Jack thought he'd made an embarrassing mistake, UMASS stopped working the basketball and grinned. "If you're gonna play, come play, but don't sit over here like Jeffrey Dahmer eyeballin' a bunch of brothers."

Lina and Levora sat in a cozy coffee shop in Cambridge long after Louise, Levora's daughter, had kissed them goodbye and returned to the MIT campus. Levora had been in town for two weeks, and Lina appreciated the amount of time she'd devoted to her when she should have been spending all of it with her own daughter.

"Lou thinks of you as a big sister," Levora assured her over a bucket-like cup of hot chocolate. "You saw her. She's excited about becoming an aunt."

Her elbow on the tiny circle of their dark wood table, Lina rested her chin on her palm and turned her gaze to the plate glass window beside her. Cambridge was a student ghetto populated by undergraduates dressed in Gortex and hunched against the cold evening as they walked past the coffee shop. Lina supposed that most of the students she saw belonged to Harvard and MIT, and although the two schools were no Stanford, they did manage to turn out some of the finest minds in the country. One day, Louise would be one of those minds, and Lina couldn't help worrying a little about how her behavior might influence the smart young woman who'd been the closest thing to a real sister she'd ever had.

"Do you think I'm setting a bad example for Louise?" she asked.

Levora looked confused. "How so?"

Lina met Levora's gaze directly, hoping to gauge her true feelings with her next words. "I'm pregnant and I'm not married."

"And . . . you're afraid that I'm going to knit a scarlet 'A' and pin it to your turtleneck?" Levora chuckled. "You're not some horny high school kid who got herself in trouble, doll. You're twenty-nine years old, and you have the resources to properly care for a child. Yes, it would be nice if Jack was a part of the equation, but until he comes to his senses, you're all this baby's got. Well, you, me, Louise, Ben and Errol—it takes an island to raise a child, love, and you've got one. So no worries, okay?"

Lina reached past their cocoa cups and empty cheese-cake plates and grasped Levora's hands. "Thank you for coming. It really means a lot to me."

"Anything for you, kiddo, even Massachusetts in April. It's spring everywhere else in North America, but there's still snow on the ground in New England. Everything's backward here."

Lina chuckled. Three decades in the southern hemi-sphere outweighed the time Levora had spent growing up in the northern. She sounded like a true native of Darwin.

"It would be perfect, you know," Lina said wistfully. "We could spend September to February on Darwin, and March to August here in New England. Jack could practice law six months here and then teach sailing or something the rest of the time on Darwin."

Levora peered over the top of her glasses. "That might work for a few years, but you can't split time on two continents once your sprog begins school. I'm all for showing a kid the world, but a child also needs stability. Would you be willing to consider moving here permanently? You could always visit Darwin during the summer when your kids are out of school, and Louise will be here for a couple more years, too, so it's not like you wouldn't have any family at all here, and . . ."

Levora's voice faded into background noise as Lina's attention strayed. She had wrestled with the notion of resettling in Massachusetts, Nahant to be exact. The Commonwealth had its charm, but it was not her home. It was a whole different world, a whole different ocean. The only reason she'd be willing to move would be Jack, and for now, as things stood between them, that just wasn't enough. Shaking her head, she stared at the glop of melted marshmallows and cocoa in the bottom of her cup.

"Maybe you shouldn't be thinking that far ahead anyway," Levora suggested, gently reclaiming Lina's attention. "Jack hasn't exactly come around yet, has he?"

"We still talk, still see each other. That's something. We tried to get together once, but . . ." She gave a dismissive shake of her head.

"But what?"

"We can't keep our hands off each other," she laughed sadly. "We turn into a pair of howler monkeys in heat and nothing gets resolved about the baby."

Levora patted Lina's hand. "Maybe—and I'm not saying this to be cruel, doll, 'cause I got nothing against Jack even though he abandoned you once already and you shouldn't forget that—but maybe he doesn't want this baby."

Lina smiled through a trickle of unexpected tears that she quickly swiped away. "He wants us, Levora. He just doesn't know it yet."

"What makes you so sure?"

Lina hoped that her reason made as much sense to Levora as it did to her. "Whenever we talk about the baby, Jack always says 'him.' From the first, he never referred to the baby as 'it.' Only 'him.' "

A light but steady rain pattered against the tall, wide window nearest Lina as she gazed at Hyde Park. She'd chosen the Berkeley Hotel solely for its views of London's spectacular little park, but she hadn't factored in the weather, which seemed to reflect her mood. She had literally piles of work stacked on the table before her, and still more awaited her in the cozy study of her suite, but she found it impossible to focus on contracts and legal maneuverings with Jack crowding all other thoughts out of her head.

She picked up the morning's *Daily Mail*, which she'd discarded earlier after deciding to get cracking on the business that had brought her to London. An item in the celebrity pages caught her eye, a long-winded paragraph about singer Lucas Fletcher and his American wife, Miranda Penney. The couple, and all of Conwy, Wales, it seemed, were rejoicing in the birth of their second child, a son they named Reilly.

Lina tossed the newspaper atop her work papers and resolutely surrendered to her sodden view, her hands clasped possessively over her abdomen. "Reilly," she murmured. "That's a nice name for a girl or a boy."

Her back sank further against the arm of the comfy sofa as she brought her knees closer to her chest. "Your father thinks you're a boy," she told her baby. "Let's hope not, if for no other reason than to avoid calling you Henderson, Robinson or, God forbid, Johnson." She giggled, her still mostly concave belly moving beneath her hand. "Perhaps we should call you Bullseye." Her merriment faded as she recalled the steamy night she'd pinpointed as the moment of conception. She'd been wonderfully out of her head, her whole self and soul given over to Jack. Even now, so many weeks later, the memory of that occasion weakened her knees and started a flame of yearning that melted her insides.

Just as much as she loved the child she had yet to meet, she missed its father. She knew that she should be with Jack testing out names, not alone in yet another hotel on yet another island. Darwin, Nahant or Great Britain, the island didn't matter. Lina wanted only to be with Jack.

She replayed their angry parting—her angry departure, rather—on Nahant, and tried to justify the abruptness of it by calling up the way Jack had left her on

Darwin. She reluctantly admitted that the two events couldn't have been more different. "I didn't have to go," she mumbled under her breath. "I never gave him the chance to properly digest the news. I left because I didn't want to give him the chance to leave me again."

Lina winced at the painful memory of Jack's disappearance from Darwin. For nearly a week after, she had haunted the island, a mere ghost of her former self, visiting the places she had learned to love anew by sharing them with Jack. He had ruined her precious spot high above Tuanui Bay. She'd been unable to enjoy the first light of each new day without hoping that it would bring Jack back to her.

After Edison Burke's deplorable behavior on the island, she'd decided to meet with the Coyle-Wexler execs in Boston herself rather than subject the island to another version of Edison Burke. The prospect of a good fight had actually helped her forget about Jack. Until she'd come face to face with him in the Coyle-Wexler boardroom.

She covered her face with her hands, even though there was no one in the room to see the scorching blush heating her face. As long as she lived, Lina was convinced that she'd remember the hot rush of joyous desire that had exploded within her when she saw Jack sitting at the conference table. She crossed her arms and allowed herself a satisfied smirk at the way she had handled the surprise. Jack had played the moment cool, too, but she'd caught the confusion in his eyes and the slight lift of his brow before he'd been able to work his face into a placid mask of indifference.

In so many ways, he'd told her that he wanted her with him there in Nahant. Had she given him a chance to cool down, Lina was certain that he'd want their baby, too. "But only on Nahant," she sighed. "And that, my darling," she said to her belly, "is the problem."

CHAPTER 17

This time, the conference room was almost completely empty when Lina walked into it promptly at ten, the time Reginald had designated for this latest meeting. Jack, Reginald, Edison Burke and a transcriptionist were clustered together at the end of the table farthest from the double doors. This time, Jack sat two seats away from Reginald's left while Burke occupied the chair at Reginald's right elbow.

The men politely stood in deference to Lina, who opted to sit directly opposite Jack. They exchanged a look, Jack mutely conveying that he had no idea what the meeting was about.

Reginald began by loudly clearing his throat. "Ms. Marchand," he said with a glance at Jack, "or Lina, if I may, we—"

"You absolutely may not," she said.

Jack stifled a dry chuckle. If Reginald had meant to intimidate her by facing her three on one, he was about to be disappointed. Just as she had at their first meeting, she immediately established the hierarchy in the room by denying Reginald the use of her nickname.

"*Ms.* Marchand," Reginald began again with a frown, "we have a very grave issue to discuss."

In a white wool jersey dress perfect for the cool but sunny morning, Lina was radiant with the famous glow attributed to pregnant women. Other than the glossy sheen of her hair and the warm glow of her skin, she showed no outward signs of her condition. It had been two weeks since their lunch date, and Jack could not stop looking at her.

Lina held his intense stare, struggling to read his thoughts. She wondered if there would ever come a day when the sight of him did not jumpstart her heart, or make her belly leap in happy circles. He looked so different than he had from the first time she'd seen him in the conference room. His hair was slightly unruly, his jacket unbuttoned, and even more amazing, his pricey tie didn't match his ridiculously expensive suit. Tempted to look under the table to see if he even wore shoes, Lina might have done it if Reginald's booming voice had not stolen her attention.

"We've made no headway in isolating the component that gives Darwin tea its weight loss properties, Ms. Marchand, and as you know, we're rapidly nearing the end of our twelve-week trial," Reginald said. "It is not my intention to walk away empty-handed from this situation, not after all the time and expense Coyle-Wexler has devoted to it."

"Then I wish you all the best in the next two weeks," Lina said cheerfully. "I've always believed that desperation, not necessity, is the basis of great scientific discovery."

Reginald exchanged a sly look with Burke. Jack sat up a little straighter, unsure of what was going on. "Your relationship with Mr. DeVoy has created a conflict of interest, Ms. Marchand," Reginald went on slickly. "The non-disclosure of your personal interactions with Jack constitutes fraud on your part, and therefore makes any agreement between J.T. Marchand and Coyle-Wexler Pharmaceuticals, Inc. hereby null and void."

Jack launched himself to his feet. "Are you seriously trying to pull this, Reginald?"

Without looking at him, Reginald said, "Sit down, Mr. DeVoy."

"It's Mr. DeVoy now? If you think you're going to get away with—"

"Mr. Wexler," Lina snapped, cutting Jack off, "surely you can do better than this. What you got is all you're going to get. No more time and no more tea. It'll take more than a petty manipulation of circumstance to make me even consider revising our original agreement."

The old man smiled, and Lina thought he bore a sad resemblance to a frilled lizard. "I thought it might." He turned to Jack. "I'm sorely disappointed in your lack of good judgment, Jackson. You started your career here at Coyle-Wexler, and I had stellar hopes for you. I'm not going to live forever, and someone will have to take the reins someday. I'd hoped that that someone would be you."

A rapid, muffled thudding distracted Reginald. "Are we having an earthquake?"

Burke reached down and grabbed his own thighs, quieting the eager tapping of his knees against the under-side of the table. "Sorry," he smiled awkwardly.

Jack ignored Burke's obvious delight at his turn of fortune. "Are you letting me go, Reginald?" he asked, his calm exterior camouflaging the fury bubbling under his skin. "Are you actually using me as a brokering chip against Lina?"

"For all I know, Jack, your pillow talk with this woman might have jeopardized Coyle-Wexler's interests," Reginald said with a victimized expression. "How do I know that it won't happen in future deals?"

Lina's unflappable composure kept Jack's growing temper in check. "What do you want from me, Mr. Wexler?" she asked.

"You know what I want, young lady. I want the rights to cultivate and harvest that tea on Darwin."

"Jack has served you well and faithfully for years, and now you mean to trade his career for my tea?"

Reginald gestured toward the transcriptionist, and her fingers froze over the keys of her typing machine. "That's one way of putting it. This is strictly business, my dear, and business is like a war. Sometimes the com-mander-in-chief has to sacrifice a general to the cause."

Jack's ears steamed. *All these years,* he thought furiously, in his mind's eye watching everything he'd worked for swirl away. *I've gone from one end of the world to the other acquiring his products, I've sat back and shut up when he's needed me to, I've made excuses for him . . .* He heard Lina's voice in his head, simply stating what he was finally acknowledging. *I've been his pet, and now that lying, back-stabbing, deceitful—* "Don't do it, Lina," he blurted toward Lina. "Don't give him the tea."

Reginald laughed in disbelief. "Do you know what you're saying, Jack? You're the one who'll lose everything if Ms. Marchand does not surrender the rights to Darwin mint."

"You're clever to play on my emotions, Mr. Wexler," Lina said. "I love Jackson DeVoy. You're not wrong to gamble on that. If you'll spare his position, I'll happily give you the secret to Darwin mint tea."

Jack felt as though he'd been kicked in the gut. "Lina, don't give in to him."

"One more word from you, DeVoy, and I'll have you escorted from the room by security," Reginald said. He knuckled away a dab of drool as he turned back to Lina. "You'll surrender the rights to the tea? Just like that?"

She cocked an eyebrow. "Just like that. Do I have your word that you'll spare Jack?"

"Yes. Indeed, yes."

"I want it noted on the record."

Reginald motioned toward the corner, and the transcriptionist's fingers began dancing across her keyboard once more.

"Lina, don't do this," Jack pleaded, stretching his arms toward her across the table. "Don't sell out Darwin to protect me."

"Tell me the secret, Ms. Marchand." Reginald greedily leaned forward as though he could taste her answer. Burke leaned in, too, likely hoping to catch the crumbs from Reginald's mouth.

Jack issued an earnest appeal to Lina. "I don't deserve your loyalty, so don't do this."

"Does Darwin's tourist trade deserve it?" Burke interjected. "Our campaign is ready to go. Jack loses his job and Darwin loses its number-one economic resource if you don't give us what we need, Ms. Marchand. It's not like you aren't getting anything in return." He shoved a red folder at her. "Our original offer still stands, minus the use of the properties in Europe and the apartment here in Boston." He cast a sly, knowing glance at Jack. "We were fairly confident that you wouldn't need us to provide you with room and board here, that you'd make other, more comfortable, arrangements."

Lina held Jack's gaze, and he thought he glimpsed a spark of impishness in her eyes. "Mr. Wexler," she began, still pinning Jack with her bright eyes, "the secret to Darwin mint tea is that there is no secret."

Silence. Then the transcriptionist jumped back into action. The skip of her fingers over her keys was the only sound in the room until Reginald sputtered, "Wh-What? *What?*"

With cool reserve, Lina rose from her chair and clasped her hands at her back. Jack knew that she was a savvy negotiator—her undefeated record was as good as his. Actually, it was one better. Jack folded his arms over his chest and relaxed back into his chair, eager to see how Lina would handle Reginald.

"You and your wife were on Darwin for six weeks, Mr. Wexler. Please, correct me if I'm wrong," she started casually.

"This isn't a courtroom and I'm not some young lawyer with the hotsie-totsies for you," Reginald said derisively. "You're not going to talk circles around me, so don't even try it."

"How many automobiles did you see on Darwin?" she asked before catching Jack's eye and mouthing, *Hotsie-totsies?*

"Four, perhaps five," Reginald guessed. "I hope this goes somewhere fast, Ms. Marchand, I'm really losing patience."

"Did you visit the beach?" she continued. She passed Jack's chair, close enough for him to catch the faint scent of her hair.

"That whole island is beach," Reginald answered.

"Did you reside in a homestay?"

"There's no hotel on Darwin, so of course. We rented a bungalow about a mile outside the town center."

"Did you take meals in your room, or did you eat out?"

"We ate out, for the most part." Reginald's face screwed into a childish pout. "How much longer are we going to play this game?"

"And the tea your wife enjoyed every day," Lina said, unruffled by Reginald's impatience. "Was it delivered?"

"No," Reginald stated loudly enough to startle the transcriptionist. "My wife picked it fresh every day, said it tasted best fresh from the valley. She brewed it herself, right there in our little kitchen."

Lina stopped at her seat and rested her hands on its back. "*Darwin* is the secret, Mr. Wexler, not the tea. You and your wife walked everywhere. A mile into town for meals and a mile back to your homestay, a quarter mile to and from the beach, a mile to and from the mountain where your wife picked the tea.

"Darwin has no taxis, no buses, no hired cars. There are no fast food restaurants, and our cuisine comes primarily from the sea, so it's naturally low in fat and high in protein. You and your wife ate healthy foods and moved your bodies. That's how she transformed her figure, Mr. Wexler. It had nothing to do with the tea."

"If that's true, *Ms.* Marchand, then why is it that Millicent continued to lose weight even after our return to the States?"

"Your wife and I had a lovely conversation at your nephew's wedding," Lina said pleasantly. "She has quite a number of hobbies. Tennis, swimming, hiking . . . as a matter of fact, she mentioned that she's planning to get a bicycle. You dine with her regularly, so I'm sure you've noticed that she's cut processed sugars, alcohol and trans fats from her diet."

"She's no fun," Jack smirked.

Reginald turned purple. "It was the tea, I tell you!"

"The tea has nothing to do with your wife's success," Lina persisted calmly, "unless she tends to retain water. Perhaps your research team has discovered that Darwin mint tea has mild diuretic properties."

Reginald slammed his hands on the tabletop and shot to his feet. "You could have told us that ten weeks ago, missy!"

Unfazed by Reginald's display of temper, Lina smiled, and it almost looked sympathetic. "Would you have believed me if I'd told you that there was nothing in the tea . . . but tea?"

"This time next year you're going to be sorry you ever tangled with Reginald Wexler, Ms. Marchand," he promised through gritted teeth. "When Burke launches his campaign, tourists won't come within ten miles of Darwin's shores!"

Her eyes flashing, Lina dropped all pretenses of politeness. With the stealthy swiftness of a magician, she produced three large photographs and slapped them onto the table. "In the past two and a half months I put aside all my other clients and devoted my considerable resources and energies solely to Darwin. I've visited the ministries and departments of tourism in the United Kingdom, Spain, France, Italy, Germany, Canada, Japan—I've been all over this planet bolstering Darwin's reputation as a vacation destination. While you were trying to squeeze a miracle from a tea leaf, I was securing my island's economic future."

She slid the photos to Reginald and Jack. They stared at the publicity stills, Jack's smile growing as Reginald's mouth grew tighter. The first photo showed Carol Crowley laughing and clapping with a large crowd gathered to watch Maori performers. The second showed the diverse, smiling faces of the staff physicians and specialists at the island's medical center. Studying their list of credentials, Jack noticed that several of them were Stanford and Harvard graduates. The third photo invoked bittersweet memories in Jack. It depicted the cheery counter clerk in a bright, open space offering assistance to a woman traveling with a caged chicken, while in the foreground Levora appeared to be giving directions to a relieved looking businessman.

Jack looked up at Lina, and she gave him a pointed stare as if to say, *Now you know what I was up to.*

"Darwin is bulletproof," she told Reginald. "Or should I say bullyproof?"

With a final half-smile and a flip of her hair, she turned and started for the doors.

"Wait a minute," Jack mumbled in quiet confusion, the best he could do now that he realized that this was the end of the meeting. He started after Lina.

"You're not going anywhere, Jackson," Reginald barked.

"Is that so?" Jack challenged. He kept walking, but before he reached the door, Reginald's voice reeled him back.

"I made a mistake, son, a huge mistake." Reginald left the head of the table and met Jack halfway to the door. "We've wasted so much time, so many resources on this tea fiasco. I'll need my number one out there securing new products."

"Sir," Burke interrupted, "I'm your number one now, remember? You said that you were going to fire Jack, no matter what happened today."

Reginald dismissed Burke, who left the room in a full-fledged huff. Jack was on his way out, too, when Reginald reached up to put his arm across his shoulders. "Don't pay any attention to Burke. All that nonsense was part of my strategy. I'd never let you go, son. You're my number one, my go-to guy."

Lina's words echoed between Jack's ears. *You're his pet.*

"Let's just forget about that whole firing baloney," Reginald clucked uneasily. "You do realize that it was all a charade, don't you, my boy? I never intended to let you go. I think you're due, overdue in fact, for a raise. How does fifteen percent sound? Why don't we go to my office and really hash out your future with Coyle-Wexler? I was just speaking with the board of directors the other day about creating a new position, vice president of international acquisitions. The position would be for you, Jack, and you'd work directly under me, reporting to me only. I don't want to lose you. You're the best attorney I've ever seen."

He shrugged off Reginald's arm. "Then you must not have been paying attention to what just happened in here. We got our asses handed to us. We lost. *You* lost."

"Oh, but this is only a small battle in a larger war," Reginald said, clenching his fist in renewed determination. "There's more than one way to skin a cat, Jack. The tea obviously has a placebo effect that we can easily capitalize on. Only trouble is, we still need the tea. You and I will sit down and reconfigure a plan of attack that—"

The sound of Reginald's voice became so much background noise as Jack's thoughts circled more tightly around the woman who had just walked out of the conference room and possibly out of his life. Nothing Reginald offered compared to the scent of Lina's hair, the taste of the soft skin of her throat, or the melody of her voice. Lina had taken on Coyle-Wexler and won. Hell, he'd seen her take on the Pacific Ocean and win, so in retrospect, Jack realized that Reginald had never stood a chance. Neither had he.

And yet, Jack had no regrets about how it all had turned out. Lina was the only attorney to have never given him what he wanted; when it came to business, that is. In every other way, she'd given him everything he needed.

Reginald could offer nothing that would mean more to Jack than the one thing he really wanted: to spend the rest of his life with an island goddess.

"Let bygones be bygones, Jack, and take your rightful place at my elbow. And one day, I promise, I'll turn the reins of Coyle-Wexler Pharmaceuticals over to you. What do you say?"

Jack offered the old man a quiet smile. "Edison Burke has been diddling with Carol Crowley of PharmaChemix for the past two years. He's the one who's been feeding her information on the products Coyle-Wexler's been pursuing. Check with Milt McCrary down in the technical information department. At my request, he's compiled a log of phone calls made from C-W to PharmaChemix on dates that correspond to our product acquisition meetings, and a file of outgoing e-mails detailing our meetings regarding the Darwin mint tea. Your new number one is probably in his office right now, telling Carol that the mint's a dud. You'll know for sure by the time I walk down to the elevators."

Reginald's eyes widened as Jack exited the room and started down the corridor. "You're leaving? Where are you going?"

An image formed in Jack's mind, one of Lina dressed only in a silky sarong and moonbeams, her belly growing pleasantly round with the child they had made. "I'm going home, Reginald," he called over his shoulder.

"When will you be back?"

"I won't."

"You can't go, not now," Reginald called after him. "What will I do without you, Jack?"

"Frankly, old man, I don't give a damn." At the elevators, Jack pressed the down button. While he waited for the car, he stripped off his tie and shoved it in his pocket. Reginald was hurrying toward him, but was intercepted by the pale, stoop-shouldered figure of Milt from technical information. Jack watched Reginald stare at the sheaf of papers Milt handed him, and then crumple them in his hands.

"Burke!" Reginald bellowed, his arms stiff and his hands fisted at his sides. "Someone find Edison Burke and send him to my office. *NOW!*"

Jack started whistling a sunny little tune that deafened him to Reginald's further rantings. The elevator arrived just as Reginald's secretary came trotting after him, her graying hair bouncing out of place. "Mr. Wexler wants to know when you'll be back," she panted as Jack stepped into the empty car.

Still whistling, Jack pushed "L" for the lobby. The secretary used her hand to bar the doors from shutting. "Mr. DeVoy, please," she implored fearfully. "Mr. Wexler wants to know when you plan to return. He's on a tear, screaming about corporate espionage and fraud. I've got to tell him something!"

Jack chuckled, and then sighed. "Tell him to have my mail forwarded to Darwin Island."

The rain that had saturated Jack's loose-fitting linen trousers and shirt left the blacktop driveway slick and glossy. The soles of his hiking sandals slapped their way closer to the treehouse. He shook his wet hair out of his eyes and wiped his dripping nose on his sleeve. He hadn't bothered to secure a room or even tried to get a ride to Marchand Manor upon landing on Darwin. With his one carry-on bag in hand, he'd trudged through the rain to get to Lina.

He left his luggage slumped against the picket fence, swung open the unlocked security gate, and climbed the spiral staircase. Hoping against hope that what he wanted to see would be awaiting him at the top of the stairs, his stomach knotted tighter with each step. He held his breath as the rain-slickened, narrow planks of the tree-house floor came into view, followed by thinner branches of the tree that supported one end of a jute hammock.

Jack exhaled sharply when he saw the ebony loveli-ness of the long, sinuous form resting in the cozy middle of the hammock. Lina wore a sheer white sleeveless shift that looked casual, comfortable and painfully sexy all at once. As Jack quietly approached her, his eyes raced ahead to trace her legs, starting with her delectable toes.

Her bare, smooth calves were next, and Jack's hands ached to caress them up to her thighs, and still farther to the supple meat of her gorgeous backside. One of her arms hung over the edge of the hammock, treating Jack to a lingering look at its unaffected grace and beauty. Her black hair pooled at the head of the hammock, but her face was hidden behind the document she held before her eyes. Its length and blue backing sheet told Jack that she was reviewing some sort of contract or legal brief.

He took two more steps and his shadow fell over her, alerting her to his presence.

She lowered her papers.

Her mouth opened, and she might have formed his name. Jack couldn't tell for sure because no sound came out.

Lina dropped the contract she'd been trying to proof-read and it fluttered to the floor. She carefully eased herself into a sitting position, her eyes never leaving Jack. For a long time she couldn't decide if he was actually standing before her, or if she was staring at her most realistic daydream yet. For hours she'd lain there in the hammock, trying to work, when all she could think of was Jack and how much she'd missed him in the week since she'd last seen him.

She'd returned to Darwin determined to keep her focus forward, on herself and her baby. She'd resolved to never spend a single minute wondering about what could have been with Jack, or worse, what should have been. The days were easy with Levora and the rest of the islanders celebrating both her pregnancy and her success at keeping Darwin safe from Coyle-Wexler's plans for economic revenge.

The nights were altogether different. Night was a place where Lina had little to no control over what her heart would stir up in the kitchen of her mind, serving her easily digestible memories of the first time she'd seen Jack, or the way he'd looked at the helm of their rented yacht. As the time without him progressed, the menu of memories became more sumptuous and harder to resist. She'd dreamt of the night of the beach party, and the sizzling moments they'd shared atop the lifeguard station. She'd awakened in a hot, breathless sweat with her body quivering in remembrance of the intoxicating pleasures she had shared with Jack.

From that moment on, every thought of him had set her nerve endings on fire, oversensitizing her flesh to even the slightest contact, creating a constant yearning that only Jack could ease.

Even worse, the harder she fought to push thoughts of him aside, the more firmly his memory rooted itself in her heart.

Her baby was the only one to whom she confessed her love for Jack. The little person growing beneath her heart was all she had left of him, and that was the only regret she had whenever she thought back on the months she'd spent with Jack.

But now, with him standing before her in his rumpled clothes, his rain-darkened hair and woeful expression tinged with hope, Lina dared to believe that her one regret was about to vanish.

Jack fell to his knees, and only partly from exhaustion. More than twenty hours of travel had finally delivered him to Lina, but it had been a hard-fought finish to a whirlwind week of activity that had seen him resign from Coyle-Wexler, consolidate his finances, liquidate many of his assets, and transfer ownership of his car to Anderson and his house to his parents. They had taken a full day of convincing once they'd gotten over the shock of what Jack planned to do.

With all that accomplished, the purpose of his drastic life changes had brought him to his knees before Lina, who raised a hand to move a wet lank of hair from his left eye. Her whispery touch seemed to have the same effect on both of them. Jack's hands fisted on his thighs as he breathed in deeply through his nose. Lina's heart rate increased, setting the skin at the hollow of her throat to fluttering.

"I don't want you here," she managed over the hard lump blocking her windpipe.

Jack's jaw stiffened as if he'd just received a physical blow.

Lina stared beyond him as she mentally composed what she wanted to say to him, now that the moment she'd been longing for had arrived. There were so many things, the least of which was that she loved him. But there were things he had to know first, before she dared put her heart's wishes in his hands.

Jack watched her face as the music of Darwin played around him. The sweet percussion of falling raindrops was a calming complement to the harsh rustle of leaves stirred by the not quite cool breeze. The random cry of a large bird and the twittering responses of many smaller ones reminded Jack of the time he'd spent with Lina on the island during his first visit. They were the sounds that made him think of home. And now Lina didn't want him there.

She finally met his gaze. "I can't keep saying goodbye to you. And I won't ask you to stay. So really . . ." Her voice broke, her throat working visibly to force out the rest of her words. "There's no reason for you to be here."

Still on his knees, Jack took handfuls of her dress, kneading her hips with his knuckles. He tugged her to him and buried his face in her abdomen, pressing his lips to his baby's temporary home. "This is why I should be here." He cupped Lina's face in his hands and crushed his mouth against hers, "And this is why," he insisted through his kiss.

Lina kept her lips pressed together as long as she could. But Jack's fervent coaxing broke the resolute seam and she welcomed him, shivering when his tongue touched hers. She returned his kisses, allowing him to deepen them as his hands moved over her thighs and slipped under her dress. His thumbs traveled along the waistband of her bikini panties, and Jack chanced a glance at them. The prim white cotton pushed his buttons harder than if she'd been wearing nothing at all, and he drew Lina closer against him, aching to feel her even through their clothing.

Although she hung one long leg over his hip, Lina braced her hands on his chest, discouraging more intimate contact. "We can't do this," she whispered against his seeking mouth. "I won't."

Slightly panting, Jack drew his face from hers but remained within kissing distance. "I came here with open hands. I'm not here to take anything from you, or to convince you come back to Massachusetts with me. I want to be with you. If it has to be here on Darwin, then so be it. I don't want to be merely the father of a child. I want to be his dad. And I want to spend the rest of my life with his mother."

"You say that now, Jack, but—"

"I don't have anything to go back to," he told her. "What I couldn't carry, I gave away. Everything that means anything to me is right here." He pressed his forehead to hers and tightly gripped her hips. "Whether you want me or not, I'm here on Darwin for good. I'll start that sailing school I've always wanted, or make muffins with Levora. I'm not going anywhere, Lina."

A gasping sob tore from her then. "I want to believe you. But you've left me before. And then you let me walk right out of your life."

"I've made mistakes." He blinked back the sting of tears. "I won't make any more. I just want to do what's right."

"And popping up on Darwin is the right thing to do?"

"Yes, if I expect you to accept this." He reached into his pocket and pulled out a water-stained jewelry box. He opened it, and the diamond ring within it managed to catch enough light to throw dazzling stars into the overcast day. "Jaslyn Thérèse Marchand," he began. "Will you marry me?"

Lina had no care for the glittering ring. She had eyes only for the man kneeling before her, who'd come to her with open hands and a single plea that she had failed to read in his eyes when she'd first seen him.

He loves me, she told herself. And to her most heart-felt delight, she believed it.

"Lina, will you be my wife?" Jack asked, a nervous edge to his voice.

"Yes," she managed through a fresh fall of happy tears. "Oh, God, Jack, yes!"

Her hand shook as Jack slipped the half-carat emerald cut diamond with its platinum band onto her finger.

"It might not seem like much, but it's priceless," he explained. "This was my grandmother's engagement ring. It belonged to my mother's mother, and my grandfather worked on a fishing boat to pay for it. It was brutal work. My grandmother used to say that a half ton of haddock and cod paid for this half carat diamond. My grandfather was a crusty, plainspoken, second-generation Italian-American, and every time I imagine him as a young man in love, walking into Shreve, Crump & Lowe to buy this delicate little ring for the woman who became my grandmother . . ." He stroked a thumb over the ring. "This ring represents everything you tried to teach me about home and family. When I told my parents that I wanted to marry you, my mother insisted that I give you this ring. If you don't like it, I'll get something—"

Lina vigorously shook her head. "It's perfect. I love it. I love you!"

Jack took her in his arms and kissed her, and Lina pulled him onto the hammock. Her dress was soon lost to Jack's demonstrations of just how much he'd missed her, and his wet clothing soon followed. Wearing only her long, silky hair, a rapturous smile and the sparkling engagement ring, Lina welcomed the love of her life to the new life they would share on Darwin.

EPILOGUE

"You have to give us the password!" squealed a chorus of gleeful voices. The faces they belonged to lined up in an uneven row along the railing surrounding the treehouse that had become less Lina's office and more of a command center for an army of Darwin's feral children.

Jack, hands on the hips of his low-slung cotton trousers, worked his face into an exaggerated scowl of impatience. "Louisemawk!" he shouted up.

An eight-year-old, dressed in the short grass kilt worn by Maori warriors, peered over the railing. Blue-black spirals and dots meant to represent a warrior's facial tattooing sloppily covered the nut-brown skin of his face. Clearly the leader of the youthful marauders, the little boy shouted, "That's the old password. You have to give us the new one!"

Grinning, Jack stared into hazel eyes exactly like his own, and the child grinned back, shaking his long honey-blond hair from his face. "If you didn't change the password every ten minutes, I'd have a better chance of remembering it."

"It's wicked easy, Daddy!" chimed the sweetest voice Jack had ever heard, that belonging to a six-year-old girl who was too short to peer over the top of the railing, but whose sun-bronzed belly poked against the posts.

She pushed her forehead against a post, and long tendrils of her golden-brown hair floated on the warm breeze. Where the boy had his mother's jumbled dialect, the little girl had more of her father's Boston accent, which was refreshed every June, July, August and December, when she visited her grandparents, aunt, uncles and cousins in Nahant.

"Would you give me a hint, Thérèse?" Jack pleaded with the little hazel-eyed girl.

"It's in Maori, Daddy, and—"

"Don't tell him any more!" the eight-year-old warrior commanded, emphasizing the order by clapping a hand over Thérèse's smile.

"Jason, you know my Maori is weak," Jack complained. "Couldn't you pick something in Italian?"

Thérèse peeled off her brother's hand and pointed through the posts to something just beyond Jack. "Mommy's coming! She'll guess the password."

Jack turned to see Lina strolling down the nikau-lined path, a ginger-eyed toddler with a mass of maple curls propped on her left hip. The nattering of the children high above him faded into empty noise as he watched her approach, and each step she took toward him carried him back to his favorite moment at the treehouse.

He'd just arrived on Darwin after a whirlwind week spent transferring his worldly goods to his parents and brothers. With nothing in hand other than the clothes he'd purchased with Lina and a one-way ticket to Darwin, he'd fled New England, and he'd stopped only when he found himself standing at the top of the treehouse stairs.

They had spent the next few days making up for all the kisses they owed each other. Now, eight years and four children later, as Lina stepped up to him to transfer their curly-haired son into Jack's arms, Lina kissed him, and Jack figured that they were just about caught up.

"Harry and Beth are back from their swim at Tuanui Bay," Lina said. "They're changing back at Marchand Manor. Your parents and Anderson are already in town, so we can walk in together to meet them at the Taiko Café." She frowned slightly at Jack's disheveled appearance. "I thought you were going to change and dress the children."

He tipped his head toward the treehouse. "I don't know the password so I couldn't get up to collect them."

Lina looked up, counting heads and bellies. Jason and Thérèse were accounted for, as were their cousins, eight-year-old Harry Jr. and his five-year-old twin sisters, Constance and Corinne. With 18-month-old Heath in his father's arms, Lina was one child short. "Where's your sister?" she asked Jason.

"Charis is up here with us, Auntie Lina," Constance said. She drew away from the railing for a second and returned pulling a three-year-old along with her.

"Charis," Lina said, "why are you naked?"

"She's always naked," Harry Jr. laughed, himself one grass kilt short of copying Charis.

"Come on down, guys," Jack said sternly, "so we can go to the house and get cleaned up and dressed to meet Grandma and Grandpa."

As one, the children protested, stomping their feet and banging their makeshift weaponry against the railing.

"Have it your way, then." Lina stepped over to the bottom of the staircase and keyed in a series of buttons on the electronic console embedded in one of the posts. The treehouse that had once been her primary residence had become her office after she married Jack and moved back into Marchand Manor. She'd tried to use the treehouse for an office, but as her tribe increased in number, so had its dominance of the treehouse. It was now the children's favorite play area.

When she returned to Jack's side and slipped an arm around him, she rather loudly said, "I suppose it's just you, Heath and me meeting Grandma and Grandpa for ice cream this afternoon." As she and Jack started away from the treehouse, Lina turned to wave at the warriors. "Jason, see to your little sisters and your cousins, darling."

"We want ice cream, too!" the children clamored, Jason loudest of all. "Mom! Dad! We can't get down, the gate won't open!"

"I know." Lina smiled up at the children, and as he watched her face, Jack felt his chest inflate with love for her.

"Let us down, Mommy," Thérèse pleaded, her stern tone an exact imitation of Jack's.

"Sure," Lina said with a sly glance at Jack. "If you tell me the password."

"What language is it?" Harry Jr. called down, his young face the spit and image of his father's.

"English," Lina answered, her eyes still on Jack. "I'll give you a hint. It's a boy or a girl."

"How can a password be a boy or a girl?" Jason wondered aloud.

Jack wondered the same thing, at least until Lina lovingly ran a hand over her abdomen. Jack's mouth fell open with a soft pop. Lina leaned around Heath to kiss one corner of Jack's mouth.

"Bullseye?" Jack laughed weakly. "Again?"

Smiling broadly, Lina wrapped her arms around Jack's waist and rested her head on his shoulder. "What did you expect?" she teased softly. "You run around half naked on this damned rock of ours, just waiting to seduce your unsuspecting wife, knowing full well that something like this could happen . . ."

Jack knew the rest of that speech, so he cut her off by touching his fingers to her jaw, and bringing her mouth to his. With their son, daughters, nieces and nephew chanting "Bullseye!" high above them, Jack and Lina kissed, sealing anew their devotion to each other and their growing family.

The End

ABOUT THE AUTHOR

Crystal Hubbard is the author of the Winters Sisters series, which is comprised of *Suddenly You, Only You, and Always You* and the Love Spectrum title *Crush*. She is also an award-winning children's book author. The mother of four, Crystal resides in St. Louis, MO., where she enjoys cooking, tennis, fishing, yoga and mixed martial arts. Visit her online at *www.crystalhubbard.com* or e-mail her at *crystalhubbardbooks@yahoo.com*.

Coming in April 2008 from Genesis Press:

Choices by Tammy Williams

Excerpt:

CHAPTER ONE

"I changed my mind, Daddy. I don't wanna do it."

Ryan Andrews looked down as tiny hands wrapped around his leg. Those words hadn't surprised him, but his shy son actually standing inside Oakwood Primary School was a miracle, so they couldn't turn around now. Plus, it was stifling out and the air-conditioning felt great.

Ryan gazed into troubled brown eyes. "Don't be scared, Justin, it's going to be fine." He drew a deep breath. Disinfectant, a hint of fresh paint, and books hot off the presses mingled together. "You smell that? That's the smell of school. Look around." He pointed to the happy children, books, and alphabet that made up colorful borders atop the off-white walls. "Don't those kids seem to be having fun playing and learning all sorts of new things?"

Justin shrugged.

"Son, class starts on Monday. I dropped everything to bring you over to meet your teacher because you said you were ready." Ryan shuddered at the thought of the unfinished dusting and other chores awaiting him. "I know you can do this."

"But she might be mean. She might not like me."

"She's going to love you. You're the best little boy in the world. What's not to love?"

Justin shrugged. "I dunno."

"Well, I do know. Your kindergarten teacher will be just like your grandmas—old, caring, and crazy about you." Ryan only hoped showing up out of the blue on the hot summer day wouldn't paint him in a bad light with the teacher and make things worse than Justin already thought they would be. "You ready to meet Mrs. Boyd?"

Justin said nothing. His grip tightened around Ryan's leg.

"I promise, it will be fine." Music drifted from a partially open door at the end of the hall. Maybe that was the classroom. "Come on, let's go."

The rumble in Lara Boyd's stomach made concentrating on the half-finished mobiles before her an impossible task. Marvin Gaye harmonizing about a grapevine didn't help matters. For one always spouting the merits of a complete breakfast, hers should have been more than a strawberry Pop Tart and an almost-full pot of her must-have French vanilla coffee. Rubbing her hollow tummy, she glanced at the clock on the wall. Twelve-thirty. A toaster pastry was not created to keep one going for four hours.

Tired muscles cursed her as she stood from the small, square table used as her base of operations. Paint, glitter, and glue covered her hands and drizzled along the front of her t-shirt and the flaps of the colorful plaid over shirt. Lara chuckled, imagining she looked like a fudgesicle dipped in rainbow sprinkles. At least no one could accuse her of not throwing herself into her work.

Lara gazed about the classroom, finding the two things she prided herself in giving every child who walked through her doors—education and fun. From the beginner readers and fairy tales filling the colorful wooden shelves to her left, to the toys, blocks, and veritable who's who of *Sesame Street*—she loved Ernie— lining the three-foot high shelves to her right, to the eight computers loaded with the best and coolest 'kid-approved' learning software, she had managed to create a kiddie learning wonderland. Teaching kindergarten at one of the top school districts in South Carolina certainly had its benefits, but teaching in itself was the biggest perk of all.

She bubbled with anticipation like a good little child at Christmas. In four days, a stream of giggly, enthusiastic, and oftentimes scared five-year-old boys and girls would fill the kid-friendly space. Monday couldn't get here fast enough.

The growling in her stomach sidelined Lara's excitement about the coming school year. Though the scent of what remained of her French vanilla brew filled the air and teased her tummy, her liquid addiction couldn't compare to a ham and cheese sandwich. Quitting time had officially arrived.

Impersonating Gladys Knight and the Pips kept her mind off her empty stomach as she completed cleaning up. With the room in order, and her hands back to their paint-free state, Lara spun from the sink with a hearty 'toot-toot' to find a tall, blond, extremely handsome stranger standing just inside the door. The curtain came crashing down on her little show. Her hand covered her pounding heart. *How long had he been standing there?*

"Oh, I'm—I'm sorry," he stammered. "I hope I didn't frighten you."

Was he kidding? Lara's suspicious eyes stayed on him. His contrite tone and the doe-like sincerity in his dazzling baby blues showed he was indeed earnest. He seemed a bit flushed, too, but that might be the heat. It was a real scorcher today.

She tabled her sarcastic retort since he appeared to be punishing himself enough. "It's okay," Lara said, "I'm still breathing." Albeit just barely. She wasn't startled anymore, so why wouldn't her heart stop racing?

Giving the stranger a once-over, she found the answer to her question in every inch she covered. A half-buttoned, way too long denim shirt couldn't conceal straining biceps beneath a white t-shirt or the jean-covered muscles making up his upper thighs. He couldn't possibly be a member of the stuffy school board Principal Styles mentioned might make impromptu visits before the students arrived. Male board members were old, short, and on the rotund side. This man was young, early thirties, and at least six feet, two inches; not at all the board member type. Plus, board members didn't look this good in jeans.

Near-debilitating hunger became a thing of the past as she shamelessly took in her fill of the bountiful dish before her. Specific long-dormant body parts stirred to life. The tip of her tongue bathed her dry lips. The man smiled. Her pulse quickened.

As if on cue, the Supremes' "I Hear a Symphony" played. Butterflies invaded her stomach and heat fanned her cheeks. She hadn't felt this attracted to a man in over six years, and never to a white man—except for a soap star she'd have had to be dead not to notice. But impossible crushes didn't count. This man was right here, and she couldn't keep her eyes off him, or help envying the t-shirt that had the great fortune of being pressed to his magnificent chest.

Careful scrutiny of his many enticing physical attributes brought Lara's attention to a pair of tiny hands wrapped securely around his Adonis-like leg. Her heart went from pounding to swelling at the cute and very appealing picture. Finding the ability to move, she stopped the Motown CD and strolled to where the stranger and his small companion stood.

The scent of lemon furniture polish flooded her senses as she approached. After smelling vanilla coffee, watercolor paint, and glue half the day, the citrus aroma was unmistakable. Lara smiled. She obviously wasn't alone in using the beautiful but hot summer day to clean. "Can I help you with something?" she asked.

Crystal-clear blue eyes stayed trained on her face. "Huh?"

"Can I—"

"Oh, I'm sorry. Yes, I'm, uh . . ." His head tilted. "You have some white—" He rubbed a spot on his chiseled right cheek.

Lara wiped the spot with the collar of her shirt. That explained the staring. And she thought it was because he found her attractive. She had to stop presuming. "I was just finishing up," she explained, motioning around the room.

Instinct drove her fingers along the sides and back of her dark brown hair, but good sense brought them back down. She had a new flip-wrap haircut she couldn't style without a mirror, and there was no point in making matters worse. *God, how I must look to him.* She should have worn her hair in a ponytail—and *buttoned* her over shirt.

The man's gaze stayed on her face as he reached into his back pocket and extended a piece of paper. "I'm looking for Mrs. Lara Boyd's classroom," he said.

"You've found it, but I'm not a Mrs."

Surprise registered on his face. His penetrating eyes took in every inch of her multi-colored, paint-splattered frame, leaving her feeling exposed and strangely wanton.

Thick eyebrows drew together. "*You're* Lara Boyd?"

"That's what my mama told me," she answered, not quite sure what to make of his statement. "I don't think she lied, but if she did, I've been living this lie for twenty-nine years."

"I'm sorry, it's just—You don't look like a kinder-garten teacher." His gaze traveled the length of her body once again before returning to her face. "At least not any of the ones I've ever known or seen."

I don't look like a kindergarten teacher? What did he think a kindergarten teacher looked like? Sure, her appearance could be considered strange with rainbow-colored clothing and polka-dotted skin, but she found his reaction a bit disconcerting. Was he paying her a compliment or putting her down?

After two years in Denburg, had she finally met one of South Carolina's infamous hicks? The city boasted cul-ture, big business, great shopping, and nice beaches, but it was still the South. The Confederate flags she encoun-tered on a near-daily basis remained constant reminders if she dared to forget.

Lara studied him closely. He didn't seem hostile, maybe a little wound up, but—Who was she kidding? When it came to men, she couldn't tell what was what anymore. Not since her ex-fiancé, Foster, and his *love*. Men! Why did they have to be so complicated? Was it any wonder she preferred the company of children?

"I'm not doing this well, am I?" said the stranger.

"That depends." Lara folded her arms. "If your inten-tion is to insult or perplex me, I think you're doing a bang-up job."

His crestfallen expression said it all. He wasn't a racist hick, but his behavior still baffled her. Maybe he was a member of the school board and just taken aback by her unteacherlike appearance. Then again, he wasn't in a suit.

327

The owner of the tiny hands clinging to his leg peeked around the man's right side. A small replica of the enigma standing before her grabbed Lara's attention. The big brown eyes shining in his handsome little face marked the only discernable difference between him and his jumbo counterpart. Her heart warmed instantly.

She waved at the boy and smiled. "Hi, cutie. What's your name?"

"Justin," he murmured before slinking behind the leg again.

The man touched Justin's shoulder. "He's a little shy at first meetings. Well, second and third meetings, too. My name is Ryan Andrews, and Justin is my son," he shared.

"He starts Monday," Lara said, remembering Justin's name from her list of students. "I guess that's what's on the sheet you gave me."

"I think you're supposed to keep it."

She tucked the sheet in her shirt pocket. "I am."

"We, uh, we were out of town until last night, so we missed Tuesday's Meet and Greet, but I still wanted to get him acquainted with his new teacher." Ryan extended his right hand. "I really feel I should apologize to you, Ms. Boyd. You just aren't at all what I expected."

"So you've said."

An electric surge swept through Lara at the touch of his hand. Her head screamed to let it go, but she didn't listen.

"My—uh, my words weren't meant to offend or said to confuse you, honest."

His caressing thumb on the back of her hand worked wonders in convincing her of his sincerity.

"I just didn't know kindergarten teachers were so . . ." Ryan wiped his sweat-glistened forehead. A shiny, gold band caught Lara's eye. "I didn't realize the way they looked from when I was five had changed so much," he finished in a rush.

A tight smile concealed her disappointment. How could she *not* know he was married? The sight of Justin's tiny hands around his leg and the smell of furniture polish screamed 'settled'! One look at a gorgeous man, one tingle of long-forgotten feelings, and her ability to reason flew straight out the window. Ryan's last words had sounded like a compliment, but she was in no position to wonder, because it didn't matter.

He was married!

Her reaction to him disturbed her on many levels, but she could handle it. So what, he was drop-dead gorgeous with an athletic body and a dazzling smile. He was still just a man, and a *married* one at that. She could, and would, rein in her raging hormones. She had no choice.

Lara rescued her hand from his dangerous touch. "No need to explain," she said with a smile she didn't feel. "I'm sure a vanilla-spotted black woman in bad plaid and old jeans wasn't what you were expecting."

Curious brown eyes peeked at her for the briefest moment and then disappeared behind denim-clad thighs. A sincere smile touched Lara's lips. That Justin was a real cutie. She'd have to work with him on that shyness.

"As I was saying," she said, "it would have thrown anybody, so think nothing of it."

Ryan nodded, his appraisal of her without shame. The seductive turn of his lips sent a titillating shiver shooting down Lara's spine and a wave of disgust crashing through her belly. Her attraction to him and struggle to keep it under wraps was one thing, but as a married man, he had no business being so overt in his attraction to her.

"So, will your *wife* be joining us?" Lara asked.

Every trace of color drained from Ryan's face. She'd definitely hit a nerve. *Good! Serves him right.*

Justin peeked from behind his father's leg. "My mommy's in heaven," he murmured.

What? Her gaze shot to Ryan's adorned finger. *Heaven?* "I'm . . . I'm sorry." Lara looked from his hand to his face and back again. "I thought—I just figured that—" She groaned. "I'm sorry."

Ryan's thumb rubbed against the top of the band. He cleared his throat. "It's okay. You didn't know."

A dark cloud of tension filled the classroom. Booming silence hovered. Lara shut her eyes and prayed for the floor to open and swallow her whole. Ryan was a widower, and she all but accused him of cheating on his wife.

Justin sniffed the air. "Ms. Boyd, do you really have vanilla spots?"

Adult laughter filled the room, evaporating the almost stifling anxiety. Ryan leaned forward. "He's at the age where he takes things literally," he whispered against her ear.

330

The feel of his warm breath sent more tingles racing down her spine. *Did lemon furniture polish always smell this good?* Lara nodded. "Yes, I recognize that," she said. Stooping to Justin's eye-level, she reached out to him. He emerged from behind his father, accepting her proffered hand.

"I think you smell my coffee, sweetheart. My spots are just a little white paint." She glanced at her shirt. "And red paint, and blue paint, and glitter, and—you get the picture." Lara chuckled. "I do think I'm as sweet as vanilla ice cream, though. Well, on second thought, maybe chocolate ice cream."

Justin laughed. "You're funny, and you're pretty, too."

"I don't feel very pretty right now, but thanks. You're quite a handsome guy yourself, and so charming." She figured Justin's charm came from the same place he got those beaming brown eyes. Ryan could be the picture beside the word *gorgeous* in any dictionary, and he lit her fire for sure, but he wasn't the smoothest cat in the world. Justin was a different story. Lara smiled. "I'm going to enjoy having you in my class."

The boy's face lit up, as did his father's.

"Wow!" Ryan praised. "I have never seen him take to someone so quickly."

Lara brushed her forefinger against Justin's nose. The boy giggled. "I'm a teacher, we're a special kind."

"I can believe it."

Their eyes met and held as tension of another sort sparked around them like so many hanging live wires.

"Look, Daddy, there's Elmo, and Ernie!" Justin exclaimed, breaking the highly charged moment. His eyes brightened with familiarity as he pointed at the row of plush toys on the shelf.

Lara shook the small hand she held. Justin didn't seem so shy anymore. "You like Ernie?"

Justin nodded so hard his body shook. "I love him. I like Elmo, too, but Ernie's the best."

A kid after her own heart. "You want to know a secret?"

Justin nodded.

"Ernie is my favorite, too," she whispered loud enough for Ryan to hear. "Shhh, don't tell Elmo, I think he gets jealous."

"I won't," Justin said in the same loud whisper. Lara stood to her full five-feet-nine-inches of height to find Ryan staring and smiling. Her knees trembled, but thankfully didn't give way. *Keep it together, Lara.* Still holding Justin's hand, she walked to her desk and picked up some sheets.

"Here's a list of all the items Justin is going to need for school: crayons, markers, a mat to take his naps on, that sort of thing," she explained.

Ryan nodded. "Okay."

"There are also some forms you'll need to fill out detailing any allergic reactions or sicknesses he might have and the name and phone numbers of individuals to call if something were to happen while he's here." She extended the sheets. "Justin can bring the forms back on Monday."

"I'll be sure to get this done," he said, folding the sheets lengthwise and tucking them in his back pocket.

"Great. Do you have any questions?"

"Questions?"

She nodded.

"Oh, questions? No, I don't—" Ryan sighed. "I don't have any questions about Justin's schooling."

He might not have questions about school, but his hesitation said something weighed on his mind and he was clearly struggling with whether or not to share. She decided his not sharing was probably for the best.

"Alrighty, then." Lara gave Justin's hand a little squeeze. "I guess I'll be seeing you soon, Mr. Justin."

"Yes, ma'am," Justin replied with his full-body nod.

"Okay, buddy, I think we should let Ms. Boyd get back to her finishing up." Ryan held his hand out to Justin as he spoke to Lara. "Thank you for your time and everything."

"You're welcome," she said, following them to the door.

Ryan turned around. Again, he seemed to want to say something. He stared at her for a long moment before releasing a heavy sigh. "Good day, Ms. Body."

He left so quickly, Lara wondered if his Freudian slip had registered with him. She smirked. It could have been worse; at least that slip made her feel good. Ryan Andrews may have more charm than she thought. One thing was certain: He definitely had her attention.

Ryan's smile grew wider with his every thought of the breathtaking Ms. Boyd. He'd expected Justin's teacher to be a blue-haired granny, but he couldn't have been more wrong. *'I find you incredibly attractive.'* Why was that so hard to say?

Justin's peals of laughter brought a momentary end to his pensive state. He shook the boy's hand as they continued to the car. "What's so funny, big guy?"

"You called Ms. Boyd 'Ms. Body.' "

Ryan stopped mid-step. "No, I didn't."

"Uh-huh." Justin nodded.

Ryan slapped his forehead, sending a stinging spray of sweat into his eyes. He welcomed the discomfort as just punishment for his inexcusable behavior. Practically offending Lara with his wacky behavior was bad, but to call her Ms. Body? *Ugh.* He pinched the bridge of his nose and discovered he smelled like Lemon Pledge. His hand dropped. *This just gets better and better.* Something told him to shower first, but did he listen? No. He thought he was meeting an old lady. One that smelled too much like mothballs to notice anything else. *Damn.* He grunted.

Justin tugged on his hand. "You okay, Daddy?"

"I will be. I hope," he said walking again.

Ms. Body. Ryan sighed. The title suited her. The oversized plaid shirt demanded attention, but so did the traffic-stopping curves underneath. A paint-stained canary yellow t-shirt tucked inside equally discolored faded blue jeans never looked so good. And her face.

Cola-colored eyes, high cheekbones hinting at Native American ancestry, and full, kissable lips perfected her beautiful countenance.

The father in him had to be restrained from smoothing away the paint staining her pretty face, but the man in him wanted any excuse to touch her creamy, milk chocolate skin, and run his fingers through her silky, dark hair. Lara was absolutely stunning, even with assorted paint splatters. And her way with Justin. His son wasn't one to be so friendly and talkative when meeting people, but Lara drew Justin right out, just as she did him.

In the three years since losing his wife, he hadn't been attracted to any woman. He saw attractive women while out running errands, and a few tried to make a play for him, but he'd never been interested. All he could think about was his Shelly. But Lara . . . Ryan sighed. Lara definitely interested him, and in more than just a physical way, although the physical currently took center stage.

Ryan looked with gratitude at his concealing shirt. If Lara had seen what she stirred in him, not only would she think him a jerk, but a pervert, too. Images of her shapely, long legs wrapped around his waist played in his head. The bulge in his jeans tightened. He hadn't felt this way in a *long* time.

"You were wrong about Ms. Boyd, Daddy," Justin said.

Ryan shook away his lascivious thoughts. "I was wrong?"

"Uh-huh, about her being old. She's young, pretty, and nice. I really like her."

"Me, too, son." Ryan turned toward the window of Lara's classroom. "I really like her, too."

2008 Reprint Mass Market Titles

January

Cautious Heart
Cheris F. Hodges
ISBN-13: 978-1-58571-301-1
ISBN-10: 1-58571-301-5
$6.99

Suddenly You
Crystal Hubbard
ISBN-13: 978-1-58571-302-8
ISBN-10: 1-58571-302-3
$6.99

February

Passion
T. T. Henderson
ISBN-13: 978-1-58571-303-5
ISBN-10: 1-58571-303-1
$6.99

Whispers in the Sand
LaFlorya Gauthier
ISBN-13: 978-1-58571-304-2
ISBN-10: 1-58571-304-x
$6.99

March

Life Is Never As It Seems
J. J. Michael
ISBN-13: 978-1-58571-305-9
ISBN-10: 1-58571-305-8
$6.99

Beyond the Rapture
Beverly Clark
ISBN-13: 978-1-58571-306-6
ISBN-10: 1-58571-306-6
$6.99

April

A Heart's Awakening
Veronica Parker
ISBN-13: 978-1-58571-307-3
ISBN-10: 1-58571-307-4
$6.99

Breeze
Robin Lynette Hampton
ISBN-13: 978-1-58571-308-0
ISBN-10: 1-58571-308-2
$6.99

May

I'll Be Your Shelter
Giselle Carmichael
ISBN-13: 978-1-58571-309-7
ISBN-10: 1-58571-309-0
$6.99

Careless Whispers
Rochelle Alers
ISBN-13: 978-1-58571-310-3
ISBN-10: 1-58571-310-4
$6.99

June

Sin
Crystal Rhodes
ISBN-13: 978-1-58571-311-0
ISBN-10: 1-58571-311-2
$6.99

Dark Storm Rising
Chinelu Moore
ISBN-13: 978-1-58571-312-7
ISBN-10: 1-58571-312-0
$6.99

2008 Reprint Mass Market Titles (continued)

July

Object of His Desire
A.C. Arthur
ISBN-13: 978-1-58571-313-4
ISBN-10: 1-58571-313-9
$6.99

Angel's Paradise
Janice Angelique
ISBN-13: 978-1-58571-314-1
ISBN-10: 1-58571-314-7
$6.99

August

Unbreak My Heart
Dar Tomlinson
ISBN-13: 978-1-58571-315-8
ISBN-10: 1-58571-315-5
$6.99

All I Ask
Barbara Keaton
ISBN-13: 978-1-58571-316-5
ISBN-10: 1-58571-316-3
$6.99

September

Icie
Pamela Leigh Starr
ISBN-13: 978-1-58571-275-5
ISBN-10: 1-58571-275-2
$6.99

At Last
Lisa Riley
ISBN-13: 978-1-58571-276-2
ISBN-10: 1-58571-276-0
$6.99

October

Everlastin' Love
Gay G. Gunn
ISBN-13: 978-1-58571-277-9
ISBN-10: 1-58571-277-9
$6.99

Three Wishes
Seressia Glass
ISBN-13: 978-1-58571-278-6
ISBN-10: 1-58571-278-7
$6.99

November

Yesterday Is Gone
Beverly Clark
ISBN-13: 978-1-58571-279-3
ISBN-10: 1-58571-279-5
$6.99

Again My Love
Kayla Perrin
ISBN-13: 978-1-58571-280-9
ISBN-10: 1-58571-280-9
$6.99

December

Office Policy
A.C. Arthur
ISBN-13: 978-1-58571-281-6
ISBN-10: 1-58571-281-7
$6.99

Rendezvous With Fate
Jeanne Sumerix
ISBN-13: 978-1-58571-283-3
ISBN-10: 1-58571-283-3
$6.99

2008 New Mass Market Titles

January

Where I Want To Be
Maryam Diaab
ISBN-13: 978-1-58571-268-7
ISBN-10: 1-58571-268-X
$6.99

Never Say Never
Michele Cameron
ISBN-13: 978-1-58571-269-4
ISBN-10: 1-58571-269-8
$6.99

February

Stolen Memories
Michele Sudler
ISBN-13: 978-1-58571-270-0
ISBN-10: 1-58571-270-1
$6.99

Dawn's Harbor
Kymberly Hunt
ISBN-13: 978-1-58571-271-7
ISBN-10: 1-58571-271-X
$6.99

March

Undying Love
Renee Alexis
ISBN-13: 978-1-58571-272-4
ISBN-10: 1-58571-272-8
$6.99

Blame It On Paradise
Crystal Hubbard
ISBN-13: 978-1-58571-273-1
ISBN-10: 1-58571-273-6
$6.99

April

When A Man Loves A Woman
La Connie Taylor-Jones
ISBN-13: 978-1-58571-274-8
ISBN-10: 1-58571-274-4
$6.99

Choices
Tammy Williams
ISBN-13: 978-1-58571-300-4
ISBN-10: 1-58571-300-7
$6.99

May

Dream Runner
Gail McFarland
ISBN-13: 978-1-58571-317-2
ISBN-10: 1-58571-317-1
$6.99

Southern Fried Standards
S.R. Maddox
ISBN-13: 978-1-58571-318-9
ISBN-10: 1-58571-318-X
$6.99

June

Looking for Lily
Africa Fine
ISBN-13: 978-1-58571-319-6
ISBN-10: 1-58571-319-8
$6.99

Bliss, Inc.
Chamein Canton
ISBN-13: 978-1-58571-325-7
ISBN-10: 1-58571-325-2
$6.99

2008 New Mass Market Titles (continued)

July

Love's Secrets
Yolanda McVey
ISBN-13: 978-1-58571-321-9
ISBN-10: 1-58571-321-X
$6.99

Things Forbidden
Maryam Diaab
ISBN-13: 978-1-58571-327-1
ISBN-10: 1-58571-327-9
$6.99

August

Storm
Pamela Leigh Starr
ISBN-13: 978-1-58571-323-3
ISBN-10: 1-58571-323-6
$6.99

Passion's Furies
AlTonya Washington
ISBN-13: 978-1-58571-324-0
ISBN-10: 1-58571-324-4
$6.99

September

Three Doors Down
Michele Sudler
ISBN-13: 978-1-58571-332-5
ISBN-10: 1-58571-332-5
$6.99

Mr Fix-It
Crystal Hubbard
ISBN-13: 978-1-58571-326-4
ISBN-10: 1-58571-326-0
$6.99

October

Moments of Clarity
Michele Cameron
ISBN-13: 978-1-58571-330-1
ISBN-10: 1-58571-330-9
$6.99

Lady Preacher
K.T. Richey
ISBN-13: 978-1-58571-333-2
ISBN-10: 1-58571-333-3
$6.99

November

This Life Isn't Perfect Holla
Sandra Foy
ISBN: 978-1-58571-331-8
ISBN-10: 1-58571-331-7
$6.99

Promises Made
Bernice Layton
ISBN-13: 978-1-58571-334-9
ISBN-10: 1-58571-334-1
$6.99

December

A Voice Behind Thunder
Carrie Elizabeth Greene
ISBN-13: 978-1-58571-329-5
ISBN-10: 1-58571-329-5
$6.99

The More Things Change
Chamein Canton
ISBN-13: 978-1-58571-328-8
ISBN-10: 1-58571-328-7
$6.99

Other Genesis Press, Inc. Titles

Other Genesis Press, Inc. Titles (continued)

Other Genesis Press, Inc. Titles (continued)

Daughter of the Wind	Joan Xian	$8.95
Deadly Sacrifice	Jack Kean	$22.95
Designer Passion	Dar Tomlinson	$8.95
	Diana Richeaux	
Do Over	Celya Bowers	$9.95
Dreamtective	Liz Swados	$5.95
Ebony Angel	Deatri King-Bey	$9.95
Ebony Butterfly II	Delilah Dawson	$14.95
Echoes of Yesterday	Beverly Clark	$9.95
Eden's Garden	Elizabeth Rose	$8.95
Eve's Prescription	Edwina Martin Arnold	$8.95
Everlastin' Love	Gay G. Gunn	$8.95
Everlasting Moments	Dorothy Elizabeth Love	$8.95
Everything and More	Sinclair Lebeau	$8.95
Everything but Love	Natalie Dunbar	$8.95
Falling	Natalie Dunbar	$9.95
Fate	Pamela Leigh Starr	$8.95
Finding Isabella	A.J. Garrotto	$8.95
Forbidden Quest	Dar Tomlinson	$10.95
Forever Love	Wanda Y. Thomas	$8.95
From the Ashes	Kathleen Suzanne	$8.95
	Jeanne Sumerix	
Gentle Yearning	Rochelle Alers	$10.95
Glory of Love	Sinclair LeBeau	$10.95
Go Gentle into that	Malcom Boyd	$12.95
Good Night		
Goldengroove	Mary Beth Craft	$16.95
Groove, Bang, and Jive	Steve Cannon	$8.99
Hand in Glove	Andrea Jackson	$9.95

Other Genesis Press, Inc. Titles (continued)

Other Genesis Press, Inc. Titles (continued)

Last Train to Memphis	Elsa Cook	$12.95
Lasting Valor	Ken Olsen	$24.95
Let Us Prey	Hunter Lundy	$25.95
Lies Too Long	Pamela Ridley	$13.95
Life Is Never As It Seems	J.J. Michael	$12.95
Lighter Shade of Brown	Vicki Andrews	$8.95
Love Always	Mildred E. Riley	$10.95
Love Doesn't Come Easy	Charlyne Dickerson	$8.95
Love Unveiled	Gloria Greene	$10.95
Love's Deception	Charlene Berry	$10.95
Love's Destiny	M. Loui Quezada	$8.95
Mae's Promise	Melody Walcott	$8.95
Magnolia Sunset	Giselle Carmichael	$8.95
Many Shades of Gray	Dyanne Davis	$6.99
Matters of Life and Death	Lesego Malepe, Ph.D.	$15.95
Meant to Be	Jeanne Sumerix	$8.95
Midnight Clear	Leslie Esdaile	$10.95
(Anthology)	Gwynne Forster	
	Carmen Green	
	Monica Jackson	
Midnight Magic	Gwynne Forster	$8.95
Midnight Peril	Vicki Andrews	$10.95
Misconceptions	Pamela Leigh Starr	$9.95
Montgomery's Children	Richard Perry	$14.95
My Buffalo Soldier	Barbara B. K. Reeves	$8.95
Naked Soul	Gwynne Forster	$8.95
Next to Last Chance	Louisa Dixon	$24.95
No Apologies	Seressia Glass	$8.95
No Commitment Required	Seressia Glass	$8.95

Other Genesis Press, Inc. Titles (continued)

Other Genesis Press, Inc. Titles (continued)

Other Genesis Press, Inc. Titles (continued)

Other Genesis Press, Inc. Titles (continued)

Uncommon Prayer	Kenneth Swanson	$9.95
Unconditional Love	Alicia Wiggins	$8.95
Unconditional	A.C. Arthur	$9.95
Until Death Do Us Part	Susan Paul	$8.95
Vows of Passion	Bella McFarland	$9.95
Wedding Gown	Dyanne Davis	$8.95
What's Under Benjamin's Bed	Sandra Schaffer	$8.95
When Dreams Float	Dorothy Elizabeth Love	$8.95
When I'm With You	LaConnie Taylor-Jones	$6.99
Whispers in the Night	Dorothy Elizabeth Love	$8.95
Whispers in the Sand	LaFlorya Gauthier	$10.95
Who's That Lady?	Andrea Jackson	$9.95
Wild Ravens	Altonya Washington	$9.95
Yesterday Is Gone	Beverly Clark	$10.95
Yesterday's Dreams, Tomorrow's Promises	Reon Laudat	$8.95
Your Precious Love	Sinclair LeBeau	$8.95

ESCAPE WITH INDIGO !!!!

Join Indigo Book Club©
It's simple, easy and secure.

Sign up and receive the new
releases
every month + Free shipping
and
20% off the cover price.

Go online to www.genesis-
press.com and click on Bookclub
or
call 1-888-INDIGO-1

Order Form

Mail to: Genesis Press, Inc.
P.O. Box 101
Columbus, MS 39703

Name _____
Address _____
City/State _____ Zip _____
Telephone _____

Ship to (if different from above)
Name _____
Address _____
City/State _____ Zip _____
Telephone _____

Credit Card Information
Credit Card # _____ ☐ Visa ☐ Mastercard
Expiration Date (mm/yy) _____ ☐ AmEx ☐ Discover

Qty.	Author	Title	Price	Total

Use this order form, or call 1-888-INDIGO-1

Total for books _____
Shipping and handling:
  $5 first two books,
  $1 each additional book
Total S & H _____
Total amount enclosed _____
Mississippi residents add 7% sales tax